DEFEND

TRAVIS TAYLOR

SUMMARY

DEFEND

A catastrophic event looms over the world. Through all the turmoil, NASA stands up a crew to reduce the size of asteroids to a manageable and survivable size. However, unbeknownst to the world an on-earth threat looks to take advantage of the crippling situation and assume power over major governments. Bryan Reed, a NASA crew member, finds himself volunteering to do much more than breaking space rocks.

1

Prepare The Runway

IF I HAD it my way the crew and I would have executed the plan already. The last week has been unpredictable. With bad weather and terrorist threats, the mission keeps getting delayed.

Today is not the day. It's November 15, 2038, three-day's past launch. I hardly know what to do with myself. Three days ago, I was ready to leave my family, but now I really don't want to leave them. I'm pacing in my room watching the news even though it's practically the same as yesterday.

"...and today they are expected to execute the mission. Over to you, Caleb. Thanks, Becky. If you remember..."

I work for NASA in a recently new division. Ten years ago, NASA discovered asteroids heading towards Earth. Nine years ago, even more were discovered. Although NASA has tracked objects in the past they had never seen so many at one time. The last eight years has been the start of NASA's operation Defend. Seven years ago, the plan was revealed to the public. The mission would include going to space in an armed spacecraft able to launch missiles at the asteroids.

No citizen could really understand the magnitude of the situation until the plan was released. Basically, the earth is going to be bombarded with meteorites and possibly asteroids, and human life has a slim to no chance of survival. That is, however, without Defend the operation of reducing the size of matter before impact. The impending doom has led many countries to build bunkers and safe houses, they have stored food, and supplies, and have made plans for rebuilding cities. Count the blessings of seeing these things years before.

The glass tablet on my table chimes. I jump and turn around. I hope for the best as I swipe the green button to the right.

"Hello," I answer, attempting to sound calm.

"Bryan, you are departing in ten hours," a man's voice commands. "You know the departure procedures; do you have any questions?"

"No," I reply.

The phone goes silent. Apparently the man hung up. He didn't even say bye. Some people seemed to have lost their manners these days. I wonder if it has to do with losing hope. With so many problems around us, it seems inevitable.

Wow, I am going to be leaving in ten hours. I don't know if I should get too excited though, what if later they call it off. The weather isn't that great, but we don't have much time. This is all getting stressful even for me. I haven't even been to space before, only the simulators have prepared me for this. I can't be alone when I get stressed. I should meet up with everyone, they must be talking about our new departure.

There are seven members of the Defend spacecraft. Three others man a supply carrier. We all have very different backgrounds but work well together.

I exit my room, and head down the hotel looking hallway. All budget money went to the Defend spacecraft leaving employees with subpar workstations and amenities. While walking and texting through the hallway, a crew member steps out of his room,

"Hey how are you Josh?" I say enthusiastically.

"Oh, I am good," he says with a face full of uncertainty.

"You got the call?" I ask.

"Yup," he replies with certainty in his voice.

We begin to walk together to the lounge. Josh is an interesting guy. He doesn't say too much but I know he likes robotics and works on various robotic projects at home. Once, I thought I overheard him say he participated in a battle bot competition.

We arrive at the lounge and a few crew members are there. The large room has pictures of past astronauts and quotes hanging on the walls. There is a blue faux L-shape leather couch in front of a 45" T.V. built into the wall. Blue cushioned chairs around a few white tables are occupied by some employees I don't know.

"Bryan there you are," Susanne says as she breaks her conversation with Yochi.

"Hey, are you excited?" I ask..

"Yeah, I am. I think everyone is, well most of us," She says.

I started training Susanne three years ago. We have become close friends. Sometimes her family and mine will get together for dinner. Although most of the crew have known each other for at least two years, Susanne and Yochi are the only ones I hang out with after work. And I don't know three supply crewmen very well. They came on nine months ago.

The news on the T.V. grabs my attention,

"The weather is not going to let up for the next day or so,"

"Ah great, I really had my hopes up this time," Yochi says disappointed.

Yochi is a short Asian American who always seems to be optimistic. He is one of those people that can brighten up your Monday.

"Oh, don't worry we're still going no matter what the weather is," Rick replies barely having entered the room.

Everyone stares at him puzzled. Rick heads straight to the fridge to grab a soda.

"Oh yeah, I have been following several weather forecasts. So, when I got the call a few minutes ago I challenged their judgment and sources of weather updates, they told me it was tonight or never," Rick says.

Everyone quiets down.

"What do you think the chances are of us getting up there?" Josh questions hesitantly.

The door opens fast.

"Chances are good and good is great when the window of opportunity is not so great," Captain Dane says, as he walks in with the Co-captain, Jessica Jet.

Everyone has their eyes on him

"Congratulations everyone. Today is the beginning of our journey to save what we know and love. We leave as men and women, fathers and mothers, sons and daughters, but we will return with the title of hero," Captain Dane says hardily. "Let's not waste time doubting, there are enough people around the globe doubting and laughing at us. We must remember what we have worked and trained for. Years of simulation have been tested. Millions of equations have been created. The greatest technology has been harnessed, the greatest crew has been entrusted. Don't forget for one second the reason you are here today," he finishes.

He gives a heartfelt smile and walks into the kitchen, Jet follows him. We each look at one another surprised to get an impromptu pep talk.

The next few hours the crew and I are being examined by doctors. None of us seem to be different than two days ago before our last hopeful departure.

I get a glimpse of the spacecraft, while walking back to my room. I can see engineers and maintenance crews running around the craft. I am glad they are doing some final inspections. We are going to need everything to go perfectly under such a tight window. It's four hours before takeoff and I have time to call my family. My wife Samantha and my son and daughter are on the video call, but there really isn't any more to talk about since last night. The reality of the actual event, and my departure, keeps us from saying much more than "I love you" and "I can't wait to see you", all through our tears.

Now, three hours before, the crew gathers to eat. Few words are exchanged besides Rick and Yochi debating about the better of two soccer teams. Two hours before takeoff we sit down to be briefed on the weather and take-off circumstances.

"Everyone will be on the craft 45 minutes before departure. 30 minutes before departure everyone must be seated at the main deck," Ron Sparks, head of NASA's ground control, commands us. "The weather will challenge us beyond our practices," He continues "With winds ranging from 10 mph to 40 mph we must be even more precise and quick to adjust,"

The craft itself is a larger, bulkier version of the aircraft F-117 Nighthawk. It wasn't until about 4 years ago the designs of the rocket we were going to be on changed to this completely innovative departure system. The craft propels itself on an inclining track before being propelled in increments until complete lift off. Right at lift off the craft's propulsion takes over, allowing it to enter space. All of which I hardly understand but it's as much as I am allowed to know according to my supervisor.

"After you stabilize yourself in space we will direct you to the first coordinate to release the first set of missiles. Does anyone have any questions?" Ron finishes.

No one does. Everyone leaves to go to their rooms to prepare for departure.

As I get back to my room there is a note between the door handle and door. The note is to wish everyone luck. I toss it on my bed but something catches my eye. Something is written on the back of the card. I pick up the card and read,

"Don't sweat the small stuff," With the initials J.F. below it.

I sit down on the bed and examine the hand writing. It is, it really is Jake Farr's handwriting. But he has been gone for almost three years now.

Once on the crew, Jake, and I had become good friends. One night he told me he was going to meet up with some old friends. He never showed up to work the next day and I later found out he was missing. Investigations are still being done. I have talked to his wife, and very little evidence has been found. Some speculate he is trying to sell NASA's information to other organizations or terrorists. He would never do that and anyone that really knew him would know that. He is still alive and by this note he is up to something. I tidy up my room, grab some items, and head off to the departure room.

I can't wrap my head around Jake being alive and how he was able to write on the back of the note. Or is someone messing with me? But who? Who would play a joke about someone missing, and coming back to... to what I don't even know. My head is swirling and I realize I better focus on the mission at hand.

I am doing this! I am boarding the Defend craft and launching out to space to defend the world. There are so many possibilities of outcomes to this mission. There is less than one percent chance of the best outcome for earth, that being, pebbles hitting the earth. Those who are optimistic are expecting car size pieces of meteorites to hit the earth. Although the damage will be horrendous, there are plans set in place to rebuild and strengthen the communities. I am confident that it will be awful for the next 3 years. Lives lost, extensive power outage, broken sewers, contaminated water supplies, and the list goes on. Modern civilizations will be shattered around the world.

I reach the door of the terminal and take a deep breath. When I push open the door, my crew is there putting on their suits. No one says anything. Occasionally, eyes meet but no one wants to talk. Dane looks upbeat. He sees me looking at him, he gives a little smile.

"Well, I'm ready," he says.

"Yeah me too," Rick chimes in.

"Let's get this done," says Jet.

"Done right," Yochi says.

It appears everyone is excited. That makes me feel better.

"You bet we'll get it done right" Dane says enthusiastically.

"Years of education, simulation, and practice have brought us seven to this point. The next few days will allow mankind to live on and have a hope that we can make a difference if we try,"

We all agree just before James Finly rushes in. James is our public relations guy.

"Alright!" he belts out enthusiastically and then notices our countenance.

"Oh sorry did I interrupt something?"

"What is it?" says Dane understandably.

"The media is ready to hear a few words from you and your crew. You're on in two minutes," James replies.

"Alright, thanks Mr. Finly," Dane says with a half-smile.

Everyone gathers their things and heads out to the tarmac. As we step outside the cool breeze reminds us of the weather conditions. Gray clouds are marching through the Texan sky with intimidation. The reporters and cameraman are in a hanger waiting for us.

Camera flashes abuse our eyes. We all stand side by side as James begins addressing the media.

"Thank you for joining us for this special moment. As NASA has continually strived to prepare for these next few days, they have found these 7 men and women capable of accomplishing a mission beyond anything NASA has accomplished in the past. The captain of mission Defend has prepared to address you and I will answer your questions at the end of his address. Here is Captain Dane Floyd,"

Everyone claps respectfully.

Dane walks up and shakes James hand and smiles big for the people.

"We all have dreams,"

Bursts of flashes go off.

"We live for a purpose better than living itself. We work for good outcomes and we work hard for justice. We strive to know more so we can do more. Our lives revolve on improving, such as technology and expanding our understanding of the past, present, and future. In our day we have been given a great challenge in which our lives are threatened greatly. The 6 crewmen behind me and I have been by the world's side, hoping, praying, and believing that our dreams, purposes, and day to day labors will not be in vain! Today we leave.... but we stand firm and true to our purpose,"

I can't see his face but Dane seems choked up.

He continues "We would like to thank everyone for their support and prayers. This is a great day and we will tell our children about this day. We will tell our children about what strength people can have when they believe rather than doubt. Our mission as a whole begins now, but in a way, will never end,"

The cameras intensify with more flashing.

James goes up to the podium. "Alright, we have a few minutes for questions,"

Hands and people rise swiftly. James chooses a man in a blue dress shirt and gray pants. The man stands confidently,

"Mr. Finly, tell me how it is possible that your "spacecraft" is going to blaze through the approaching storm. Many Scholars have run their numbers and disagree with the likeliness of any air, slash, "space" craft making it through the intense atmosphere,"

"Well that's a great question and the answer is we are confident in our hybrid rocket with unique characteristics. This design has gained our respect and we will count on it being four times more stable than your average rocket," James explains proudly. "I would like to share more, but at this time many specs of the Defend spacecraft are highly sensitive and must remain confidential,"

Another person grabs James' attention.

"Yes ma'am" he acknowledges her.

"At this point of time, are we only to expect small sizes of meteors to enter the earth's atmosphere?" James takes a moment while looking at her, and then everyone,

"At this time, we expect car-sized meteors to hit the earth's surface,"

Many people appear unphased as they likely have already known this from previous reports.

"Alright, one more question," James says.

Then an old, balding, short man in the front row beckons to talk,

"Alright, we may not die from impact, but do we know what chemicals may be on the rocks? Is it possible other casualties will be because of gasses brought with the foreign objects?"

James tightens a little and stands up straight. "We have not detected any meteors or asteroids with dangerous chemicals or gasses. Perhaps we won't see any evidence until these objects are broken into pieces and reveal more before falling into our atmosphere,"

"And so, we have more time before the gasses reach us and we die more painfully?"

James quickly replies "We highly doubt those circumstances, but in that situation, direction will be given and our current certified shelters are sufficient,"

The old man continues thinking out loud. "...the gasses would seep within the earth and ruin the soil–"

James speaks over him "Well that's unlikely, Alright, the Defend crew must depart now, thank you for your time,"

Cameras shoot off.

All at once two security personnel come through each door.

People are swiftly funneled out awkwardly. Then, I hear booms and automatic weapons somewhere in the distance.

Something isn't right.

A swarm of national guard's cattle us into a room nearby.

2

T ruths Above

"Everyone please stay calm," says one of the well bulletproof suited guards.

All of us begin looking at each other with confusion and some fear.

Captain Dane pipes up, "Sir can you tell us what is going on?"

"I'm receiving word now," the guard says as he holds his finger to his ear.

We wait a moment.

"I'm receiving information that a radical group is attacking NASA. Although they are not close to us now I am told that we can't waste time getting you on the Defend ship,"

This is crazy! I heard about some people who believed this catastrophe is our destiny and the way God will choose the righteous. So now people are trying to interrupt us from attempting to do something good.

"Ok, although there is not any known terrorist nearby we are going to create a formation around your crew and walk to the craft,"

There are 8 guards and they begin talking about the formation.

"Okay, does everyone have their things?" asks the guard.

We all confirm we do.

"Alright, stay within our perimeter and put your heads down,"

Now I see the guards' name badge. Sgt. Jorge. He opens the door and has his assault rifle ready. Five more guards follow Sgt. Jorge out to the messy abandoned hanger. They begin to make a semi-circle. The guard next to me instructs us to follow the others.

As I step out, I can see the hanger has been secured with more guards at the other doors. The last two guards bring up the rear and all 8 make a circle around us.

"Remember to keep your head down and keep walking within the perimeter," Sgt. Jorge says.

We all move together. Now, we are exposed to the wind and we can see the dark monstrous clouds are ready to drool. The ship is about 100 yards away. I can still hear pops of gun fire, but then I hear squealing tires too close to us for comfort. I want to look back, but don't want to slow down.

"Keep your head down!" Sgt. Jorge yells.

I look back through the guards to see a van coming up next to us. It's probably ten feet from us when its window shatters. The driver, another national guard yells, "There's a sniper! I'm gonna stay next to you until he is neutralized,"

Now more windows shatter and shots increase.

"Just keep it in idle, we'll keep walking," Sgt. Jorge yells back.

The driver, trying to slouch, puts his thumb up.

"We're almost there," Sgt. Jorge yells back to us.

The bullets stop. We continue walking until the driver, Sgt. Jorge, and the other guards begin turning their heads to each other.

"We all need to run!" says Sgt. Jorge

The circle gets a little bigger and we begin running. I'm panicking in my head. I wish I had one of those ear pieces. What the heck is going on?

We're about 20 yards from the ship and then I look up to see a drone plane. I fear that it's not manned by the National Guard. Then the plane dips. I would run faster but I'm in a herd.

Just before I reach the runway I see the drone spit a missile out from its underside.

My heart drops and Susanne looks at me with despair. I don't know whether to watch or not, but I do.

As it comes closer, it redirects its path and meets another missile I didn't realize was in flight. Only fifty yards away a ball of fire erupts. The van stops and so do we, to take cover from the flying debris.

"They neutralized the sniper and the rocket launcher," says Sgt. Jorge. "Go ahead, we have done our part, the rest is up to your crew," He looks at Captain Dane and then at the ship.

"Thank you, Sgt. Jorge," says Captain Dane.

We all thank the men and hurry to get on board. The spacecraft is on a track that begins parallel with the ground, but then angles and slopes up perpendicular. We enter the spacecraft by climbing the stairs to a door on the top of it. Ground control is waiting for us on the monitor.

"We are so sorry about that!" says Ron Sparks.

"We're glad you're okay,"

"We are all fine. I think we just need a minute to breathe," Rick blurts out.

"I understand that," Ron says kindly. "However, we need you to move quickly so that you're able to beat the worst of the storm,"

We look at each other just wanting to breathe, but understanding the circumstance we begin taking our places.

Within minutes everyone has gotten comfortable.

"Controls look good, all systems up and running," Yochi informs.

"Systems are in sync and ready for designated launch," Susanne chimes in.

"We are closing the doors," says Jet.

Ron Sparks comes on the monitor, "Alright let's get you guys up there already, huh?"

"Alright, we're ready to launch. Countdown, sixty seconds," Captain Dane straps into his seat.

The control board adjusts for him automatically.

"What is the situation with those radicals?" Rick blurts out.

We all kind of look at him like this isn't the time to ask that.

"It could be better, but don't worry about it. I need your head on the mission," Ron Sparks replies.

"Thirty seconds to launch" an automated voice puts us in reality.

I check my seatbelts. We're looking ahead at mostly charcoal clouds. I can see just out of the corner of the window a bush blowing, giving me the idea that the winds and gusts have picked up in the last few minutes. I can hear the ship revving up with the amount of power it's ready to release. We are all looking straight ahead ready for the rockets to kick us to the monster above.

Lightning flashes in the distance.

Bang!

The rockets burst and we're moving down the runway track only to quickly adjust upward. The monitors show that the track rockets disengage our spacecraft right before we leave the track.

We begin cutting through the gray clouds and the crafts' exterior is taking on a suit of water. We can feel the wind's rejection to our goal. The ride is not smooth and Rick begins breathing heavily. The computer is relaying numbers back to Dane. Then, the sky is clear in front of us and we can see the stars and a passing satellite, possibly recording us for the world to see. The external rockets burn out and drop back to earth.

Now gliding in space, we begin to receive directions to begin releasing missiles. Everyone takes their places. Susanne and I sit down at our computers to bring up previously prepared files.

"This is amazing," Yochi says as he peers out the windows.

"Just think, in a day this area will be immersed with rocks," says Josh staring out the front.

"I can't believe we made it through that storm. I thought we were dead for sure," Rick says, still feeling under the weather.

"It was brutal," agrees Jet.

I can't figure out Jet. She doesn't talk enough to know who she is and how she got here. She usually doesn't chit chat and goes straight to work.

"Alright, it looks like our coordinates are still valid and we are ready to begin launching missiles," Susanne breaks my thought of Jet's strange personality.

"Great, let's inform ground control and the supply shuttle," Captain Dane says. "Ground control, this is Captain Dane speaking. We have confirmed coordinates and we're ready to initiate the launch of the first set of missiles. Over,"

"Copy that. Continue with operation, Defend," Ron Sparks confirms,"

I begin programming the first missile, "Initiation of the first missile of operation Defend, November 15th 2038, in three, two, and one,"

A monitor shows the missile disengage from its chamber and stream out from the ship.

"Woohoo!" Everyone cheers.

"Good job, now only 67 more," Dane says with a smile.

Josh and Jet are doing a tour of the ship for the media. Captain Dane, Rick, and Yochi are talking about mining asteroids next year. Susanne and I have got 28 missiles out in the last two hours. Only six more before we need to reload more. That is the worst part. We'll have to transfer them from the supply ship and load them in the launch chambers. Most of the first set of missiles will break up the biggest asteroids while the second set will identify and reduce the sizes of the next biggest fractures produced.

"Only six more," says Susanne.

"Well you two will have a good break because the supplies won't be around for another 45 minutes," Captain Dane says, passing by.

. . .

"So, what do you think is going on with the radicals at NASA?" Susanne asks me.

"I hope it's under control. I can't imagine them still fighting," I reply.

"I don't know, they somehow had the ability to get a rocket launcher on the premises. I wish people weren't so crazy. We're just trying to help humanity. Is that so much to ask," She says, covering her face in frustration.

"Yeah it's amazing how strange people get when they feel their lives are immensely threatened. Some people stick to their values even closer while others throw them out altogether," I say.

"I was watching a program a few months ago and it was talking about people's ideas and their views since the announcement of the threat to the earth. There are tons of crazy people out there," Susanne exclaims.

I give her my full attention.

"Yeah, I think a lot of people have lost hope. I still believe there is a God watching over us. He may have given us a trial, but he has also given us a tool to face it," I reply.

"Yeah, I guess that's a good way to look at it. I wish more people could accept hope instead of despair," She says.

"We have two more" I look back at the screen.

"-- And so there you have it, the Defend ship," Josh and Jet come around the corner while talking to the media.

"Well, thank you for your time and service. Let the crew know we are grateful for their service and we hope you all return safely," says the man on the thin glass monitor. They sign off.

"Josh, how about we go mining asteroids next year?" says Captain Dane.

Josh laughs, "Yeah that sounds good. I heard there should be some coming near earth," Which is true, some are expected to come near earth for the next ten years at least.

"Alright, the last one for now is out," I say as I hit the button.

Cheers are exclaimed.

"I will update ground control," Captain Dane says.

"I am taking a nap. Wake me up when the supply ship is five minutes out," I tell them.

"Don't worry about it, we will load everything and take care of it," Captain Dane says.

"But...the system will need–" I'm cut off by Susanne.

"I can do that!" "Alright, thanks. Wake me up when the hard work is over," I chuckle.

I strap down in my cot and just think of the day. I can't believe we almost died before getting on the ship. I wonder what is going on down there. What if there was a nuclear war and there is nothing to actually go back to. I wonder how my family is doing. I'm sure everything will be ok. I just need to clear my head and reset from the last few hours. It only takes a few minutes for me to pass out.

THERE IS A TON OF NOISE.

There is panic and fear in people's voices.

I'm shoved and I awake to my entire crew in front of my cot.

As I sit up everyone is staring at me including two guys from the supply shuttle. One of the men I don't know calls me over.

"Bryan, come on," he says sternly.

I unstrap myself from my cot and stand up. Everyone is quiet and I see fear and confusion on everyone's face. Now I see the second man has a gun pointing into the room.

"What is going on?" I ask.

"Bryan, you know what I need you to do, right?" The first man asks.

"I know to do my job, but I can do it without a gun drawn!"

"No, Jake told you and you agreed," He replies angrily.

"What? Jake has been gone for years and no one has heard from him," I say clearly offended.

The man glares at me. "Come with me,"

I leave my room with everyone standing, baffled.

I hear the door close behind us as we walk to the front of the ship while the other man stays with my crew.

"You know my name, right? I am Carl Dagoon. I knew Jake for some time. You are right, no one knows where Jake is and few people care. He was supposed to have sent you a message but in the end, went back on his word and foiled our agreement,"

He stops and looks at me.

"I have no idea what business he had with you," I sternly say to him.

"I can tell you don't know anything," Carl walks to the control panels and begins accessing the system.

"Your friend Jake was going to make an agreement to help destroy government leaders around the world. But we don't need Jake any longer,"

"I am not going to help you," I back up.

"Fortunately, we don't actually need you any longer, except for our plot. The only thing left to do is fire off the missiles to the government buildings and bunkers. I have your password and identity already and you will look like the one to have sent the missiles," He says with a smirk.

I make a rash decision and jump at him and we both slam into the wall. He throws me to the ground and I quickly roll to my feet.

He pulls out a taser gun. I begin to back up.

With no hesitation he shoots and I am on the floor. Pain throughout my body runs a riot. He walks back to the control panel and puts in a thumb drive. I try to get up but he sends another jolt into my body.

Gasping and shaking I can only watch him set the system to launch rockets to continents, countries, and then government buildings. He is prepared, so prepared to launch to specific places. He must be working with a strong organization.

"The rockets are meant for asteroids, if we don't destroy the asteroids what good would your plan be.? Everyone will be dead in the end," I exclaim trying to get up.

He turns to me.

"You are right. If I hadn't brought extra rockets our purpose would be in vain and ignorant. This is a time for change and opportunity. We should all work with nature and the change it brings to life,"

I use a chair to help me get back on my feet.

"Before Jake got cold feet in the best part of the operation, he performed a service on these missiles. He knew the locations to send them and how to program the missiles into the system without giving any hints of their existence. Not many people know how to do that. He had talent in hiding things, like himself the last three years,"

I manage to pull out a prong discreetly.

"Conner!" Carl yells. "Let's go!"

Carl hits a few more buttons and the missiles are preparing to launch in only a matter of minutes. Conner comes around the corner.

"Everything is ready?" He asks while grabbing his helmet.

"Yes, we are ready to return," Carl says.

"It appears we only have 30 minutes until the first missiles hits Russia, China, Iran,--"

"All those will be shot out of the sky!" I say glaring at him.

"Okay, we will see," He says as he pulls out a silver box. "It's unfortunate that some good people must be buried under a better cause,"

Oh no!

Carl has a syringe!

I begin to stand up and Carl reaches for the taser and then realizes I'm no longer barbed.

It's too late. I'm already arm's length when he raises the syringe.

I plow into him and grab his arm. We both hit a glass monitor.

He pushes me back into a chair and I fall over it onto my knees.

I hear screeching metal from the back of the ship.

Carl quickly reaches for his helmet and nods to Conner. Conner pulls out a cylinder object and tosses it into the monitors. Within seconds smoke is being spewed out all over the main controls.

Carl and Conner exit the ship.

Captain Dane peeks his head in.

"They're gone," I yell out.

Everyone rushes in.

"Grab a blanket!" Captain Dane says and he moves quickly to the front of the ship. Rick grabs a first aid kit and dumps its contents on the seat.

"Alright get the doors ready," Rick calmly instructs.

He immerses himself into the smoke, fumbles the smoke bomb a little, but manages to scoop it up and closes the box. Jet is at the door.

Josh comes running in "I've got a blanket,"

Yochi points out Rick tossing the first aid kit out the doors.

"Turn on the vents, Yochi," Captain Dane says. "This stuff is thick. It's coating the glass monitors and the windows. Grab some cleaning supplies. Oh, Bryan I'm sorry, are you alright? We saw the whole thing through the security link," He helps me get up.

"Yeah, I'm okay, thanks. The missiles are about to launch though. We need to contact the Governments. We need to warn them!" I say, desperately trying to convince everyone that I am not in on Carl's operation.

"This smoke is a pain," Rick exclaims.

Captain Dane hurries to the monitor. "If we can't get this stuff off, I won't be able to see the coordinates and operate the landing system," Captain Dane informs.

"So, what? We won't be able to land?" Rick looks at Captain Dane.

"We will have to land manually," Captain Dane replies back.

"Well, this keeps getting better," Jet says.

"Contact ground control Jet," Captain Dane orders.

Jet starts calling ground control.

"It could have been a lot worse," Captain Dane says with a sigh.

"Ground control, this is Defend, we have a code red situation," Jet says intensely. There's no response.

"So, did all the missiles get launched?" I ask.

"We loaded all of the missiles and shot them off when Carl got on board," Susanne says.

"But, now we have extra and they're programmed to launch any minute," Jet says, while trying to get a hold of ground control.

"This will definitely start a war between all nations," Josh says.

I quickly move to the missile control panel.

"I'll try to stop the launch, but that sounds too easy for all of Carl's hard work,"

"Maybe ground control could warn the governments and intercept the missiles," Yochi says.

"That's a great idea. How's that coming, Jet?" Asks Captain Dane.

"I'm having a hard time getting through," Jet shakes her head.

"Hey guys, it's coming off," Rick says excitedly as he scrubs the monitors.

"Bryan, how much time do we have before they launch?" Captain Dane says as he jumps on the controls.

"We have less than ten minutes," I reply.

"What do you think the problem is?" Susanne asks.

"I wonder if ground control is in trouble," Says Jet.

Captain Dane looks up from the controls. "Gosh, I hope not. We need them to get back to us soon,"

"We will be responsible for the missile attacks. America, and the others will be responsible; nations will turn against us," Josh says with distress.

"Bryan, can we disarm the missiles manually?" Josh asks.

"There wouldn't be enough time," I reply.

"Ground control this is–" Jet is cut off. The monitors show an incoming call.

"Accept call!" Captain Dane calls out.

"This is ground control to Defend, can you hear us?"

"This is Defend we can hear you," Captain Dane says with relief.

"I'm sorry we could not get to you sooner. We have been under attack and our systems keep being interrupted. We also believe you may have trouble landing at NASA. You have to land in a secluded field," Ground Control says.

"Sir, we have a bigger problem. The supply ship crew set up the system for missiles to target main government buildings around the whole world," Captain Dane explains simply.

There is a pause.

"Can you stop the missiles from launching?" The man asks.

"We have tried everything to stop them. There isn't enough time to manually disarm them either. You must warn the Governments so they can intercept the missiles," Captain Dane says.

"There is less than eight minutes" I say, stepping forward.

"We will get on it. Is it possible to get each missile's destination?" The man asks.

"Bryan?" Jet turns to me.

"It will take me a few minutes," I reply. I jump back on the monitor.

"We will have them sent to you soon," Jet relays to the man.

"Alright. You and your crew were supposed to head back 15 minutes ago; this doesn't give you much time when you land to make it back to NASA," Ground control says.

The connection glitches for a couple seconds

"I will be right back, stay on the line," Ground control hangs up.

No more than a minute goes by before we get called back.

"This is Ron Sparks. Captain, are you there?" A voice comes on.

"This is Captain Dane and the crew," Captain Dane answers.

"Listen, we don't have a lot of time. I need your crew to head back immediately. Unfortunately, we won't be able to get you and your crew to your families on time, so we will take you and your crew to the closest bunkers available," Ron declares, appearing somber.

"Copy that," Captain Dane says and then hesitates. "Is everything okay there?"

"To be truthful, things are kind of berserk down here. You should know since you will be in the mix, you may be targeted during your landing. We have a tactical team picking you up, but from the last few hours, we now know there are a lot of terrorists on our soil. They got into our system which we just regained control of before calling you. Even the military is calling them highly advance," Ron says as he sits back in his chair.

"Well, that's the thanks we get, huh? We will be on our way no," Captain Dane says as his eyes trail past the monitor.

"I have a landing zone ready. You will be landing in Texas. The coordinates have been sent to you. I probably won't see you and your crew for a couple days so I'll say thanks now for your crews' hard work and sacrifice," Ron says.

Captain Danes' eyes zero in on the monitor.

"Not to interrupt but, I sent the coordinates to you and we have five minutes until the missiles launch," I inform Ron Sparks.

"Thank you, and good luck crew," Ron Sparks signs off.

"Jet, prepare the ship to land at the appropriate coordinates. Crew, you know the drill,"

WE ALL DISPERSE to different parts of the ship and begin picking up loose objects and closing the cabinets. I see a blinking light from the missile panel and go check it out.

"Missiles launching in five, four, three, two, one," The system informs.

"Captain, the missiles are launching," Everyone stops and looks out the window. The missiles slowly move out of their chambers, almost taunting us and saying, "We are what you couldn't stop,"

A few of them begin changing direction with small pulses of air pushing them towards Earth.

After a minute goes by, everyone finishes cleaning. I secure a closet when I hear Jet telling us to take our seats.

"The ride will be rough, it's a big ship," Captain Dane says as we strap ourselves in.

"Don't forget to breathe and think happy thoughts," He adds.

"Ok. Systems ready. We are heading back," Jet informs.

I peer out the windows and take one last look at space and its vast beauty. I hope we land relatively fine. Jet engages the propulsion units.

As we head back towards Earth there are a few missiles we can see still right before metal shields cover the windows.

"Here we go. We are about to enter the atmosphere," She says.

We begin feeling a wobble and then some turbulence. Jet reverses the propulsion for a slower entrance. Warning signals begin popping up on the screen.

"What are those about? What is going on?" Josh says worriedly.

"The ship is just feeling the stress," Captain Dane says.

Rick is the only one looking quite calm with his eyes closed. The ship starts to really shake and then there is a huge bump.

"Jet, kill and detach the propulsion," Captain Dane says sternly.

There's another big jerk. Jet slides her fingers over the monitor and hits a few buttons. We hear metal bend and break.

Josh is looking very uncomfortable. I wish I could close my eyes, but it makes me sick. I can't focus on anything because of the shaking.

"Detach the outer wings, now," Captain Dane continues to instruct while monitoring the system.

Jet brings up a screen of the ship and simultaneously selects the left and right wing tips. With a button, the wings fly off. After those fall off, Jet does the same with the mid-section and lastly the base of the wings and the back section of the ship. Now it's just the capsule and us.

Still rumbling quite a bit, the cabin rings with alarms of possible problems.

"Not too much longer until we let the parachutes fly," Captain Dane insures while looking at Jet.

Jet is looking straight ahead, appearing tense. She starts breathing heavily. Her hands grip the arm rests.

"Jet, everything is okay. Be calm and take a deep breath," He instructs.

Then Rick, while his eyes are closed, calmly reassures her it will be okay. Jet still grips the chair. Captain Dane takes over the control panel.

"Hold on tight," He says as he deploys the first parachute.

Our velocity decreases so fast we all jerk forward hard in our seats. A section of the shield begins to separate over the windshield. I can see we're in a bunch of clouds. Captain Dane quickly types on the control panel.

"Dang it!" He says.

He releases the two side parachutes.

We feel a smaller drag.

"We might land on the beach, just a heads up," He yells over all the noise. There's static and then a voice begins coming through it.

"I think it's ground control," Susanne pipes up.

It comes in clearer.

"Run into the trees. Tactical teams are meeting you as well as some unknown helicopters. Can you hear me?"

"Yes, we can hear you–" Captain Dane says before being interrupted.

"Our tactical team has yellow marked on their helmets. Do not go with any other soldiers," The voice commands.

"Copy that," Agrees Captain Dane.

The call ends. Captain Dane looks at us

"We are landing in 3 minutes,"

"Are we going to be shot at? Asks Josh.

"I don't think we'll be shot at," I say, hoping to convince myself as well.

"Yeah, they would have blown us up in the air by now," Captain Dane says not really helping any of us feel safe.

"Why would there be other people wanting to take us or kill us within an hour of asteroids hitting the earth?" Asks Yochi, confused.

"Maybe for ransom, maybe they can get some good deals for releasing heroes," Rick blurts out.

Captain Dane throws a hand in the air. "Okay, alright, that's enough. We don't care why the other people want us. They won't get their hands on us anyways," he says.

Static again floods the capsule.

"Crew of Defend, this is Jake Farr, I and a few others are here to help you. Let the tactical team know. We will be in the brush so don't let them shoot in there,"

We're all confused; we look at each other in disbelief. The static goes dead.

"Wait, is this the guy that left the notes?" Asks Susanne.

"Yeah," I say in disbelief.

"Bryan, do we trust him? You know him the best," Captain Dane asks as he looks at me seriously.

I'm not sure what to say, it has been so long, a lot could have happened.

"Well, I would hate for everyone's safety to be in my hands. It has been almost three years since I have talked with him. He could be different from how I knew him,"

Then, I pause. "But I think we should trust him,"

The capsule begins alerting the distance to the water. Captain Dane presses a few buttons above his head.

"Alright everyone, get ready we are going to be landing in the shallows of the beach which means the waves will be on us. Hopefully the waves won't push us around too much," He says.

I can see outside a little through the broken panel. The computer counts down the meters. It's hard to tell but I think we're moving diagonally, sort of fast.

Captain Dane reads my mind, and says "Hold on we're descending. Touching down in three, two, one!"

Splash!

3

Imposters

WE DROP through the water and then ram the sandy bottom. Our bodies tense up as the impact attempts to yank us out of our seats. We sit for a few seconds in silence.

The waves pound the back of the capsule.

Captain Dane sighs, "Is everyone ok?"

We all look at each other.

"Yeah," Susanne replies.

"I have a headache," Josh complains.

Another big wave hits us. The capsule rocks forward and back.

"Let's get out of here," Captain Dane says as he unbuckles himself.

Everyone begins to do the same.

Captain Dane opens a box on the wall by the door and smacks a red button. The hatch pops open and gas emits from the seal.

After waving the gas away, Captain Dane climbs through the exit.

"Oh yeah! Fresh air!" He says.

"Alright, I'll jump out first, test the water, and make sure there aren't any reefs or rocks," Captain Dane volunteers.

"Do you see any helicopters?" Inquires Yochi.

"Uh…no…nothing in the skies," He says as he looks around.

He peers out over the side of the capsule and jumps.

Josh is up next. I faintly hear Captain Dane say it's safe.

"Actually, Susanne, why don't you go next, I'll be last," Josh says as he climbs down the ladder.

Susanne looks confused. "Okay," She says hesitantly.

"Dude, Josh, you're such a gentleman," Rick says sarcastically.

"Guys, come on!" Captain Dane yells to us.

Susanne hops out and I hear a splash.

"Yochi go ahead, I think Jet needs a minute," I say as I look back at her.

She is looking at the controls and the screen.

"Are you okay Jet?" I ask.

She takes a moment to reply.

"Yeah. I just…I just wish I hadn't frozen up. What good am I when it comes to the moments that really matter?"

"Woah! Hey, Jet these things happen. Everyone has moments of overloading stress. It's okay though because Dane was able to, –," I try to comfort her.

"--and if Captain Dane wasn't there?" She asks, frustrated.

"I'm next,", she says as she pushes past me. Rick is already on the ladder.

"Hurry up or get off," She says, trying to be polite.

"Okay, okay," Rick says.

I hear his entrance into the water.

A wave hits the capsule and it rocks. Jet holds on at the top of the ladder. Once the rocking stops, she jumps out and into the water. I jester to Josh to go ahead of me.

He hesitates and then denies my offer. "Go ahead, Bryan,"

"Alright," I say.

I pull myself up the ladder.

The sight of the water and beach is amazing. For the last few weeks,

I have only seen the city and walls of the NASA facility. I jump into the water feet first.

Although it is somewhat cold, it's refreshing. I only swim a few meters toward the beach before I feel the sandy bottom. Jet and Yochi are just getting to dry land and Captain Dane, Rick and Susanne are waiting, knee high in the waves.

I can finally stand up, so I turn around to look at Josh. He is at the top of the ladder just looking at the water.

"Josh, what are you waiting for?" Captain Dane yells.

Josh begins climbing out and just before he jumps a big wave hits the capsule. Josh slips and the door swings, smashing his leg on the way out. His back splashes into the white foamy wave. I hear gasps behind me. I start swimming towards him. His head comes up and he is gritting his teeth. I grab Josh from behind and head towards the beach.

Rick, Susanne, and Captain Dane help me pull Josh onto the beach. We are almost out of the water when Jet begins yelling and then we hear the sound of helicopters.

"Let's hurry," Captain Dane says.

"Don't forget, make sure those guys have yellow marks on their helmets," Rick reminds us.

I can see men dressed in swat gear inside the helicopter. Two men repel down as a second helicopter lands. We get Josh to dry land finally. Yochi and Jet start asking us what happened.

Susanne begins pulling Josh's pant leg up. Just below the knee is an enormous bruise.

"I think you have internal bleeding," She says.

"Are you guys okay?" One of the swat guys asks as he runs up to us.

"Most of us," Captain Dane replies, and then he notices the absence of yellow on the man's helmet.

"Well, we need to get you out of here, there are only 35 minutes left," The man ensures.

I look at the man and then the helicopter that dropped him. It's hovering and pointing in our direction, but then abruptly ascends. Another helicopter lands on the beach a little ways behind us.

"Come on everyone, let's go," He says sternly.

The second swat member has made his walk to us. None of us are sure what to do.

I try to stall, "Uh, so where will we be sheltered?"

"It's just over the ridge, we need to leave now!" The second swat member says.

As I look at Captain Dane I hear a roaring of gunfire. I crouch down fast and cover my ears. The chopper in the air is shooting repeatedly. I look toward its target to see three more helicopters are darting toward us, returning fire.

"Alright everyone lets go!" The impersonators order.

Both have their guns pointed at us.

"Come on, move it!" They yell.

Susanne and I try to help Josh up. One of the men swiftly grabs Susanne's shoulder.

"Leave him,"

The second man rounds us up from behind and begins pushing us with the barrel of his gun.

The helicopter above us moves over the trees and is taking heavy fire. We all start moving towards the chopper on the ground. One of the friendly choppers flies to the left of us, over the water and then hovers over the grounded chopper.

Yochi, Josh, and Jet take off, sprinting toward the trees. As they run, the man behind us points his gun up at them.

"No!" I exclaim as I lunge at him.

A few single gun shots go off just as I reach him. I tackle him to the ground and quickly sit up to punch him.

I pause when I notice two bullet holes in his vest and him in agony. I get off of him and grab his gun. I turn to see the other man and he too is squirming on the ground in pain. Captain Dane grabs his gun.

The uninvited helicopter takes off over the trees, but doesn't get too far before combusting into flames. All three helicopters land on the beach. The second enemy helicopter we were heading towards, powers down. I can't see anyone inside it. It may have been a drone.

Susanne runs over to Josh while Captain Dane and I keep the two men on the ground.

"Don't you think about getting up," Captain Dane says as he points the rifle at the imposter.

Jet, Yochi, and Josh come out of the tree line. But, they aren't alone. Five other soldiers are behind them, holding rifles.

"Are you guys okay?" I ask.

"Yeah," Jet replies out of breath.

One of the three life saving helicopters has landed now.

The yellow marked swat team quickly runs up to the five random soldiers with rifles, who quickly put their hands up. The five men are walked over to us.

One of the swat members runs up to us, "Are you guys okay? We didn't have much of a choice but to shoot over your position,"

"We are okay, but Josh has internal bleeding and he needs immediate attention," Captain Dane says, as he hands his prisoner to a swat member.

Sgt. George, the swat member in charge, looks at Josh, "There is a facility close enough we can get him to, but first we need to take care of these guys," He looks at the five similarly dressed men.

They are now unarmed and on their knees. I walk over to them expecting to find an old friend.

"Do you know these men?" Sgt. George asks me.

"I just might know one of them," I reply.

Immediately one of the five guys looks up at me and it's him, Jake Farr.

He just smiles lightly at me.

I stop and stare while my mind races through memories.

"What's going on Jake?" I ask him seriously, still confused of what I should expect from him.

"I hoped I would have the chance to explain everything, and now I can," He says.

"Why did you leave...and come back?" I am now sounding upset.

"Listen, we can't chit chat here, we have less than 25 minutes to be sheltered," Stg. George exclaims.

"Everyone needs to get on a chopper,"

"He's right," Jake says.

"However, I do have a bunker, five minutes walking distance that everyone can come to,"

"No, no, we have government approved facilities. Everyone needs to come back with us," Stg. George is appalled.

"Actually, I think I am going to stay with these men," I say, half unsure about my decision.

"I'm sorry Bryan but I have orders, you must come with me," Stg. George insists.

I look around at my crew as they look at me like I'm out of my mind. I walk in-between the swat team into the circle with four strangers and an old friend. I then feel like that's exactly where I need to be.

Stg. George stares at me with a hard glare and then it turns to rolling of his eyes.

"Whatever, he can do as he wants. Everyone else, let's go before we become powder,"

His swat team follows him carrying Josh and the two imposters.

Yochi comes over to me and places his hand on my shoulder.

"Good luck. I hope to hear from you again," He then jogs off towards the chopper.

Rick, shakes my hand, "Are you sure you want to do this?" He asks.

"Yeah, I will be fine. Thanks though," I say with a small smile.

He walks off.

Susanne, Captain Dane, and Jet all come up.

"We too hope to see you again, soon," Captain Dane says.

"Yeah, don't get lost in the woods," Jet slips in.

They both head for the helicopters.

Susanne has some tears in her eyes. "It's been one crazy day, hasn't it?" She says quietly.

"I hope you know I appreciated serving with you. Don't lose that hope you have always had. That is what was the best part of trying to save the world," She smiles and gives me a hug.

Two of the helicopters begin to leave.

"Thanks, I have enjoyed the journey with you. We will see each other again," I say as she lets go of me.

She and a swat member board the last helicopter out.

As I watch them fly overhead, I begin to tear up.

"This probably wasn't the way you wanted say goodbye to your crew," Jake says as he walks up to me.

"It wasn't easy for me to leave my friends or family either,"

I look at him and can tell he really means it.

"But you will understand soon enough why I did it. Follow me, I'll show you what you need to know. I have a lot to tell you,"

4

The H.E.R.O Initiative

WE WALK for about 5 minutes into the woods before I see a concrete structure on a hillside with a metal door.

"This is it," Jake says. "This is where I have been most of the last few years,"

"Hiding?" I ask slightly upset.

"More like preparing," He replies.

Jake swipes his watch over a silver box. A door opens up and we walk in.

"What have you been preparing for? The sky falling?" I ask.

"No, I had that security when working for NASA. While working for them though, I found another threat to humanity. An organization that is going to feed off the disaster that is only minutes away,"

"Carl is in that organization. Why didn't you warn me?" I begin to be more upset.

"I wasn't sure who was in the organization. I suspected they had more people than just..." Jake pauses.

I look at him and he looks at me.

"Then just who?" I ask.

"Uh, well me, but I can explain," He says quickly putting his hands up in front of himself.

"I hope you can, because you are sounding pretty crazy right now with your hideout and knowledge of an organization trying to blow up capitals, you have been stalking me with notes and hacking into NASA's communication system. Please, explain!" I'm irate!

He looks at me and then at his personnel standing around. I see some place their hands on their guns. Jake raises a hand up and tells them it's okay.

"Okay, I know it all sounds bizarre but I have a good reason for keeping secrets the last few years. When I was still working with you, I began meeting up with these people who were working on new technology. They showed me sketches and blueprints of weapons and machines that were very impressive. I wanted to get in on the project. Only a few weeks before I disappeared, I was asked to get addresses of all the major capitals so the organization could present these new machines and weapons to them and get buyers. So, that task was easy because most of those addresses aren't hard to find. By the way, the way I met these people had nothing to do with me working at NASA, so I thought. A few days after getting what they wanted they told me someone from inside their organization had found the coordinates of multiple government bunkers and were planning to attack them after this disaster with stolen equipment from the organization. I was then asked to provide coordinates of all the bunkers that could be attacked. I gave them that information thinking we would defend the governments and get back what was ours. It was only a few hours later, after doing some snooping, that I put together what they were really trying to do,"

"They are trying to take over governments themselves," I say beating him to the punch. "I know that from Carl," I add.

"Exactly! That is when I chose to leave the organization, but not without some compensation," Jake says as he walks me over to a garage door.

He punches a code in, and the door spreads apart in four directions. We walk into a much bigger room, or warehouse. It is filled with heavy metal machinery. Jeeps, four-wheelers, motorcycles, tanks, and... mechs. I look at him with disbelief. I couldn't believe my eyes.

"I organized a group of old military friends and we were able to snatch a small amount of their equipment," Jake says proudly.

"Let me ask you, how many people do you have working for you?" I ask curiously.

"Well, first of all, they don't necessarily work for me. We all work together and compromise to reach the best solution to problems. There are just over 200 personnel that work in this place and less than 5,000 within H.E.R.O," He replies.

"Hero? Your organization is called Hero?" I try to clarify.

"It stands for Helping Everyone Restore Order. We are a little full of ourselves, but it is what it is," He says smiling.

"Okay, I see what you're trying to undertake. H.E.R.O is going to protect the governments from this other group of crazy people," I say with skepticism.

"Exactly," Jake says.

I start walking around the warehouse examining each of the different vehicles. "Even though these are pretty intense machines you don't think the governments can handle themselves?"

"Under normal conditions they could probably do just fine but this organization has a plan to use a type of Electromagnetic Pulse. They're EMP is highly sophisticated in that it affects all machinery without a special device. The device is within all of their own equipment," Jake says as he pops the hood on a jeep.

There seems to be some different components attached to the engine I haven't seen before.

"Would they be able to change the chip so that now your stolen vehicles won't be immune to their EMP?" I begin testing his plans.

"Great question, it is plausible but not likely. We..," He pauses and begins to whisper. "We have people on the inside that tell us there hasn't been a change," Jake nods.

A loud buzzer goes off.

"The first meteorites are hitting earth," An automated voice informs.

"Let's go to the satellite room and see what we are dealing with," We walk into the room and there are big screens and a few people on computers.

"It looks just like NASA's system," I say as I walk around.

"Yup," Jake says. "We get to see what they see,"

"Sir, it looks like we may have an approximate 5 hours of a large number of meteors," One of the technicians says.

"Alright, do we have a damage percentage report?" Jake asks.

"Not yet, Sam hasn't got back to us on that," The technician says.

"Okay. Let me know when it's in," I keep hearing thuds above us.

"How large are the meteorites that are falling?" I ask the tech.

"Well the largest ones are the size of cars but that doesn't mean we can't have bigger ones later on," He says.

"Right," I agree.

Jake begins to walk out of the room, so I follow.

"What else should I know?" I grab his shoulder.

He jesters to continue following him. We continue walking into a room with large lockers. He sits down on a bench.

"My wife knows I am alive,"

I am shocked. How could she know and be okay with Jake gone?

"How long has she known?" I ask.

"About 6 days after my disappearance. I told her that I would like to keep it this way. I told her everything that had happened. I need all this to be confidential,"

Questions continue to flood my mind.

"Why didn't you go to the government and tell them?" I ask him. "They can handle terrorists better than some retired marine friends,"

"You're exactly right. After I stole the vehicles and equipment, I was trying to figure out what to do next. I decided to tell the government what I found and how I found the organization. I was locked up for days, then weeks, and then months before they believed me. I was able to show them what I stole and they knew that there was a more powerful technology being crafted against them," Jake says with confidence.

I know he is telling the truth, but it's so frustrating not having been in the loop and finding out what happened the last three years in just 30 minutes.

Jake looks at me. "The government officials did let me see my family, secretly, and I still do from time to time. Bryan, this base is secretive to most government personnel. It's a new division. The U.S. government is still trying to catch up to the technology these people have,"

"Who is this group? Is it a country or is it a company gone crazy? Who is behind all this? I say very intently.

"They call themselves Rev, supposedly short for revolution. This group began when someone made a breakthrough in technology and then decided to hold it from the world. Why? I'm not sure. They grew by drawing in people who care much less about anyone outside of Rev,"

He pauses.

"Bryan, I know it has been a tough day for you. I know all this is overwhelming but you have to trust me,"

I look at him and take a moment.

"I do. I believe you Jake. This is kind of crazy and I wasn't sure about all of this at first. But I believe you! I know I can trust you," I give him a tired but heartfelt smile.

"Thanks," He says with relief and a smile.

He stands up and we make our way to the door.

"I'll let you get some sleep now. In about 8 hours we will need to head out," "Where are we going?" I ask while following him out of the locker room.

"I figured you would like to see your wife and your kids," He says.

"Of course!" It's been a day since I have seen them but a month since I have been with them.

We walk through a hallway and round a few corners.

"This will be your room for today," Jake says as he swipes a card over a padlock and it turns green.

A lady walks up with a bag. "Here are some clothes and essentials you requested, Officer Farr," She says as she hands him the bag.

"Aw, perfect timing. These are for you Bryan. Go ahead and make yourself at home. There should be a watch in here, that's how we keep in touch around here. You can set your watch for 7 hours so we can get ready and go at about 5am. Your family still lives in Colorado, right?"

"Yeah, they do," I reply as I walk in my room.

It's a little cold, but it's nice.

"Alright, I'll see you in a bit," He says as he closes the door.

WHAT A DAY. I haven't been so tired since serving in the Marines. I haven't been shot at since then either.

I look in the bag and find the watch. It's black and sleek with no buttons on it. I tap the screen and it takes me to a clock. I tap it again and it brings up three app icons. One is a map, an app menu, and a distress call. I find the clock again and set an alarm for six hours. I look at the clothes in the bag and they are a uniform style I had seen a few people wear around here. I find some soap, toothbrush, and toothpaste, so I go into the bathroom and get cleaned up. By the time I get to bed I can hardly keep my eyes open. For a few minutes I am saddened because today is when the earth will be drastically altered. Societies will be cleaning up broken buildings, roads, and homes for the next few years. My eyes are heavy and my mind is exhausted. I give up thinking and I fall asleep quickly.

THERE'S a noise and it continues in a pattern. Oh yeah, it's the alarm I set. I rollover and find my watch on the nightstand. "It's still dark in the room," I think to myself. Then I remember it's because I am underground. I wish I could go back to sleep for another day, but I drag myself out of bed. I stand up and get ready. As I begin pulling my thoughts together, I'm getting excited to see my wife and kids. I have a boy that is six and a girl who is two, almost three. I miss being with them a lot. My wife and I have been married for eight years in December. I can't wait to get back home.

A BUZZ GOES off on my watch. I pick it up and see that Jake has sent me a message.

"Breakfast in five then go out the room and turn right then continue down the hall. You will find it from there,"

I pack up my clothes and put the watch on. I sweep the room for anything else of mine and then remember to make the bed. I switch the lights off and head out of the room.

As I walk down the hall I see some other people heading the same way. There's a semi large room with tables and chairs. I get in line and begin picking my food from the buffet. Everything smells really good. I get some eggs, sausage, and toast. I grab a bowl of fruit and a cup of milk and walk to one of the tables. As I sit down a young man comes up to me and asks if he can sit down. I have no objection.

"Go ahead. I'm Bryan, what's your name?" I say making sure his visit isn't awkward.

"It's James, I help manage the supplies in the armory. I heard you were one of the astronauts to go into space. What was it like?"

I sit there and stare at him for a second and then look down. I debate whether to mention being attacked.

"Well, it is pretty cool to see earth from way up there and be surrounded by absolutely nothing. Neither the takeoff nor the landing were my favorite parts," James smiles and nods. "That's awesome!"

We both eat our food and more people trickle into the room. My mind becomes enveloped in the machines I saw yesterday. I wouldn't mind trying those out.

"So, what do you do here?" James interrupts my daydreaming.

"I actually don't work here. I just kind of got here by chance. I'm heading out in an hour,"

"Well you're lucky to get in here without having a job. This is a highly classified facility,"

"Yeah, it definitely is. It must be neat working here," I say.

"I like it," James replies.

I feel a hand on my shoulder.

"Hey Bryan, how's that breakfast?"

It's Jake.

"Better than I have had in the last month," I chuckle a little.

"So, you have met James. He is a good worker and has been here just over a year," Says Jake.

"Yeah he's nice," I reply.

"Unfortunately, we can't chit chat all day, we have to get going," Jake looks at his watch.

"Well how is the air outside?" I ask. I almost forgot about the meteorites.

"The skies are clear of any significant falling debris. Your NASA team did great. There is one little thing that's interesting though. I'll tell you on the way. Come on," He begins walking.

"It was good meeting you James," I say as I pick up my bag and follow Jake.

WE WALK OUT of the mess hall and follow some yellow arrows labeled 'Hanger'.

"Alright, we decided to try flying out to Colorado. It may be a little risky, but the sooner we get you home the better," Jake says.

"I appreciate that, but I don't want to put anyone at risk," I say plainly.

"To be honest, we have a sweet jet that came in a few weeks ago and we have hardly been able to use it. We need to see what kind of maneuvering abilities it has. This jet can get us there in about one and half hours," He says with excitement.

"Okay, sounds good. Like you said the faster the better," I smile.

We walk down another hall and Jake stops at a door.

"Here we are, the hanger," He says as he leans forward in front of a camera. It takes a few seconds, but the door opens.

"Does that have eye recognition?" I ask, slightly impressed.

"It's actually more than eye recognition. The camera also senses your flesh and deep eye tissue for functionality. This prevents any access through dead body manipulations," Jake says, while walking into the slightly cold hanger.

"Take this jumpsuit and helmet," He says while pulling another off the wall for himself. I grab the jumpsuit and helmet and follow him to the jet. It looks quite sleek but hefty. It is a gray green with a black bird symbol on the side. It probably has a wingspan of 40 feet. This jet has been equipped with rotating engines. This technology is getting more common for the additional vertical take off option.

"I am impressed! This is pretty nice looking," I say with shock.

"Yeah there are supposed to be some more coming in a month. They are top notch military grade fighters," Says Jake as he steps onto a ramp leading into the jet.

"What is the firepower of this monster?" I'm always interested in new weapon technology.

"Twenty large missiles and 10 small missiles as well as dual machine guns.

We are inside the jet. The interior is quite spacious excluding the four-wheeler in the middle. I count ten seats, three on each side facing each other and four looking out the front window. Five of the seats are already claimed, four men dressed in black combat attire and a man dressed in a suit. The man in the suit stands up.

"Jake, how are you? Long time no see,"

"It's good to see you, Mr. Locke," Jake says back.

Mr. Locke shakes Jake's hand.

"This is Bryan, a good friend of mine. Bryan, this is Mr. Locke," Jake introduces me to the man.

"Right, I have seen you on the news a few times. It's good to meet you," Mr. Locke says as he turns to me.

"Nice to meet you," I say, as I shake his hand.

"Let's get going," Jake says, and he takes the pilot seat.

"Bryan, take this seat," He says pointing to the co-captain seat.

Jake pushes a button and the controls come out of the dashboard.

"Alright everyone, buckle up," Jake says as he begins checking the systems.

I put my seatbelt on and have to tighten it a lot.

"Was a giant sitting here?" I chuckle and look at Jake.

He just smiles as he continues to check everything. I look all around at the controls. There are some monitors just above the windshield. Two show the camera view of the inside of the jet and one switches between different points outside of the jet.

"All systems check. Opening bay doors," Jake flips a switch and types on the dashboard control panel.

The giant door rumbles and separates into two scalene triangles. I look at my watch. It's 6:21 am. We'll probably get there around 8 o'clock. The structure's door is now wide open and we begin to move forward. The runway starts within the structure and continues 100 yards outside.

Jake takes the throttle and pulls it towards himself. Immediately I feel the force of the engines propelling us forward.

"Lift off in, three, two, one," Jake says as he pulls it back further. I am caught off guard of how fast we begin to take off. I stare straight ahead not entirely comprehending the procedure.

Our wheels are off the ground. We exit the structure passing trees not far from our wings. With no warning, we make a quick ascension. The sky is hazy and the haze is denser in some areas than others. As I look down over a few cities, I can make out that there are some buildings damaged badly. I even see a fire or two. Before long we are too high up to make out any more of the city's damage. I think about the informative and instructional videos that have been given in preparation for the catastrophe. One thing that stuck out, was making sure to shut off gas lines where possible to reduce the chance of fires. It just takes one house fire to light a neighborhood ablaze. With everyone taking shelter and roads possibly being damaged, there is no telling how long it would take for first responders to arrive at a scene, if at all.

Jake turns left, making me brace myself a little.

I turn and look at Jake. "What do you call this beast of a machine?"

"It is the Falcon X50," He replies with a big grin. "Do you like it?"

"It has some boom to it," I reply.

"You haven't seen anything yet," He says as he pulls the throttle back more.

A red light turns on around the base of the throttle stick and I begin to sink into my chair. "This is about 8,500 mph," Jake says as he does a quick look at me.

I just raise my eyebrows and nod.

We go about 30 minutes at this speed and say little to each other. The sky is still hazy looking. We're flying over a desert. It has a large dark fractured meteorite shattered all over it. Jake looks at it too.

"Woah, that's a huge meteorite," He says. Jake slows down the Falcon. The next 10 minutes we see numerous meteorites scattered all over.

"We'll be there in 5 minutes," Jake says as he veers left and cranks up the speed again.

WE REACH THE CITY, Dunken. It looks mostly intact. The roads are cluttered with meteorites and bits of chipped buildings. We come up to the airport and the runway is speckled with pebble size meteorites.

"Can we land on that?" I ask Jake.

"Well, we probably shouldn't try a normal descent, but this Falcon does hover. We can try a tight spiral descent and hopefully push out the debris enough to clear a nice landing zone," Jake replies while searching the controls.

"I just haven't had a chance to practice it," He adds.

I cock my head and think he shouldn't try it right now.

"It's the blue switch under the yoke," One of the guys from behind says.

"Thanks!" Says Jake as he finds the switch. "Ok, I'll just get over the runway and try this out," He says.

I grasp the armrest to brace myself.

"There must be an auto pilot on here that can land this," I try to change his mind. "I'll do that if this doesn't work," He says with a smile.

Jake descends and gradually decreases the speed. We're above the runway and Jake flips the switch.

"Hold on everyone," He warns us all. He turns right then left quickly. We are at a 95-degree angle, spiraling down 100 feet. Jake drops the speed more and levels the Falcon perpendicular to the ground. We are now looking off center down the runway towards hangers. He lands the jet with a little wobble.

"Not bad Jake, not bad," Mr. Locke says from behind.

I notice one of the doors to a hanger is open. A couple of men stand at the door watching us.

I turn to Jake. "Do you know those guys?"

"Yes, they're expecting us. You are always so curious and attentive to your surroundings Bryan. I like that, but don't ever let it become worries. You are in good hands," Jake replies.

Everyone begins to unbuckle their seatbelts.

"I am allowed to worry. There is a lot going on that makes me have valid reasons to worry," I give Jake a piece of my mind.

Who does he think he is? "Well, trust me enough when I say that you don't need to worry, unless I tell you to," He says confidently.

"Okay," I say sarcastically.

5

Fort and Fun

THE FOUR COMBAT men begin grabbing gear and unloading a four-wheeler. "Charles, Robin, take the quad down the route and scout out the area. I doubt there are any Rev's here, but who knows what is happening now in the world," Jake orders. The two men jump on the vehicle and speed off.

"The rest of us are meeting up with more H.E.R.O.'s. They have some vehicles for us,"

We walk to the hanger where a man in heavy armor meets us.

"About time," He says as he smiles and gives Jake a solid handshake.

"Roy, this is Bryan. We're taking him home 8 miles out from here," Jake says.

"Hi, it's good to meet you Roy," I say, a little intimidated by his large stature and heavy armor.

"Likewise, Bryan. You have some guts running up to space and taking out those asteroids at the last minute. I appreciate your service,"

"Thank you. There wasn't much of a choice," I laugh a little.

"Roy, I was told you had some vehicles and men that I could barrow for this little rendezvous," Jake walks into the hanger looking around.

"I do. We would be happy to assist you. Over here we have a June Bug that holds 8 people and equipment. We also have four Tigers," Roy says as he points to some four-wheelers.

The June Bug is a long, lifted truck with what appears to be a heavily armored roof.

"Well those would work but what about that one," Jake replies pointing to a nice dune buggy equipped with a machine gun.

"That's probably not necessary," Roy says.

"Well you never know," Jake replies.

"I don't want you driving that around town, people will never come out of their bunkers," Roy says as he puts his hand on the June Bug.

"Fine, we'll take this June Bug," Jake says with disappointment.

"I'll give you two of my guys. They know the city inside and out," Roy motions two men towards the truck.

"We shouldn't take too long," Jake says as he climbs into the driver's seat.

I begin to hop in the passenger's seat when I hear Mr. Locke clear his throat.

"Bryan, do you mind if I ride up there with Jake, I need to talk to him about some business."

"Oh, yeah, that's fine," I climb down and head to the rear of the truck. I don't really mind where I ride as long as I get home. I jump up in the back of the truck and sit down with four soldiers. Two are Jake's and two are Roy's.

As I look around the truck I realize how excessive all these men with their gear seem to be just to get me home.

I try to make light conversation. "It looks like I am underdressed," I say with a chuckle. One of the guys gives me a half smile.

. . .

THE TRUCK ROARS AND RUMBLES. We roll out of the hanger and head out of the gates of the airport. One of Roy's soldiers directs Jake periodically from behind the passenger seat through the grated barrier.

A few minutes down the road we are in the heart of the city. I look out the back of the truck at the streets and buildings. The streets are filled with debris from the meteorites. I wonder if it is this bad everywhere else. My wife and I have had a house here for almost three years. The past two years I have hardly been here during my intense NASA training.

A radio crackles in the front cab and I hear Jake talking. I can't make out what the conversation is about. A green light above our heads turns yellow. I look at the men in combat attire, they check their rifles and slightly adjust their gear.

"What does that yellow light mean?" I ask.

"It's letting us know there may be a threat. A red light will mean there is definitely a threat," One of Jake's men explains.

"Of course it does. Two minutes from home," I'm annoyed.

The truck takes a hard right and I almost fall out of my seat. A speaker turns on in the back and I hear Jake's voice.

"We are taking a different route than planned. We will most likely run into combat on the way out. Don't worry Bryan, we are almost there,"

I look over at the men with their stone faces. I once was like them. Being in the military at age 20 made me like that, fearless, and focused. I only served 4 years and now after being out for over ten I have lost some of that discipline. A part of me wishes to become strong like that again. However, that entails a certain lifestyle that I don't know how would affect my family life.

The tall city buildings are now a few blocks behind us. We must be coming up on the city's bunkers. This one bunker can hold 4,000 people. I think there are a few others that hold a little less around the city.

We make a left and the truck comes to a stop. This is it, I get to see my family. I get a little teary eyed just thinking about what I and they have been through. I follow the men out the back. They stand on guard checking each direction.

"Alright Bryan, we made it," Jake says.

"Let's get in there," He walks over to a metal door and opens it.

A dark stairway leads down to another door. We make our way down to the door. I go to open it and it's locked. I see a button that must be a buzzer. I press it and I hear nothing. I press it again and then a camera unfolds from the wall.

"Who are you?" A voice comes through a speaker.

"Bryan Reed. My wife and kids are here. My wife is Samantha Reed. Please, I need to get in."

There is some silence. The locks click and the door opens. A man stands with a rifle. Jake walks up from behind.

"I'm Officer Farr, I am here with Bryan."

"Okay follow me," The man behind the door says.

He opens the door wider and three other soldiers stand nearby. I notice Mr. Locke and two other men come along.

The building is bland with gray cement walls everywhere. As we walk down a hallway I see a man and then my wife and kids come out of a room. I run to them. I gush with tears and my wife does too. I give them a huge hug. We kneel there on the ground for a minute embracing each other. Once the waterworks turn off we stand up.

"Bryan, let's go into a room for a few minutes," Jake puts his hand on my shoulder.

"Yeah, that would be good." I say trying to put myself back together.

We step into my family's room and close the door.

"Jake, I can't believe it's you," Samantha looks at him then me.

"It's a long story," I tell her.

"How did you get here so quick," She asks me.

"Jake was there at the place we landed and helped us. I decided to go with him and he took me to a nearby bunker. Luckily he had a plane to fly me here,"

Some static is heard from Jakes radio. He turns it louder.

"This is Jake, what is your status Charles?" The radio crackles.

"We're...taking fire...few blocks down...your location. We don't think...Rev," Well that doesn't sound too good.

"Chase, Jeff, give them back up," Jake commands.

"Yes sir," The two soldiers that came with us run out of the room.

"We should probably be going soon too," Mr. Locke says as he looks at the time and then at Jake.

"Yes, but before we go I need to ask you something, Bryan. I was wondering if you would consider joining the H.E.R.O. initiative?"

I freeze. I don't know what to say.

"If you choose to accept, your family would be taken to a facility of high security and their needs provided for."

"Well, I don't know. We... would have to talk about it," I say completely taken by surprise.

"What is H.E.R.O.?" Samantha asks.

It's an organization created by the Government in response to a group of terrorists. It stands for Helping Everyone Restore Order," Mr. Locke explains.

"So, combat?" Samantha puts her hand on her forehead.

"Yes," Jake says.

I grab my wife's hand and look into her eyes. I can see the anxiety she has from the thought of me being away right now during such a crazy time.

"Jake, we really need to talk this over, together, privately," I say to him.

"I definitely understand. If you would give me a call in a few days that would be great," Jake says.

He begins to turn towards the door. "Oh yeah, every soldier gets to go home at least every 3 months for a week and sometimes more. Here is a video of the facility," He hands me a small memory chip.

"Thanks, I'll call you," I say, almost in a whisper.

Mr. Locke opens the door and Jake and him walk out.

"It's so good to see you all," I say tearing up again. We hold each other for a minute and then I pick up my soon to be three-year-old; sweet little girl.

"Dad, who were those people?" My six-year-old boy, Tate, asks.

"One of them is a friend from work. The other was a man I met today," I tell him.

"How have you been buddy?" I ask him, trying to forget everything that just happened.

"This place isn't very fun. Mom says we can't go outside to play because the air has dirt in it," He says, sad and serious.

"I bet in a couple of days the air won't have any dirt in it, and then you can play outside," I try to cheer him up.

"You can play on the playground here. I'm sure there are kids playing on it right now," Samantha says smiling at Tate. "He made some friends yesterday,"

Tate looks up at her. "Okay. Dad will come play too?"

He quickly looks at me with his eyebrows raised.

"Yeah, of course buddy," I hand Caroline to Samantha and help Tate put on his shoes.

It is great to be back with my wife and kids. I love my family so much.

"I'm right ready!" Tate announces.

Samantha laughs. "He has been saying that lately, for dinner, baths, and everything. Tate you are such a goofball,"

I pick up Tate and put him on my shoulders.

"Alright, Caroline, are you ready to go?"

She smiles, "Yes, daddy!"

Samantha picks her up. "We're off, like a dirty shirt,"

We walk out the door.

"Hold on, I need to lock the door," Samantha pulls out a card. She swipes it in front of a black box on the door. I think to myself it's kind of strange she needs to lock the door. She can tell that I question the need.

"There have been some unwanted guests in some of the rooms," She says as she catches up to me.

"What? Really? How many days have people been down here?" I'm surprised. "Two days, for most," She answers.

"People are desperate for anything that will help them get ahead in life after they return to their homes. Money or electronics are the targets of course," She says.

That's ridiculous. I didn't put my family in one of the best community shelters for them to worry about that kind of thing.

"So where is this playground?" I ask, trying to not worry about burglars.

"It's just around that corner," Samantha points ahead.

"Yup, it's a big yellow door," Tate informs me.

"Tate, is your favorite color still pink?" I tease him.

"No!! I don't like pink. My favorite color is red," he says, a little more upset than I expected.

Samantha looks at me with a smile and shakes her head.

"Don't be causing problems already," She laughs.

Caroline reaches for her mom to pick her up.

"Caroline, what is your favorite color?" I ask her.

"Gween," She says with a big smile.

"Do you know what my favorite color is?" I ask.

"It's pink!" Tate shouts and chuckles.

"Nooo," I smile at him.

Caroline shrugs.

Samantha looks at me. "It's blue,"

"Yeah, it's blue," I say excitedly.

We turn the corner and I see the very bright yellow door.

"Now what's mine?" Samantha asks with a smirk.

I am pretty sure it's purple. "Of course, it's purple," I say trying to make it sound like a ridiculous question.

She laughs and then just smiles at me.

"It's still purple, right?" I ask, smiling back.

She gives me a hesitant look and then laughs. "Yes, it is,"

I put my arm around her. Tate starts to wiggle as we get to the door so I let him down. Tate grabs the door handle and uses all his strength to open it. We walk into a pretty good size room with kids squawking and running. There are probably 15 kids.

"Dad, come on," Tate grabs my hand and pulls me onto the astro turf.

"What do you want to do first?" I ask him.

It's been awhile since I have gone to a playground with Tate.

"First I want to show you the monkey bars. I can do them almost all the way," He says as we reach the ladder that leads to the monkey bars.

Tate climbs up the ladder. He grabs the first rung. "Okay, I'm going to go," He says.

I stand near him ready to catch him. He hangs on the first rung and then grabs the second, third, and fourth. He loses momentum and hangs from the fourth rung.

"Good job buddy. Now try for the next bar."

I shuffle my feet a little closer anticipating him dropping. He flails trying to keep his hold and regain momentum.

He then kicks me, on accident, in the groin.

I back up quickly, but with a hand out to catch him.

"I'm going to drop," He warns me.

I put my hands around him and he lets go.

"That was great! I'm proud of you," I say putting him on the ground while trying to hide my pain.

"Tate!" Samantha calls from behind. We both look that way. She waves us over to the bench she is at.

"Let's go see what mom wants,"

We both walk over, but I am much slower and more waddlely.

We walk past, Caroline who is playing with some foam blocks.

"Tate, I see a few of your friends over by the slide. Do you want to go play with them?" Samantha asks.

"I was playing with dad," He says.

"I need to talk to him for a few minutes. Once we're done talking you two can go play again.

Okay?"

He looks at me and I nod.

He then looks at his friends and back at mom.

"Okay," Tate runs off towards his friends.

I take a seat next to her.

"How are you doing?" Samantha looks at me with a smile.

I chuckle, "Oh, so you saw what happened,"

"Yeah I did. I thought I would give you a few minutes to recover," She says to me.

"Thanks,"

I WATCH Tate and his friends as they run around on the playground.

"He is growing up fast," I say.

"Yeah he is. Lately he has been really interested in books," She says to me.

"That's right, I remember you telling me that a few weeks ago. How's he doing with reading?"

I start thinking of how much I am missing from his life.

"He gets a little better each week. I have really been working with him. In a year or two at this rate he could easily be at the top of his class,"

I look at her. "Really? We could have a genius in the family," I joke.

She smiles and lightly backhands me, "Well, you never know,"

We sit there for a minute just watching the children pinball around the playground.

"So what do you think of this job opportunity?" Samantha asks me.

I was waiting for her to initiate it. "It sounds like it would be good for our family's security. However, I wish it didn't mean being away from you guys," I reply hoping she won't take it one way or the other.

"I knew you would say something like that. If it is a government secured place, then yes it might be good. However, you will miss more and more time from Tate and Caroline and Me," Samantha's tone begins to get more intense.

"And that's not what I want. I don't even know if I would want to go back into combat," I tell her.

A piece of me wants to be a part of it all and do what I did really well for four years. I always want to be with my family but without this job their quality of life could be jeopardized.

Samantha leans forward with her elbows on her knees and clasps her hands.

"You still need to tell me how Jake is back," She says, slightly cocking her head towards me.

I remember the fact that I know so much more about the situation than she does. I begin trying to explain to her Jake's disappearance. She gets a confused look at the part about H.E.R.O.'s but I just continue. I tell her about the other group Rev and their plans to overtake governments, which also led me to tell her about all that happened from the time I left NASA and landed in Texas.

"Oh my gosh. You almost died!" She looks at me seriously. I sit there in silence. I can't say she's wrong about that.

"I know you are afraid to let me go do these kinds of things but this world deals out unpredictable experiences. I was supposed to be up in space days before meteors came, not hours before. I was supposed to be part of a safe team without any terrorists," I tell her plainly. "All I know is that I am trying to be the best I can be, for you and the kids and... my country," I try to reason.

There's a pause in our conversation as some people walk over and tell us that Tate is the cutest. The couple has a little girl with them. The conversation doesn't last very long before they leave.

Samantha turns towards me. I look at her. "Bryan, I love you. If anything were to happen to you my world would be shattered," Her eyes have tears building up.

"Honey, I love you. You mean the world to me. Our family is the happiest thing I have ever had. I would never give you guys up,"

I hug her for a few minutes as we both let out some tears.

We sit there holding hands for a few minutes while composing ourselves.

"Tate," Samantha yells.

He comes running over a little out of breath.

"Are you guys done talking?" He asks with some excitement.

"Yes. You two can go play now," She says to him as she fixes his hair.

I stand up.

"Come on dad. We can go on the slide," Tate says as he pulls me by my hand.

We go down the slide a few times and then play tic-tac-toe one and half times before a steering wheel distracts Tate. He asks me if I flew the ship that went to space. I told him I didn't, but I exaggerate the excitement of blowing up asteroids. After a few minutes of Tate pretending to steer the playground, I ask him if he wants to try the monkey bars again.

"I'm too tired to do that," He says.

I laugh and I look at Samantha. She waves me over.

"Hey buddy, let's go see what mom and Caroline are up to,"

I pick him up and put him on my shoulders.

"We need to go back to the room and do some school work. I'm sure dad would love to watch you do your math and reading," Samantha says looking up at Tate from her seat.

With some reluctance Tate replies, "Okay,"

Samantha grabs Caroline and we all leave.

ONCE WE GET BACK to the room, the kids wash up and have lunch. Caroline and Tate have peanut butter and jelly sandwiches and then Caroline takes a nap while Tate does school work. I help him with his math and reading for 20 minutes before he starts getting tired. Tate lays down on his bed and Samantha and I lay down on ours. The four of us are out like a light.

6

S ide Quest I Guess

I WAKE up and hear my wife talking to Caroline.

"How long have I been asleep?" I ask sitting up.

Samantha looks at the clock.

"Three hours,"

"What?" It's past three o'clock.

How could I have slept that long. I never take naps that long.

"I am sending the kids over to a friend's place so we can talk some more," Samantha says as she brushes Caroline's hair.

Tate comes out of the bathroom. "Dad, you're awake. You were sleeping forever," He says as he comes over to me.

I put him on my lap. "I guess I'm getting old," I say as I tickle him.

There's a knock on the door.

"Oh, that's them. Come on Tate," Samantha says as she finishes up Caroline's hair.

I walk over and open the door. A lady with her two kids stand there.

"Hi, I'm Bryan," I say politely.

"Hello, I'm Paula," The lady says with a thick southern accent.

Samantha walks up next to me and our kids walk out the door.

"Thanks so much for watching them," Samantha says.

"It's no problem, I need to get the wiggles out of my two anyway. We'll be back in an hour or so," Paula says as they leave.

I close the door and look at Samantha.

"What exactly do you want to talk about?"

She walks over to a monitor and grabs the remote. "Remember the USB Jake left with us?" She asks, turning on the monitor.

"Yeah, what about it?"

"I was watching what was on it and it is a nice place that the kids and I would stay at," She said, but something in her voice didn't seem right.

I sit down and watch the video with Samantha. It shows the grounds with trees, grass, and a high wall around it. It is probably 5 acres or so with a couple large buildings no more than 3 stories high. Then it shows the underground and it is almost more beautiful than the above grounds.

Almost a year after the announcement of Earth's destruction the economy received a big hit. You could tell that many people saved more and the appearance of new technology decreased. Having worked at NASA over the years made me realize that a person could find a lot of new technology mostly in pockets of government organizations. This is obviously one place money is going.

The video ends with kids in a classroom and the words "Your kid's future begins here,"

I sit there for a minute watching the menu screen.

"Well, what do you think?" I ask Samantha.

She looks at me. "I have to show you something else,"

She grabs the computer sitting on the table.

"There are cameras outside along the perimeters and the residents have access to them. I wanted to see what it looked like outside and saw some strange footage,"

She opens a screen and begins playing the recording.

"Just wait a minute and look at this blue car," She insists.

I look at her then back at the screen. About thirty seconds go by and then I see it. A dog jumps up on the blue car parked against a wall. I look closer and notice that it's not your average dog with different parts of it shining or reflecting light. There is something off about it.

Then I notice it.

"That tail isn't moving like a normal dog's tail would," I say out loud while still examining it.

"Well watch its eye," Samantha points to the screen.

The eye facing the camera gleams red and then blue then green.

"It has to be robotic," I turn to Samantha.

She leans back. "Are they coming for us?"

"No, I don't think so. I mean what good would I do for them?"

"Well they tried to get you when you landed and used you for their cover on the ship,"

"But...this is ridiculous. They should be after Jake. I have nothing to do with them,"

"Unless they are trying to use you as ransom to get close to Jake or take you, a hero, hostage for money," There's silence for a moment.

"So, what does that mean for us?" I ask her, looking at the screen again.

"If they want you for any kind of gain then they might be willing to come for me, Tate or Caroline,"

I turn my head towards her. "So, you need protection,"

"I know you would do all you can to protect me and I would do everything to protect you; but this isn't a burglar or something like that. This is war, and from what you have said and what we have now seen, the war is literally at our door," Samantha grabs my hand.

"So, we are going back into this military thing," I say putting my other hand on hers.

Her eyes begin to fill with tears. I pull her into my chest and we sit there for a while.

I hear a buzz, like an old doorbell. We both sit up.

"What is that?" I ask Samantha.

"It's from the bunker supervisor," She stands up and goes to a cabinet. She opens the cabinet door and pulls out a cell phone.

"I missed a call from them. I'll call them back,"

"What time are the kids supposed to be back?" I look at the clock.

"Pretty soon," Samantha puts the phone on speaker.

"Hello, this is Samantha Reed. I got a call from you,"

"Yes, your husband has been left a package from the guy he was with earlier," A man says over the phone.

He sounds strange, but I don't know the man so it may just be nothing.

"Oh, okay we will come pick it up," Samantha says.

"Thanks," The phone goes silent.

"What do you think Jake left for you?"

"I have no idea,"

We head out the door and lock it behind us

We are walking down a hallway when we see Paula with Tate and Caroline. "Well hey, I was just coming back. Your kids were just as sweet as can be," She says.

"Oh, I am glad. Thanks again for watching them," Samantha picks up Caroline. I grab Tate's hand.

"Where are you guys off too?" Paula asks.

"We need to pick up something from the office,"

"Well, okay. Tell Dalton I say hi," Paula says bubbly.

"Okay," Samantha says with a big fake smile.

We continue down the hall.

"Who's Dalton?" I ask.

"Just some guy Paula thinks is cute,"

"I see, but I thought she was married,"

"She is in the middle of a divorce," Samantha says as she points to a door.

I open the door and we walk into another hallway, but it's small with less rooms on each side.

"Where are we going?" Tate asks.

"I got a package delivered and were going to pick it up,"

"Is it something cool?" Tate makes an excited face.

"We will find out," I smile at him.

"It's the green door on the left," Samantha says.

I knock on the door. We stand there for a minute before hearing the door unlock and then it opens a crack.

"Bryan?" The man asks immediately.

"Yes, I'm Bryan," The man opens the door and jests me to come in. The four of us begin walking into the room.

"Excuse me Bryan, but maybe you should have your family wait outside," A sharp, but not overdressed man says from the other side of the room.

"I prefer them to be with me if that's okay," I say looking at him determined to have them here.

"Alright then, Bryan please take a seat up here," He says pointing at some chairs in a semicircle. There are two men and a woman already sitting down.

"I am just here for a package," I say hesitantly moving towards the chairs.

"Oh yes, we do have a package for you, but we also are going to ask a favor of you," He says.

I take a seat and look back to my wife and kids still by the door.

"Okay, so you may or may not know me. I am Drake Stanger, in charge of keeping this bunker safe. I am a former Marine. Each of you have some kind of military training and have been selected to help in a security situation. A few hours ago, there was a sighting of a mechanical...dog," Drake says with hesitation.

"If you have seen the footage already, raise your hand,"

We all raise our hands.

"Great, I will let it run in the background as I keep talking," He uses a remote and the video is projected onto the wall.

"This is nothing I have seen before. It is a threat to the people I am supposed to protect. I want it out of the area. Have any of you seen this kind of technology?"

The four of us sitting down look at each other, but no one seems to have any experience with this kind of thing.

Then, a man raises his hand. "I have seen the studies about this technology and experiments that haven't quite panned out,"

"Okay, but nothing like this. I am going to show you a video of one of our drones scanning the area trying to track this...dog," Drake says, still trying to figure out what to call it.

A new video hits the wall. The view is from about 40 feet above the ground moving approximately 15 mph.

"Here the drone has found the dog, and is following it. Right here the dog stops and seems to scan the area. It only takes a minute before the dog senses the drone and bolts around a building," Drake forwards the video a little.

"The drone eventually found the dog two minutes later in a distant car. When the drone went towards it, a green laser flashed over the drone and its camera. Soon after, the camera lens was damaged and before sending out another drone to recover the first, the drone's signal was gone,"

The video plays again from the start.

"Has anyone been out there since?" The woman sitting next to me asks.

She has mid-length brown hair and a leather jacket on her lap. She was probably in the marines too.

Drake looks at her.

"No, that's where we come in. We are going to retrieve the drone and hopefully clear the area of that dog,"

"Alright," Says a guy who's been leaning back in his chair with his arms crossed the whole time.

"Well, just know we have no idea what this thing is capable of. It could be extremely dangerous. We need to think about the fact that it looks as though it's made of metal and it could withstand some gunfire," Drake informs.

"Are we all willing to go forward and find this thing?" Everyone, including myself confirms to be on board.

Drake does a jester to the man that opened the door.

"Dillion, will you grab the gear?"

Dillion disappears into a room. Drake looks at me as I stand up.

"Bryan, this is probably a good time for you to send your family back to their room," He does a quick glance at them.

"Yeah, I will," I walk over to my wife and kids still by the door but having found objects for chairs.

"Well, I guess I am getting started a little earlier than we had planned," I help Samantha up from a short bucket.

Her face displays a concerned look.

"Be careful," she says.

"I will. I will be back right after I am done here,"

She grabs Caroline and puts her on her hip.

Tate looks up at me. "Where are you going? You can't go out there. There is a mean dog that might bite you," He says with a serious face.

"I will be okay buddy. There will be others out there with me," I assure him.

Samantha grabs Tate's hand. I give Samantha a kiss and they leave.

"Okay, here you all are," Dillion says as he brings out a rack with body armor hanging off of it.

The vests are military grade.

"These are the best out there for military personnel. Please respect them, they are expensive. There should be enough different sizes so each of you can find your best fit," Drake says moving the chairs against the walls.

"What about my package?" I ask and think this probably isn't the best time.

"Here it is," Dillion says as he pulls a long metal case out from behind a desk.

"The man you were with earlier told us to give it to you after 4 o'clock. He is kind of a strange guy. You might not want to open it," Dillion says, jokingly.

The metal case is dark green and worn. It is about a foot and half wide, half a foot thick and 4 feet long. There are four latches along the seam of the case.

"Thanks," I take the case from Dillion.

It's just as heavy as it looks.

Everyone is keeping an eye on me and the case as they sort through the body armor. I take the case to the chairs along the wall and set it on the seats. I'm thinking it's a gun or two. I wonder if Jake knew about this dog thing. I unlatch the case and lift the lid. It's a suit. An armor suit that is…It's impressive with S.W.A.T. like qualities. After a minute of just staring at it, I turn to look at everyone else who seems to have been looking at the suit too. They look back at their suits.

"And I thought these were the best there was," One of the guys says, looking around for Drake.

I chuckle lightly and hear others laugh too. I pick up the suit and examine it. There is a small amount of metal plating over the chest and on the outer forearms. Just below the knee down to the shin is metal plating too. I am excited to put it on.

"Five minutes and we are heading out. I will give you a gun walking out the door," Drake says.

I put the suit on, first the bottom half then the top. It fits snugly but it is still flexible. I notice a handgun and magazine in the case. I put the mag in the gun and put it on the holster on my waist. There isn't a helmet or anything else in the case so I close it. I walk on over to the rack feeling powerful like when a child gets a new backpack or shoes, invincible! I pick up a helmet from the rack and try it on. It's a little loose so I'll try two more. The third helmet fits just fine, so I take it off and put it under my arm.

DRAKE WALKS to the door all suited up. "Alright, let's get going. I have some guns waiting for us at the outer door,"

The four of us look over each other quickly, nod, and walk out the door. As we walk down the hall we get a little acquainted. The woman is Janet and she was in the marines, but started in the army. She is probably in her late thirties and is obviously still fit for combat. Ben, is a former special ops. He is probably in his mid forties tall and dark. The other guy who just crossed his arms during the briefing is Victor.

He was in the army up until last year. Victor is likely in his early fifties and looks tough as nails.

We follow Drake to the door leading outside where two men stand with a large metal box at their feet. Drake stops in front of the door and turns towards us.

"Each of your helmets have walkie-talkies. Just turn them on and we'll all be able to communicate through them as it is likely we will split up," He says as he turns on his own helmet.

We follow his example. Drake jesters to the two men standing now behind the metal crate.

"These are your weapons. AR-15's with three magazines," The men hand out the guns to us.

"Up to this point I didn't know if we should take grenades. What are your thoughts?" Drake asks.

"Why not. It may not just be that dog out there. It's obviously a scout. I think the more fire power the better," Victor says, looking at everyone.

"I'll agree with that," Janet says.

Drake looks at the two men, "Okay, that makes sense," We each get one grenade.

"So, this is a shoot to kill, right?" Ben asks.

"Yup. Don't hold back," Drake puts his helmet on.

He nods to us and opens the door. We file out making a fan shape covering each other's backs. The door we went out is different from where I came in. It's an alleyway. I'm scanning our nine o'clock. Nothing in sight. The wind is blowing softly. It's going to be a little cool tonight I can tell.

"Clear," We all chime, one after the other. Drake stands up straight and looks at a blue car. Actually, that is the blue car in the video. I look back at where the camera is. Just above the door is a camera.

"Looks like it's a heavy little sucker," Drake says.

We all look at the car and bent the hood.

"How much do you think it weighs?" Victor asks.

"I'd say 200 plus," I say looking over at him.

"Oh yeah, no doubt. Maybe 300," Ben says, raising his eyebrows.

"Either way let's drop that muttel," Janet says.

"Muttel?" Drake asks, confused like the rest of us.

"Yeah, it's a metal mut," she says nonchalantly.

We roll our eyes and she just smiles a little.

"First let's clear the blocks around here and then move outward," Drake gets us focused again.

We nod and begin calling out the direction we're going.

"I will take Goose Street and head south," I inform them looking at the next street to the east.

"Alright I will head down...what is that, Pelican Street?" Janet says, looking west.

"Yeah it is," Drake confirms.

"Okay, and I will head south down that as well," Janet adds.

Drake nods and then looks at Ben and Victor, "You guys got the north side of those streets. I'll be on the rooftop with a sniper, watching over east and west,"

We turn quickly to look at him.

"Wait, what?" Victor says shocked and confused. "You're going to leave us on the ground while you're in the nest,"

"It's not like that," I am going to have a better view of East and West.

"Shoot man!" Ben exclaims.

"Whatever, let's just go. That thing is probably gone anyways," Janet says.

We begin to disperse. I can't believe that. He will recruit a bunch of Vets and then sit in the safest place. Then again someone should have the eagle eye.

"Oh yeah, I'm sending a drone out so don't shoot it," Drake says from behind.

IT'S BEEN 20 minutes and no sign of Pluto. That's what we named it about five minutes ago. I begin to loosen up a little expecting to find nothing now that it has been an hour and half since the first sighting.

"Anything?" Drake comes through the radio.

"Nada," Janet replies.

"A whole bunch of trash," Victor says.

"Nothing on my side," Ben sighs.

"Yeah, I've got nothing," I confirm.

"Wait. What the..." Ben comes back on. "I've got something in the distance.

Drake, can you see my 11 o'clock? It's about 100 yards out from where I'm at,"

There's silence.

"I see it. It's our target," Drake replies. "Alright everyone, get to Goose and Spruce,"

I look back down the street I walked for 20 minutes. Spruce is the street north of the bunker. I start jogging and I begin to feel the weight of my suit.

"Ben, the dog is on the move. It's heading north," says Drake.

"Towards me?" Ben sounds surprised.

"I just got to Goose. I've got your back," Victor assures Ben.

"Janet, Bryan, what's your location?" Asks Drake.

"I just got past the north corner of the bunker heading over to Goose street," Janet sounds a little winded.

"I'm on the east side of the bunker," I reply.

"I lost the target. I last saw it on Spruce just behind a computer store. I'm sending the drone out there,"

I'm coming up behind Ben. "Any glimpse of it?"

He turns his head around.

"Nope," Victor keeps his eyes forward and runs across the street.

Then Janet follows behind.

"What's the plan?" She asks. We look at each other.

"Let's split into pairs now that we know the general area it's in," I say peering around a corner.

"That sounds good," Says Ben.

"Drake, any sign of the dog?" Victor asks, walking over to a parked car. He stands on top of it to get a better view.

"No, the drone doesn't appear to see any kind of movement. Head down the street,"

We take a moment and decide Victor and Ben will go together down Goose and Janet and myself will take the street east of Goose. If we can catch it from both ends of a street it will be a quick execution. The sky is darkening and the wind is still blowing gently. The temperature is dropping.

As Janet and I move down Maple street we walk slowly around parked cars trying to stay hidden.

"The drone picked up something and it's not a cat," Drake informs us.

"Where at?" I ask.

I look up to see if the drone is nearby, and it is. The drone is 40 feet high about 50 feet north.

"It's on Maple and Spruce. It's heading towards Bryan and Janet,"

I immediately lay down on top of a windshield and peer over the top of the car. Janet moves up alongside the parked cars.

It feels like it has been an hour but it's only been a few minutes when the large dog comes down the abandoned street. It's a sort of blue silver and has defined components to its mechanical make up. I look through my scope and find its head slightly bobbing up and down. Its eye is blue and glowing.

"I've got Pluto in my sights," I let everyone know.

Janet slips between two cars just a little further up from me.

"We are on the corner of Maple and Fur," Ben says.

"We'll stay low until you give us the go," Says Janet.

"Alright, I just need it to head a little further south," I reply.

Another minute or two goes by. The dog just scans vehicles and shop windows and walks on slowly. I look behind myself thinking that this could just be a lure.

"Drake, how's it going? Any other activity going on," I look back towards the dog.

"Nope, It's quite everywhere else,"

"Bryan, I'm ready when you are," Janet says anxiously.

"Right, Victor, Ben can you see it?" I ask.

"We've got eyes on Pluto,"

"Okay, on my count. One, two, three," I fire a few shots.

The dog bolts behind a vehicle.

"Did we hit it?" Victor asks.

"I hope one of you did," Drake says.

"I'm sure we did. It probably has some resistance with it being made of metal and all," I reply as I roll off the car's windshield landing on my feet.

"Pluto is camping behind the green sedan," Ben says.

"I think it's time for a grenade," Victor replies.

"That sounds like a good idea," Janet says.

Victor must have thrown it because I see something fly underneath the sedan. No sooner does the dog dash from its hiding place and turns the corner. The blast bumps the car up a little and sends shrapnel flying.

I sprint towards the dog's fleeting direction. Gunshots go off and I quickly press my back to the wall of a building. Bullets break glass, on a car 20 feet away. The dog must be just out of sight around the corner.

"Grenade!" Ben yells.

I can see him on the opposite corner pulling the pin. Just as Ben goes to release the grenade into the air a beam of green hits his face. The grenade lands short and closer to me. I run to a business's doorway.

Boom! The windows rattle.

I look first then run back to the corner to see the dog is off again down the street.

"What happened?" Janet asks frantically.

"That thing put a laser into his eyes," says Victor.

"Guys, it's getting away," I say sternly.

"Janet go ahead. I will take care of Ben," Victor insists.

I am chasing the dog and just as it turns and stops, I raise my gun to shoot. Its mouth opens and a green light beams out making me turn my face and pull up my gun. I shoot into the sky and then I hear the strange noise of its rubber feet pounding towards me. I look again and shoot quickly. A few rounds hit its right shoulder and then its chest. Still the mechanical beast sprints at me. It is only then that I realize how big it really is. Just its weight will take me out if not its jagged chrome teeth. I stand frozen as it bounds closer, faster and faster.

"Move!" I hear Janet yell.

Just as the dog leaps towards me to smash me into the cement, I dive onto a car hood. The dog side swipes the car, breaking off the mirror. I hear Janet unloading her rounds. I look at the unstoppable dog making its way for Janet. I grab my rifle with both hands and aim.

"Neck, neck" I keep repeating in my mind.

I shoot a few bullets out before having to reload. Janet stops shooting which means she has to reload and she doesn't have enough time. I reach for a mag but feel the pistol in hand and decide to go with that. I lift it up just as the dog reaches Janet. She moves to the side as it pounces. She jams the rifle into the dog's jaws but it catches her vest with its strange paw. Janet falls to the ground, her head barely misses being crushed. I have a clear shot as she is now three feet below my target. I shoot two shots on its neck before it backs up a few steps and faces me. I land two more on its head. Janet pushes herself off the sidewalk underneath a truck. I keep shooting.

It looks at Janet then at me. It must have calculated its best option within the situation because it charges me again. It is about 30 feet away. My pistol is now empty and I have to reload my rifle. I decide to take a chance. I pull my grenade off my belt and put my finger through the ring. I take one second to decide my placement and then pull the pin. I throw it ten feet in front of me into the base of a building and dive onto the same hood as before.

Boom! The grenade goes off just as I roll off the hood onto the street looking for the dog. I hear a thud and the car next to me slides an inch into the street. I put another mag in. I stand up ready to shoot. I look left then right, nothing. Then I notice a repetitive noise just on the other side of the displaced car. I cautiously step forward, finger on the trigger. As I peer around the car I see the mangled legs of the beast. They twitch forward and back. It's lying there on its side.

"I think we got it. It's pretty mangled," I try to inform the others. "Nice work everyone," Drake says.

I look up at the drone flying above.

After watching the mechanics of the dog slow down and stop I run over to where Janet took cover. She isn't under the truck though. She comes around the truck with her rifle in one hand and a hand holding her side.

"Are you okay?" I walk up to her.

"I think I dislocated a rib," She hands me her rifle.

"Hey nice job," Victor comes up to us with Ben trailing behind.

Ben is blinking and squinting with his hand above his eyes.

"Sorry we hung back. It blinded me. I should recover though, hopefully," He says. We walk over to the broken four-legged tank of a dog. Its blue and silver shell is broken and jagged from bullets and the grenade. Holes in its armor expose its gears and wires.

"Dang! That grenade did it in," Ben says lightly kicking it.

"Check out the car," Victor points to the large indentation across its middle section.

"Hey team, should I send a vehicle to pick you and the dog up?" Drake asks over the radio.

"Yeah, I think we would appreciate that," I tell him.

"Yeah there is no way we are going to drag this trash back," Ben says.

"Alright, it will be a few minutes,"

WE STAND AROUND WAITING for a truck to pick us up.

The sky is darkening and the wind has stopped. I look at my watch and see the time is 4:48. It's been about ten minutes since we talked to Drake.

"We're not that far from the bunker. They should be here by now," Victor says.

"We could have walked back by now," Ben adds.

I bend down and grab the hind legs of the dog. I pull to see how heavy it is. It slides a little making a heavy scraping noise.

"What are you doing?" Janet asks, giving me a look as to say, you're crazy.

"I wanted to see how heavy it was,"

We definitely couldn't get it back in a timely manner.

"We should just hotwire one of these cars and get it over there ourselves," Ben starts looking into car windows.

"Hold on, don't break any windows" I say, putting my hand up.

My watch's screen gets brighter so I look down at it.

I received a message from Jake. "What do you think? Are you on board,"

I would reply back right now, but it's kind of a bad time.

Another two minutes go by and then we hear a truck's engine.

"Hey team, there you are," Drake says happily.

"Finally," Ben says.

The truck stops next to us and Drake and four other guys jump out.

"Let's see this thing," Drake walks around the car.

"Wow. That is a beast!"

"Yeah, I hope I never have to face one again," I shake my head.

"You guys are a good team. Thanks for keeping everyone safe," Drake looks at the four of us standing next to each other.

We look at each other and agree.

"Drake?" Someone says from another walkie-talkie.

"Yeah this is Drake. What is it?" He says turning around.

"There's a vehicle entering the city and I cannot confirm its origin. I don't know if it's a threat or just those guys from earlier,"

"Is it a military vehicle?" He looks back at us.

"Yeah...hold on, let me check another camera," There's a pause.

"Okay let's load this up and go," Drake says seriously.

Everyone but Drake and Janet help get the dog in the truck. It is just a normal truck and not enough seats so Victor, Ben, Janet, and myself sit in the bed of the truck with our dead foe.

As we pull away from the battle scene I hear Drake's conversation begin again. The tiny window makes it hard to hear so I put my ear closer to the open window.

"...not a U.S. military truck but it looks combat ready. I suggest you get back now,"

"Copy that, we are already on our way," Drake puts the walkie-talkie down and speeds up.

We're not far from the bunker now, but twilight has snuck up on us in all the commotion. We slow down to wait for a garage door to open.

"The vehicle, a military truck, is pushing 100mph down Goose St. They'll be here in a minute!" I hear the man on the other side of the radio say.

We pull into the larger than expected garage and the door closes behind us.

"Get the dog into a secure room," Drake says as he stops the truck.

I quickly jump out to catch Drake.

"Drake! These guys are probably looking for this thing. We can't risk them breaking in and endangering the lives of civilians," I say grabbing his elbow.

"I can do whatever I want," He pulls his arm away. "Besides Bryan, I am not going to endanger civilian lives. They can't get to them or the secure room!"

We hear a truck's tires roll to a stop accompanied by squeaking brakes.

"They're here," I say quietly turning around to face the garage door. I check my gun to make sure it's ready.

"Everyone, take a position. Guns up!" Drake orders. There are probably 9 of Drake's guys. They each find cover and point their guns at the garage door.

We wait there for a minute before hearing pounding on the door. It stops and then with no warning the door explodes. Shrapnel flies everywhere leaving a large jagged hole in the doorway. Smoke slowly drifts towards us.

The smell takes me back to my days in the field. It must have been C4 I tell myself. I think of a time we used it to break through a wall that led to a hoard of contraband weapons.

I focus back to reality. Just in time too, because a grenade bounces then rolls into the garage. I spin myself back behind a cement pillar.

Bang!

I wait a second and then look at the damage. One of Drakes men lies against another pillar. Another man holding his side tries to crawl for cover. Green lasers break through the smoke from the outside. My first thought is, more mechanical dogs. I look over at Drake behind the grill of the truck. He has his rifle on the hood. He fires a shot and then a couple rounds come back scattering on the truck. I turn and look for a target. Five guys break through the smoke and shoot as they take cover behind crates, barrels and cars.

I shoot at a soldier behind a barrel. The bullet punctures the barrel and water pours out. A guy from behind a car aims at me. I hide and watch powdered concrete spray in front of my face. Like a switch everyone on my side fires. A car's tire pops, lowering it half a foot closer to the ground.

"Janet, you got a grenade?" I ask.

"Yeah!" She yells back

"Victor, let's take them out," I look at them as they shoot from behind some cars parked beyond the truck.

Janet stops shooting and crouches. She comes up holding the grenade. She nods at me and jesters to the left side of the garage door or what's left of it. I nod back. She takes another look at her target and pulls the pin. With a solid throw she lands it under a car.

The explosion is big!

For a few seconds there's minimum gunfire. I turn to find the rest of the soldiers. As I search for them I hear gunfire. A force pushes me backwards and I fall to the ground. Pain fills my chest and the wind is knocked out of me. Struggling to get up I roll over onto my side and stay like that.

I hear bullets whiz by and a grenade bounces somewhere. The blast sends shrapnel into my back. I hear another grenade but further away.

The shooting stops.

The smoke has cleared for the most part and I can see outside. It's dark and I can see a truck's lights. A hand grabs my arm. It's Drake, helping me to my feet.

"That should be all of them," He says.

The truck outside drives off. Those of us that remain, stand up and slowly walk towards the door with our guns ready. As we approach we find the streets deserted. My watch flashes blue.

Jake is calling me?

I press accept, "Hello?"

"Bryan, are you okay?" Jake's voice is surprisingly super clear.

"Yeah I am fine but we just got attacked by five guys. I think they are from Rev," I pause, realizing I may have indirectly told a group of people something confidential.

I walk back into the garage to talk freely.

"Bryan, I need you to get out of there a soon as possible. Have you and Samantha decided what you are going to do?" He says kind of tense, which isn't like Jake.

"Yeah we want to take your offer. We think it is the best thing for us to do,"

"Great. I will be there in 15 minutes to pick you and your family up,"

"Alright, I'll see you then," I wait for him to end the call.

I walk over to Drake quickly, seeing I only have 15 minutes to get my family ready.

"I am leaving soon, in 15 minutes. I'm sorry about your men," I say looking around at the few men lying on the ground.

"Wait, where do you think you're going?" He says wrinkling his forehead.

"My family and I have a...job offer and it requires us to leave immediately," I begin to walk away from him but he grabs my shoulder.

"You guys can't go out there. I can't let you. There are probably more of those men out there,"

"I know there are more guys out there and my new job will be to eliminate them," I pull away from him and walk off.

7

 New Home

SAMANTHA, Tate, and Caroline are with me at the door I entered this morning. With suitcases in hand and a feeling of urgency we stand there waiting.

"Jake should be here soon," I look up from my watch.

"Whose Jake?" Tate tugs on my body suit I'm still in.

"He is a friend of mine. He dropped me off here this morning," I look down at him and smile.

A few guards stand nearby watching me. They look concerned, probably because I look like a mess. The last few hours have been a bit strenuous. One of the guards, begins to look around as if someone is watching him. Then he walks up to me.

"So where are you going?" He says calmly.

I look at him for a second trying to decide what to say and how to say it.

"I work for the government and I have an assignment elsewhere," I say, sounding like it's not a big deal.

"Ah, so a pretty secure job? That's cool," He looks like he is about to turn around and then stops.

"You wouldn't happen to be working in the military, would you? The vest and all, the fact that you are working for the government," He says with an eye squinted and a small nod.

"It's military. Why?" At this point I'm wondering if he is part of Rev.

An insider looking to punch my card.

"I am looking to get out of here. I want to join the military. I have no family and I have nowhere to go after this place lets people out,"

He looks serious and a little scared. I take a moment and look at the other guards and look back at him.

"I can mention it to the man picking me up but I have no say in this whatsoever," I whisper to him and step back.

He nods and walks back to his original post.

I BEGIN to feel the activities of the day wear on me. The adrenaline has died down and I am getting tired. Just then a Humvee pulls up. I wait to see Jake step out then I open the door. He looks beat up as well. A cut above his eye with a bandage and a slight limp as he walks over to me.

"Alright, do you guys have everything?" He asks, taking a suitcase from Samantha.

"Yeah, this is all."

We put the suitcases in the back of the Humvee.

"Great. I forgot to tell you we don't have any car seats so you will just have to make do," He closes the back door and walks to the side of the Humvee then opens the door.

Samantha stops before getting in. "Where exactly is this safe house, Jake?"

He looks at me then her and leans into her ear. I could barely hear but he whispers, "Texas".

Samantha picks up Caroline and steps into the Humvee. I help Tate up and then just before I step in I remember.

"Hey Jake, there's a guy inside there, who's a guard and he was wondering if he could...uh. Well, he wants to be in the military and he was wondering if he could come too," I try to not make it sound awkward, but in reality, it was a strange request from a random guy.

Jake raises an eyebrow. "Okay, let's go talk to him really quick," He looks at the driver. "Wait here I will be back in a minute,"

We go back inside where we find the man. He quickly stands up from his leaning wall position.

"Who is it?" Jake asks.

The man looks at me.

"This is the guy," I point to him.

The man does a quick smile and puts his hand out to shake Jakes.

"Hi I'm Ed. I want to–"

Jake stops him. "Have you been in the military?"

"No, but I have done security for a few places," He says looking confident that it has some weight to military training.

"Okay, well this is bigger than the military. I won't even ask where you worked only because it doesn't compare to what you are wanting to join. I can't overstate the danger you will be in. There won't even be a leave date for a couple of years. Day in and day out you will be using your gun and dodging bullets," Jake tilts his head a little as if to say, "hopefully dodging bullets,"

"Are you sure you want to join the H.E.R.O. initiative?" Jake stares at him. The man swallows hard. His nostrils flare and his jaw tightens, but then it releases.

"If it is for the freedom of this country I will be with you guys to the end," He says with more seriousness and confidence I have seen in most men.

Jake looks back at me then back to Ed. "Alright Ed, you have just joined H.E.R.O,"

They shake hands.

We head back outside after confirming Ed has nothing to take with him inside the bunker. Outside is cold and dark as though it mourns the death of men who died that day. As we pile into the Humvee the driver tells Jake and everyone that there will be some obstacles on the way back to the airport.

"Luckily this Humvee is the sturdiest around," Jake tries to reassure us.

THE STREET LIGHTS aren't on anywhere. The roads are black as can be. My mind imagines enemy surprises jumping out in front of the Humvee. Our driver, Chad, turns the headlights off and puts night vision goggles on. Every once and while Chad would press on the breaks hard and turn onto another street.

I peer over the tall front seats and see the GPS system that has red dots randomly scattered throughout the city.

"How do you guys have a GPS without any satellites?"

Jake looks back at me. "It's a system of small receivers on buildings and to strengthen that we have drones sending signals from above,"

IT'S BEGINNING to feel extra-long to the airport due to detours to dodge vehicles and camped out soldiers.

"I should probably brief you and Ed on what has happened today," Jake says, slightly turning his head around.

"After dropping you off at the bunker, we made it back to the airport. Only 45 minutes later we discovered Rev troops trickling into the city,"

I stop him. "Why are so many troops here? This isn't a large city,"

"We can't be sure exactly what their strategy is but we know that they are going to try and take over as many locations as possible. Now, back to what happened. They sent some troops out to the airport and although we took heavy damage, we survived. It was then that we found out you and others were in danger,"

"How did you know that?" I ask, puzzled.

He holds his wrist up and points to his watch.

"Your watch has a sensor that detects gunshots and explosives. It's a good way of knowing and tracking danger on our team. If someone gets shot and is unconscious, at least we can find them. It's quite useful,"

Finally, we get to the airport. We drive through an opening in the chain link fence, the road leading to a hanger. The hanger's large doors open and a dozen soldiers stand waiting.

"Grab your things and walk directly to the jet. We aren't safe here and there's no time to lose," Jake says as the Humvee pulls up to the doors.

I look at Samantha who is worried. I don't blame her if she is, for the fact that this is all out of her comfort zone. Heck, I am uncomfortable that my family is close to danger.

"ALRIGHT I'LL TAKE Tate and this suitcase," I say opening the door.

"Are you sure we are going to be okay?" Samantha grabs my shoulder.

I stop and look back at her. "We are going to be just fine. All these men have the proper training to keep us safe. Now come on, we need to be quick,"

I carry Tate and the suitcase to the jet. As I'm walking past the men in the doorway, I hear them say to each other, "...Only a matter of time before the real fire power is on the ground," I wonder what they are talking about.

I put Tate on a seat that is extremely too big for him, but this is a Jet for the military so I don't expect anything different. Samantha comes in with Caroline who is asleep.

"Here, I'll take her, you buckle up," I offer.

We try to transfer our sweet angel without waking her up. After buckling her in I remove some clothes from our suitcase and stuff them around Caroline and Tate. That should help them from sliding around too much.

Three men board the jet and begin securing loose objects. I go out of the plane to see if I can help with anything. I stop on the stairs and see Ed walking by with a couple other soldiers toward the second jet.

Then my ear catches a conversation. Jake is talking to Roy at the foot of the stairs.

"...well, Africa will have to wait a few days. We can't make it there tomorrow," Roy says.

"Unfortunately, you're right. On the up side we have a few days to train some more men," Jake says and then looks over at me.

"Let's get going, we can talk in a few hours," Roy says as he too looks at me, then jogs off to another jet.

Jake heads up the stairs towards me.

"Africa?" I give him a confused look.

We walk into the jet and he closes the door.

"Yeah, there are some big things going down there," He says.

"Is your family buckled up?" Jake asks as he heads to the pilot seat.

"Yeah they are," I say, following him.

I feel like he has so much to tell me, but there hasn't been a good time to do it.

I sit down in the co-pilot seat but he turns to me with a look like, what are you doing?

"Bryan, don't you want to sit with your family?"

I wait a second to reply.

"Sorry, I do but I just feel like we should be talking more about what is happening around the world. I just feel as though there's never enough said about what we're up against," I confess.

"Listen Bryan, I know this has come all at once and that you have many questions, but I want you to know that I can't tell you everything right now at least. Technically you haven't filled out any papers as to our contract, so I am not supposed to inform civilians of all the details. Once we get back to base you can sign the papers and then your family will be safe and we can inform you completely on what you will be up against. We will also begin training,"

I am a little taken back. Civilian pff. Yeah, I may be out of the military but...pff. Whatever, I guess it's fair and I know how "top secret" things go.

"Okay sounds good," I say getting up and putting a smile on my face.

"Thanks again for joining. We all need you," Jake says as I walk away.

I sit down with my family and buckle up. The day has been long and the time with my family has been short. Soon we'll be separated again and my wife will be left to raise our kids alone. How much of this should I continue to do? Will I know my kids when they are older and will they know me? My wife waves her hand in front of my face.

"Bryan. Are you okay?" She asks.

"Yeah, I'm just tired and thinking of...yeah stuff," I blink a few times to help me focus, on what's going on around me.

"Look, they are both out," She smiles while looking at Tate and Caroline.

"Yeah they are beat. Probably not as much as me though," I chuckle.

Samantha stares at me.

"Are you going to be okay with this?" She puts her hand on my face.

I stare into her eyes. "Yeah. I mean I will miss watching these kiddos grow up, but yeah I'll be okay," I put my hand on hers.

"You won't miss everything. Every three months we'll spend time together and hopefully in a few years you can get out. In the meantime, I will take lots of pictures. Maybe you could do a video journal and send it once a week or something," Her eyes start to well up with tears.

I try to wipe them away, but I can't keep up with them.

I HADN'T EVEN NOTICED, but the jet is on the runway.

"We're taking off. Hold on tight," Jake announces.

The jet rumbles a little bit before the engines thrust us back.

For a while, we don't say anything to each other. I mention to her what Jake told me about signing paperwork when we land. After a few more minutes of silence, I mention to Samantha that I will be leaving for the field after some brief training. She inquires more about where I will be going, but I tell her that I don't know enough about it right now.

· · ·

THE REST of the flight we talk about our home in Colorado and the things that are there. It became clear to me that nothing too valuable is there. If someone ransacked it, they would at most enjoy a car and some nice furniture. Of course there are some electronics that were also expensive, but it really came down to some simple items that reminded us of special times. Both Samantha's and my families are in various places throughout the States, so it really was only the house that tied us to Colorado. In the end we concluded that once things are back to normal we will settle down somewhere else.

THE JET LANDS on the same runway I left from this morning. We roll into the large garage and the massive metal doors close behind us. I remove the clothes around the kids and put them back in the suitcase, messily. We unbuckle Tate and Caroline and carry them off the jet. We follow Jake and the four other men, who have picked up our luggage, out of the jet. Just at the foot of the stairs are a couple men dressed in uniforms, military officers. When I get to the bottom of the stairs, I look at them and nod, expecting to walk past them but one of them lightly grabs my bicep.

"Bryan, we would like to take care of some things as soon as possible," The man looks me directly in the eyes.

"Of course, sir. I will just get my family settled in, and then I will come see you," He nods and lets go of me.

"Bryan, Samantha, this way," Jake says as he and another man carry our bags. We walk through a door, exiting the garage, when I notice a man in a white lab suit pushing a cart. I get a glimpse of some blue liquid in glass cylinders underneath a white sheet. I wonder what that is. My weary and imaginable mind could only come up with wild ideas. I ignore them and keep walking. We go through a few more doors and then reach a hallway that looks like a nice hotel.

"Bryan, you and your family will be staying here for the next few days. We will have an escort for them so that they can get any of the services in the facility," Jake jesters to the man carrying a piece of luggage.

"Hi, I'm Sal. I am pleased to be at your service for the next few days," Sal does a little bow.

Jake hands us a box. "These watches will let you into your room. Bryan, please go see the general in 8 minutes. Just follow the map on your watch. I am sending it to you now," Jake says as he walks away tapping on his watch.

I look back at the door, but I don't see any box to swipe my watch over. I take a step closer and the door beeps and opens, sliding into the wall.

"Wow," Samantha exclaims. "You don't see a door like that every day,"

I look at her and smile. "That's what special people get," I give her a wink.

We walk into the room which is much more spacious than what I had yesterday. I lay Tate on the bed. He looks at me through heavy eyelids and then succumbs to sleep again. I head to the bathroom to wash off my face.

"So, are you taking care of the paperwork and then coming right back?" Samantha asks from outside the bathroom.

"I don't know. I hope that's all I am doing tonight," I turn on the water and run my hands through it a few times. Once it's warm I splash the water on my face. The run off is brown and swirls into the drain. I dry my face and notice my watch blink. A map message pops up on it.

"Alright, I should get going," I say, as I walk out of the bathroom.

"Don't be too long," says Samantha, with a half smile while changing the kids.

"I'll try to be quick. I love you" I say and then kiss her goodbye.

I WALK through the halls looking down and up continually trying to follow the map on my watch. A few minutes of this and I feel lost. The watch takes me through two double doors. A few guards stand along the walls. One of them stops me.

"Bryan?" He asks

"Yes," I answer.

"I'll show you the rest of the way,"

He takes me around a corner to a solid metal door. He punches a code into a keypad and the door opens. A pungent smell fills the air. Almost like chemicals and power tools. We get to another door and the same process is done. We reach a dark room full of computers and busy workers.

"Go to the large glass windows and you'll find a door there. Stand in front of the door and your ID on your watch will be processed, allowing you access," The guard says pointing it all out.

"Thank you," I say and begin walking through the aisles of computers.

I give quick looks of what is on each monitor, as I pass by. Global temperature, remaining usable satellites, messages from bunkers, and some programs running random numbers. I wonder what satellites would still be functional. It's hard to imagine any satellite made it through the hurling debris.

Once I get to the glass door I stand there in front of it. The door beeps and I hear the lock retract. The door swings open by itself and I walk right in. Five men sit at a table watching me come in.

"Thank you for coming, Bryan. This shouldn't take long. You can call me Officer Crawford," A well uniformed man at the head of the table says.

"Thanks for allowing me to serve in this organization,"

And taking care of my family, a big reason I want to serve, I think to myself.

"We will just get right into it. This isn't going to be quite like the Army or the Marines. It also won't measure up to the special forces. What you are walking into is a whole new combat," The head officer says, looking very serious into my face. He leans forward in his chair.

"I will give you a look at just one picture to help emphasize what I am trying to say," He presses a button on his watch and looks up at a screen to his left.

At first, I am confused as to what I'm looking at. Then my imagination says it's a high tech metal armored alien. My logical side says it's just a sculpture or costume from a movie.

"What exactly is that?" I say pointing to the screen and looking at the officer.

"That Bryan, is the enemy. It's a walking nightmare. Tell me, what is your real initial thought of what it is? Give me the truth," He says leaning back in his chair.

I swallow and take a moment.

I give a subtle smile and raise my eyebrows.

"It looks like an alien or something from a movie,"

Officer Crawford gently pounds his fist on his arm rest.

"Exactly. This enemy is using fears of all kinds to manipulate people to bow down. This is just one example in Africa. So, what I am trying to let you know is that you will face challenges not yet ventured,"

I look at the screen again. The alien imposter is covered in metal not patterned after military armor. The helmet covers the face completely. It comes to three points above and towards the back of the head. The front of the helmet comes to a point below the chin. The rest of the body is covered in flowing metal shields and blades.

"The question is, Mr. Reed, can you stay focused with new concepts and technology popping up at a moment's notice? You will have to quickly analyze and adjust your combat to tackle diverse threats," He says, putting his fingertips together in front of his chest.

I look at him and the rest of them at the table. "I will do all I can to be the soldier the government needs me to be," I stand at attention for a few seconds and then ease up. The group of men look at each other and then they nod.

"Great. Thank you for your service. Once you sign these papers you will take an oath and be expected to carry out all our orders. Your family will be transported to a safe facility,"

I quickly scan the papers on the table in front of me.

No red flags stand out, so I take the pen and sign it.

It's done.

The war is on.

I pass the papers to the closest officer.

An officer stands up and helps me perform the oath while raising my right arm to the square.

"Great. Thank you again Mr. Reed. We will expect you to be at training tomorrow morning at 7:00 am. I suspect you will do well in training and therefore should leave in 3 days to Africa," Officer Crawford looks at the picture of my new enemy.

I walk out of the room, but head around the outside of the computers this time. When I get to the door that I came in through, the same guard that escorted me in is there waiting. He opens the door and follows me out.

"Welcome to H.E.R.O, Bryan. My name is Brock Benzinger. I will be there tomorrow, on your first day of training," We walk through the room that smells funny.

"Okay great. Hey, do you know what that smell is?" I say looking around the room.

"Oh yeah, there is a room nearby used for experiments. They use chemicals and who knows what," He says walking on.

Once I get back to my room, my wife is fast asleep on a bed and the kids are sharing another bed. I brush my teeth and set my watch for 5:30. After laying down next to my wife, my mind becomes occupied wondering more about the picture I saw. I wonder about this war being different from what previously has been fought. As interesting as the topic is, my mind fades away and I fall asleep.

8

T rain The Body, Mind, and Emotions

THE MORNING COMES. I'm feeling sore from yesterday. My chest especially hurts doing pretty much anything. I can't quit before I get started, I think to myself. Despite being sore and achy, I am pretty excited for training. I figure I should eat a little before I get to the training so I dabble on my watch looking for a map of the facility. I find directions to everywhere I would need to go in the building. With a kiss to my wife and kids, I head out.

I reach the mess hall where less than a hundred people are also getting their food. After a few minutes in line, I grab my bowl of oatmeal and an apple. I notice a row of tables with a few people and decide to sit next to a group consisting of two men and a woman. As I grab a chair, I ask if it's alright to sit down.

"Depends. Where are you from?" A darker skinned man points his spoon at me.

"What do you mean?" I say pulling out the chair and sitting down anyways.

"You are from...let me guess, the Navy?" He says with a smirk.

"No, actually I am from space," I stir my oatmeal.

"A space soldier. Ha, that's a good one,"

"My name is Jade. I used to be in the Army," The woman says, staring at me with her dark green eyes.

"I am Vince. I was just admitted to Special Forces but the H.E.R.O initiative found me before I started training," The other man says.

He looks like he is in his late 20's.

"And you?" I ask the man that spoke first.

"Marines for eight years. Pretty much seen it all. The name is Eli,"

"It's good to meet you all. I served in the Marines a few years ago. Recently I have been working for NASA. My name is Bryan,"

The three of them look at each other.

"Told you," Jade says looking back down at her food.

I take a bite of my oatmeal.

"So, you were on the Defend spacecraft?" Vince asks.

I look up from my bowl.

"Yeah, I helped with the missiles and such," I take a few more bites.

"Wow. That's pretty cool. Thanks for saving the world," Vince says with a serious face. He goes back to eating his food.

"Well, boys, we don't have much time until we have to go to training. I'm assuming you are training for combat, Bryan?" Jade asks while getting up from her seat.

She gathers up her dishes onto her tray.

"Yes. I will be there," I look at my watch then up at the three of them. "Do any of you know where you are being deployed after your training?" I'm curious if they were told the same thing I was.

"No. Not sure. I hear it can be pretty much anywhere around the world. Why?" Eli replies.

"Well, I just heard that Africa is a possibility," I say, not sure if I'm allowed to.

Vince looks up. "Could be anywhere boys. We'll see you in training,

Jade," He says with some food in his mouth and waving to her as she walks away.

A MINUTE later Vince finishes and gets up and then Eli too. It looked like Eli just didn't want to be alone at the table with me, because he still had uneaten food. Oh well, what do I care. I look at the time again. I have only five minutes to get to training. I get done with my food and take my tray back. The mess hall has only a few people left in it. I see a few people heading out a door and suspect they are going to the training, so I follow them.

Not far from the mess hall are some large metal doors. Above the doors hangs the words "Helping Everyone Restore Order," I walk through the doors to see rows of people standing on the concrete floor. The ceiling is about 20 feet high with metal beams showing. On the walls hang weapons from different cultures and eras.

There must be 100 soldiers lined up in rows facing the front of the room. I follow the trend and step into line. An officer stands in the front of the room watching us trickle in.

I see Jade a few rows from the front. Vince and Eli are standing next to each other only two rows in front of me. A few minutes go by and then I notice a few officers, including Jake, walk into the room to meet up with an officer already at the front of the group of soldiers. My row has filled up and a new one begins behind me.

AFTER A MINUTE of conversing with each other the officers stand side by side. One of the officers steps forward.

"Attention!" He orders.

Boots smack each other as everyone follows the command.

"Listen up soldiers! Today you will go through a physical and start your training. Each of you have been chosen because of experience, focus, bravery, and proven patriotism. We expect you to keep those characteristics throughout your service and always. Do not share confidential material with anyone not of H.E.R.O. Be very basic in any conversation about your work," The officer paces slowly back and forth in front of us. "Before you find out what your schedule is for today I want to leave you with one thing," He stops pacing and looks straight into the middle of us.

"Once you are out there in the field you are going to be seeing things you've never seen before. Be prepared and be creative in how you approach each scenario," He stops staring at us and keeps pacing.

"Some of you will be training here longer than others. This does not necessarily mean you are lagging. Be patient as we put soldiers out at specific times in specific places for the purpose of strategy against Rev. You are now free to follow the schedule that has been sent to your watch. If you have any questions you may ask them to any of these officers or myself," He steps back in the line of other officers.

EVERYONE BEGINS LOOKING at their watch. A few people head towards the officers to ask questions. I look at the schedule assigned to me. First thing is a physical, second, is the gun range. I click on the map for the clinic. As I begin walking out the door, I notice a third of the group also heads my way.

Once in the clinic I see a line and stand in it. A nurse comes up and he hands me a clipboard. I fill out my medical history which takes about five minutes. The line is moving pretty quick, but I don't see many people leaving. Soon enough, I get called in. A new nurse leads me to a room where curtains divide one soldier from another. Normal procedures are taken and then they start bringing out needles.

"Oh, what are these shots for?" I ask curiously.

"Your records say you will be going out of the country soon, so we are required to give you a vaccination to help protect you from any diseases. Don't worry, they have a good track record," The nurse says with a soft smile.

"Alright, great," I say.

I just wonder if there is anything else inside the shot. The nurse lifts my sleeve up and she injects me with the vaccination.

"Alright, you are good to go," The nurse says.

"Thanks. Have a good day," I say walking out.

Next on my list is the shooting range. I keep wondering if they're going to have us shoot any large weapons. I do like the big guns. Then again, we are only inside and underground so probably not. I walk down the hall away from the clinic to a large garage door. I stand in front of the door looking to see how to open it. I see a black box with a pin pad and swipe my watch in front of it. At first nothing happens. Two seconds pass, then the hallway lights dim. I back up a little, not expecting a mood change. A rectangular section of the wall slides into itself and a monitor comes into view.

"Bryan, you are now beginning gun training," A man says on the monitor.

"You will need to eliminate all targets and you will be graded on your performance,"

A new wall slides out behind me, blocking me from backing up.

"You will begin with a Beretta and then be given a M4. Use your shots wisely as circumstances change from one simulation to another. You may only carry two weapons at a time for training purposes. The whole simulation should take less than five minutes for experienced soldiers," The monitor goes black.

A tray slides out from the wall about waist high. On the tray lies a helmet and the Beretta with a magazine clip next to it. I grab the gun and look it over quickly and put the magazine in. A short buzzing noise signals the garage door opening. I quickly put the helmet on and I walk in with my gun pointed and ready.

On the right, ten feet in front of me there is a 4 foot by 4 foot slab of concrete standing up like a makeshift wall with crowbars sticking out of it. On the left, 25 feet ahead, are a stack of metal barrels. I make my way to the makeshift wall and just as I get to it, a dummy pops out from behind the barrels. I quickly shoot it once in the chest. The dummy slowly retracts from where it came.

· · ·

MAKING my way to the barrels, I see a light come out from behind a corner. I get to the barrels and take cover. The light is from a monitor.

"Nice reflexes. Now be prepared for the rest. Each target will have a number on it and that is how many times you must shoot it," The monitor goes dark but the voice is still there.

"When you hear "take cover" find the nearest obstacle to shield yourself from rubber bullets. Your timer begins now," The voice stops.

It's dark everywhere I look. I walk forward with my eyes adjusting from looking at the monitor.

Now I'm making out objects in the room. There's a large crate ahead on my left. A car door leans on a barbed wire fence a few feet in front of me. There is a noise ahead of me and I see something moving in the dark.

"Take cover!" A voice yells at me.

I look quickly and decide the crate is my best option. I hurry over to it just before hearing an indistinguishable number of thuds somewhere behind me.

Crouched behind the crate, I decide there must be a target close that I didn't see. I peek up and there is a dummy just behind a car with the number two on its chest. Then, I see a gun barrel move, located where the dummy's arm should be.

I duck down.

I hear a thud on the crate just above my head.

I pivot around the crate and fire two shots. The room gets a little lighter and I can see the dummy fall back into a cupboard.

I walk past the car and see two more targets jet out from hiding, one with the number 3 and the other 2. I place three into the correct dummy just before hearing, "Take cover" again.

I slide behind another concrete slab.

The noise of a machine gun goes off. The car, ten feet directly behind me, gets pummeled with rubber pellets. I get up to shoot, but the second dummy is out of sight. Slowly, I move forward and the lights above me gradually get brighter. Similar to when I beat the dummy behind the car and the lights got brighter, I wonder if this dummy is done or out.

I begin to think I have missed my opportunity. Just before succumbing to that thought, the dummy pops out and I hear, "Take cover".

I shoot twice anyways and then duck and roll to my right behind nothing.

Expecting to hear a machine gun and get multiple bruises I stay crouched with my head down.

No noise or bruises come. I look up, first to see that I'm out of ammo and second that the dummy is withdrawing back behind a wall. I guess I didn't miss it.

A door opens up and a glow of green appears within the doorway. I walk to the door and see that it is a small hall to another room. Sitting against the wall in the hallway is a M4. I pick it up and move on.

As I walk, I check the safety and good thing, because it was on. The lights are now brighter than before and the room I'm in is basically a big box with four doors on the other side. One of the four doors is abnormally big though. I notice tracks coming from each of the door ways. The three normal sized doors open and sporadically dummies come out from them, mostly with ones but sometimes twos on their chest. I take out each one without missing. The doors close and the big door opens. A vehicle comes out on the track with a turret on the top. Behind the turret is a dummy with the number four on it. I shoot it four times before it backs up into the door it came from.

The lights in the place turn on completely and a door opens up close by on my right.

Through the doorway a man walks up to me.

"Great job Bryan. You really knew what you were doing," He says grabbing the rifle and shaking my hand.

"Thanks. I thought I was going to be rustier," I give him a smile.

"Well, it was good," He says walking me out of the room. "By the way I'm Officer Dillion," We step into a hallway where he places the rifle down.

"It's nice to meet you," I say respectfully.

We keep walking, turning a corner.

"So just to review your performance. You didn't miss any targets or waste any ammo and that's impressive within itself. However, your time was 6:28. That's about a minute and half longer than we would like to see,"

I nod my head at what he is saying, but still think I moved pretty fast.

We reach some double doors and then we stop.

"I'm sure tomorrow you will do better," Dillion says with a smile.

I walk out the doors feeling a little upset my time wasn't better, but whatever, I am just getting back into the swing of everything. I look at my watch and see that my next activity is the track, for physical training. That isn't for another 20 minutes and it isn't very far from here, so I decide to take my time.

WHILE WALKING down a hallway I see a door that says "Weapons Hall". I open the door that leads into a long hallway. The walls have blue prints for different weapons every few feet. Pistols, shotguns, rifles, rocket launchers, and all sorts of attachments, each with concise notes and specs. I get halfway down the hall and hear a beep from my watch. It appears my schedule has changed slightly. I am supposed to go to physical training as soon as possible and then to vehicles and weapons training.

I head back down the hallway the way I came in. When I step out into the main hallway, I see more people are heading to the field. I see Jade walking and get her attention.

"Well, look who it is," She says.

"Hey, how did you do in the simulation?" I ask.

"I haven't had any simulation. I have done the physical and the gun range so far today," She says, a little confused.

"Oh, I thought," I pause. "Never mind. I thought the simulation was the gun range but I guess not,"

"How did you do on the simulation?" She returns the question.

"Well, I didn't miss a target, but I was slower than what they wanted," I reply.

We reach the field with everyone else. It is partially outside to my surprise. It has a track that is probably half that of a normal track. An officer stands by, giving orders.

"If you are just getting here, time yourself on running eight laps. Be quick soldiers,"

Jade and I start our timers and begin an easy jog.

"What's your time usually?" Jade asks.

"My average time is 6:20. What is yours?"

"I am normally around 6 minutes. I am going to pick up the pace in a minute," She says.

I just laugh.

Just like Jade said a minute later she picks up her stride. I try to keep up, but she stays ahead. I observe the other soldiers around me and most of them are faster than myself. The soldiers consist of men and women of various ages. I would say most are in their 30's. Seeing the number of soldiers around, I realize that H.E.R.O. needs more soldiers. I wonder when they will start bringing in masses of soldiers from the marines and army. They are going to need them eventually.

I DO my eight laps and turn in my time to an officer holding a tablet. "Reed, Bryan, 6:17," I say panting.

"Alright, make it faster next time. Good job though. Head over to the center of the field and they'll instruct you from there," The officer says, pointing with his pen to the crowd of soldiers already in the center of the field.

"Yes sir,"

I walk over to the field, just as everyone is told to give 20 push-ups. I quickly get in the group and start doing push-ups.

"When you are out in the field, this is what you are going to be doing a lot of. You are going to get knocked down and then push yourself up again and again. You need to be quick and accurate soldiers!" An officer walking up and down rows yells at us.

Another officer yells "Up, Down" over and over.

· · ·

WE FINISH the 20 and then move into jumping jacks. I can tell that these are experienced soldiers because of their perfection in executing each command. No one is getting grilled because they aren't doing the exercises properly. We finish jumping jacks.

"Alright, jog in place now and listen up. Our next exercise is going to require you to make some room from those that are around you. Make a space 3 yards from each person by you,"

We all spread out.

"Okay, you will all roll forward. Hopefully you all have done this before or else it's going to be a disaster. On the count of three you're going to roll, then stand, then roll again."

I can see some soldiers looking over at each other.

"One, two, three, roll," The officer orders.

I put my right shoulder forward and dive. I don't do it as smoothly as I would have liked, but I do it without hitting anyone. I land on my feet and then roll again. The second roll is even worse than my first..

"I saw a lot of poor rolls. Let's do it again," The commanding officer yells. "Jog! On the count of three do the two rolls again,"

He counts down from three and we do the rolls. I think I perform better this time around but he makes us do it again. After everyone figures it out we go back to push-ups. Once done, he gives us a breather.

"Now, take two minutes and then meet me over at the pull-up bars,"

I pace back and forth with my hands on the back of my head.

"Whoa, it feels good huh?" Jade says as she walks over, trying to catch her breath too.

"Yeah, I guess," I smile.

"It's been a while since I was put through this kind of training," I say.

"Not me. I was still in the marines when they brought me here and I still do it every day,"

We start walking to the next station.

"How long have you been here?" I ask, curious how long people have been getting recruited.

"A month tomorrow," she says.

"What have you done since being here?" Now, I start hearing my questions as an interrogation.

"I work out and study some of the weapons and vehicles. I also clean and have various duties around the facilities,"

We get to the line for the pull-ups. I offer for her to go ahead but she declines.

The officer looks at the time and then starts his instructions.

"This is really simple, so listen up or you're going to look like a fool. Once you get to the front of the line, you will state your name and then proceed to the bar. Do as many pull-ups as you can. Another officer will record your score and yell right or left depending on your score. I'll tell you this now, where you are placed depends on your score plus your height, weight, and speed from today's mile. Alright, let's begin,"

A woman soldier goes first, doing 16 pull-ups.

"Right!" Yells the recording officer.

The next is a man and he is told right as well.

It keeps going like this with a few people being put on the left.

I step up to the front and state my name. Once I reach the bar, I take a moment to focus. Out of all the results of the previous soldiers I am pretty confident that I don't want to be on the left. I jump and grab the bar and begin. I hit about 13 and start to fill the burning in my arms. I try to concentrate on the number 18 to block the sensation in my arms. I reach 18 and decide I have one more left in me and then one more after that. I drop half way up on number 21. I step forward waiting to hear the direction I will go, left or right. The officer marks something on his tablet.

"Right!" He yells. I step over to the right feeling accomplished.

I watch Jade, hoping she comes to the right, 'cause in my mind the left is weak. She pulls up 15 times and then starts to struggle. She is able to pull out 2 more for a total of 17. "Right!" Yells the officer.

"Nice job," I give her a fist bump as she walks over to the group.

"Thanks," She says, pacing a little.

The rest of the group goes through the exercise. In the end there are 13 people on the left and 41 people on the right. The officer giving all the commands walks up and stands between the left and right groups. "Great work everyone. Now you are divided as to your level of strength. If you are on the right you have a total level of strength meeting or exceeding our expectations. If you are on the left, today you did not meet those requirements and need to work harder in all your areas. Now, just because you are on the right side today doesn't necessarily mean you will be there tomorrow. Keep training hard because our expectations will continue to rise as the challenges in the field will too. Now you are free to go but we encourage you to spend some time in the gym today. We will see you tomorrow back here at 7:30 am," He finishes and walks away looking at his tablet.

"Well what is on your schedule Bryan?" Jade asks, looking at her own watch.

"I believe I have vehicle training now," I double check my schedule.

"Today, I have some cleaning to do I guess, but you will really like the vehicles if you haven't already seen them," Jade says, starting to walk towards the building.

"I have only seen a few and I didn't get much time to look at them," I say, walking the same way.

"You're going to want to go through those doors and take a right," She says pointing across the field to two metal doors.

"Thanks. Have fun cleaning," I smile and walk across the field.

I open one of the doors and head right, like Jade said. The walls are plain cement bricks. On the walls hang pictures of military vehicles from the first to the present. I reach a large garage with metal plated vehicles everywhere.

"State your name," An officer says.

"Reed, Bryan,"

He stares at me, then down at his tablet.

"Alright, go down this way to the office. Officer Farr is waiting for you," He says pointing at some doors.

"Thank you," I reply and continue down the hall.

I am only halfway to the office when Jake walks out with energy.

"Bryan, it's good to see you. You look like you got some rest,"

"Same with you," I say jokingly.

Jake smiles. "It was a busy day yesterday. It's good to be back at base," He puts his hand on my back and leads me toward the vehicles.

"So, here's the plan. We are going to leave for Africa tonight. We'll land on a Navy ship, where we'll get some rest before heading out again,"

"Already? You don't think I need some more training? They say I am slow at the field simulation," I look at him a little curious.

"Bryan, I won't put you in any situation that you aren't trained for. Your training report came through and it says you're in shape for a mission. Now let's finish up today's training with these advanced vehicles," He raises his hand up towards the heavy vehicles.

"This is a new Humvee we built, called the Juggernaut. It can only get up to 55 mph but it is loaded with a retractable machine gun turret and hidden missiles. It's a pretty safe metal box. It can hold 6 people inside," Says Jake.

The Humvee is a tan color, as many military Humvees are. It looks a little bigger all around than the ones I am familiar with. Jake walks over to the next vehicle.

"Here is the June Bug, you rode in yesterday. It is made to carry troops to and from battlefields. It also has a roof that can separate, creating more room to operate a large gun. It's a hard shell that can withstand a lot of fire power. Over here are some smaller vehicles for up to two people,"

He shows me some four-wheelers next.

"This is almost your basic four-wheeler. We just call it the Runner as it is durable and quick. This other one is longer, a little bigger, and can hold more equipment. We call it the Tiger. It holds 50% more gas than the Runner,"

"This last one has only been out in the field a few times and is still proving itself. It's called the Cougar. It's pretty amazing. It looks large and bulky, and it is, compared to the other two. However, what makes this unique is its four jets that stabilize it. It also has some power to set you higher when you jump into the air,"

I am amazed. Jets on a four-wheeler. It looks pretty sleek for a military four-wheeler. It's a dark green matte color with a black seat. The jets or boosters are in the front middle and back middle. Jake explains that when activated, the jets unfold and point slightly outward, towards the sides of the four-wheeler.

"Can I try it out?" I ask.

Jake looks at me. "Well, yeah of course. It's new to you so you do need to be trained on it,"

I jump on the four-wheeler and Jake shows me the functions. I start up the Cougar and hear the engine roar. I take it in between vehicles inside the garage while Jake opens the door to the outside.

"Bryan, come outside," I hear Jake yell.

I finish driving around a tank and head outside.

"How does it feel?" Jake asks with a grin.

"It is nice. It isn't as heavy as I thought," I say jumping a little to show its ease of movement.

"Alright, so make sure you have the balance sensors on. That will allow the jets to help restore your balance if you are about to roll or something. Just make sure you hold on tight, you'll do fine,"

I nod my head and take off. I ride over some alternating bumps, testing the suspension. As far as I could tell the jets didn't go off on those. I head over to some small mounds and the Cougar takes them nicely but I can tell it likes to stay close to the ground. After that I see a jump. It isn't very big, probably three feet high. I decide to take it and see what the jets do for me. I ride past it to get a good sense of what I am dealing with and then turn around to face it.

I take one moment to analyze and then I crank the throttle.

I gain speed and hit the jump going about 40 mph. As I glide through the air I realize I am tilting a little. Then I feel the jets kick in and level me out just before landing. My heart is racing. I drive up to Jake.

"That was awesome!" I exclaim.

"Well good, I'm glad you enjoyed it,"

"Did Rev come up with this?" I ask, curious of who the creator is.

"No. This one was by us," He says.

"I'm glad you like it but we need to keep going through some more vehicles,"

I drive the Cougar back in the garage and he closes the door.

"Over there, we have some basic military jeeps and right here are the mechs," Jake walks over to another room of the garage and turns on the lights.

The mechs are huge. A metal box with a glass window the shape of a rounded corner triangle all sitting on top of two metal legs. They stand about 15 feet high and have no arms but gun barrels instead.

"Yeah they're beautiful. Try not to drool on them," Jake says lightly pushing me.

"So, what can it do?" I ask, still amazed.

"These were built to get up close and personal. It becomes a lot easier to push the enemy back when you have one of these stomping towards them,"

I walk around one of the eight mech's. On the back of the mech are rungs like a ladder.

"Why don't you get in it really quick and try it. You probably won't be using it for a while, until we really train you, but it's always good to be a little familiar just in case,"

I look around for a ladder, so I can actually reach the rungs and get in it.

"Look at your watch," Jake says, pointing to his own.

"My watch?" I question, thinking I have little time until my next scheduled event.

"When you approach a mech you can use your watch to turn it on and give the command to lower, so you can get in it,"

A button appears on my watch screen, "Use Mech" it reads. I tap it and back up. The mech turns on and then I tap "Lower Mech". The mech lowers and I climb up. I open the hatch by sliding it forward. I lower myself down onto a seat. The controls are pretty neat, there are two joysticks, one for directing the mech and the other for aiming the guns. There are also two pedals, one makes you go forward and the other backwards.

I like it. It is well designed, but I can see how some practice with it would be necessary for combat. I climb out and down hanging from the rungs and dropping to the ground.

"That is awesome. I can't wait to get trained on that," I say walking out of the room with Jake.

"I'm glad you like all of the vehicles because you are going to be using them a lot,"

"What time is it now?" I ask.

"It's just past two. I think you have the rest of the day with me. I want to get a jump start on briefing you and your new team on your next task,"

"Great! I am feeling more in-tuned and ready to get out there. Today has been a good day," I say with a smile.

Jake looks at me.

"I thought I saw a difference in you when you walked in,"

"Well I think a lot of things just fell on me all at once. Now that I have processed it, I can prepare for a mission,"

We walk out of the garage and into another room where groups of six or seven soldiers discuss what sounds like missions.

We go through some doors and I start asking Jake about the operations planned to tackle such a massive terrorist group.

"When we decided to create this organization, it was unthinkable how we would tackle such a large group. With the downsize of the military back in 2034 and red tape in the U.S. on certain defense programs, things weren't looking ripe for a strong operation. Also, I didn't even know and still don't know, who the leader of Rev is. Along with that, every time an option was brought up it seemed to be that it would lead to division within the nation and we didn't need that on top of the end of the world. So, we decided to make this group with the best of the best. We had to keep this quiet because we didn't want anyone to spill the beans that there was a counter group specifically against Rev. Anyway, knowing our numbers would be low until the world saw what was going on, we decided to hit main areas of concern. As we find out about different tactics Rev is using, we'll consider how much manpower it will take to eliminate them,"

I nod my head.

"Okay, so once the world sees Rev out and about, we will call in more forces like the Army, Marines, Air Force, and Navy?" I try to confirm what he said.

"Yes. However, like I mentioned the other day. The vehicles other forces have will be vulnerable to EMP attacks," Jake opens a door leading into an office.

The room is approximately 30 feet by 20 feet. A projector and some whiteboards are placed around the room. In the middle of the room are three soldiers sitting around a table.

"Well, look who decided to show up, Jake and his space cowboy. Just kidding. The name is Jace. It's a privilege to meet you Bryan.," a six foot, rough looking man says.

He stands up and we shake hands. I am five foot eleven so we were almost the same height.

A thick built man stands up and shakes my hand.

"Hi Bryan. I'm Luke, it's nice to meet you,"

He is also about six foot, which makes me feel even more out of place. My body is just tone, so these two guys are making me feel small.

Walking up to me now, is a woman about five foot eight.

"And I'm Erin. I'll have your back when these two guys trip and fall," She says smiling and patting Luke and Jace on the shoulders.

"Okay, so everyone is getting along. That's good," Jake says.

"Now, everyone sit down. I have some things to go over,"

Jake walks over to the projector.

"You four and myself will be one squad. This is how it will be for a long time, so start liking each other now. Your missions will rely on excellent team work. You can't just think about yourself, but about the whole team. If one of you is down, the whole team is weakened. If you end up alone during a mission, you won't have much of a chance. But you all know this because of your previous experiences. So, onto the good stuff,"

He turns on the projector.

"Your first mission will be in Africa. Why? Rev has placed some troops there staging an alien presence. They are using fear to control less powerful countries. This same tactic is being used in other countries as well. You will be up against this,"

He changes the slide to the metal man alien the officers showed me last night.

"This is what people are seeing and believing to be an alien. Like I said, it's staged so other people are pretending to be civilians and try to convince the others they must follow the alien or else they will die," Jake changes the picture to another angle of the "alien".

"It is critical that we get in there quickly because some civilians are rebelling and are dying while making no gain on the situation. Although there are some that rebel, we fear that in a short amount of time, enough people will believe or conform to what they are told to do. This would make Rev larger and stronger,"

Erin raises her hand.

"Can we get some drones out there and blow up the alien figure?"

Jake switches the slide to an aerial view. The picture shows a group of soldiers circled around the alien, facing outward. The crowd of people look at the soldiers' nucleus.

"This was yesterday. The last picture we got because on the next trip the drone took was its last. The drone didn't return," Jake pauses.

"Rev has the technology to see these drones coming or any missiles for that matter. We will be on the ground taking out as many soldiers as possible, before taking out the alien imposter," He says.

The four of us chuckle lightly.

"So, are we going in there with just the five of us?" I ask curiously.

"No, but we will only have about 20 more soldiers. They aren't going to be on the front lines though," Jake turns off the projector.

"We will meet tonight at 7:00 pm to head out. We will be flying to a navy ship, some ways off the coast of Africa. Once there, you will get some rest just before our mission starts. You're now free to leave. Use the rest of your day wisely," Jake says waving his hand like "get out of here".

I stand up with everyone else, but hesitate to leave.

"Alright Jake, I'll see you tonight," Jace says leaving with Luke and Erin.

"Well, this will be my first combat against aliens," I joke.

"Yeah, Bryan, this is going to be really interesting," Jake says, staring at me.

"I hope you aren't upset with me for leaving or recruiting you," He says, solemnly looking right at me.

"What? No. I...want to help," I try to reassure him.

"I just needed all the men I could get. I knew you would be a great soldier to take on this new kind of combat," He starts walking towards the door.

"You should go spend some time with your family. I am sure they would like to see you with the remaining hours you have, for the next few months," He leaves.

That was really weird. Jake just sounded super depressed or something all of a sudden. I hope he is feeling okay. I am just now wondering where his family is and if he has seen them much. I'm sure he is fine, I tell myself.

I WALK BACK to my room and don't see my wife or kids. I check the box that had watches in it and they're gone. I figure Samantha has her watch on and I can message her.

My message goes through and I sit on the bed waiting to hear back from her. It's then I realize I have a message, it appears to be an updated report of the catastrophe caused by the meteorites.

"Damage Report", It reads.

"Washington State: Space Needle and many skyscrapers destroyed.

California: Water Treatment facilities compromised. Earthquakes ripple throughout the state.

Missouri: Kansas City virtually destroyed.

New York: The port was heavily hit.

This is not an encompassing report. More will be shared as news is received,"

That is the end of the message. To think that the next decade is going to be trying to restore cities and communities is depressing. Yet maybe focusing on a simple common good will help people forget less important differences and politics will not cause unnecessary contention between various groups.

I still haven't heard from Samantha, so I call her. After one ring she picks up.

"Hello," She says hesitantly.

"Samantha, it's me," I say.

"Bryan, are you done with your training for today?" She asks. "Yeah I am. I only have a couple hours though before heading out on my first mission,"

There is a pause.

"Wait, tonight?" Samantha asks.

"Yeah we have to leave tonight. Where are you? I'll come meet you there,"

"We're just at the theater. The kids are watching a movie,"

I didn't know they had a movie theater here.

"Alright, I will be there soon," I end the call and look for directions to get there.

AFTER FIVE MINUTES of walking the halls I get to the theater, where mothers and a few fathers watch their kids. Samantha is standing against a wall near the entrance.

"Hey, how's it going?" I walk up and kiss her.

"It's good. The kids have been here most of the day. How has the training been?" She hardly looks at me.

I think she is upset, because I will be leaving tonight.

"Training was good. We did some physical exercises and they recorded our scores. I didn't do as well as I have in the past, but it wasn't bad. I did a simulation. I met up with Jake and learned about some vehicles. Oh, and I also met my new squad. It consists of two men and a woman plus Jake and myself," I try to make it all sound interesting, but for her it's just my job that takes me away from the family.

"Are you okay?" I ask.

"Yeah I am fine," She says quickly. "I just wish we had more time together. I have only seen you for 24 hours and then you have to go again,"

There is silence for a minute.

"I know this is hard. I am living it too. But we both agreed this was a good idea considering the circumstances," I say.

She looks at me.

"I know, but it sucks," She walks over to the kids sitting on a couch and tells them I am here.

They look back towards the door and then, rush over to me.

For the next few hours I play with them, we build towers with blocks and I give them piggyback rides. I was able to give them a little tour of the facility. When dinner rolls around, we get to eat together.

"Dad, how long are you going to be gone?" Tate asks while prodding his mash potatoes.

I look over at Samantha and then back at him.

"Well, after a few months, I'll be back for about a week or so to see you guys,"

Tate takes a bite of his food.

"I will probably be in this job for a few years," I begin tearing up.

Just the thought of not being here and missing their lives makes me question my choice of joining.

"Don't worry Tate, I am sure we can see him over the computer like we have done before," Samantha tries to reassure him, but I think it's really for me.

Her eyes get watery too.

"Yeah, that was fun," Tate says taking a really big bite of potatoes.

I smile through my tears. I look at Samantha who is trying to do the same.

Once we finish dinner, we head back to the room. I gather a few things together to take with me. A picture of our family and a sock puppet Tate made for me today. Caroline made me a nice pasta necklace, but I figure it would just break apart if I try to bring it.

· · ·

THE LAST 30 minutes before heading out, Samantha and I talk about what she learned today from the instructor who is over the families of soldiers. The kids will have classes four times a week and have some activities that are optional on the other 3 days.

Like always, time seems to fly by when I am with them. I kiss Samantha and the kid's goodbye.

"I'll be back in a few months if not sooner," I say with tears in my eyes.

I walk out the door and just a few steps down the hall before falling on my knees. I just cry and ask myself what I am doing. I pray that my family will be watched over and I will be able to return to them. The tears keep coming and then after a minute, I feel a comfort that it will all be okay. I stand up and wipe the tears off my face. I take a moment to concentrate on my new task at hand. At that moment my mind switches to combat ready and I head to my departing flight.

9

Outskirts of a Nightmare

I WALK INTO THE HANGAR, where four Falcon X50 jets and one jumbo jets sit, surrounded by soldiers. I see my squad standing by one of the Falcons and head over to them.

"Bryan, how's it going?" Asks Luke with a light smile and he shakes my hand.

"I'm good. I'm ready to get out of here," I say feeling a boost of excitement.

"Yeah, we are too," Jace gets up from tying his boots.

"Jake should be here soon."says Luke.

"He better be or else it's going to be a bumpy flight, because I don't know how to fly that thing," Jace says looking at the jet.

"No one is going to be flying my bird except for me," Jake ducks under the tail of the jet.

"Alright, we got our team together. Let's get out of here," Erin gets up from sitting on a tool box.

"I have your combat suits inside, as well as the guns and ammunition. Let's get on the jet and I'll let the others know we are ready to go.

The five of us board the Falcon.

"This is Jake and Squad 7. We are ready for take-off. Over," Jake says while doing a quick check of his controls.

"This is mission control. We are just waiting to hear back from Platoon 283. Once they're ready we will give you the green light. Over,"

Jake gets up from the pilot seat and heads to the back where we begin examining our combat suits.

"Well what do you think?" Jake asks.

"These are impressive. This is an inch thick of...what kind of material is this? Erin asks.

"It doesn't have much of a name yet. We just call it Q5,"

"Wait, are we testing this material out?" Jace sounds worried.

"No. I wouldn't allow that," Jake sounds offended.

"It has proven itself. It is a material the government has been working on for years. Lightweight but durable,"

"Sounds pretty cool to me," Luke says.

"This is mission control. The rest of your company is ready to go. You may depart from home base. Over,"

Jake heads to the pilot seat. "Great. Let's buckle up and get to our Navy friends,"

"Shotgun," Luke says as he heads to the co-pilot seat.

"Hey Jake, who else is in our company?" Jace asks.

"We have 15 other soldiers flying on a jumbo jet, carrying some vehicles. We also will have another Falcon X50 coming along," Jake replies.

"Prepare for liftoff," Jake drives the jet onto the runway.

The engines roar. The jet moves forward slowly to get into position. After checking a few more switches Jake begins picking up speed.

No more than a minute goes by and we lift up and begin soaring in the air. The sky is dark. I can see some lights in some buildings far away. I wonder if people are already going back to their homes. I sit in my chair looking at the guns and ammo. It appears seats have been removed from the jet to accommodate the supplies.

. . .

FOR THE NEXT few hours we just talk a little about what to expect or what guns are our favorites and share a little about ourselves.

A few times, we got a heads up that meteors are falling around us and we all watched out the windows at their glowing appearance. We couldn't tell if any hit us due to the loud engines, but if they did hit us they weren't very big.

We arrive close to 2 o'clock in the morning on the Navy ship. When we land, we are met by three sailors. Once off the jet, we are escorted to our rooms.

"Get some sleep. We will be up in six hours," Jake says. We all jump into our cots. Not much else is said and we go to sleep.

I WAKE up feeling a little sick, but try not to think about it, afraid it would make it worse. We all get dressed in our combat suits and head to the dining hall. Sailors stare at us everywhere we go. I guess I would too if I saw some heavy armored soldiers on a navy boat. Most people don't know what our business is about, but they sure are interested.

IT'S ABOUT eight now and we finish breakfast and our whole company meets together in a room to discuss the day's plan. The room is a little cozy with all of us in there. Two columns of long tables, with 5 chairs at each, fill the room. The chairs get filled up and few people stand along the walls.

Jake stands in front of the room with four other officers.

"Okay, listen up. We'll all be landing on the same beach and then from there we will be dispersing in slightly different directions. The Navy will be dropping off vehicles as we land. Once we do land, clear the area and then grab your needed supplies and vehicles. Platoon 321 will head north east. Platoon 283 will head south east. Squad 7 will go directly east," Jake shows everyone on a monitor, drawing out paths on the large digital map.

"I want you to talk to those who have information about strange activity in the area. If they don't have anything important or relevant to our mission, move on. I don't want you to spend more than 15 minutes in a town. We will then meet up here around four o'clock," He says pointing to a place on the map.

One of the officers taps Jake on the shoulder and whispers something. Jake jester for him to speak.

"My name is Officer Blake. I first want to just thank you all for being willing to serve in this organization. Second, I want to hand out a chip that goes inside your watch. He passes around a box of small chips. This, when activated, will allow you to select a language or region in which you would like the language to be translated into another, such as English. It will save information for 30 hours, unless you choose otherwise," Officer Blake steps back with the other three officers and Jake steps forward.

"Thank you, Officer Blake. I forgot to mention that you should not go any further than the rendezvous point for any reason. This could ultimately cause us to scramble the whole mission. Now, I think that's about it. Everyone, be on a Falcon in ten. Dismissed!"

Everyone begins walking out of the room. I start following the others when Luke grabs my arm.

"Jake wants us," He says pointing to the front of the room.

We walk over there, just behind Jace and Erin.

"Hey, I need some hands," Jake hands us some green briefcases.

"What are these?" Jace asks.

"Computers, grenades, and some rifles. What else?" Jake says, as though Jace has never seen military briefcases.

We each get two briefcases except Luke who has three.

"That's it. Let's get going," says Jake as he leads us out.

We walk out of the room and out onto the main deck to our Falcon. We load up the luggage and buckle into our seats.

Once we are given the clear, we take off with the rest of the platoons.

"Jake, have you ever used one of these language translators?" Erin asks.

"No, but supposedly they are pretty accurate. It should be quite interesting to see it in action."

"Does anyone know another language? We could try it out," I suggest.

"I know some French," Luke says.

"Well let's see. Actually, hold on. Let me set mine up," Jace taps on his watch. "Okay, go ahead I'm ready,"

"Je voudrais un peu plus de nourriture," Luke says with ease.

A few seconds later the translation comes out.

"I would like some more food." A woman's voice projects from Jace's watch.

We all look at Luke.

"Well, it worked," Luke admits.

We all smile and shake our heads.

I LOOK out the front window and see trees intermixed with buildings just on the edge of the beach. We descend lower and lower until we reach the beach and then we spin around a few times before landing.

The five of us grab our helmets and rifles. Jake opens the door and I jump out first. My boots sink into the sand as I clear the landing zone. The rest of my squad comes out and they follow my path up the beach. We reach a patch of grass and stop.

"It looks like the area is clear," I hear Jake say through my helmet's headset.

"Let's grab our gear and go,"

The other platoons evacuate their aircraft and begin preparing for their departure from the beach.

We grab a few duffle bags, computers, two tiger quads, and a Humvee. Jake and Luke take the Humvee while Jace and Erin ride together on one tiger and I on the other. The tiger I ride is equipped with a GPS system showing important landmarks around the area. With a nod to the other platoons, we take to the streets through the city, east as instructed.

Surprisingly there are quite a few people out. I guess more than I expected. It's now three days after the falling meteorites. This city has some damage, like an exercise ball sized hole in the side of a few buildings, but other than that, it's minimal.

It is when I take a turn around a street corner that I realize the difference between this tiger quad and a regular one. The tiger's longer frame makes one think differently about how to turn to clear obstacles.

As we get closer to the outer edge of the city there are some native soldiers stationed behind barricades. The soldiers stop us and one of them walks up to Jake's window. It's only a few minutes later, before we are moving again past the barricades.

I hear Jake over the headset, "It looks like multiple planes and helicopters have been in the area for about two months. Recently, it's been quiet, causing suspicion among locals. It's best to assume Rev has a strong force here,"

The next 45 minutes we drive from the city and further into the wilderness. We've passed two small towns where in one, an entire house had been decimated by a meteorite. Pieces of wood and other debris litter the ground around where the house was. The air has an odor resembling burnt wood, moist dirt, and burnt hair.

It's now 11 o'clock and we have reached halfway to the meet up location. The five of us stop in a small town where curious men and women stop and stare. Jake stops the Humvee in front of a little market. He gets out and looks around. A short hair, black man dressed in a tan shirt and tan pants with a hand on his gun, holstered on his waist, walks up to Jake. I'm assuming he is a police officer.

"Hello, we are from the United States military. We are in search of some wanted men," Jake says while tapping on his watch.

He probably is trying to get the translator on. However, the officer begins to speak in English with a noticeable native African accent.

"Are you going to Yaounde?" He asks.

Jake looks back at us and then to the officer.

"Yeah, how'd you know?"

"We have had some strange people come to our town trying to recruit men for some job there. Next thing we hear, city structures were being put up quickly and strange things were happening inside them.

Someone just got here this morning saying they saw an alien," The officer pauses and looks around.

"The man swears that aliens landed. He also said people are trying to leave the city, but the aliens have taken control of soldiers to keep people there," The officer doesn't sound overly convinced of it and is skeptical of the wild claims.

"Well, we will be looking into that. I want you to assure your town that there are no aliens nor are they being controlled by aliens. It's a terrorist group. Do not succumb to their lies because it's all just a trick," Jake says.

The officer nods his head.

"Is there anything we should know?" asks Jake.

The officer shakes his head. "No, that's all I know,"

Jake thanks the officer and jumps back in the Humvee. The engine roars as he takes off. Jace, Erin and I follow him out of the small community.

ANOTHER 30 MINUTES go by before reaching another town. We get the same story. We fill up on gas that we brought in the Humvee. Once I see the fuel I realize I had seen the gas before. Back at base a man was pushing a cart of it. A clear bluish brown.

"Jake, what kind of fuel is this?" I ask.

"It's a concoction put together by Rev. We actually are limited on the supply we stole from them,"

He says draining one tube of it into the Humvee.

"Can't Hero just reverse engineer it?" Luke asks.

Jake walks over to the tiger quads to fill them up.

"They have been trying to, but for some reason they can't quite figure it out,"

He finishes putting a quarter tube of the fuel into each quad.

"That seems bizarre," Erin says.

"Once I heard someone in the lab say they couldn't match everything within the solution to any elements known to man," Jake says, walking back to the Humvee.

"Are you serious?" I ask, really questioning what he just said.

"Yeah. It's what I heard once," He looks directly at me. "Now let's get on the road again," He climbs into the Humvee.

One hour later we slow down at the last town before Yaounde. The town is scarce of people. Once we stop, I get off my quad and stretch. As I crack my neck, I see someone on a rooftop pointing a rifle at me. I stop. I look slowly around to find more soldiers watching us.

"Jake, we have snipers on the rooftops," I hear Erin say.

"Be calm," Jake says to us.

"Hello. We are U.S. soldiers here to help," Jake says kindly, as if he didn't know there were snipers.

A few soldiers come out of a brown brick building with their guns pointed at us. Almost, as though for dramatic effect, a man on the second level of a building, possibly an officer, walks out slowly from the dark inner building into the bright sunlight.

"How do we know you are from the U.S.?" The officer asks with his hands behind his back.

"You could be part of Yaounde's terrorists," He continues

"Take off your helmets and open your vehicle's doors. I will have my men determine whether you are my enemies or my friends," We take off our helmets, while hoping they don't blow off our heads. How do we know whether they are working with Rev or not?

The soldiers come down a few steps to the street and surround us. A few of them check the Humvee and examine the quads. One of the soldiers searching the vehicle walks back to the officer. For about two minutes they talk to each other in another language.

The officer then turns to us.

"Thank you for cooperating with me. I know you are from the U.S. now, but, what is your business here?"

Jake walks around the Humvee to face the officer better.

"We know that a terrorist group is here in Yaounde. We have a mission to eliminate them from your soil. They have capabilities that are even challenging for the U.S. military," Jake says.

The officer walks down the stairs to the street.

"They are challenging. My men and I were stationed in South

Africa only three days ago, when a bomb dropped on the entire base. We were on an assignment to oversee that civilians retreat to bunkers, when we found out our base was gone," His face shows discomfort.

"We are so sorry to hear that. What made you come here?" Jake asks.

"We flew here the day after the meteorites, because Yaounde has been a whisper of strange events. We were hoping to find out some more information. Once we got here we learned that the terrorists are holding hostages. Many people fled from here to go to bunkers closer to the city. Now, we are just holding our ground. There are too many soldiers there in Yaounde. Each day more people are succumbing to the terrorist. Aliens are what some call them, but I won't be fooled," The officer says.

"How many soldiers would you say there are?" Jake asks.

He looks at his men.

"About 500 soldiers and growing," One soldier says.

Jake looks back at us.

"You and four others cannot defeat such an army. Even adding my 18 men wouldn't make much of a difference," The officer tries to convince us.

"We are with a larger company, but you are right it won't be easy or quick. What was your name? I don't believe I got it," Jake asks.

"My name is Officer Zuzika," He says firmly. "You are?"

"Officer Farr" Jake says as he goes to shake Zuzika's hand.

"We are in a time crunch so we must go now, However, I want you to send me intel if you catch wind of anything that may be useful. We will be about 4 miles out from here,"

"I will, Officer Farr. If you need any assistance, we will be here,"

We put our helmets on and drive out of the town.

A short drive later we pull off the road and into the brush. Once we get a way in, we stop.

"These are the coordinates we were told to come to," Jake says getting out of the Humvee.

I get off my tiger quad and stretch again. Riding a quad for four hours is a lot more tiring than I thought. Growing up I never rode them much but always found them to be cool. Now, not so much.

"Let's search the area to make sure we are alone," Jake pulls his rifle out of the Humvee.

I detach my rifle from the quad and check it over.

I walk through the jungle, pushing large lush leaves out of my path. The foliage is excessive, making me think how easy it would be to hide mines or IED's, improvised explosive devices. Maybe, I don't have to worry so much this far out of the city but it's good to remember, the closer we get to Yaounde. I try to pay attention to things out of the ordinary, but colors of flowers and bugs seem to have more weight on my mind. Everything here is a new environment to me. I try to stay focused and keep scanning the area as I walk further and further away from the vehicles. I stop for a second and observe a large tall trunk. It stretches high up, before its branches disperse into the canopy. While panning the tree tops I notice an oddly formed hole letting a large ray of sunlight through. My eyes follow the ray of light down occasionally accompanied by gnats zipping around.

WHEN THE RAY of light meets the forest floor, a round object lays halfway in the ground. Thinking it's a meteorite, I continue walking closer to it. Now five feet away I see that it has strange symbols written on its black surface. I stop and then slowly move around the meteorite. Its oval shaped. On one end of the meteorite is a perfect one inch by six-inch lateral cut and another perpendicular to the first, making an addition symbol. The more I observe it, the more peculiar it appears. There are a few holes around the egg- shaped stone, in some kind of pattern.

I look around to see if anyone is nearby but the rest of my squad is still on their individual searches. I pause for a moment and try to relax so I can think this through. Okay I found something out of the ordinary, which was the purpose of my search. Should I continue, as it isn't an immediate threat? Or should I stop here and tell the rest of my squad?

I grab a stick and put one end of it into the ground so that it sticks up about three feet. Then, I go a few steps out and search for anything else that seems strange. Only a minute later, I decide there won't be anything else more important than the odd egg shaped meteorite. I run past the stick in the ground and then look back to make sure the strange object is still there. I continue back to the vehicles.

"Jake, Erin, Luke, Jace, I found something you should all see. I don't believe it's an immediate threat, but it's got to be important," I say into my headset looking around for them.

"Where are you Bryan?" Jake asks quickly.

"I am back at the vehicles," I reply.

"Everyone, get to the vehicles now," Jake orders.

LESS THAN FIVE MINUTES LATER, Erin comes through some trees and the rest only seconds later. Jake, breathing a little heavy, takes off his helmet.

"I just...I just saw...a snake. It was huge. Right in front of the path. Sorry, what is it you found Bryan?" He says helmet under his arm and leaning his gun against a quad.

"Follow me," I turn and walk back on the path I first made through the trees.

I scan the area as I walk, making sure I don't go off to a different area. Then, I recognize my stick I planted.

"This way. Don't get too close, I don't know what it is,"

We push through some final leaves and into the low brush, where the egg shaped stone lays.

"That? That's a meteorite, Bryan," Jace says relaxing his shoulders.

"No, it's something else. Look closer and you'll see strange symbols. It has perfect holes and cuts in it," I say, shaking my head and pointing at it.

The four of them circle the object, examining it.

Jace, Erin and Luke take off their helmets.

"I see what you're saying," Jake says placing his helmet on a branch.

"Look at it. It's like this was made by someone. The perfect holes and the shape, it's too neat to be natural," Luke's face show's that he is amazed.

"Woah! Look at the back," Erin is looking at the addition sign.

Jake walks around to see what she is pointing out.

"Okay, this is the strangest meteorite I've seen," He says.

"What is this thing?" Erin asks.

"I have no idea," Jake replies.

"If we could understand these symbols, we could know for sure," Jace says, crouched down and observing the object.

"I have never seen those kinds of characters before, but I might have something in the Humvee that can translate written text. If it's a real language, we'll know what it says," Jake says, but he just stares at it.

"What if it isn't a real language? What if it was put here by Rev to make someone think it was an alien object? It would help their story out," Erin considers with a raised eyebrow. We all look at each other.

Jake and Luke leave to get a computer and the three of us stay looking at the mysterious object in question.

"You don't think it's a bomb, do you?" Jace asks.

"No. I mean I guess it could be but it didn't come to mind because I found it by seeing a beam of sunlight through the treetops. As my eyes followed the path of light, it led straight down to this," I use my finger to show my thought process.

"Huh, that is true. The light falls right on it," Jace confirms.

"So, it probably fell out of the sky, but it's not a meteorite. It could be a bomb made by Rev that ended up being a dud," Erin suggests.

"That could be true. I mean they seem to have a lot of new inventions. This could be a faulty one," I go along with the thought.

We begin hearing some roars and hums.

The noises get louder and louder.

They're vehicles.

I hope it's our company and not Rev. I can tell the vehicles have come into our camp. The engines shut off and we hear some voices. Just as I was making out what was being said Luke comes through the brush.

"One of the platoons is here. Jake said we will come back once we get situated,"

I grab Jake's helmet off the branch and the four of us walk back to the camp.

Once back at camp we find the soldiers in platoon 283 are putting up tents and unloading supplies.

"Let's see what Jake wants us to do. Oh, and don't act suspicious. I don't think the officers want everyone spreading rumors about this black egg," Luke says, while leading us to Jake.

Two other officers and Jake are looking at a map on the hood of a Humvee, when we approach them.

"There's your squad," One officer says.

"Let's finish this and then I have something to discuss with you guys," Jake says pointing to the map. The other officers look at him and then each other and then at us. "Alright then," Officer Cortez says. I get one of the officer's names from reading his badge. Jake points to the map and slides his finger over it.

"We'll take the right, you two and your platoon will take the middle, and platoon 321 will take the left. The objective will be to scope out the city and find areas of high security. If we are lucky, we will be able to mark safe zones within the city limits," Jake looks up at everyone.

"We should have gotten a tank in there," The other officer, Officer Benson says, taking his hand from his chin and making a fist on the hood.

"We talked about this. Our vehicles may not be the smartest move at the moment. We'll be better off relying on our soldier's boots, than easy vehicle targets," Jake reassures him.

"Okay, when do we leave?" Officer Cortez asks.

"We'll wait for the 321 platoon. We won't have a lot of time to scout out the area but it will suffice for today,"

Jake looks at us and then back at the two officers.

"Now for the other concern we have. We found something when clearing the area. It isn't an immediate threat but it's oddness concerns me. Follow me," He walks past us and we follow him with the officers in behind.

The other soldiers continue working with only a few noticing our posse leaving, into the trees.

"Where exactly are we going?" Benson asks just before we break through the last set of trees to the clearing, where the questionable object lies.

"What in the..."

"It's not a meteorite," Jake cuts Cortez off.

"If it's not a meteorite then what is it?" Says Benson, sounding a little unconvinced.

"We don't know where exactly it came from or why it's here in the middle of nowhere. However, there are symbols on it" Jake points out. "There are also holes that appear to be perfectly cut out of this object,"

"And if I may, Jake, we were talking after you went back to the Humvee. The canopy above has a hole in it where it seemed to drop through," Erin jumps in.

For a minute the two officers just observe the black egg shaped object. Their heads tilt and they squint trying to comprehend its purpose.

"I don't know," Cortez shakes his head.

"How do we know this isn't a bomb?" Benson asks one eye a little wider than the other.

"We don't know much about it. We don't even know its weight or the material it is made of," Jake shrugs.

"I was just about to get my computer and a transcript translator when you guys pulled up,"

Cortez nods his head. "That's a good idea. Since we are waiting for 321 let's do that now. I don't like the idea of camping by such a strange object,"

"That could be a bomb," Benson adds.

"Luke, you saw where the computer was right?" Jake asks.

"Yeah,"

"Will you go get it, please?"

"I'm on it sir," Luke jogs back to the camp.

"Let's not tell the other soldiers about this. This could really mess with their minds. We can't do a long show and tell and then have them creating strange ideas about what this might be," Cortez says, waving his hands in the air.

"Yeah, I agree," Jake says.

Jace, Erin and myself just nod.

"I guess that's true," Benson says. His face is getting a little red.

"Are you okay?" Cortez asks him.

"Yeah. I just need a minute," Benson walks a few feet away looking off into the trees. Cortez has a curious look on his face.

"This is definitely something we'll want to take back to the base," Jake looks at Cortez.

"Yeah, but depending on what it is, it may make that difficult. If it's a bomb, how does it work and will it blow up on us,"

Luke comes through the thick forest carrying a silver suitcase.

"Some soldiers were asking questions. Just to let you know," He says looking at Cortez.

"I'll go back and make sure the camp is getting put together right. Let me know if you get anything," He says walking Luke's path back.

"Alright let's set this up and see what we can find," Jake opens the suitcase.

A few minutes go by and we anxiously wait.

"Okay we're set. Jake grabs a video camera looking tool and then runs it in front of the symbols on the eggs black surface. I step around to see the computer screen. The symbols show up with red lines and dots around them.

"Anything?" Jace asks.

Jake just keeps scanning the symbols.

"Are there any more symbols on this?" Jake asks.

Not on any visible parts. Maybe the section that is buried in the ground," Erin says.

Benson walks back over next to me. He squints looking at the computer screen.

"It doesn't look like it's getting anywhere," He scratches his head.

Jake stops scanning and begins tapping a few keys.

"There, let's see what it finds now," The computer appears to be processing the data. Each symbol is flipped around in different directions. With no pattern, a few symbols get copied and placed into a bar down below the rest. Some symbols stay black while others have parts of their structure turn red, almost creating a symbol inside the original symbol.

Once all the symbols have been processed, the computer brings up a new tab showing the results.

"Well look at that," Jake says, excitedly.

"What did you get from it?" Jace walks around to see the computer.

Erin and Luke do the same. "

"These symbols here are from African languages. Not all are the same language though which makes this strange. According to the translation it made out, sun, four, death, shadows, and peace," Jake says just staring at the screen trying to comprehend the meaning of the words.

"What? This is crap. This has to be a hoax or something. What does that even mean?" Benson rants on. "Death and peace don't go well together,"

Jake looks at him. "Will you just relax? It is only five symbols out of 21. The rest could just take a deeper diagnostic before getting a clear message,"

Benson backs up. "Alright, but I think we should just focus on some more important tasks at hand,"

Jake stands up and looks at Benson. "Will you please go get Officer Cortez?" He says sternly.

"My pleasure, sir," Benson walks off into the trees.

Jake kneels down again in front of the computer.

"Oh," He says moving the mouse.

"What? What's oh?" I ask, not seeing what he sees.

"I didn't realize that it's still processing the symbols in the background. It has added two more,"

He refreshes the tab with explained symbols. "Help and people," Jake reads aloud. "I have no idea what this is," He stands up.

Officer Cortez comes through the trees.

"I heard you got a few symbols to translate," He hurries over to the computer.

"Yeah, nothing very good. It's not giving us a clear message yet," Jake says, standing up.

Cortez looks at the computer for a minute, crouches, and then starts tapping keys. "You could lift it up and see if there are more symbols on it,"

Jake looks at all of us and then back down at Cortez. "I could, but no one is sure what it is. I guess you could say we're afraid it's a bomb," Jake says plainly.

Cortez takes a minute to think. "Bryan, you are an explosives expert. Would you say this is an explosive device?"

Everyone looks at me. I begin examining it again.

"This would be a unique design for a missile due to the fact that it doesn't have any fins. If it was meant to be dropped from a plane and explode, it hasn't and this area is an unlikely place for it to happen, especially since no one has talked about bomb raids," I say while convincing myself more and more that we were safe to move it around.

"Good points, but what if someone just laid it here," Cortez questions.

"It being partially sunk into the ground means it's either been here awhile or it did fall. The hole in the trees convinces me it fell, but all other factors say it's not likely a bomb,"

Cortez stands up and looks at the black egg. He then looks at his watch.

"I can side with that. Let's keep this quiet and leave it here for now. We have things to do,"

Jake nods in agreement. "Yep. Let's get back to camp and get ready for a view of the city,"

We walk together back to camp.

Back at camp my squad and I eat and then begin packing weapons onto the quads. I can't get that object off my mind. It is so interesting. Everything about it. It's design. It's location.

"Bryan,"

Jake calls breaking my train of thought.

"Come on, the other platoon has arrived. We are going to discuss the plans of scoping out the city,"

I follow Jake to the center of camp.

The platoon carries one of their men onto a table.

"What happened to him?" I ask Jake and I nod towards the man.

Jake looks over at the men tending a bloody leg.

"Don't know,"

He then calls everyone to listen up.

"Alright soldiers, let's bring it together. Officer Thompson, we are glad you and your men could join us. It looks like you have a wounded soldier. I think we should start with you telling us what happened. Do we need to worry about a potential threat?" Jake asks sternly.

"No, there is no threat. It was a village not too far from here. They must have thought we were Rev's men. We were taking fire before we could even stop to talk to them. A few men were shot while on the quad, but only one sustained open wounds," Officer Thompson looks a bit disappointed in his report.

"We are glad the majority of you are okay," Jake says.

He then nods to Officer Cortez. Cortez steps forward from the large circle of soldiers.

"Now that we are all here, let's go over some rules. First, no one leaves camp alone or without permission from their own Officer. Second, report anything out of the ordinary, whether it's a soldier, an object, or whatever," Cortez turns slowly in the middle of the circle, while looking each soldier in the eye.

"Do I make myself clear?" He yells.

"Yes sir!" We all yell back.

Officer Cortez pulls a large monitor out of a Humvee and places it on top of the vehicle, high for everyone to see.

"This is a map of where we are. Today we are going to head three miles out to the edge of the city. Our objective today is to only scout out the most outer west area. At any point of spotting enemy soldiers, you are commanded to remain undetected and report the sighting,"

Cortez begins drawing on the monitor.

"This is the section we will secure today. Tomorrow we will continue deeper into the city. Remember our objective is to stop Rev's operations. One of their biggest threats is brainwashing people or paying them off to be soldiers for the reign of an "alien". We hope to release as many prisoners and even those soldiers that are scared of defying Rev. Unfortunately, we will not convince everyone and souls will perish. But remember, we are Helping Everyone Restore Order. Together we are Heroes," Cortez says with emotion.

Many of the soldiers nod and some vocally agree.

"Gear up. We're out of camp in twenty minutes," He says while grabbing his rifle.

10

G o Stealth

AFTER LOADING up a few cases of ammunition and water onto the quads, my squad takes a moment to eat.

"Back to MRE's and energy bars I see," Jace says disappointedly.

We just eat energy bars to hold us over for a few hours.

"Jake, do you think it's likely we'll be seeing any Rev soldiers today?" Erin asks before taking a bite of her bar.

"It is possible. You have to consider how big the city is and know how many soldiers there are. Personally, I can't imagine we will see any soldiers on the outskirts where we will be," Jake says, eyeing a second bar.

"That's a good question. How many people could have joined such an organization?" Luke asks, throwing away his wrapper.

"That is unknown," Jake grabs another bar and stands up. "Get your helmets on. It's time to go,"

Jace and Erin get onto one tiger quad facing forward and Jake gets on facing the rear. Luke and I jump on the other carrying ammunition and supplies. We meet up with the other platoons who are also on quads.

"Can you guys hear me?" Jake says through the radio system.

We each sound off that we can.

"Great, we'll follow the others a little way down the road into another area of trees. That's where we will ditch the quads and move in on foot," Jake informs.

Our squad takes up the rear on the dirt road. As we cruise at 30 mph I see something furry on the ground. And then another.

"Jake, do you see that?" I ask.

Jake looks over at the side of the road.

"It looks like chimpanzees. They're dead," he replies.

"I wonder who did this. I don't think locals would," I say.

"Well if it's Rev they will be answering to this," Jace chimes in.

TEN MINUTES GO by when the whole troop veers right down off the road into the thick tree line.

"Jake," Another commanding officer comes on over the radio.

"Make sure you guys hide our tracks. Over," It's Officer Benson.

"Sir, we'll do our best," Jake says.

"Well Bryan, Luke, try to hide the tracks from the road to the trees. Be quick about it though and hopefully that will be enough," He relays to us.

Luke and I park our quad in the trees and get off.

"The soil is too moist to just brush it with a branch," Luke says.

I look at it. "Well, what do we do?"

"Let's lay down a dead tree right across the tracks and throw some branches on it," He says.

I think for a moment. "That would hide our tracks but in case we need to exit in a hurry our passage would be blocked," I say.

Luke pauses. "Let's see if laying the log down and rolling it would be enough weight to remove the tire tracks," I say.

"Alright," Luke agrees. "Now to find a log," He says.

We begin looking around. It doesn't take very long before we find one covered in some moss. Together we pick up a section of the corroding tree and carry it up to the road.

"Okay, that was heavier than I thought," I say.

"Yeah, a little. So, we should roll it down slowly so we don't have to do this again," Luke says.

"Let's try it,"

We both get below the log and let it roll somewhat slowly down to the tree line. We stand up and examine our work.

"It looks good to me," Luke says.

I nod. "Let's move this log back into the trees and throw brush in this gaping hole leading into the trees,"

We hear some static over the radio.

"Are you two about done?" Jace asks.

"Yeah, we just got done putting up a sign pointing to our location," Luke says.

I smile.

"Really funny. Just hurry up," Jake says unamused.

After covering our entry point we jump on the quad and follow the beaten path to the others.

"Alright let's move out," Officer Cortez says as we jump off the quad.

I take a canteen of water and follow my squad into the thick jungle.

The sky holds wisps of faded orange clouds above the horizon. The sun is lowering and letting its rays play in the sky. Every step I take is upon some plant. The jungle doesn't allow for silent movement even for experienced soldiers. A group of monkey's chatter in the distance and insects hum here and there as we tread over the jungle floor. There is almost a serenity from all the sounds of life.

"We are 100 yards from the nearest buildings," Officer Cortez says pulling me back to reality.

"Start spreading out. Remember we are not to be seen,"

Each soldier puts 10 feet between them and the soldier to their right and left, making a long line in width. We continue to carefully step through the jungle until we reach the edge where the trees and bushes become less and less.

"Hold your position," Officer Cortez says, raising his hand. "Look for anyone, civilians or soldiers,"

Five minutes go by and not a soul is to be seen. The real city looks to be a couple more miles away. Skyscrapers shadow this outskirt village.

"Everyone but Dobson and Calder get down and crawl to those homes. Once there make sure they are empty," Cortez says.

We follow the commands strictly and head to the village. The ground is cool to the touch, but not quite muddy. We crawl through the last bit of jungle into patches of large grass. We close in on the homes where the grass is no longer tall or even there. Most of the small homes are made with mud, straw, and scrap items like metal, and plastic. A few are made with bricks and mortar, with tin roofs.

We get on our knees and nod to each other that at this point it's clear to go forward. Luke takes the lead and we, Erin, Jace, and myself follow behind him, against a wall of a brick home. He stops at the doorway where a sheet dangles, slightly swaying back and forth. I step around Luke to be directly in front of the doorway. He reaches across the sheet and I give him the signal.

The sheet is quickly drawn back.

I search quickly, but there's nobody. I step in to look for any helpful clues.

"Nothing, nobody," I whisper, lowering my rifle.

Luke comes in. "Let's keep searching the houses nearby," He says.

We searched twenty more houses and found no one or much of anything interesting in them.

"Well, this town is cleared out," Officer Cortez says after we report back to him.

"It's getting dark, we should head back to camp," says Officer Benson, but he turns and looks at a home down the road.

"I want to have some of you stay here overnight. Groups of two stay in two different houses. Keep at least one soldier watching at all times. I want to know if there is any activity this far out of the city," Officer Cortez orders.

"I will stay," Jake says.

"No, Jake I need you at camp so we can get a solid plan ready," He says.

"I will stay," I say.

"I'll stay too," Says Jace.

"Great, thanks for making it easy," Officer Cortez says.

"Okay, two more down the road. Who's up for it?"

It takes a second, but two more soldiers volunteer.

"Let me give you some advice. Any troops that are out here in the middle of the night will have more men than you and more power. Don't engage unless they do. I just want you to lay low and observe. It's pretty easy, don't mess up soldiers. Everyone else, let's move out,"

Jake hands Jace and I a pouch.

"If you get hungry, don't eat each other," He just smiles.

I look at Jace. "You wouldn't be that tasty,"

He gives me a light shove.

"See ya guy's tomorrow," Jace says, waving to Luke, Erin and Jake walking back up to the jungle.

"Alright, I have a deck of cards, do you want to play?" Jace asks.

WE HUNKERED down in the nicest house we could find. It has brick and mortar walls and a tin roof. The interior is mostly bare with a bucket in a corner and a cloth hanging on the wall. The cloth has some neat patterns using green, yellow, and black.

The next hour we play some card games as the sky darkens overhead. We begin seeing the little details of the home, cracks in the walls and vines creeping through some of them. Nocturnal animals and bugs begin taking the stage. Sounds of frogs and birds heading back to their nest fill the silence of the ghost town.

I GIVE up on the card games after losing almost every game. We open the food rations and eat all of it. It reminds me of my previous years of being in the military. I try not to think much of those years. They were tough. The challenges of a soldier are difficult and can be mind altering.

It's almost eight o'clock now and I'm starting to feel the weight of the day come over me.

"Jace, do you want to sleep first?" I ask.

"Pff, I have been on watch duty enough times to know what that means," he says, alluding there is something unfair about it.

"I'll take the first watch. Three hour shifts whether you got sleep or not," He says plainly.

I laugh. "It seems like you have been on too many stake outs,"

He smirks. "You could say that. I actually enjoy it though. There is something about taking time away from everyone else and enjoying the quiet," He says as he stands up to peer out the window.

"I can understand that," I say while laying on my back.

"Well, wake me if you need me, but if not see ya in three hours,"

He just raises his rifle a little as he continues to look outside. My eyes fall heavy and my conscious mind only slightly considers my family and tomorrow before succumbing to sleep.

I wake up, startled.

"What!?" I say quietly.

"Wo, calm down," Jace says.

I rub my eyes and my face, unexpectedly rubbing dirt over them.

"Wow, I hope I sleep that good," Jace says sitting up against the wall.

"It's been three hours?" I say in disbelief. "Did anything happen?"

"No, just some animals roaming around. I think I saw a big cat, so if you need to use a bush do it now while I'm awake," Jace lies down with his rifle over his chest.

"I can wait," I stand up to look out the window. "Sweet dreams,"

· · ·

THE NIGHT IS NOISY. A lot of creatures making small noises creating a strange symphony. I look out the window to find the moon slightly covered by the clouds. The houses around are lifeless. The curtains in the windows dance gently as the wind finds its way through the poorly constructed houses.

After some time, I sit back down against a wall and think about my family. I hope they can get into a new enjoyable routine. My poor wife has to figure out new schedules and make new friends. It won't-

I hear a snap behind the house and whip around aiming my gun at the window.

I move slowly to the window. I check left, then right but nothing is there. I step back and relax. Just as I turn and step again, I feel something thick and round under my boot.

I jump and turn around to see what it is.

A large python is slithering into the house and heading for Jace. I try to use my rifle's barrel to move it from getting on him but the snake's muscles and flexibility ignore my protest. The body is about six inches in diameter.

I debate shooting it, but I consider the enemy and whether they will hear it.

I try harder to use my gun to deter the snake. It's now on Jace, with the rest of its body still sliding through the doorway. I put my gun down and start pulling the mid-section of the snake away from Jace. The snake starts wrapping its body around my foot. I decide I can't successfully get this snake out without Jace's help.

"Jace," I try waking him up.

He doesn't move a muscle.

"Jace, get up," I say more sternly.

He rolls over and I see his eyes slightly open.

"Jace, there is a huge snake on you,"

He jerks and lifts his head up.

"What? What is going on?" He says sitting up.

"There's a python on you. I am trying to get it out of here," I say, still trying to pull the mid-section of the snake backwards.

Jace finally realizes the snake is on him. He quickly moves away from the snake.

"Help me take it outside,"

Jace helps me grab the snake's body and drag it out onto the street

"I don't know what exactly its goal was, but I'm glad we aren't sharing the house with it. Sorry to wake you up," I say as we drop the snake a few feet from the house.

"I guess it's better than being squeezed to death," he says.

We walk back into the hut and Jace checks for any other snakes, while I watch the python outside. It slithers slowly into the road I guess heading for another house.

"Do you hear that?" Jace asks.

I stop to listen.

"Like a hum?" I ask back.

"Yeah. It sounds like a vehicle in the distance,"

I listen again.

"You think so?"

Jace gets up to look out the window.

"Yeah I am pretty sure. Do we have any way of contacting the other soldiers?" He asks.

"I'm not sure what their channel number is,"

Jace goes outside only to run back in.

"There's a Humvee coming," He exclaims.

Beams of light flood the dark and abandoned road.

The vehicle gets closer and closer moving at an easy pace. Before it gets close enough we move out of sight. Just listening we can tell it's right in front of the house. Without warning the truck stops.

Both of our eyes go wide.

"Why'd they stop?" I whisper.

Jace shrugs and mouths he doesn't know.

We listen. Voices chatter and I think I hear a laugh.

I crawl to the door and let one eye move past the door frame. First thing I notice is that it is a huge Humvee. It looks armored beyond need. Second, there are soldiers gathered around something a few feet in front of the Humvee. I see one of them pick it up while the others move out of the way. It's the snake's tail. I move back to the window.

"They stopped to move the snake out of the road," I tell Jace.

He nods "They shouldn't be long then," He says.

Then I think. "What if they see our footprints?" In my mind I start freaking out.

The vehicle revs its engine.

"I think they are leaving," Jace says.

The voices stop or are drowned out by the truck. Jace looks out the window. I watch his reaction to the size of the Humvee. The truck begins to crawl away, so I get up and watch it leave down the road. The Humvee has two machine guns mounted on the side facing us. The top of the truck must be 10 feet tall.

"Did you see that truck?" Jace asks.

"If they have more of those and who knows what else, we will be out matched,"

"Well, it's all about strategy, right?" I try to be optimistic.

"Why don't you take your break now," I say.

"Great now that I'm wide awake," Jace lays down.

The next hour, I just imagine how the next few days will go. The strategy we will have to have, to take out a large army, will nearly be suicide. I bet it's ten times the size of our company. I bet they have jets or helicopters, while we only have Humvees and quads. I start to lose hope, but then I shake my head and concentrate on winning this war.

It's almost three o'clock and I start to feel the lack of sleep. So, I play with my watch to see what it can do out in the middle of Africa. I wonder if I can send a message to my family, but then I worry that my signal will be located by Rev. I decide to leave my watch alone in case something I press sends any kind of signal to a tower nearby, being monitored.

ANOTHER HOUR of boredom and fighting the negative thoughts. This is why people have to sleep and they sleep during the night. Your mind gets tired and despair is left to tempt your thoughts. Sometimes, I wish I could just stop thinking. I try, but like always, I seem to be thinking of one thing or another. I just keep thinking, maybe the sun will rise soon and we can get this day going, but I know there is still a few hours till that happens.

During a session of sleepy head bobbing, my watch blinks and buzzes. I shake my head and blink a few times to focus my eyes. A message came through from Jake.

"We will be there at six o'clock. We will bring you guys food. The day's plan is to keep checking the houses on the outskirts and set up camp somewhere within," The text reads.

I think to myself the possibility of getting an hour's worth of sleep before they come. That would be nice. There is only less than an hour left before Jace's three are up. So, I wait eagerly, which makes the time go slow.

To distract myself, I start looking at every part of my gun. I admire the design and the decades of building a powerful tool.

Finally, it's 4:30 and I decide to wake up Jace.

"Jace, it's time to get up," I shake his shoulder a little.

He turns his head towards me and then lets it fall back into place. I decide to let him have a few minutes to gather his mind together. As predicted, a few minutes go by and he finally sits up.

"What time is it?" He asks.

"It's 4:38 to be exact," He gets up and stretches.

"Any more activity out there?"

"No, it's been quiet for a while now,"

"Too quiet?" Jace asks. I give him an unsure face.

"Maybe," I get up too, and stretch.

"Oh, Jake texted me letting me know that they will be here at six o'clock. He said they are going to be moving camp here today,"

"Alright, sounds like a plan. Oh, yeah, he texted me too," Jace says, and yawns.

"And they are bringing breakfast," I remember.

"Good, cause I am starving," He says standing up.

"So, did you tell them that Rev does patrol at the night?" He asks.

I start to think about it and then realize I should have mentioned that.

"Well, I haven't, but I will message him right now," I say tapping my watch and bringing up my messages.

I pass on sleeping and we just wait for Jake and the rest of the company to arrive.

THE SUN RISES and a new day begins. Birds chirp and the dew sets on the grass. I'm feeling tired. My eyelids begin to fall and my mind tries to fight the idea of sleep. Then my watch vibrates.

I jump up.

"It looks like the company is here," I say as I go outside.

Jace follows me out. We walk to the last section of huts before the grass and tree line. We see the other two guy's half a mile down. I wave my rifle in the air towards the trees to signify they can come down. Without warning we hear a roar of engines and the Humvees and quads break out of the jungle. We stand there as they drive up.

A Humvee comes straight towards us and brakes, ripping up grass as it comes to a stop. Jake and Officer Cortez step out of the Humvee.

"So, what exactly did you see last night?" Cortez asks.

"A few patrolmen. They were driving a large Humvee decked out with thick armor and multiple machine guns mounted onto it," Jace says.

"They had stopped right in front of our post, so we got a good look at them. The men didn't seem as suited up as one would think, coming out of that machine," I add.

Jake looks at Cortez.

"Any reason why they stopped where they did?" Jake asks.

Now, Jace and I are looking at each other to see who wanted to explain the strange experience. I assume I should since I was awake for most of it.

"There was a python snake that snuck into the house we were in and started to get on Jace while he was sleeping. I eventually woke him up and we dragged the python to the road. A few minutes later the soldiers came by and stopped and got out to investigate or observe the meandering snake,"

Jake and Cortez just look at us like we ate some bad berries.

"Okay, well then," Jake says.

Cortez steps past us and between two houses to the street.

"There aren't many houses that will give us protection. We will have to search out the best buildings and then pray they will be enough,"

He walks back to his Humvee and gives the company orders to move into the town three blocks in.

Jace, Jake and myself get into Cortez's Humvee. I quickly receive memories of past years in the military. The smell and the design of the inside are the same. My mind comes back to reality when we come to a stop.

"Alright, grab some gear and put it inside those two houses for now," Cortez points to the nicer homes on the block.

I grab a silver suitcase and a duffle bag to start with. After making a few trips and clearing out the Humvee, Jace and I start searching for some sturdy houses in the surrounding area.

Each house is approached as though someone is in it. After confirming that no one is them, we inspect its make up and whether it can hold up against machine guns.

After checking over 100 buildings we find about 8 with potential and a few that have at least two walls sturdy enough to hold up for a short period of time. We take notes and map out the locations. A few other soldiers come back with other houses fit enough for cover so Jace and I go check them out. Walking through 20 or so homes we find that 3 have appropriate protection. We report back to Cortez to finalize the decision.

"Sounds good. We won't be sitting around here long anyways. We have to give the people back their city within two weeks. Every day we need to be moving a couple miles," Cortez says when we return to report our findings. "Multiple cities around the world are facing a similar attack from Rev. We need to be quick about this so we can move on to the next city,"

It makes sense that Rev is trying to take over more cities. I wonder where they are and if the same alien figure is the tool.

"Hey, where are Luke and Erin?" Jace asks.

"They're setting up a lookout at the jungle's edge," Jake says as he comes walking into the house.

"It's amazing there weren't any casualties when Rev cleared this town. No bodies or blood was left behind," Jake lays his rifle against a crate.

"Yeah, that is strange. Perhaps a strategy was carefully crafted to persuade everyone to leave. That would also make it easier for Rev to entice them to become part of an army," Cortez stares back at Jace and me.

"You said the soldiers that got out of the Humvee didn't quite look... like soldiers," He stops.

"Do you think those soldiers you saw last night were possibly locals? Locals given guns and vests," Jake finishes Cortez's thoughts.

"We could be up against hordes of brain washed civilians before even getting to Rev's troops," Cortez opens a map on his tablet.

I look at Jake and Jace. We could be in for more than we thought. Even if these are just quickly made soldiers, the armor on the Humvee would give them time to just hide and shoot. I can only imagine they have more Humvees like that, with relatively unlimited soldiers.

"We need Falcons in the sky," Jake says.

"It's likely they will have some jets or helicopters too. We wouldn't last long," Cortez says, still looking down at his tablet.

"I know we have the firepower to take down any aircraft. If we need some Falcons, we will call them in, but to start out like that was never the plan. We need to figure out where Rev is and how they are containing the civilians," He says.

A static signal comes through the radio channel I'm on. Then, Erin's voice comes in clear.

"Officer Cortez, we have two vehicles coming your way from the southeast. They're about ten minutes from your location. Over," We all look at each other.

"And so, it begins," Cortez says, briskly walking outside.

11

D issolving Corrosion

Cortez is yelling orders at everyone. Jace and I grab a few crates left against a house and bring them inside.

"Erin, can you tell if they're coming directly toward us or are they doing random patrolling? Over," Cortez asks over the radio.

A moment later Erin gets on.

"Let's be honest, they're probably coming for us. They aren't moving fast necessarily, but they have been on the same street the whole time and it's not the main road,"

I grab the last crate and move it while Cortez says something over the radio I couldn't hear.

"We should get a Humvee set up with the turret," Jace says.

I agree and we both jump on the Humvee to set up the turret.

Everyone finishes their tasks and takes positions behind walls.

"Everyone should have their headsets on," Cortez yells out to the entire company.

He presses a button on his ear piece.

"Alright everyone, we have approximately 5 minutes until the enemy is on us. Wait for my queue to engage. Jace, Jake and Bryan take the Humvee and drive around the block. I will have you come up from behind the vehicles if things head south," He says.

"What do you mean?" Jace asks before getting cut off.

"I am going to try and talk to the soldiers. If they are locals, maybe I can convince them to not fight,"

I jump off the Humvee to talk some sense into Cortez.

"Hey, how do you expect to approach these soldiers?"

He looks at me like I'm out of place.

"Bryan, get back in the Humvee. I don't have time for chit chat. We have to give them a chance before we begin attacking locals," He says.

"But we don't even know if they are locals. That is just an idea. You can't just assume," I say trying to be realistic.

He walks into a house and opens a crate. Inside lies a large vest. It must weigh 40 pounds considering how Cortez handles it.

"Get back up there and get to the next street. You should be able to get a video signal of what Erin sees. That way you can stay out of sight until we need you," He puts the vest on and grabs his helmet and rifle.

I back up in disbelief. He is crazy.

Once on the Humvee I take position on the turret. Jake drives us down the road to park on the corner northeast of where we camped.

"Jake, what is he thinking?" Jace asks.

"We just don't want to be an enemy to locals. We are outnumbered and if we can get a few more allies and take soldiers away from Rev, then we will. It's a necessary risk," He says.

"Erin, are you there?" Jake asks over our channel.

"Yes, sir," Erin replies.

"I need you to send your video feed to Humvee 2390 ASAP," Jake requests.

"I'm on it. I'll also send the camp surveillance feed since I don't have the height to see between all the buildings,"

Then I hear Cortez.

"They're right here. Coming around the corner,"

"Erin, we got your feed," Says Jake.

"We are ready to be there in a moment's notice," Jake tells Cortez

"Thanks. Jace, Bryan you guys were right, these Humvees are intense," Cortez says and then pauses. "Alright, they are stopping. That's the first good sign,"

I pull myself down into the Humvee to watch the live feed. Soldiers spill out of the monstrous Humvee. They have their rifles pointed at Cortez with himself raising his rifle in submission. They take his rifle away. Through Cortez's mic we can hear commands being yelled at him. He gets on his knees while saying over and over he wants to talk. "Who else is here?" We hear them ask.

"I have come to save you. I have come to save your people!" Cortez yells.

The soldiers look at the person apparently in charge just getting out of the Humvee. It's hard to make out what their officer in charge says but he walks up to Cortez.

"We know about the group that invaded your cities. We want to help you escape," We hear Cortez say.

The leader says something back.

"We are American," Cortez says.

The leader steps back to talk to his men. After a minute, he walks back to Cortez and hits him over the head with the butt of his rifle.

"Ah shoot!" Exclaims Jake.

"I can take a shot at him," Erin says.

"Not yet," Replies Jake.

The leader signals the Humvees to come forward.

"We have to move in there," Jace says.

Jake doesn't say anything. It looks like the soldiers are searching the street.

Jake looks back at me, "Get up there!" Then he starts the vehicle and punches the gas going south on the street east of camp.

"Everyone, engage the enemy and secure Officer Cortez. I repeat, do not let them take Officer Cortez,"

I'm up on the turret now with my heart pounding. I look over to see frames of movement in between houses as we floor it down one street over. The sound of gunfire echoes throughout the streets. We come up to the end of the street where we take a hard right turn. Dirt spits out from underneath the tires.

"Bryan, watch our men, focus on the turrets," Jake orders.

As we make the last turn I think of only targeting turrets. Without warning we slow down. Something happened. I start to make out what Jake is saying.

"Hold your fire!"

"What?" I say, completely confused.

"Jake, come here," I hear one of our soldiers say.

Jake stops the Humvee behind the enemies two black beefed up Humvees. No guns are going off and everyone is still. I can't see what is going on. Jake jumps out with his rifle in hand and helmet on. As he walks around the two other vehicles being secured by our company he lowers his weapon.

"The men have surrendered," Jake tells us.

"We need medics now. Get Officer Cortez out of here," He orders others.

I get down from the Humvee to get a better idea of what's going on.

Jake is talking to one of the enemy soldiers.

"Are you a local?" Jake asks.

The man looks upset, frightened and confused.

"Yes,"

"How did you get these vehicles and guns?"

The man starts to point to the city.

"Men have invaded our city and taken us captive," He lifts his pant leg revealing a metal band around his ankle.

"They track us and they say if we run off, this band will inject poison,"

His facial expression is now hopeful we can help. Jake looks around at each of the local soldiers.

"What was the reason for coming out here? Do they know we are here?"

"We were sent out for basic patrol until we got orders that redirected us to this location. When we saw your Officer we called it in. They will be coming soon,"

The soldier steps back and looks around.

"They are stronger than us. Possibly you too," He says starting to hyperventilate.

"Calm down. We can work together. We can stop them," Jake says quickly trying to comfort the terrified soldier.

"We could try cutting the bands off," One of our men says.

"That's true," Jake replies.

The fearful soldier shakes his head.

"They are too strong,"

Jake ignores him and orders an electric saw.

"We can try to get it off," Jake says looking at the man.

Medics tend to the wounded soldiers, including the local Rev officer.

Jace helps the wounded get inside a house. It's not long before we get a saw set up. As they do that, Jake takes Jace and I to the side.

"So, it seems like they're locals. Do we cut their bands and let them go or have them fight with us?" Jake asks.

Before we can answer Erin comes on the headset.

"Jake, are you there?"

"What is it Erin?"

"We have more vehicles coming your way. They are moving fast,"

Jake turns around and looks at the men in line to get their bands cut off.

"We don't have time for this," He runs over to them.

Jace and I follow behind.

"Alright stop, we don't have time to cut these off. Rev is on their way. I'm sure this time they're not sending locals,"

He says sternly.

"Everyone, get up and grab your guns,"

"Jake, this is Officer Benson. I suggest you get in your vehicles and fight this out. You won't have a chance on foot. Not to mention they have some drones coming your way as well,"

Jake looks around and then spots one of our soldiers. "What is the vehicle count, Jenks?"

Jenks thinks quickly.

"Uh...five, no six. That's not including those Humvees," He points to the monstrous vehicles.

"Well, break it down for me, what vehicles do we have including those two?" Jake asks.

"We have three quads and five Humvees. The rest of the vehicles are with Officer Benson. We won't have enough space to fit everyone in a vehicle," He says while counting in his head.

Jake walks into the house with the wounded. I start talking to Erin.

"How much time do we have?"

Her voice is barely heard through static.

"Erin, can you hear me? Luke? Officer Benson, are you there?" I turn to Jace. "Hey I can't get a good signal with Erin, Luke, or Officer Benson. Will you try? Ask them how much time we have before Rev is on top of us," I say quickly.

Jace tries a few times but he can't reach them either. As Jake comes out of the house, I run over to him.

"Jake, I can't get a hold of Erin, Luke or Officer Benson."

Jake looks concerned and tries himself. He has no luck.

"Crap, we are getting pinched. Nothing is going our way," He grabs a soldier by the arm. "Get up to Officer Benson and see what is going on with their radios. We can't hear them," Jake commands.

"And ask them how much time we have," I include.

The soldier runs off.

Jake walks over to the enemy's Humvees we just acquired, and checks them out. A massive metal box containing a turret on each side and one on top. The interior holds 4-6 soldiers. The ceiling has a seal on it but it's not the American seal.

"Well, I guess this will have to do," Jake says, jokingly. Considering it's more than our Humvees have we couldn't ask for more under the circumstances.

He stands up on the Humvee.

"Listen up soldiers. I need eight of you to stay here and stay down unless I say otherwise. Your job will be to keep the wounded alive. Obviously, we need some to be medics, so let's say our four medics and four others. The rest of you get in a vehicle. Only two per quad. Six in each of these Humvees and four in each of our own,"

"What about us?"

The local soldiers step forward, "We will fight them with you."

Jake looks at Jace and me.

"What do you think?"

"We don't have enough room for everyone. Give them their guns and have them stay here," I reply.

Jake nods.

"There isn't enough room for everyone to be in a vehicle. We will give you your guns back and you can stay here," Jake says and orders the weapons to be given back to them.

A moment later Erin, Luke and the messenger we sent comes sprinting into the street.

"Jake, they are coming!" Erin yells.

"We have five minutes," Luke exclaims.

"Alright everyone, move, move, move! The objective is to eliminate any other vehicles, no questions asked," He quickly looks at the other soldiers as if thinking "sorry if they're your own,"

"Jake, how are our guys going to know that these two vehicles are friendly?" I ask.

"I guess...uh... we'll put duct tape on these doors," He quickly thinks up.

Jake lets everyone know through the headset. With a few soldiers replying back, we agree the headsets are working down in camp.

Gray duct tape is quickly applied to the doors and to the hood of the enemy's Humvees.

"Alright, it looks good," Jake says. "Let's go!"

We take one of the enemies' monster Humvees. I take the gunner seat up top, while Erin, Luke, Jace, and Jake ride inside.

"Luke, be my navigator," Jake says as they climb in.

"Jace and I will grab a gun on each side," Says Erin.

We are the first to pull away from the camp.

"Everyone, split up. Remember not to shoot the Humvees with duct tape X's on the hood and doors,"

A few seconds later, I see the front of a Humvee like ours, without duct tape, inch forward from behind a building.

"I've got a visual of the enemy up ahead, on the right," I yell.

I point my gun at the corner of the building, where just behind it should be the driver. I pull the trigger and the building corner breaks apart creating a dirt cloud. The enemy bolts forward into an alleyway.

We narrowly missed colliding with the driver side as it continued past us. Strangely enough there was no one in the gunner seat of the Humvee. As we pull onto a parallel road to the enemy Humvee, I begin to understand the situation. We have been tricked into to following a decoy, because now we have a fully manned Humvee behind us.

"Jake, that was a decoy. Make a right," I yell as I turn around to the rear to exchange fire with the opposing gunner.

Our vehicle takes multiple rounds before we make a hard right turn.

"We have contacts on the north side of town, two Humvees," Luke says to our company.

"Copy that, we'll be over in a second," One soldier says.

"We've got contact in the east," Says another.

"They probably have a tracking system for all their vehicles to coordinate with each other," Erin says.

Rev turns the corner we just turned and we exchange fire again.

"Make a left here," Jace says.

Jake does and then all of a sudden Jace jumps out of the Humvee. He rolls a few times before getting to his feet. He slips in between two houses.

"Jace! What are you doing?" Jake yells.

"I'm better on foot,"

I just stare down the road waiting for Rev, but they don't come.

"I found the tracking signal and I'm deactivating it now," Luke says.

We make it to a large intersection with no sign of Rev.

"Does anyone have a visual?" I ask my squad.

"Nothing," Jake says.

Then, I hear someone breathing in their mic.

"Hey, Jace here. The Humvee following us stopped on the street west of you about half way down. They are just sitting there. The gunner is alert and keeps checking every direction,"

"Jace, get a few shots on the gunner and make it count," says Jake as he begins turning left towards the stopped Humvee. I check each direction for sneaking vehicles or foot soldiers like Jace. Not a minute later, I hear rifle rounds go off. Then machine guns. Our Humvee jets forward and takes a hard left onto the street. The enemy is engaging Jace.

I tightly clutch the trigger.

My bullets rip through the backside of the turret opporator's vest.

He falls limp in place.

We drive on the right of the enemy Humvee, allowing Erin to gun the driver side directly. But this was only a mirrored action by Rev, which causes Jake to swerve into two houses. My body slams into the turret shield as we slow down abruptly.

Our Humvee stops on top of the rubble.

Palm leaves and sticks are in my face, so I spin around to face the enemy.

Dust rising from the debris we caused makes it even more difficult to see.

"Jake! Get us out of here!" I yell when I realize that we are sitting ducks.

Through the hazy dust screen, I see Rev angle the driver side gun for a perfect shot at me. I duck behind my small barrier and pray I don't get torn apart. The bullets begin thrashing my gun and shield. I debate lobbing a grenade but fear my hand will be cut to shreds. I think I hear our tires spinning, then gripping slightly on the rubble. We make little progress backwards. Then a grenade goes off and the bullets stop hitting my barrier. A second grenade goes off ripping metal off Rev's Humvee.

We finally reverse off the pummeled houses and onto the road. I see Jace concentrated and delivering all his rounds into the passenger side of Rev's Humvee. I turn to my machine gun to find it completely pulverized. Realizing I am of no use up above, I try to open the hatch to get inside the Humvee. However, it doesn't budge.

"Erin, I can't get the hatch to open,"

"Erin is down," Luke says. "Hold on, I'll get it,"

I keep an eye on the enemy not knowing their condition. A moment later, Luke opens the hatch and I slip down into the cab.

"Thanks. What happened to Erin?"

Luke begins assessing her.

"Some shrapnel to the face,"

"Bryan, get out there and help Jace," Jake says, turning only his head towards me.

I can see through the rearview mirror, he too got shrapnel in the face. I grab a rifle and head to the back door where I slowly open it and peek out. Once I see the coast is clear, I jump out and take cover behind the remaining walls of the first house we hit.

"Jace, how many soldiers did you leave me?"

"Hold on," He replies.

I approach the Humvee with my rifle ready. Jace opens a door on the opposite side. I hear one gun shot.

"None," Jace says.

We meet each other at the back of the defeated Humvee.

"Thanks for getting that gunner off of me. I was almost torn to pieces," I say, pointing to the gunner seat of our Humvee. The top is heavily beaten by the 50 cal rounds.

"I know how much you hate the attention," He nods.

We jog back to our Humvee and swing open the doors. Jake is in a cold sweat with glass lodged in his face. Blood drips from each wound.

"Crap, you don't look so hot," Jace says.

"I think they'll be okay but I need to get them to the camp now," Luke says, as he starts moving Jake to the passenger seat.

"You two should probably stay out here, it sounds like we still have a few of Rev's men challenging the other soldiers,"

We nod and close the doors.

Luke speeds off.

"Well, should we take this Humvee?" Jace points to the one behind us.

I look at it and then back at him.

"Nah, we need duct tape to signal to the others it's us. Not only that, but it's all torn up. And I thought you liked to be on foot?"

Jace smiles at me and we head down the street at a good pace, making sure to stay alongside the houses.

We keep listening for our soldiers and their positions. A few streets down we find an abandoned quad and Rev group exchanging fire with one of our Humvees. Luckily, we happened to be on the back side of Rev. I give Jace one of my two grenades and he sprints to the other side of the street. He lobs the grenade just under the driver's side of the Humvee. I unload on the top gunner just before someone mans the side gun and fires back. I take cover behind a wall just in time to see Jace aim upwards above me 30 feet and shoot. I look at his target to find some kind of drone falling diagonally onto a roof.

"I think that was an armed quadcopter drone," He says over the mic.

"Jeez, Thanks again," I reply.

I hear a Humvee driving down the street. Jace and I both look and see one of our Humbles ramming one of Rev's. Shots are fired into the Humvee and they declare it neutralized.

Jace and I move on down the street to quickly make sure the soldiers aren't in need of anything. They thank us and give us some ammo and a grenade. We head off to find more of Rev's troops.

We hear some distressed soldiers are pinned down further east. We pick up our speed and find ourselves in an abandoned market. The street is full of buildings that have open fronts. Rev is down the road with two Humvees against two of ours. It looks like our firepower couldn't hold up and we only have a few trying to stay alive. Jace and I are looking around figuring out how to make a difference against two heavily equipped Humvees.

"The roof," I say swinging my rifle around to my back.

"Higher ground just might do it," He says.

We gather some crates together and quickly pull ourselves up.

"We are here on the roof tops. It's just the two of us so, we will have to get creative," I try to assure the pinned soldiers.

We make our way down to where the action is.

"It's about time. Half of us are gone," a soldier says.

Rev's two Humvees have the gunners shooting sporadically with a few of their men creeping up on ours.

"Let's jump on the Humvees and take out the gunners and then use them to take out the ones on the ground," Jace says, moving his hand around for illustration.

"Alright, who has the furthest guy because it will be trickier not to get noticed by him before it's too late,"

The two Humvees are angled right next to each other making it possible to jump onto one and then to the next, but not onto both at the same time.

Jace seems to be thinking.

"Dang, we don't have time to think," He says looking at Rev's men getting closer to ours.

"We'll just take out the gunners from here," We both start aiming.

"I've got long," I tell him, as I aim at the turret furthest away.

"I've got short. One, two, three,"

We begin firing.

I don't miss a shot and my guy rolls off the roof onto the ground while trying to swing around to aim at me. Jace's man cowards before he dies as well. We back up a little hoping to not be spotted by the men on the ground. The two Humvees start pulling away.

Gunshots start going off below, Rev's foot soldiers exchange fire with our company.

We run on top of the buildings to get closer to where our guys are at. The enemy has no coverage from us up here, so we pick them off easily.

The two Humvees drive off. We wave down to our men and make our way off the rooftops.

"What's your damage?" Jace asks them.

"Four of our guys are dead and we have one wounded," A soldier says.

"Sorry we couldn't get here sooner. We got wrecked on our first encounter, leaving us on foot," Says Jace.

"Yeah, it looks like we are in the same boat," The soldier looks back at their Humvee.

"Maybe one of them works," Jace says. "Go ahead, take your wounded back to base. We'll continue on foot,"

We begin turning away when they give us one of their men.

"The name is Greg," The soldier introduces himself.

He seems fairly young and spry.

"Greg, you'll need to listen very closely to us and do exactly what we say. We may sound crazy, but it won't be as crazy as dying," Jace says as we continue to walk up the street.

"So, what you're saying is, that if I don't do exactly what you say I'll die?" Greg reiterates it.

"Yup," I confirm.

THE THREE OF us lurk between some buildings making our way back to base. We don't hear anymore calls for help and the streets are quiet. It appears this battle is over.

"This is Officer Benson. I finally got my radio working. It looks like Rev isn't on our streets anymore. We have a break for now. If you have any wounded, bring them to base quickly. It's impossible to know how long we'll have until reinforcements come,"

"Great, I'm glad the man with the eyes on us finally can help," says Jace.

"Well, I guess we know we don't have to lurk anymore," Greg says.

Jace and I look at him as we are still in lurking mode.

So, we walk more relaxed, but only alongside the buildings, just in case.

· · ·

WHEN WE GET TO CAMP, it appears we have lost a lot of men and vehicles. Greg splits off to his platoon.

"Let's find Jake and Erin," I nudge Jace.

He agrees and we begin checking houses for them.

I decide Luke might have his helmet still on and try him on the radio.

"Luke, how's Jake and Erin?" I say still popping my head into different doors looking for them.

"They're okay. A few stitches, that's all. We are down where Officer Cortez is," replies Luke.

"Alright, we will be there in a minute,"

When I walk into the house, I try not to let my face show how bad they look.

"Bryan, I heard I left you as a sitting duck," Jake jokes.

"Yeah, pretty much," I laugh lightly. "Luckily Jace diverted some attention onto himself, so it's all good," I give Jake a light kick on his boot.

Jake sits up.

"It sounds like we got pretty torn up out there. 12 men dead, six others wounded including ourselves," He says disheartened.

Officer Cortez walks up to us.

"Hero's is what we call you two. The both of you helped two other platoons while on foot. Needless to say, that's impressive. I'm going to ask you two a favor. Take a couple men and retrieve whatever vehicles you can. We are going to need as much firepower as possible,"

We confirm that we will take care of it and head out.

THE REST of the day is spent retrieving vehicles and trying to figure out what is wrong with them. We placed sniper's closer to the center of the city and by the end of the night we were well secured, thanks to the reinforcements of the locals, we'll call rebels.

Things were looking up. When I finally lay my head down it's just past ten o'clock. Today was pretty intense. I saw what kind of power

Rev's Humvees could deliver and what that must mean about other machines they have, like mechs and who knows what else. Jace did say there was a quadcopter drone that appeared to have guns. I feel as though there are no limits to this war.

12

D esolate, Distraction, and Deceit

I WAKE up in a cold sweat and panting. I hear people moving around outside.

I realize I had a crazy dream about fighting Rev's men. The hundreds of soldiers running through the streets to our position. I shake my head and get up to stretch. It's six o'clock in the morning.

When I walk outside I see a few soldiers working on some vehicles and more loading up supplies. After a few minutes to fully wake up I search for Jake to get my orders.

Jake, Cortez, and Benson are huddled together in a nearby house. I pop my head in to see if they have some place they want me to be.

"Bryan, come on in," Cortez invites me.

I walk in and look over at the T.V. screen displaying a map of the area.

"We were just discussing ideas of how to best get into the city. We have some of our scouts reporting large blockades here, here and here," Cortez points out on the screen.

"Most likely, this is the same around the entire city. Every main street is under surveillance and blockade, making it difficult to move any large vehicles into the city,"

"A couple days of fighting could get us through there, but we don't have the time, men or supplies to spend on the outskirts of the city," Jake chimes in.

"Yeah, and it doesn't help that we are limited on air support. The Navy said they would help, but we just heard that they are busy with some of their own problems. We have just a couple of our own Falcons to assist us," Benson informs.

I just keep looking at the map and back at them trying to gather all the information.

"Well, this doesn't sound like we are going to be able to make it through the barricades head on. What is the plan then?" I ask.

They look at each other then back at the map. "Good question," Replies Cortez.

After a short pause, he begins describing what he thinks, while pointing to the screen, illustrating a plan.

"It seems like our best bet is to send a group through the alleys and try to cause some commotion as a distraction,"

"Distractions are good, but for a limited amount of time," I agree with him, but acknowledge there is caution within his plan.

"That's distraction number one. Distraction number two is only a quick air strike on this barricade. Following the air strike, we will put heavy fire on them and open the path. Once through, we would most likely be sandwiched from reinforcements, making it difficult to reach our distraction team. If we can't reach the small team, it will end up being a suicide mission," Cortez finishes, withdrawing his hand from the screen.

"Our plan gets us through the barricade, but not to the city," Benson helps clarify.

I think for a minute, surprised they are asking for my advice, but then again why not. When you have a good plan, but it's not fully developed, fresh eyes open up avenues not yet explored.

A minute goes by where we are all looking at the map.

"Why does the distraction team need to be picked up? Why do they need to be helpless?" I say, while stepping closer to the map. They all look at me with a little puzzlement.

Then I continue.

"The distraction team may be the strongest asset. Once we break the barricade our caravan needs to make a dash through here," I point on the map of a different section of the city off to the east side. "The caravan will draw attention due to its size and potential power. They will be the bigger distraction,"

They look at me, concentrating intently and then it clicks.

"So, our troops will be on foot and able to make it into the city. It's highly unlikely that any of our vehicles will make it to the city, let alone, get to the building," Jake exclaims.

Then another idea pops into my head.

"We need someone who knows the city. One of the locals. They will lead us into the place where the "alien" is," There is a moment of contemplation.

"Well, the plan isn't that different from what we had, but I think that your variation is a better way to reach the goal," Cortez says, rubbing his chin.

"We will just make sure we have a strong team on foot," Jake says.

"Well, let's figure this out. How many men do we need on foot?" Asks Cortez.

"At least four," Jake replies.

"They need some heavy weapons and gear to make it through the city. And four seems a little low," Benson adds, looking at Jake.

I start feeling like I'm out of the loop on something.

"Don't forget a local soldier for our guide," I say.

"Right. Then five at least, because I want the four to be our men," Cortez redefines the group.

Then Cortez looks at Benson.

"Only because I saw them do so well yesterday, I want Jace and Bryan on this team,"

Benson nods his head.

Cortez turns to me. "Bryan, who do you think should be with you guys on foot?"

I take a moment to think.

"Well I would like my whole squad, but if I must pick, I would have Jake and Luke plus the local," I say feeling bad I had to exclude Erin.

"What the heck. Jake, your whole squad will go and one local man for directions," Cortez declares.

We finish up some last-minute details and wrap up the meeting. We plan to head out at 7:30am.

Officer Cortez briefs the entire company and we start preparing and packing up the Humvees. Our squad checks over our weapon supply and decides to grab a rocket launcher. We also grab a few grappling hooks and ropes, in case of high walls. We find the most knowledgeable local with the best fighting skills. He seems a little hesitant, but willing to do the job. We eat a quick meal and get together to set out on foot.

It's 7:25 am and we are half a mile east from camp. The sun is up and creating long shadows out of the short houses. We pass two Humvees, broken down from yesterday, as we cross from alley to alley. We start reaching larger buildings where it doesn't feel as deserted. Before you couldn't find a chair to sit on, but here, there are a few on the porches. Every once in a while, you could find a car on the side of the road.

Twenty minutes have gone by and we have only made it a mile. While making our way here the conversation of what exactly we will find in the heart of the city has been discussed. The local man didn't have much of an idea as to what they have been doing inside a particular section of the city, as it has been blocked off for three days now. Rumors of locals being led into the area and never returning, have been passed around amongst the different local bunkers.

We are walking through an alley, created by two tan brick buildings, when Jake has us hold our position. I see the left side of his face, which had the most shrapnel damage. The medicine he took has been working well for him. The stitches look loose and the wounds are looking like they've had a couple days of healing, when it's been only hours.

Jake crouches down, so we do the same. Then I hear it. It's a truck not too far away. The truck gets closer and closer at a decent speed. As it gets closer I can tell it has no intentions to stop. The truck speeds by going left, past the alley. A trail of dirt rises high after the truck. I can't tell what kind of vehicle it is, but I know its not one of the monstrous Humvees. We wait for the dirt to clear out of our view before moving on.

"Officer Cortez, look at my location. We just found a truck heading west. I don't know where it's heading, but it is on the outside of the barricades. Over," Jake says over the radio channel.

"Copy that. We'll keep our eyes peeled,"

We go a mile more and find ourselves at the border, with patrolling foot soldiers. Men are on rooftops, spaced out a couple blocks away from each other. We wait there a few minutes to watch the pattern of patrolling vehicles, but no one comes.

"Alright, so what's the plan?" Luke asks.

We look at Jake.

"Move slow and stay hidden. We want to get past the barricade line before causing any ruckus. We are a few blocks from the actual line of road blockades," He then turns to slowly look around the corner at the man a couple buildings down.

"Alright, on my queue I will send one of you over at a time. Walk as softly as possible to kick up the least amount of dirt," Jake says.

"Jake, we know how walking softly works," Jace replies with a look of disappointment.

Jake has Erin go first. When the soldier on the roof rotates away from us Jake sends her. Then, Jace goes across. The soldier rotates back in our direction. It's about another two minutes before Luke and the local soldier, Dingane, run across together slightly kicking up dust.

Luckily, the Rev soldier doesn't turn around. Jake and I debate whether we can make it too. We decide we can and we sprint across the street into the alley. We wait a moment to make sure we didn't alert the soldier. After a minute, we decide he has no clue.

The six of us move on, a couple more blocks, where there are soldiers on every other rooftop and vehicles patrolling at jogging speed.

"It looks like this is where the fun begins," says Erin.

"You better believe it," Jace says, checking over his weapon.

"Cortez, we are at the road with barricades, a mile to the east. Give us five minutes to devise our plan then call in for an air strike. Over," says Jake.

"Copy that," Cortez responds.

"Make sure your earpieces are in, we need to split up. Jace and Luke take the other side of this building on our left. Bryan, you'll take the right side of this building," Jake begins drawing in the dirt.

"Erin, and Dingane stay here with me. We'll each get into position and then on my word we'll each take out a man on the roof. Once you take out your guy, sprint across the street. I want to get at least two blocks past this one. Okay, any questions?"

None of us do. We break off to our different positions.

I MAKE my way to the south alley. I peek around the corner and see my guy at his post. He looks like he could be a local, but what does that even mean. How do I know what a local person looks like compared to another man? I guess I just feel bad having to kill people that potentially could be forced to do something they don't want to do.

I shake the feeling and focus. I have a job to do and sometimes I have to make imperfect choices that lead to success. I can't assess everyone to find out their back story.

I shake the feeling again. As I crouch behind some trash cans, I line up my cross hairs over my target. I say a little prayer that I'm not killing an innocent man who has a family and is forced to go to war for something he doesn't believe in.

Jake asks if we're in position and ready.

We all confirm we are.

Seconds later he gives the word and simultaneously the bullets fly and for a few seconds I sit there.

Whether it's nerves or confirmation my guy was down for good, I'm not sure. I finally get to my feet and leave the alley.

I can see everyone else has just reached the other side of the street. I sprint fast to make up lost time. Just after entering the alley, I hear bullets hitting the brick wall next to me. I run faster and go straight on through the next street to the second alley.

I hear people yelling behind me in the distance. I just keep sprinting until I get to the street.

"Jake, where are you?" I say into my mic.

"The third street. Where are you?"

"I'm on the second street," I reply wondering why they went ahead.

"Bryan, get up here. The streets are fairly clear. If you don't hurry we'll miss our window,"

I begin to sprint again moving through the street to an alley on my left. This alley is long and has a few short walls I have to hop over.

As I make my way down it, I can't see anyone. I keep moving past rotting garbages and dark doorways to the third street.

As soon as I get to the street, I hear vehicles behind me on the last street I was on.

"Jake, where are you guys?" I say peering up and down the street.

"Your 10 o'clock, Bryan," Jake says quietly.

I look to see him standing against the wall in an alley to my left. I double check the street and then run to meet Jake.

"Can't you keep up today?" He says half-jokingly.

"Sorry. I'll do better,"

I tell myself I need to focus. Then without warning Jake pulls his gun up and I spin around to see him take out a soldier walking on the roof across the street. People start yelling to each other and Jake pushes me further into the alley.

We are behind the rest of the squad, who sees us. They get the clue and they start running too. Down the alley we run, sometimes jumping over garbage and other objects. We stop before the next street, just in time, because a Humvee is moving at a jogging pace not too far from us.

"We have a Humvee coming our way," Luke informs.

"One rocket should take it out," Erin says, swinging her rocket launcher around from her back.

"Or, we could try and hijack it and make it further into the city," Dingane says.

For a second it doesn't sound too bad, but then we hear soldiers running down the alley behind us.

"There isn't time. Blow it up and we'll keep running," Jake orders.

We crouch against the wall as Erin waits for the Humvee to roll across.

Unexpectedly, the Humvee comes to a stop some yards before the alley.

"What's going on?" Jace asks quietly.

But then bullets break our silence as the soldiers behind us spot Erin. The bullets scatter around us and we immediately turn to fire back.

"Erin, Jace, keep your focus on the truck," Jake orders.

The rest of us begin exchanging fire down the alley.

A second later, one soldier tosses a grenade pretty close to the refrigerator I'm using as a shield. I lean against it and the grenade goes off rocking the refrigerator.

Dingane takes out another soldier ready with a live grenade, forcing the grenade to drop to the ground. Two seconds later the grenade goes off, blowing garbage and junk everywhere near another Rev soldier.

I look back at Erin for a moment. She is laying down on her stomach in position to fire a rocket at the Humane.

Luke, Jake and Dingane begin alternating firing at the soldiers in the alley. I look down the alley for a closer position. Not much is there, but I see five more soldiers coming. Just as I pull my head back behind the fridge, I realize what I saw a soldier holding. A machine gun and tripod. "Heavy machine gun coming our way!" I yell. I grab one of my two grenades and nod to Luke. He gives me cover fire and I pull the pin and lob the grenade.

Boom! The explosion echoes into the buildings next to us.

"Nice throw," Dingane says.

We move up closer while the soldiers are trying to orient themselves. Through the dirt polluted air, we fire at the silhouettes of soldiers.

We determine they are all dead just before we hear machine gun fire behind us.

We swing around and see Erin on the ground, out of position, and a stream of bullets coming from outside the alley at an angle.

"Is she dead?" I ask myself.

Jace grabs her arm and pulls her away from her lethal position.

"Jake, we have more guys coming," Informs Luke.

Then we see the Humvee's grill moving into sight. "Move inside!" Jake barks, as he charges a doorway with two wood boards blocking the entrance.

His force breaks the boards and he falls inside the building onto the floor. We follow him in, making sure not to step on him. Jace and Erin get inside after us. Erin appears to be okay and still has the rocket launcher in hand and still loaded.

For the moment, we are safe. That is, until we hear yelling and Dingane, the last one in, who tells us to run.

We make a beeline for another room just as bullets pelt the building, some breaking through the wall.

"Alright we have to get to the roof or the top floor. These buildings are close enough that we can jump to another one," Says Jake.

"You guys find some stairs and I'll hold them at the door," I offer.

They nod and head off to find the stairs.

I take position behind a wall of the inner room. Only moments later, do I hear footsteps coming alongside the building.

I know there's got to be at least six guys outside.

I see a rifle on the edge of the door frame. Whispers get exchanged in the alley.

I stand ready.

I give them just a peek in, making them feel as though it's clear.

Then, just as one of them is about to creep in, I pop out just enough and fire.

I pull back just as I'm seen by another soldier who fires into the door frame in front of me. A minute goes by of exchanging fire from doorway to doorway.

"Bryan, hold them off for another minute or two, then come up the stairs," Jake says through the headset.

"Copy that,"

The soldiers begin busting more boards off other doors and windows in other rooms on the first floor. Then just as I'm distracted, a grenade rolls into the first room. I jump back and duck for cover behind the wall.

Boom!

Dirt flies past me and sizable chunks of the wall hit me, pushing me onto the floor.

With my adrenaline running a little more, I push off the ground and dive for the next door way. The soldiers rush into the building and I decide it's time to go.

"Jake, where are the stairs?" I ask while running from room to room.

Then, I make it to a hallway where I find them. The stairs are a gray metal and thy're rickety as I run up them.

"In the hallway, a couple rooms back into the building," Jake tries to explain.

"Got it,"

"We are on the third floor, Bryan," Erin says just as I reach the second floor.

I continue up and notice the soldiers are at the base of the stairs on the first floor.

"What's the plan guys? They're coming up the stairs,"

I reach the third floor, where I only see Erin waiting for me. Bullets are shattering the windows of the building on the other side of the street.

"Let's go!" Erin yells, as she pulls a pin and tosses a grenade down the staircase.

We are running through a fairly open floor plane. It looks like a business was in operation here at some time. We dodge desks and copiers, all out of place. The floor is littered with paper and books.

"The last balcony on our left is our exit. Jump diagonally to the next building's corner balcony," Erin informs me.

I see the balcony and begin preparing my mind for the leap. I veer left, jumping over one last tipped over trash can. The doors are open and a curtain gently blows in the wind. I run through the doorway and jump up and off the waist high banister.

I notice my landing is a few feet lower than my departure and anticipate a rough landing. My right foot steps down onto a thick stone banister like the one I jumped off. My head nearly misses the wall above the door frame and my body continues forward smashing into the corner of the door and wall.

I quickly recover and block out a slight pain from the collision.

When I turn around to see where Erin is, she is just jumping off the banister. However, to my surprise, she isn't facing me, but a Humvee down below. She doesn't look like she will make it to the balcony. With her rocket ready, she shoots in mid-air down three stories at the Humvee. The kick of the blast corrects her short jump and she falls right into me and we break through the door, falling to the ground.

Bullets fly through the doorway and a grenade bounces off the wall, exploding in the air, not too far away.

We get up and shake ourselves off.

"Woah," Is all I say, being impressed with Erin.

I decide almost anyone could do that jump, so I push a table onto the balcony.

"Hopefully that makes it a little more difficult," I say.

The next thing we know, a soldier tries to jump on the table but hits the building and falls off.

WE RUN through the building to the other end.

"Where is everyone else?" I ask.

"In a different building. We couldn't follow them or we might have gotten shot,"

We look out the windows at the roof of another building.

"Look!" I exclaim.

The others are jumping onto the stairs of another building.

"Let's jump to the roof and then we can meet them in that building," Erin says backing up to get a running start.

I follow her method and we both leap to the rooftop twelve feet below us.

"Jake, we're coming to meet you in that building," I inform him.

"Copy that," He replies, a little winded.

The roof we're on connects seamlessly to a taller building. I notice the building has taken damage from the meteorites a few days ago. Large rocks are scattered around a few bigger sized holes.

Erin and I sprint to a window and climb through it. We hear footsteps on the floor above us. As we get to the stairs, the others are coming down.

"Hey, you guys okay?" I ask.

"Yeah, we are all fine. This street is too wide for us to jump. We need to head down to go anywhere," Jace says as he makes it down first.

Jake comes down next. "Our decoy hasn't made much of a difference at the barricades, but the jets opened it up enough. The caravan is on the move, probably a couple miles ahead of us," He says, still winded.

Everyone else comes down the stairs in a single file. Once on the main floor we get real quiet so as to not tip off anyone searching the perimeter. Softly walking, we make our way to the windows looking out to the street.

Luke breaks out a map and puts it up against a wall. "It appears we still have two miles until we hit the inner-city boundaries,"

Erin steps quietly to a door and unlocks it. As she checks the street, I assess the map with Luke.

"Dingane, where did you guys have your main base?" I ask, knowing it probably wasn't in the center of the city.

Dingane walks over and points to the map.

"Right around here. There are vehicles and weapons stocked there. There are approximately 8 locations like this one around the city.

Erin gives us the okay and runs across to another door. We each follow. Erin tries to open the door, but it's locked. She pulls out a pistol to shoot it but Jake stops her.

"I don't want to be making too much noise," He points to an alleyway and suggests we use that.

The alley is just like the previous ones, filled with garbage cans and junk, but it is different from the rest. It has a pile of rubble from the building to the left of us.

"What do you think that is from?" Luke asks.

"Probably a meteorite," Jace says.

As we walk on top of the rubble, I can see the meteorite underneath. I stop to uncover some of it. I only remove a brick or two, when Jake tells me to keep moving.

We make it to the street where small bits of meteorite lay scattered on the ground. For the next mile and half, we see large and small meteorites all over the place. Most buildings have damage somewhere on them.

Rev seems to be spread thin this far from the barricades, but the few soldiers we saw, we passed by unnoticed. It's hard to know if they are local soldiers or Rev's full-fledged soldiers.

WE ARE NOW in a building two blocks from where Dingane said there was an arsenal. A report from Cortez tells us the caravan is causing some havoc, but it sounds like we are also losing men. They were only driving around in the city for about 20 minutes, when they headed to the outskirts to lose Rev. Now, less distracted, Cortez is trying to give us directions to the rumored location of Rev's headquarters in the area.

After a few minutes of resting inside a building, we go over the supplies we have.

Between the six of us we have 4 grenades, and about 2 mags a person. We aren't too enthusiastic about our supplies while heading to the beast's belly.

"If we can get into the arsenal, we may be able to get a vehicle and make our way into the city," Dingane says. "I have a security card for some select areas, but it's better than nothing,"

We agree a vehicle would make the most sense as the area is becoming more congested with soldiers and possibly civilians.

"Can you get there yourself and bring a vehicle here? I'm worried it's going to be pretty heavily guarded," Jake says.

"Yeah, our uniforms will be a dead giveaway, even if we are seen from a distance," Jace adds.

Dingane thinks for a few seconds and swallows hard.

"Yeah, I can try. I just wish I had some back up,"

"You can do it, Dingane," Erin nods at him.

"Okay, it's a plan," says Jake.

Dingane cracks his neck and re-adjusts his vest.

"I should only be about ten minutes. Anything longer than that you should devise another plan," he says, before walking out the door.

I grab him on the shoulder. "Wait, take my earpiece so we can stay up to date on your status,"

I take off my helmet and remove the earpiece from inside. Jake looks at me with a little hesitation. Dingane takes the earpiece and then heads off.

Jake takes his earpiece out and turns the volume up louder for me to hear. A minute goes by before we hear from Dingane.

"I'm at an entrance, let's see if my card still works,"

We are all looking over at each other.

"I'm in, but I have to go through security, so, bear with me,"

Our sigh of relief for Dingane getting through the door is retracted at the news of having to go through security.

We can hear a small conversation about Dingane's purpose inside the arsenal.

"I have orders to grab a vehicle and a few men to patrol the outskirts," Dingane answers.

"ID please," One of the men requests.

"We need to be getting the people running within our borders," Another soldier says.

"Alright, go ahead. Make sure your tracking device is working before taking the vehicle. If you take it and it stops working, you need to call in every 30 minutes or just bring it back. That's easier," The first soldier instructs.

"Yes sir. I do remember the protocol," says Dingane.

A door shuts on Dingane's end.

"Okay, I made it through. Now which vehicle do we want?"

We all let out a sigh of relief.

"Good work. We probably want one of the big black beasts," Says Jace before Jake can speak.

"Yeah, that's what we want," Jake says anyways.

"Oh man," Dingane says with amazement.

"They have got some new equipment in here.

"Like what?" Jake asks.

"A couple large robots. Like six of them,"

We look at each other.

"It looks like we'll have fun later," Jace says sarcastically.

"I'll be there in a few minutes," Says Dingane.

"Once we get the vehicle, we need to be quick about where we are going to go. Cortez should be sending me coordinates any minute now," Jake tells us.

"So, whats the plan? To break into the building holding the alien costume and...what?" Jace asks.

It's a good question. Are we here to stop one man or many and if it's many then how do we do that.

"Listen, we need to find out what is going on here. We are afraid more than just manipulation is happening here,"

"Like what?" Asks Erin.

Jake looks to the side.

"I think he is here," He avoids answering.

"No Jake, tell us what you know," Jace puts his hand on the door preventing Jake from opening it.

Jake steps back and stares at Jace then looks at the rest of us.

"Mutations. We think there are people willing and probably not willing to be mutated into beasts,"

"We already knew they were working with mutations," Luke says.

Jake looks at him.

"This is different. Not just small changes like being able to sleep less or being able to run longer. Imagen thicker bones, skin and stronger resistance to pain,"

We are all a little taken back. I can hear the Humvee outside.

"We should go," Jake says.

Jace moves his hand off the door and we follow Jake out of the building.

We climb into the vehicle, Jace being the last, after taking a moment of thinking what he just learned.

With Dingane in the driver's seat and the rest of us a little crammed in the back, we head into the city. The buildings get a little nicer, but there are still meteorites lying on the ground amongst broken brick and glass. It is apparent that someone has had the job of moving the large meteorites off to the side of the street.

This drive makes me think of how much faster it would have been if we had a vehicle from the beginning. But then again, we also couldn't have gotten this far because of the barricades.

After a few blocks, people start appearing like actual civilians.

"What do these people do in the city? Luke asks.

"Whatever the soldiers want them to do. Construction, computer work, monitoring surveillance," Dingane says.

"And all these people are okay with this invasion?" Erin asks dumbfounded.

Dingane puts a hand in the air like he is unsure.

"People promised to work if they got a spot in a bunker. Once they made the promise, they can never leave until the soldiers allow them to. However, they believe now that there is an alien that controls the city, so they never really expect to leave,"

We all sit in silence for a few minutes.

"Dingane, I have the coordinates," says Jake and then tells Dingane the latitude and longitude. "By the way did you turn off the tracking system?" Jake says, looking up on the map where to go.

"Yes, I turned it off,"

While Jake and Dingane talk about the coordinates I tell Jace and Luke about Erin's amazing mid-air rocket to Humvee shot. They both agree they would have liked to have seen it.

"What kind of mutants do you think we'll see?" Jace asks us.

"Probably part animal or maybe insect," says Luke, without much thought.

"I can't imagine what that would look like, but what the heck, why not," says Erin.

"Mentally prepare yourself for anything, because anything is possible," Jake turns to look at us and then goes back to the map. "It looks like we are right around the corner from our stop. We're going to be infiltrating the arsenal. If we gain heavy artillery there we could get to the headquarters and take out key officers. The question is how do we get in," He says while rubbing his chin.

"Officer Cortez, what's your status?"

A minute goes by and still no reply from Cortez.

"Officer Benson, can you hear me?" Jake looks back at us.

"This isn't –"

Jake is cut off by Cortez.

"We're on our last leg. Half a tank of gas and then were hoofing it. There are too many vehicles and they have eyes on us through drones. We can't get more than a few minutes away from one vehicle before another comes up on us,"

Jake sits back.

"How can we help them?" He says to us.

"There is no way we can get back here again if we leave now," says Luke with surety.

"Officer Cortez, I suggest you retreat back into the very first camp we set up," Jake reluctantly suggests.

It takes a moment for Cortez to respond. "We may have to do that, but we need to lose the drones before going anywhere. We'll never be safe if we don't,"

Jake turns back to the map.

"Do you have any maps or any idea how to get in the building, Dingane?"

"Possibly sewers," He replies.

"There is a garage, but only authorized personnel may enter and I doubt I qualify,"

"Dang it!" Jake punches the passenger seat.

"We are a block away and we can't even get in!"

"There is always a way," I say, trying to be positive.

"Let's drive by the building and maybe we will find a way," Luke says somewhat enthusiastically.

There's a pause in the conversation.

"Alright, let's go," Jake says.

Dingane drives around the building a few times from different directions.

"Dingane, all these civilians have wrist bands like you guys had. Doesn't that mean the people are being forced to do things or they'll die?" Asks Erin.

"Some are willing and some aren't but most that aren't willing aren't around up here. The people you see here with wrist bands have them as communication devices basically for receiving orders. Go here, do this, fix da da da,"

Then an idea pops in my head.

"Where is the communication control room?" I ask, somewhat excitedly.

"What do you mean?" Erin asks.

"There must be a building with a room managing messages from wristband to wristband.

"It's this one," Dingane points to a building near the one we really want to get into.

"We can send a message to everyone with a wrist band that they need to rebel and that the United States military is here to help them," I say, while seeing everyone mull it over.

"We'll work on the speech, but that isn't a bad idea," Says Jake.

"Hey, that really is better than trying to break into probably the most secure building. Plus, if that room can send messages it may control the injection mechanism that terrifies people from rebelling," Luke chimes in.

We all agree our chances of making any difference in this war are better in the communications building and trying to get people to rebel.

"How do we get into the neighboring building?" Erin asks.

"It shouldn't be as difficult to get into as Rev's main building," says Jace.

"Well, it still will have security and ID checks" Jake says.

We sit there for a few minutes trying to think of an idea.

"We could lend a Rev soldier a ride, then knock him out and take his uniform. That would allow a second person to have entry into buildings," Luke suggests.

We can't all agree on it for various reasons.

"The guy's ID would have to look like one of us," says Jace.

"It's not a bad idea, but Jace is right and we couldn't keep taking guys out until we get it right," Says Erin.

We find the imagery of Erins statement funny and chuckle a little.

So, we think some more.

Luke starts bobbing his left hand with his index finger and thumb together. Then he closes his eyes as he is doing it. We look at him confused, before asking what he is doing.

"I'm thinking of a symphony. It is one of my favorites. Someone once said that war is like a symphony and there are moments of subtlety that most people never notice, but its those notes and sounds that make all the difference,"

We are taken back a little.

"Wow, that's deep," Says Jace.

Luke puts up his other hand suggesting Jace to be quiet.

"The best way we can get into the communications building is through its garage. It must have a garage where equipment can be brought in,"

He says, opening his eyes.

"Dingane, you drive up and tell them you are there to drop off equipment and they'll let you in. Once we are in we'll jump out and take out anyone in the room,"

We look at each other.

"That doesn't sound bad," Erin accepts Luke's idea.

"We will have to be quick so that nobody is alarmed and calls security," Jake cautions.

"I think it's the only way in," Dingane says.

"Okay, does anyone object?" Asks Jake.

No one does.

"Okay let's find that garage,"

We circle around to the back of the building where a man stands in a booth in front of a large metal door. Dingane pulls up to the booth and we all cram out of view.

"Hello sir, here to drop off equipment," Dingane says calmly.

"I wasn't expecting anything till later this evening. And why do you have a Humvee?" The soldier asks with confusion.

"This equipment was supposed to be here yesterday but we got hung up with some other things. As for the Humvee, all the other vehicles were either broken or in use," Dingane lies.

"Okay, there should be a few guys inside to help you unload it. Let me just get your ID and I'll check you in,"

Dingane removes his ID from his pocket and shows it to the guard.

"Alright," he says.

We start moving again.

"Get ready," says Dingane.

"Give us the best estimate of how many people there are once you get inside," Jake requests.

The large metal door slowly rises into the ceiling.

Once in, the Humvee gets real dark. We situate ourselves ready to jump out the back of the Humvee.

"It looks like about six guys. Wait for my queue," Dingane says, as he gets out, leaving his door open.

"Wow, what's this truck doing here?" A man asks.

"Only vehicle I could get. This equipment was supposed to be here yesterday. Can I get a hand?" Dingane says.

"Three are coming," Jake says, peeking around the passenger seat.

"These doors are jammed," Dingane plays it off.

"Don't shoot unless they yell or grab a gun. Once out, Jace, Luke you two target the other three on the right side at your two o'clock. Shoot if they try to radio for help or if they run for a door," Jake says with his rifle pointing at the door.

"Here, let me get it," A man's voice is heard on the other side of the back door.

The door is swung open and the man freezes. The other two men jump back and reach for their waists where their hand guns hang. However, they stop when they realize there are too many guns pointed at them and they put their hands up instead. Interestingly, these men are white as opposed to many black soldiers encountered on the way to the city. Jace goes out first, then Luke. Jace puts his index finger over his mouth to tell the men to be quiet. Erin, Jake and myself get out of the Humvee, with our guns pointed at the men.

There are crates everywhere. Jace and Luke crouch walk behind the crates.

The man who opened the door is sweating profusely. He also looks very mad and is trying to hold his tongue.

Jake reaches into a pocket on his vest and pulls out a square packet. He tears it open and places it under the man's nose. A clear gel gets dabbed on his upper lip and then the man loses it and tries to yell for help.

Jake quickly puts his hand over his mouth and puts him in a head-lock. However, it was loud and long enough to get the attention of the men on the other side of the garage.

The alerting man passes out and Jake lays him on the ground.

The two men in front of us reach for their guns as Erin and I are slightly turned to the man on the ground. Dingane and I lunge towards them. I smack the man on the left, in the face with the butt of my rifle and Dingane throws a solid punch at the other. Both men fall to the ground and we secure their pistols.

All the while, the other three men have been walking over here yelling trying to figure out what's going on.

Then a gunshot.

"Watch these guys," Jake says running off to help Luke and Jace.

I stand there with my rifle pointed at the three guys on the ground but still looking for any surprises on the other side of the crates.

Gunfire goes back and forth for thirty seconds or so and then I hear Jake yelling orders.

A minute later, two black men walk into view with their hands up with Jace and Jake walking behind them.

"Dingane, are these locals?" Asks Jake.

"Do you think I know everyone in this city?" He says a little offended.

"I can't say,"

"We are locals," One of them says.

"Will you help us defeat these soldiers that have taken over the city and enslaved everyone?" Dingane asks.

"Do you not fear the alien?" The other soldier asks.

"We are enslaved to it. If we could defeat it, we would have. These soldiers are controlled by the alien and they control us,"

Jace steps in front of the two soldiers.

"Well now you have a choice. Fight or watch us do it for you," He says just a few inches from their faces.

"I can't help, because I know you will die trying. My family, my friends have all been murdered with little effort by the hands of the alien. Their fate will be yours too," One of the black men say.

Just before Jake was going to respond back to the man, the unconscious man comes too. Jake grabs the man and picks him up off the ground a little.

"And who are you three? Actual Rev soldiers?" Jake snarls.

"Yes, we are. Rev is the new world order," says, one of the other, white men.

"You are all fools for not accepting Rev's reign,"

Jake stops holding the awakening man and lets him slump back down.

"It will only be a matter of weeks before every continent is over-come by Rev followers. Life will be organized to help humanity be more...focused," Says one of the standing men.

"Focused? Focused on what?" Jake walks over to the man.

"Well–"

"Shut up!" The man on the floor growls trying to look back at the man standing.

"Focused on what?" Jake holds his gun at the talkative soldier.

He says nothing and just sweats profusely.

"Tell me!" Jake yells.

"Focused on bringing all the riches and comfort to our president and the district leaders," The man on the floor says.

Jake looks down at him. Silence fills the air for a few seconds.

"Bind them all. Put them in a closet. Make sure you remove their wrist bands too, I don't want them calling for help," Orders Jake.

I wonder if Jake actually believes the man. His last statement, although it could be a real objective, seems not fully honest. And why would it be.

WE FOLLOW orders and lock up the five men in the closet, bound and gagged. I walk over to Jake who has been working on the next step with Luke.

"Jake, they're all in a closet, bound. What's next?" I ask, feeling like we need to get a move on with the plan, before more people show up in the garage.

"We have a map of the building and it looks like the elevator will take us straight up to the top. We just can't stop on the way there. It's twelve floors and we need to get to the eleventh," He says while looking through the crates.

"What are you looking for?" Erin asks, standing next to me.

"Oh, I'm just trying to see what they have in here. Nothing in partic-ular. It appears to be just lots of computers and junk," He says still looking through all of it.

"Luke is trying to figure out a way to control the elevator without having to stop anywhere but the eleventh floor,"

"I figured it out. It really isn't that difficult," Luke walks up.

Jake stops looking through the crates.

"Okay, great. Let's get going then. Luke, do your thing down here and Erin, stay with him. Jace, Dingane, Bryan and myself will go to the eleventh floor,"

We all agree on the plan and split.

I ask for my earpiece back from Dingane.

"It just started getting comfortable," He says with a smile.

We get in the elevator after Luke takes complete control of its system.

"Take us up Luke," Jake says.

The doors close.

The elevator is larger than normal. These kind of elevators are for the big equipment we should find on the upper levels.

The elevator moves up, and with each floor my heart beats a little faster.

"We'll take out a few of the workers, then you guys watch the main area while I take the controls," Jake instructs.

We're now at the sixth floor.

"Officer Cortez, this is Jake. We are about to send a message to all the people in the city informing them of our presence and that we need them in the resistance against Rev," Jake sends a message via his watch.

Eighth Floor.

"Get ready everyone. Oh, and try not to damage any important equipment," He says.

"This is a great plan and all, but how are we going to get out of there once we have sent the message?" Asks Jace.

He has a point. By the time the message is sent we'll have about ten seconds max to get out of there, which is impossible.

"We'll figure it out," Jake replies.

Dingane and I just look at each other almost as if to say, nice to have known ya.

Tenth Floor. We stand ready.

My hand is so tightly gripped to my gun my knuckles are white. My adrenaline kicks in. My senses become heightened.

We reach the eleventh floor and a ding goes off. The doors open slowly and we step out strong, but cautiously. We check both sides, but nobody is waiting for us which is good and as hoped for. There's a counter up ahead along the right side of the hallway with two people sitting behind it. Just as they look over at us, bullets go through them and they fall to the ground. We rush to them to make sure they don't call security but they succumb quickly to their wounds.

Jace gets behind the desk and unlocks the door to what we hope is the communication control center. We push the doors open to a large room. The room is in the corner of the building. Two sides of the room are lined with glass panels that look out into the city. We notice, maybe only twenty computers in the room and half of them are being used.

"Get on the ground!" We yell.

"Don't touch anything!"

We corral the entire staff without firing once. We totally caught them off guard. Then I hear someone talking, trying to whisper.

"Who's talking?" I yell out and begin looking for them.

Jace finds them and beats them in the head with his rifle. It was a girl in her mid-twenties trying to send a distress signal to security. Upon further investigation of her wristband we determine it went through. We find a few with pistols and take them away.

"Everyone, take your wristbands off. Throw them over there," I instruct pointing to a planter.

Everyone does.

Jake begins working on sending a message out.

"We have been compromised, Jake," Jace says with defeat and anger in his face.

Jake doesn't say anything back to Jace, but keeps working on the computer.

We place some desks in front of the door to give us time for when security shows up.

"You will never succeed. Join us before you throw your life away," Someone says.

"Shut up. You're lucky to be alive as it is," I say getting tired and frustrated with how things are going.

Minutes go by and I am beginning to feel even more anxious about security responding to the girl's distress call.

"Guys, I got it! It's sent," says Jake.

"I will just confirm the message is received by these bands and we'll be out of here," Jace says pulling out a wristband obtained in the garage.

"Luke, can you get into the surveillance and tell us where security is," I ask.

"I disabled the elevators so they will be a little longer, from where they are coming from. I don't think I can get into the surveillance from what I have down here," Luke replies.

DINGANE IS LOOKING through the window at the city. He seems to be searching for some way out of here.

"Everyone, get up. Move to the corner of the room," I order.

Jace looks at me like, "what are you doing?"

"It worked. These wristbands received the message," Jace says with relief.

"The people on the streets, they have stopped and are looking around," Says Dingane, still peering out the window.

"How many people in this building do you think will rebel?" Jace asks Dingane.

"Just enough to cause a scene, but not enough to help us,"

There is a bang at the door. The desks hold the doors closed from a few more body checks, before cracking open a few inches.

"Jake what do we do?" I ask while aiming at the door.

Jake is walking quickly around the room as he tries to figure out a solution.

"We're under attack. We can't wait for you guys any longer," Luke says.

"Copy that. Get out of there. The message went through just so you know. Good luck," Jake says.

Dingane tells us there are snipers on the roof across the street.

"Well, get away from the window!" Jace yells

"It's thick glass, nothing will go through it," He says.

The next thing we know a bullet hits the window making a white circle of broken glass.

Dingane immediately falls backwards onto the ground.

"Wow," He says surprised, while getting up.

The men behind the door are using their rifles to push chairs off the desks.

We fire at them to slow them down.

Jake briskly walks over to the workers in the corner.

"Everyone, kneel next to each other in a row with hands behind your back," He says pointing his gun at them.

I'm really surprised he is going to do this.

But then he surprises me. He takes more of that jelly he used before and places it under everyone's nose.

"Don't smear it. It won't help," He says as each of them get uncomfortable and begin to fall to the floor.

"Bryan, keep an eye on the door. Jace, Dingane get some desks and stack them on top of each other," Jake orders us.

"We are going to go up to the ceiling?" Asks Jace, doubting Jake's idea.

"Just do it,"

The two of them begin pushing computers off the tables.

"Wait, the blinds, we should close them," Dingane stops.

"No, keep them open until I tell you to close them," Jake instructs.

I fire a few more rounds at the door, but slowly the doors begin to separate more and more. They are almost open a foot now, I begin to really fear we won't make it out.

"Jake! The door isn't holding!" I say while firing a little more.

I guess I should stop firing. I will actually need the ammo when the doors are completely open and I can get a good shot.

"Dingane close the blinds," Jake orders.

The room gets darker, but we still have fluorescent lights. He then whispers into the mic.

"After I throw a grenade, Bryan will hit the lights and he and Dingane will head for the closet. Jace and I will take cover on the furthest side of the room. Make your shots count," Jake says walking over to the doors.

He tosses the grenade underneath the desks and through the gap between the doors. As he runs to the other side of the room, the grenade goes off and I turn off the lights. All four of us get into our positions.

A lot of yelling is going on in the hallway. Then another boom goes off and I assume they are blowing up the doorway.

"Get on the ground," A soldier yells.

"Jake, you tell us when," I say, ready for anything.

I feel like the situation is crappy, but it could be worse, I suppose.

"The ceiling! They're in the ceiling," The soldier yells.

Machine guns go off.

"They're shooting the ceiling," Jake says.

"You, get up there!" The soldier commands someone.

A distinct semi shot goes off and then Jake gives the command.

"Now!"

Dingane swings the door open and I shoot a soldier facing away from me, almost point blank. Green lasers stream from a few soldiers' guns only helping me find them quicker in the dark room. I take out another guy close to the decimated doors.

The soldier who was ordered to check the ceiling is shot and falls off the stacked desks. A green laser swings my way but Jace or Jake takes him out.

Just as I decide I don't see anyone else, a soldier crouching down between two desks fires at me. I see this in my peripherals but it's too late. Bullets hit me and I fall against the wall just behind me. I decide to drop down for coverage and I point my gun in his direction. My left shoulder feels like it's been slugged with a bat going a thousand miles per hour, my head is pounding and my left ear is ringing. Dingane exchanges fire with the soldier. Then, I look towards the doors and two more men come in. They fire at Dingane who then falls back into the closest. Almost simultaneously both men are shot, one in the face and the other in the vest. They both fall to the ground.

"Jake I'm down. I think there is still one guy left, between the desks," I say propping myself up onto my side.

"Copy that. Hang in there" He says.

Dingane opens the door slightly only to get shot at. Then I hear shots from Jace and Jake.

"He's down."

I hear Jace say.

Just when I think it's clear, I hear a noise and see one of the wounded men reaching for his gun. I lift my gun up and aim the best I can with one arm but Dingane shoots before I can.

Dingane helps me to my feet.

"Bryan, where were you hit?" Jake asks as he and Jace jog over looking around to make sure the room is completely clear.

"I think it's just my shoulder and my helmet," I say looking at my shoulder where the armor is.

The matte black armor over my shoulder has a large dent in it and the coating has been removed.

"It doesn't seem to have gone through but I'm sure you will have a large bruise there. As for your head...it has the same story. I bet you have a massive headache," Jace says while inspecting me.

"Yeah, I do,"

Jake opens a pocket on his vest and hands me two pills.

"Take these,"

I nod to him and take them with the last of my water.

JACE AND DINGANE take post by the stairs. Luke informs us that him and Erin can't lose Rev on the streets. They are going to leave the city. Apparently, it's too difficult to hold off a couple Humvees when you only have two people.

"What do we do?" Jake says to himself.

I try to think of the best way out of here, but really, we are sitting ducks.

"We need back up, big time," I say leaning my back against the wall and looking down.

"We need air support," Jake says.

He contacts Cortez.

"We need air support. There is no other way out of the building. I know they said it would be nearly impossible to fly into the city, but our men can do it," Jake tries to convince Officer Cortez.

A short conversation I wasn't included in, takes place.

"Ok," Jake gets done and turns to face me.

"What did he say?" I ask.

"He said I should talk to air support myself," Jake appears frustrated and walks to the other side of the room.

I decide I will go help Jace and Dingane.

"Bryan, what's the plan?" Jace asks. "I'm starting to get worried we are just prolonging the inevitable,"

I look at him and then to the stairs.

"Jake is trying to get air support,"

Jace shakes his head.

"What's the chances of them coming into the city?" He asks rhetorically.

"We have ten floors to go. What's the chances of making it down and out," Dingane looks at us.

He doesn't have to say it, we all know there is no way to go down through the building to get out. It's like nine levels of combat and the boss is Revs' entire army waiting down on the streets.

"Listen, do you hear that?" Asks Jace.

"They're coming up the stairs," I say.

The staircase has no walls and is open to the far side of the building. It's wasted space from the stairs, twenty feet out, to the large wall with massive windows. I wonder if those windows are bullet proof.

13

T ogether and Tattered

JAKE FINALLY COMES over to give word.

"It looks like we have Falcons coming our way. They are going to take out any soldiers on the roofs and then land a Falcon on top of this building. So, that means we have to go up," He says looking a little relieved.

"Land a Falcon on the roof?" Jace asks, completely dumbfounded. "I'm not sure it's possible,"

Looking at me, then back to Jace, Jake assures him it can be done, with the right pilot.

"Well, let's get upstairs, 'cause they're coming from below and we might get sandwiched, if we don't hurry," Says Dingane moving up the stairs with his rifle ready.

We follow behind Dingane up the stairs. My shoulder is feeling worse and getting even more stiff. I just keep thinking that the pills better kick in soon or I won't be much help for the rest of the day.

. . .

SURPRISINGLY, we get to the top of the floor without any exchange of fire. Not far from the stairs are two large wooden doors.

"Bryan, why don't you open the door using your left hand and we'll move in first," Suggests Jake.

I nod and get ready. I count down mouthing one, two, three. I yank the door, but it doesn't open at all. I try again, but it won't budge. I try the other door and it's just as stubborn.

We look at each other because we can hear soldier's footsteps climbing the stairs not very far below us. Jake pushes me to the side and shoots the door, splintering the fine wood and crushing the metal handle. Jace kicks the door, jarring it loose.

The two of them open the doors quickly.

"Move in," Jake orders then grabs Dingane by the shoulder.

"Take this and do your best to slow them down," He hands a grenade to him and points to the stairs.

The three of us move down a hall quickly but cautiously. The walls have pictures of people on them as if there were successors to Rev. At the end of the hall, it opens up bigger and there is a service desk.

We are a few feet away from the end of the hallway and still no sign of anyone. Jace and Jake, each on different walls, move down to the corners checking the opposite direction.

Dingane fires a few shots down the stairs. Rev fires back at him.

I move up once it's clear and take the left side. Behind the service desk is a wall separating offices from the lobby.

"Dingane, take position here," Jake points to the lobby area.

Dingane runs quickly down the hall towards us.

"There are a lot of them," He says.

"We just need to get to the roof," says Jake while looking at his watch.

We keep moving office to office and find them all locked.

"Whether there are people in there or not we need to keep moving," Jake whispers. "Find the stairs to the roof,"

Gunfire is being exchanged in the hallway behind us.

"We better pull him out of there." I think to myself

"Jake, Jace, I'm going back to help Dingane," I say tracing my steps back to the lobby.

Once there I see Dingane on the ground against a wall using a pistol to shoot blindly around the corner. I'm confused until I notice his bloody arm.

I begin firing down the hall. It's only then that I notice we have to move out quickly. There are probably fifteen men, most of them have automatics and two are holding large shields. We have no chance of pushing them back.

"Did you use your grenade?" I ask.

He nods. "It didn't do a thing against their shields,"

I grab one of my grenades and toss it high, bouncing it off the wall and behind the shields.

Boom!

I help Dingane up and tell him to run. I shoot a few bullets and run around the service desk wall.

"Where are you guys?" Jace asks.

"Getting past the offices. Where are you?" I ask.

"Turn left and head all the way down past the cubicles then make a right," He replies.

I hear the soldiers behind me yelling in rage, ready to give it all they got. I tell Dingane the directions and tell him to go ahead. His arm is bleeding pretty bad and he isn't looking too good.

I turn and shoot down the hall just to deter them. A few soldiers fire back and then one guy just sprints down the hall shooting as though he were invincible. Hiding behind the corner, chunks of wood begin blowing off the wall.

Figuring he is just aiming high, I decide to go low. I step back one step and then lunge forward onto my knees, past the corner. I land a shot on his shoulder, causing him to lose his balance and he falls back shooting into the ceiling. Once the other soldiers realize their lunatic isn't in the way, they begin firing again. I barely avoid their shots diving back behind the corner.

"Where are you? The first Falcon has flown by already. One more and then our getaway is here," Jace says, sounding quite upset.

Thinking Dingane should be there by now I look down the stretch of cubicles and to my surprise he is lying face down.

I peek back down past the offices and the soldiers have managed to get one shield into the hallway. Bullets break up more of the wall and I breath in the dust of it. I stand and fire blindly around the corner.

Jake says something indiscernible and I look behind me. He is helping Dingane, by dragging him.

I hear a familiar sound in a short moment of silence. I back up from the hall as a grenade bounces and rolls right into where the hallways intersect. I turn and dive down towards the cubicles.

Boom!

Shrapnel flys.

My landing is hard, but I don't stay on the ground for long. I continue to run past the cubicles towards the last turn before the stairs.

Bullets scatter just as I'm turning the corner.

Jake and Dingane are struggling because there aren't any stairs, it's a ladder and Dingane has no strength.

I quickly fire back around the corner and see the soldiers have gained on us without much caution. Their numbers have seemed to increase too.

"Grab his collar and I will push from below," I yell.

I do a few more shots to hold them off a little longer, then I run for the ladder.

Jake is half way up the ten-foot ladder by the time I get my shoulder under Dingane. I put my rifle in my left hand and use my right to grab the rungs.

When I get near the top, Jace helps pull Dingane up, relieving my shoulder. Then, I realize my left shoulder is feeling pretty good.

I take one last look down the hall and see a guy peek around the corner. He realizes we are escaping. I fire with poor aim, but stall the soldier.

"Pull me up!" I yell as my hand touches the hatch.

As Jake and Jace pull me up to the roof, gunshots go off. We avoid the open hatch and then Jace tosses a grenade down and closes the door.

Boom.

"Here's our ride," Jake says as a Falcon does a spiral descent and sprays dust and pebbles up.

I help Jake get Dingane up and onto the aircraft. The pilot looks back at us and tells us to hurry. A few bullets spray the Falcon from soldiers on other roofs, I suppose. Jace fires back at the hatch we just came out of, to make sure they don't come out prematurely. He then turns and climbs into the Falcon and we close the door.

We sit down and are relieved.

THE FALCON FLIES UP QUICKLY and out range of the raining bullets. We bandage up Dingane who is on the edge of his life.

"Where are we going?" The pilot asks.

Jake looks at him with regret.

"We need to go back to the outskirts," He looks at me and I at him.

"How are we going to get back in there?" I ask.

He doesn't answer.

Dingane is coming to, a little.

"Stay with us man," Jace says.

I loosen up some. "We made it," I say quietly.

"What?" Jake asks.

I look over to him and smile. "We made it."

He smiles too and looks at Jace. "Yeah, somehow. We accomplished a lot," He says.

"Who knows what tomorrow will bring, but whatever happens, we'll get through it," says Jake.

IT ONLY TAKES a few minutes to get back to our camp. The pilot lands down. We help Dingane out and bring him into camp. The pilot stays with us talking, about how reinforcements should be here tomorrow.

"What reinforcements?" Jake asks.

"Officer Cortez told me there are a couple hundred coming," The pilot says.

We all look at him in disbelief.

"He didn't tell me that," says Jake as we set Dingane down on the ground.

"Where is Officer Cortez right now?" I ask.

"He is out scouting the area. I have to get going though. Let me know if I can help again. The name is Grant by the way. I am the most likely to do what I did earlier. The two other pilots were a little hesitant to get that close to the city,"

Jake puts out his hand to shake Grant's.

"We really appreciate it. We would have died within a few minutes if you hadn't been there,"

Grant shakes his hand.

"Just doing my job. Let me know if you need help again,"

He walks out of the house.

Dingane is looking up at us through his nearly closed eyelids.

"Thank you,"

"You're going to be okay Dingane," Jace assures him.

"I'm going to get a hold of Officer Cortez and figure out what is going on.

Someone, stay with him and get him some water," Jake says and leaves.

"We need all the reinforcements we can get," Jace says. He grabs a bottle of water and tries to help Dingane drink.

"Yeah, there would be a slim chance of getting into the city a second time. Even if we could, they have too many men for five of us to handle," I say, setting my rifle against the wall.

Dingane barely takes the water before refusing more. Jace screws on the cap on and sits down next to Dingane and assesses the wound on Dingane's arm. The fabric wrapped around his arm is soaked in blood.

"Get me the first aid kit," He orders.

I find the white box with a red cross on it. Jace opens it and takes out the gauze.

I hear vehicles pulling up, so I grab my gun and look out the door.

Jake is standing out there just waiting for the vehicles, so I figure they are our men.

"Is that Officer Cortez?" I ask.

"Yeah,"

The vehicles stop, creating a waist high dust cloud as they slow down. Officer Cortez gets out of the lead vehicle. Jake doesn't hesitate to ask about the reinforcements.

"Yes, they will be here early tomorrow morning. They don't have much H.E.R.O training but they are active military," Cortez says excitedly. "I am so glad you guys are okay. It sounded like you were in an extraordinarily bad situation,"

Jake looks back at me standing in the doorway.

"Yeah, it was almost fatal. But we were fortunate we had Grant's and the other pilots' help. We also got our message out there to every person wearing a communication device,"

Cortez nods his head.

"That has made a big impact. I dropped a couple men off in a moment of isolation while driving through the city. They reported to me, a few rebellious squads have created quite a stir in the last half hour. It's likely more rebels will follow. Once we get more men tomorrow, we will be able to put pressure on Rev and they will have to use all they have to even stand a chance against us," He says, then turns to the driver of his Humvee. "Park over there,"

"Officer Cortez, do you have a medic with you?" I ask.

"Yes. Daniel, your assistance is needed!" Cortez yells back.

A short, bulky man runs up and I wave to him to come into the house. He relieves Jace from helping Dingane.

The Humvees park and everyone begins settling in for the night. I am excited for a good meal.

The sun lowers below the horizon and nocturnal animals begin making noises. Erin and Luke get back from being up on the jungle line. While eating dinner, everyone is sharing their stories from that day. Even the spies we have in the city shared what they saw of the rebellion. One of them tells us how a few blocks became filled with rebels only a few minutes after getting our message.

· · ·

AFTER DINNER, I get called into a meeting with Officer Cortez, Jake, Jace, Erin, Luke and a few other soldiers.

A group of 15 people, including myself, meet together on the second floor of a building not far outside base camp. The building is just brick and mortar with only a table inside. Trash is scattered here and there on the dusty concrete floor. Cortez stands behind the table, where he sets up a map of the city.

"This is the map of the city and we are here. There's no doubt Rev knows our general location, but only for tonight. Tomorrow, we will have reinforcements first thing in the morning. This includes just over 200 men, additional vehicles, weapons, and food. H.E.R.O estimates we should be done with this operation within a month. We can thank the rebellion you guys created for this sped-up take-back of the city," Cortez pauses for a moment while looking into the group.

He looks back down at his map. "We'll have a platoon drive here, as that is where some reinforcements will be dropped off," He points to the northwest side of the city. "Others will be here and here. A few will be dropped off on the back side of the city to put pressure on all sides. If we make them surrender, then we can get more information about other plans they have. If not, we will exterminate them," He pauses again and begins pacing the room.

"There is one more thing I want to mention. There will be beasts or creatures, whatever you want to call them, "mutants". Rev has been working on changing humans into part animals and insects. Now, I doubt they have many. The transformation takes some time and the word from our inside guys suggest that only a few weeks ago, no actual human beings were being tested. I warn you so that your mind is prepared for what no mind could comprehend, except in stories and fantasy films. If you come across these mutant beings, you must take them out as well. Now everyone, we can take this city. Don't be hasty, just be smart and work together," Cortez steps back at the head of the table.

"Any questions?" He asks.

A soldier about five-foot ten, near the back of the room, raises his hand.

"Is it plausible to say these mutant beings will be more powerful or is it more of a fear factor to throw us off?" He says, crossing his arms.

"Once you meet one and live, tell us all about what you find out. We just don't know,"

There are some chuckles in the room.

Another person raises their hand.

"Do you want us to bring one back alive for research? I think that would be very helpful for the military to know..."

The man stops, seeing that Cortez is shaking his head.

"No, we don't want to bother with trying to haul one back to base until everything is over. Let your officers worry about that. For now, we just want to end Rev's abrasive stay,"

No one else has any questions.

"Okay, you will be directed where to go in the morning. Go get your rest,"

We begin leaving when Officer Cortez asks that my squad stay for a second.

"Tomorrow, you five will be on the far side of the city. All our attention has been from here, and its possible some of Rev's most important men will try to escape from any point that doesn't have soldiers. Your job will be to make sure no one gets past you. A few Falcons will be on that side as well,"

Jake turns to us. "I think we are up for the challenge,"

We all nod, even though today we pushed our luck trying to handle a task with just the 5 of us, plus Dingane.

"Alright, 5:30 is your departure time. We will keep in touch throughout the day tomorrow. You're dismissed," Says Cortez.

Cortez and the five of us leave the building to go back to the camp. Once at base camp, I get ready for bed. I notice that Luke and Erin kind of stick around each other a lot. They eat and sleep near each other and their assignments always seem to leave them together. It doesn't matter to me, I just started to notice it.

I brush my teeth and retire to my sleeping bag inside a dirt hut. Jake and Jace come in too, shining their flashlights around.

"It will be interesting to see what we run into tomorrow," Jake says.

"It's incredible that Rev has figured out how to cross genetics between humans and animals," Jace says.

I just can't imagine what those mutants would look like. I guess they would be different colors, leopard skin, maybe stronger, like a gorilla.

"Bryan, how's your shoulder?" Jake asks.

"It's pretty good. Still sore but I think I will take a pain reliever tomorrow morning," I reply, remembering my near-death experience.

"That was some day we had,"

They both nod. "Yeah, it wasn't too bad until those last few minutes," Says Jace.

"It was kind of fun, jumping from building to building though," Jake adds.

"Let's do it again tomorrow," I say rolling over.

"That's the plan," says Jace.

14

We Finally Meet

THERE IS a light through some haze that just won't turn off. It is blinding somehow through all of the mist in front of me. Strange shadows keep sweeping past me a few feet away. I call out to Jake, but there isn't a soul around. I'm dressed in my combat gear, but I have no gun. The sky rains with streaks of black ash.

Then, just as I look back down at the ground, a mechanical dog jumps at me!

I awake in a pool of sweat.

My breathing is rapid and my mouth is dry. I reach for my canteen in the dark and take a drink. My dream begins to fade from my memory. I look at the clock and it's four in the morning.

Trying to calm my thoughts, I think about things that make me happy. I wonder how my family is doing. I wonder what life is like under the protection of walls. Once the adrenaline of my dream dissipates, I relax and concentrate on falling asleep, which eventually works.

I WAKE up to people yelling and Jake is shaking me.

"Get up! Get up, Bryan!

A bomb goes off nearby. I jump to my feet. Jace and I quickly grab our gear and fully suit up. Once the three of us are ready, we listen to Cortez as he instructs people over the headset.

"Rev is coming our way. About 500 men. Everyone, get in a vehicle and hold this base camp down,"

I look at the clock and it's just past five. We sprint out of the hut and find a Humvee that's not occupied. But just as we get in, Cortez tells us to head further to the tree line. So, we jump back out and run past the huts.

"Erin, Luke, where are you guys?" Jake asks.

"We're heading for a Humvee," Luke replies.

"Get to the tree line. That's an order," says Jake, as we keep dashing through the streets.

"Copy that," Luke says.

Once on the tree line, we find Officer Benson and a few of his soldiers.

"Where are the other two?" He asks.

"They're coming," Jake replies.

We turn and look at the village down below.

"We just need to last one hour until back up comes," I say.

One of Benson's soldiers hands Jake a sniper rifle with a couple of magazines. "Take this, and these,"

Jake takes them.

"Great, I will give this to Luke when he gets here. But for now, let's see what's going on,"

Jake peers through the scope and narrates the commotion.

"There are at least 10 Humvees coming, one tank and..." He stops.

"Two mechs,"

He puts the sniper rifle down.

"We don't stand a chance of holding down the base," Jace grabs the sniper from him to have a look.

"How far out are they?" I ask.

"Just a few miles," Jake shakes his head.

"There are a couple drones too. They are about 500 feet high. I count four of them," Informs Jace.

Jake and Benson talk to Cortez about a plan to stay alive for the next 45 minutes.

"We can't just drive around and waste gas for 45 minutes," Benson says.

"We don't stand a chance against this army," Cortez says, losing hope.

"All we can do is retreat until we have more firepower," Benson replies

"We have to make some kind of stand. Don't we have a few rocket launchers? Even if we have to slowly retreat in the process," Jake says.

Cortez is quiet for a minute.

"Okay, that is probably the best option. Send some snipers down and I'll get the rocket launchers. However, I just called in Grant for you guys and I need you on the other side of the city," Says Cortez.

A few of Bensons' soldiers run down to the village to give our soldiers more sniper rifles. It's only a few minutes later that Grant comes spiraling down onto the field below the tree line. Luke and Erin meet us there on the Falcon.

"It took you guys long enough," Jace says.

"Hey, we got here just in time. We were helping the wounded," Luke pushes Jace.

Grant takes us up and ascends into the clouds.

"I previously found a quiet spot for you guys. Officer Cortez also told me to give you that crate when you land," says Grant.

There is a large army green crate strapped down in the midst of us. As we fly over the city, I begin to wonder if we really do have a chance against Rev. They have 500 soldiers coming down on the west side of the city. They must have more to cover the other sides, right? We are not equipped to handle 2000 thousand soldiers. We are only receiving 200 soldiers today.

The jet slows down.

"Hold on, we're going to descend," We begin the spiral descent. Once we land, unload the large crate, and make sure there isn't anything else we left on the Falcon, we thank Grant and clear the take off zone. After he takes off, we let the dust settle to assess our surroundings.

"It looks a little nicer than the other side of town," Erin says.

"Yeah, but it's still no paradise," says Luke, as if we needed to be reminded.

"Grab the crate and move it into the corner," Jake orders, pointing to the side of a building that makes an L-shape.

The four of us follow his orders.

"Let's see what we were left with," Jace says unlatching the crate. A side panel falls down to the ground with a thud, creating more dust. We all look inside anxious, like it's Christmas and we're five years old again.

"Rockets," Luke points out.

"A grappling hook and gun," says Erin.

"Grenades and a turret," Jace pulls out the turret.

"Let's go scout out the area before we get too cozy here," Says Jake.

He looks very alert as I guess we all should, but something is different about him. I guess it's a bit eerie here because it's dead quiet.

We check the building next to us and both floors are clear. There's more furniture on this side of town than the last.

"I want a mile radius checked. The quickest way to do that is to split up. North, east, south, west," Jake points to each of us with one hand and indicates where to go with the other hand. I take the south side, making my way into the alley where trash has been rotting.

There is a little courtyard off to my left with a garden that appears very dead. Some of the buildings have structures that seem like a maze. A two-story building with a sky bridge, meeting up with another building 30 yards away with a home underneath the bridge.

I keep walking through the alley, then out to the street and back to the alley to make sure I don't miss anything unusual. A few cats startle me as I investigate every small noise. It turns out, for the whole mile, there isn't one person here. I head back the way I came, still not used to the smell of the garbage.

I'm about to cross the last street before meeting back at the location, when my eye catches a man down on the right about 100 feet. I step back into the alley and peek around the corner to observe. The man is dressed in Rev combat gear and has a rifle in his hands. He is walking in my direction.

"This is Bryan, I have someone in my sights 100 feet east of the crate."

"Bryan, I'm across the street. Luke, you had the east end where are you at?" Jake says.

"I'm halfway back. I haven't seen anyone yet," replies Luke.

The man stops, looks both left and right then turns around.

"It appears the man is doing a basic patrol of the area. But he must have seen our jet," says Jake.

"Let's follow him. Maybe we can get some information out of him," I suggest.

After discussing for a minute what we should do, we agree that the man can be worth interrogating. We make our way down, with one of us always watching the street. After walking half a mile, the man walks into a building on my side of the street and closes the door behind himself.

"That's interesting. He is either a slacker or there is more than what meets the eye," says Luke.

"Probably a slacker," Erin concludes.

"Alright, let's close in on the building," Jake says, then makes a sprint across the street to meet up with me.

We cover each side of the building. The windows are the perfect height to peer into. The building itself is rectangular and not very wide, maybe 12 feet from side to side and 20 feet long. It is one story making it possible to be hoisted up and grab the roof.

"I can see a few pieces of furniture but no man," says Luke.

I look through the window and see a living room set up. I hear a door open but can't tell where it is.

"I got a visual, he just used the john," Jace says. "He has a pistol at his hip and a couple of grenades. Let's just take him out. I don't think he'll surrender very easily and I would hate for someone to get injured over one guy. It's either that or we wait 'til he leaves again and catch him a few feet from his door," He gives the ultimatum.

"You're right. Let's wait it out," Jake concludes.

We just stay low on the side of the building with shade, just waiting.

WE GET a few updates about the reinforcements. It sounds like our men were able to slow down Rev long enough so our soldiers didn't have to retreat completely back into the jungle. Air support came in and did a number to Rev's 500, but we lost two jets and even more men. However, we have men infiltrating the city right now. Reports of rebellion are on the rise.

The plan is working.

A HALF-HOUR GOES by and we are still sitting there. The man is just inside working on paperwork or something. It appears he gets some orders through his head set and begins packing a backpack.

"Get ready, I think he is going to leave," I inform everyone.

We hear his chair screech across the floor then a door opens.

"Front door in five seconds," Erin informs.

"On my signal," Jake says.

Jake and I move quietly to the front of the building. The door opens and the man walks out, closing the door behind him. With his rifle out, he just stands by the door.

Jake unexpectedly jumps out to tackle the man.

A shot goes off, but I can't tell where it made its home. They both fall on the ground and Erin gets there before me. She places her boot on the man's face and her rifle just above his eyes.

The soldier stops struggling.

"What was the last order you made to Rev?" Jake yells.

The man says nothing.

"Bind him and take him inside,"

We do.

The inside of the house has nothing unique about it but when we go through his backpack we find paperwork as previously seen through the window. Once we open the folder and examine the paperwork we find some very interesting things.

"What are these?" Jake asks flipping page after page.

The man doesn't say anything. Jace punches him across his face. The man feels the pain.

"Talk or else you'll get some more," Jace assures him.

Then he nods his head, wincing.

"Something is wrong with my mic. I wonder if it's defective,"

Then he awkwardly moves his head around.

"There is a zinging in my ear. It hurts," He exclaims.

We rip the earpiece off of him. Then he looks at Jace and mouths something a few times. Jace turns off the mic.

"Thank you. Now my superiors won't know what I am about to divulge. Those papers are the plans for more mutants to be created. They are one of Rev's lab reports about what combinations of animal genes may give the best results," The soldier says.

We are all taken back.

"I'm confused. Why are lab reports all the way out here in the boondocks?" Jake asks, with suspicion.

"I was supposed to meet another platoon out here yesterday to give them a copy of the report. My guess is it was to be used at another location," He looks down at the ground, embarrassed to reveal such information.

"So why are you still here?"

"The platoon had some issues with a group of rebels and couldn't make it," He says plainly.

"Why were you outside?" Jake asks.

"I was just told a caravan is evacuating some of their essential equipment and assets. Rev is picking me up on their way out. They said they will be here in a half-hour. I was going to do one more sweep of the area to make sure no one was around," He replies.

WE BEGIN THINKING of what we are going to do with the soldier.

"Let's tie him up and leave him here," Jace says.

"When they come for him they'll see that he is tied up and know we're here," says Luke.

"It doesn't matter. We are supposed to stop them from leaving anyways," Jace reminds us.

"Alright, we'll tie him up and then figure out what we'll do," Jake pulls out some cord from his pant pocket. We bind his wrists together and put him in the bathroom tied to the sink pipe.

"Come outside. Let's devise a plan,"

Jake walks out the front door and I grab the folder with all the lab reports on my way out.

We jog to the crate to pull out the heavy weapons.

"I'll take the turret," Jace informs.

"The rocket is mine," Erin says.

"I'll take the grappling hook," says Jake.

Luke and I look at each other.

"Let's split the extra rifle ammo and grenades," He says, seeing I got jipped.

He has a sniper rifle, so I take five grenades and four magazines.

"If anyone need's extra ammo or grenades you know how to reach me," I say dramatically.

They all smile.

"Let's make a plan. Rev should be here in about 15 minutes. Let's assume there is a caravan trying to leave the city. They will most likely be using multiple streets. I will get Grant to assess what street has the most vehicles and we'll focus on that one," Jake says.

We nod in agreement and then he continues.

"Once we get the vehicles to stop we'll give them all we got until they surrender,"

We all agree that's the best plan we have, since there are only four of us.

As Jake gets in touch with Grant, we listen to the radios of our soldiers attacking the city.

Soldiers on the North side of the city are making great progress supposedly due to a high number of rebels there. The South side is moving slowly in but just reported two mechs coming into the scene. As for the west side, where our base camp was, the casualties have been high, but the men we have there are slowly moving into the city. No one has yet reported mutants, so that's good.

Figuring someone should be on the lookout, I go into a building on the North side of the street and up to the second floor. I break a hole in the ceiling to get onto the roof. Looking at the city, I see a few of our falcons zipping by occasionally exchanging fire with turrets on top of skyscrapers. Then, I notice a haze rising in the distance outside of the city center. That must be Rev. These dirt roads don't help when trying to be stealthy.

"Guys, they're coming. We only have a few minutes before they're on us,"

"Bryan, stay there and keep giving us updates. Grant just informed me that there are two other streets besides this one that Rev is using. We are going to stay on this street because it has a large semi. The rest of us are heading up to the building we left the soldier in," Jake informs.

I look behind me to try and see them but I can't.

"Alright...I'll stay here," I say, thinking how much I hate to be left by myself at a time like this.

Two minutes roll by and the north side soldiers report having stormed a good section of the city. A minute later Rev's engines can be heard. Their trail of dust is coming closer. My heart speeds up. I slip down back to the building's second story and wait by a window.

"You guys have approximately three minutes until they're on top of you," I say as I stand and wait looking out the thin glass window.

I begin hearing a faint noise. I can't quite put my finger on it but it isn't a Humvee. I move to another window and look around outside. I look up and see helicopters coming our way just above the caravan's dust bowl.

The Humvees zoom by at full speed.

"They just passed me and they have helicopters in the sky," I tell the others.

I look out the opposite window and see the helicopters also moving at full speed, definitely passing the caravan.

I then see a helicopter to the left of my position explode.

It falls to the ground in a ball of flames.

We must have some falcons helping us. I turn back to see the caravan still moving fast down the street. The Humvees have men using their turrets to take down the falcons. Then, a semi comes rolling by. Its trailer box is a medium gray with possibly an air conditioner on the top.

"A semi just passed," I say.

"We are about to engage Rev. They're slowing down. Erin, get the first vehicle. Jace, you got the second and Luke, third and fourth turrets," Jake says, giving the instructions. "Three, two, one. Now!"

I faintly hear an explosion down the street. Even with the Humvee machine guns still going off, I hear a second explosion more clearly, probably two blocks away. After looking out a window I see a large black cloud of smoke rises above the buildings.

The last Humvee drove by a minute ago, so I leave the building. I stay next to the buildings, jogging to the other's location. A falcon swoops down and sends a missile into the midst of the caravan making a Humvee flip into a building. However, the falcon gets heavy fire from the rest of the Humvees.

"Bryan, we need you here," Jake says.

"I am almost there. The last Humvee is slowing down. I'll be there in two minutes," I keep jogging down the street.

When the last Humvee stops, a man gets out carrying something large. Thinking it's a turret and he knows I'm coming, I hide behind a building. To my surprise, he is looking up and then he takes a knee while pointing his gun towards the sky. The soldier pulls the lever, causing a large green beam to come out the end. That's when I realize he is trying to blind the falcon pilot. I reveal my position and fire only a few shots at him before the Humvee turret turns down towards me. I evade the turret, slipping back behind the building. Large rounds break off chunks of the building.

"Jake, warn air support of large lasers trying to blind them at the last Humvee's position,"

I find an alley so I can move closer up and change my position.

"Copy that," Jake says with a ton of gun fire in the background.

I find an alley right next to the last Humvee on its left side. I hear a large explosion above me in the sky. When I look up, it is a falcon falling with fire streaming off of it. I pull out a grenade and toss it underneath the Humvee and get out of the alley.

Boom!

The grenade goes off and then I hear soldiers yell in agony. The turret operator doesn't know where to look. After panning across my alley, I punch his card.

"The first and second Humvee are destroyed. The third is still active," Jake informs me.

"The Humvee directly behind the semi is taken out," I add to the list.

I move forward up the alley, jumping over trash cans. I get to another alley on my right and take it towards the street. A soldier on the other side of the street sees me and I quickly fire, but miss. The soldier takes cover and I retreat back to the alley I came from.

"The semi doors are opening," says Luke.

"Probably reinforcements," Jace says.

"Bryan, can you see what they're unloading?" Jake asks.

"Hold on,"

I see a path up to the roof by climbing back and forth from window ledges of mirroring buildings. It only takes a minute before I am on top.

I slide myself across the red shingles up to the peak of the roof and look down. The semi doors are open, but a shadow is cast down making it difficult to see what is inside.

"They haven't unloaded anything yet," I update everyone.

"Oh no, we have mutants coming from the north," Erin panics.

I look left and see two different figures sprinting across the rooftops.

"I see two on the roof tops," I pull my scope up in front of me.

My scope doesn't help in getting details, but they appear to be running fast and they're agile.

"Three more in the alleys below," Jace says quickly.

"Luke, take out the mutants on the roof," Jake orders. "Keep firing on the vehicles Erin,"

I keep an eye on the semi, waiting to see what they are going to unload. The semi shakes a little and then a lot. The men that were inside it, begin quickly exiting without anything more in their hands than when they entered. Still shaking, the gray semi creeks with stress.

Then I see it.

Tall, silver, and metal.

The famous being that has intimidated the entire city.

The alien emerges from the metal box slightly hunched from being too tall for the semi.

"Jake, guys...the alien is coming...out of the semi," I say in disbelief.

I don't fully believe it is an alien, but it is quite impressive and unordinary enough to question what I previously believed.

It must be eight feet tall. Its armor is silver with some lighter gray/blue accent near the edge of each individual piece. Blades on the forearm stick out, coming to a point near the elbows. The helmet is a full-face piece of metal coming to a point at the chin and three points on top of the head. The eyes or visor are only flat light blue triangles that cannot change from being angry. The feet are not shaped like human feet, but resemble hooves in metal form.

I hear more engines behind me and to my surprise they are our men.

"We have reinforcements," I tell the others.

A Humvee, full of our men, fire at Rev's soldiers on the ground near the back of their caravan. I look past the men down the road where more of our men are coming in quads and Humvees. It's then, I see the newly arriving Humvee being torn apart by vicious rounds of machine gun fire. My focus is now on that Humvee. Bullets rain across from side to side taking out the turret and a handful of our soldiers.

I look back to fire at the experienced enemy gunner, only to find that it's the alien.

It fires a large gun that a normal soldier would struggle holding let alone firing.

The alien quickly does something to the gun and then fires again at the Humvee's windshield.

A blue pellet sticks onto the windshield and after a second the pellet explodes. The explosion rips apart the windshield and kills the driver.

"Two mutants left," I hear Jace say.

I look back at the reinforcements behind the demolished Humvee as they begin scattering down different alleyways.

"It's going to take all of us to bring down this alien thing," I try to describe the difficulty of this one mega soldier.

I pull out a grenade and toss it down by the alien.

The alien moves just before the grenade hits the ground and hides behind a Humvee.

I'm not sure if I am more impressed by the awareness of my grenade or the relatively quick reaction the alien displayed. Immediately after the grenade goes off, the alien stands up and finds me.

I roll away from the edge of the roof, but my momentum causes me to slide down further than expected.

Bullets shatter the shingles where I had laid seconds before.

I continue to slide off the roof. I'm able to put one foot on the ground and push myself into a roll. I quickly get to my feet and notice I'm in a small courtyard.

I hear soldiers running into the alley so I push my shoulder into a door, breaking it in.

Jake said something while I broke the door down, but couldn't hear what he said. "Jake, repeat," I say softly not to immediately give away my location.

Voices of soldiers come closer.

"That door. Move in there," One of them says.

"I said, we are making our way down there. One mutant left and we're not sure where it's at," Jake repeats.

"Copy that,"

I make my way to the other side of the building. I find a door that goes outside and open it. After checking my surroundings, it appears to be clear. I leave the building and head to a window I know I crossed while inside. I quietly crouch underneath the window and wait for the soldiers to come by. It's only then that I notice a soldier's rifle sticking out around the corner of the same building.

The soldiers inside are crossing the window and I decide I will be quick enough to throw the grenade and take out the soldier around the corner.

I pull the pin and toss it into the window where it shatters the glass alarming the man around the corner.

Just in time I pull up my gun and shoot the soldier while I fall backwards onto my back. I roll away from the wall as the grenade goes off. The rest of the window shatters, raining bits of glass onto me.

As I get up, I notice the soldier I shot a second ago is reaching for his gun so I make sure he doesn't get it by landing a lethal round.

Then a gun fires behind me somewhere and I turn around to see a Rev soldier fall over, from behind a corner.

I take a slow approach and look around the corner. To my relief, it is our reinforcements.

"Thanks for that," I say walking around the corner.

"No problem, sir,"

"If you guys will take care of the soldiers, my squad will take out the alien," I say, immediately feeling weird I said alien.

"What? The alien? Is it actually an alien?" Some of the soldiers ask.

"Sorry, no. It is what they want us to believe, but it's not. It's code... Just pick off Rev's soldiers," I say taking off towards the street.

"Jake, where are you guys?" I ask, breaking down another door. "Roof tops. The alien has been returning heavy gun fire. We can only get a few shots on him before having to dodge a blaze of bullets," He says.

"I will try to distract him so Erin can get a rocket on him," I offer.

I look out around a corner trying to find exactly where the alien is. I follow a stream of bullets back to a Humvee where the alien is taking cover.

I make my way back past the courtyard I had fallen into. I have to get behind the alien so I can pull his view away from the others. Now two buildings away from the alien, I peer around the corner down the street. Rev's soldiers are almost completely gone. A few are shooting into alleys and up at Erin and Jake. I grab a grenade and toss it at the alien's feet. He quickly moves away from it into the alley as the grenade goes off. He probably wasn't affected by it much, but now I have his attention.

The alien quickly looks around the corner of his alley and fires into mine. Just the few bullets he shoots makes part of the brick wall crumble.

"Guys, I've got his attention," I say, anticipating their help.

"Hang in there," Luke says.

I look again around the corner and the alien fires again, this time the shots impale the wall my back is against and I fall forward from the bricks being dislodged.

"Bryan, are you okay?" Jace asks.

"Bryan, get up, it's coming for you," he says frantically.

Another couple rounds go through the brick wall. I get up off the ground and move away from the street.

"My rounds aren't doing much," Luke says, which frightens me, knowing that he has a strong sniper rifle.

I lean against a wall with a grenade ready. Just as the alien gets to the alley, it dives further down the street and a rocket hits the side of the building.

I hear the alien return fire and the ricochet of bullets somewhere further away. I decide to get on top of a roof and lob grenades at the alien. I find my way up, using a trash can and window ledges to another red shingled roof.

An explosion goes off up the road.

"Jace!" I hear Erin yell.

A Humvee is up in flames where the explosion went off.

I lob a grenade down and duck before being seen.

"Almost got him, Bryan. He is too quick. I have been watching his behavior and it appears he has some kind of radar that informs him of threats," says Luke.

I decide to try again.

"Erin, get ready," I say while lobbing my last grenade, this time bouncing it off the opposing building down near the alien. The alien rolls away into the middle of the street. Erin's rocket comes soaring down. The alien notices the threat only in time to not get directly hit. Only a foot or two away from the impact, the alien is propelled back towards where the last grenade exploded near a building. His metal body slams into a tan brick wall while his large gun is flung into an alley.

"Nice shot!" I exclaim.

The alien's upper body is through the wall with its legs sticking out of a cloud of dust.

"Shoot another at him," Luke says.

"That was my last rocket," Informs Erin.

"I guess a grenade will do,"

Erin slides off a roof and throws one inside the building through the hole the alien created. But then, almost immediately, the grenade is vomited back out and explodes.

"What the," Erin says. "What just happened?"

It is then that the alien begins to get up and the rubble around it is removed.

I begin shooting exhaustively into the hole through the dusty air. I hear my rounds hitting metal and then after a magazine of rounds, the alien springs out of the hole and makes a charge at me. Luke fires a bullet into its back and then another, but it doesn't do much.

The alien now only one building away from mine leaps up onto the building and begins climbing. I still try shooting at it even though I don't think it's making a difference.

Pulling itself up onto the flat roof I realize if I drop down it could just smash me on its landing. I realize that my life is about to end under the blow of some war machine known as an alien. I can see its hands, metal and deadly with almost pointed finger tips, ready to crush my skull. Half of its body armor is mangled from the rocket, making him look even more gnarly than before.

"Bryan, catch the hook," Jake says and I look down to the ground to find him. Swinging the hook on the line, he throws it up and I nearly lose my balance catching it.

"Attach it to him and we'll pull him down," Jake says quickly.

I swing my rifle around to my back. The alien looks down at the others on the ground then back at me. Its metal framed eyes make it hard to read what it might be thinking. The weight of the alien begins to show under the cracks forming in the roof it stands on. Then he steps forward and a sound comes out of it that gives me the chills.

"You are a fool. They will be coming soon and there is nothing you can do that will match their strength and knowledge," The alien says, in a deep and drawn out speech, accompanied by vibrating metal.

Then the alien jumps the gap completely, crushing the red shingles under its foot. I step back a little trying to decide how to hook the metal beast without being smashed. It takes another step towards me, but it breaks more shingles and slightly slips downward. Each time it takes a step considerable effort is made not to slip.

I have no choice except to die or make an absolutely risky move.

Obviously, I don't want to die.

I have withstood the travel to space and the blowing up of asteroids.

The first initial attack of Rev from Carl Dagoon and the attempted kidnapping on the beach. No mechanical dog could stop my journey.

All these thoughts rush my mind.

I make the decision and run towards the alien.

It takes a step forward while cocking back its right arm. I make some jukes and then stop to throw the grappling hook around its left leg.

"Now!" I yell.

The alien throws his punch, but loses momentum as his left foot slips. Able to dodge its punch, I pull my rifle off my back and move from its reach.

Jake, Luke, and Erin are pulling the grappling hook that is causing the alien to slide off the roof. At first, the alien struggles to stay on the now crumbling roof, but then decides to abandon the cause.

It pushes off the roof with little elegance and falls to the ground with a loud clank and thud. The three below scatter from its landing zone. With weapons drawn they begin yelling at the alien.

"Give up! It's over," They bark.

It appears the fall didn't have much of an effect on the alien, because it begins rolling over to get up. We all fire at the metal beast. Nothing seems to phase it.

The alien lunges for Jake, pushing him back ten feet before rolling backwards on the ground.

Next, the alien turns towards Luke, but tries to shield its face from the rounds we are shooting. With moderate strides, the alien approaches Luke and takes a swing, but Luke partially dodges it. Still being knocked against a wall and his gun flung a few feet away, the alien focuses on Erin who has already used an entire magazine.

With little options, Erin tosses a grenade down in front of the alien and he just walks through the explosion. However, it affects its right leg and the alien takes a knee.

I shoot down into the back of its head and neck, knowing those are the most vulnerable areas of anyone's armor. It quickly responds to my shots and gets up. It takes large strides towards Erin, but it stumbles from its injured leg and falls to the ground. Erin backs up now out of weapons.

The alien lies there, grunting and making efforts to get up in spite of pain. It only takes another minute to see that it's over. The beast has died.

I find a way down to a window ledge and go through a building to get down to the street. Once there, I find Erin helping Luke get to his feet.

"Help Jake!" Erin orders.

Jake is lying on the ground motionless but with his gun in hand. As I get to him he tries to lift his gun.

"Jake, it's Bryan," I say, gently pushing his gun down.

"Bryan?" He says while wincing.

"Yeah. Where are you hurt?" I ask.

He just moves his head back and forth. A few gun shots are still going off somewhere in the alleys. Jake raises his gun again.

"Jake, you're okay. We'll get you out of here soon enough,"

I begin channeling air support.

"Grant, we need you now! Come back to where you previously dropped us off," I demand.

"Who is this? Is this Squad 7?" He asks.

"Yes. This is Bryan. Jake and Jace are both in need of medical attention," I say realizing that Jace is alone.

"Bryan, I am on my way. It will be 8 minutes until I'm there. Hang tight,"

I tell Erin and Luke to head over to the landing zone, but Luke decides he can make it himself and Erin can help me with Jake and Jace. Erin begins dragging Jake by his vest. I go to the last spot Jace was and find one of our soldiers assessing him away from the flaming Humvee.

"How is he?" I ask, kneeling down beside them.

"He isn't very responsive. He must have been close to the explosion," The soldier reports.

"We have a falcon coming. I'll take him to the landing zone," I begin to pick him up.

"Do you need some help?" The soldier asks.

Seeing that it is down the road a bit, I accept his offer. To my surprise he calls for a Humvee.

We get Jace on the other side of the burning vehicle and meet up with the Humvee. Jake and Erin are both inside as well. I tell the Humvee to go without me and I tell Erin I will be there in a few minutes.

As the Humvee takes off, I notice more of our soldiers coming out from the alleys.

"Who is your commanding officer?" I ask one of them.

"Officer Blake," A man says walking up before the other soldier can answer.

"Officer Blake, can you secure this area until Officer Cortez gives you further instructions?" I ask quickly.

"I will take care of it, but for the record I don't need Cortez's orders. By the way, what is your name, soldier?" He asks, a little amused by my request.

"It's Bryan Reed. I am in squad 7. My squad has just taken out the so-called alien..," Then, I remember that I haven't even revealed its face to know for a fact that it wasn't an alien.

"Walk with me," I say quickly spinning around.

The closer I get to it the faster I walk.

"What's going on?" Officer Blake asks.

"I haven't quite proved that it isn't an alien,"

Officer Blake huffs. "You can't actually believe..."

He stops talking as he realizes the size of the metal beast. Now, up close to it and not fighting for my life, I would say that it's over 9 feet tall.

I remember that I don't have much time before Grant arrives and begin to think I should stay here instead of leaving with the others. I kneel down at the head of the unknown creature. I find a few discreet latches on the helmet. It takes some work but I finally slip the helmet off revealing the truth.

"What in the world?" I freeze.

Slight gasps are made from others behind me.

"Mutated. A giant," I say. The head is human but oversized.

"Think of how many more are out there," Officer Blake says.

"What if this is just the beginning and Rev makes them even bigger," Another soldier says.

I stand up and begin to think of what I should do. Only after a few seconds do I decide that I can't leave yet.

"Grant, take the others to get medical care. I won't be boarding your falcon," I say.

"Copy that. Good luck down there Bryan."

I need to get this mutation into the hands of H.E.R.O.'s leaders and scientists. Then, I think about all the other mutants that were here in the area.

"Officer Blake, will you have your men round up the rest of the mutants? They shouldn't be more than a mile in diameter from this location,"

He only takes a moment to think, then nods his head.

"Yes, I think that would be wise," He then gives the order.

"Bryan, what is going on? I was told you weren't boarding the jet," says Erin frantically over the headset.

"I have to stay. There are things that I need to make sure get done before leaving," I tell her with determination.

I wait for a response, but there isn't one.

"I will be fine. Make sure the others get the medical attention they need," I say.

However, I see her emerge from an alley down the road and the falcon spirals up and takes off.

While Erin makes her way back to me, I contact Officer Cortez.

"Officer Cortez, we have taken down the alien,"

"What? Is this Bryan?" He replies as gunfire is heard in the background.

"Yes, listen, we have the alien and it's not what they say it is. It's a mutated man," I try to explain.

"Bryan, what is your location?" He asks. "I don't know where exactly, but it's down off the main streets Rev was trying to escape by,"

It takes a minute for him to reply and now Erin has reached me and the giant.

"Okay, you should be able to share your coordinates with me through your watch. We will send out a falcon to pick it up," He informs me.

I quickly figure out how to share my location and send it off.

Erin's face is in bewilderment.

"A giant. That is all this was," I say kicking its metal shell.

"That's not all it is. This is a fascinating breakthrough," She says changing expressions.

"The question is how they were successful in making all the mutations of the body work perfectly together. It is fairly simple to mutate this and that, but to get a human being equally balanced in all areas is astonishing," She exclaims.

I look at her with interest in what she has said.

"Bryan, listen. If this can be copied again and again, imagine how the world would change. If Rev can make all of their soldiers like this they will succeed in taking over the world."

I begin to acknowledge her point of view.

We stand there for a minute just thinking.

"Well, I just talked to Cortez. He is sending a falcon to pick up the mutants, to take back to headquarters," I inform her.

"Alright, so that's our ride out, with a bunch of stinky mutants," She says with some humor in her voice.

"No," I tell her.

"What do you mean? Officer Cortez told us that we needed to be on our way back by tomorrow," She says in confusion.

"I know and we can get back today, but there is something we need to pick up on the other side of the city," I tell her, tilting my head slightly hoping she knows what I'm talking about.

"Pick up? What do we need to...?" She stops and then gives me a look as if to say, "oh".

"No, wait. Are you talking about that...?"

I stop her and queue her to be quieter.

"...That black...stone thing?" She whispers.

I nod to end it because some soldiers are coming with a mutant.

We stop conversing about it.

"What do we have here?" I say examining the ugly creature.

"A mutant at your request sir," One of the soldiers redundantly declares.

The mutant's body is gray with black speckles clustered randomly on the body. The skin looks rough and thick. The face is a little saggy and its forehead has what looks to be a horn forming.

"It looks like Jace got that one," I say, noticing the size of the wounds. The mutant was no match against the turret.

A falcon fly's overhead and then circles back.

"That must be it. Will you guys take that body to that falcon?" I point to it as it lands down in the same field Grant used.

"Leave it outside until we get this guy loaded,"

I ask a soldier to use his Humvee to drag the giant over to the landing zone. He agrees and we hook some straps to the armor and drag him behind the vehicle.

It takes five of us with some difficulty to get the giant into the falcon. A few minutes later the other soldiers come with the rest of the mutants.

"Thanks for your help, Officer Blake,"

He nods. "No problem. If that is all, we have to get going. The city isn't going to save itself," He smiles.

I grab his arm as he starts to turn and leave.

"Well, actually if you could spare a vehicle. We need to get to the other side of the city,"

Officer Blake looks confused.

"Sorry, but we need these vehicles. We can't cram our men into only a few. We came completely full. Besides, we need you two in the city. There isn't any more fighting on the outskirts," He starts to question our need to be on the other side of the city.

"Yes, I know but we have to pick up important equipment that got left behind," I say.

"If we could at least get a ride to the city we will find a way to continue on," Erin jumps in.

He agrees, still suspicious of our intentions.

15

S ave The Egg

THE FALCON TAKES off and we climb into a Humvee that is packed already with Blake's men. I have to lay down on my back, on the floor of the Humvee in the midst of soldiers. Erin sits on the edge of a bench.

I feel every bump in the road.

"So, where were you guys stationed before this?" Erin asks.

"We guarded some of the bunkers of important people back in Washington," One of them reply.

"It was less brutal than this place," He adds with brows raised.

"That's kind of surprising," I say with my eyes closed trying to zone out the bumps.

"Yeah, I guess," The soldier says.

"Don't you think Rev would be interested in taking Washington?" Erin suggests.

"Yeah, but they probably didn't think they could overtake it, considering the U.S. military was heavily present," I reply.

"Okay, true but then why send any soldiers there at all," Erin replies with skepticism.

"Beats me. Like I have been saying to everyone, these are some dumb terrorists with distorted minds just like the rest of the terrorists out there. They can't get very far on their delusions," A soldier replies.

The rest of the ride is quiet.

It takes about 15 minutes before Officer Blake starts talking about the main battle grounds and the artillery Rev is using.

"Five mechs, two on the east side and 3 on the north side, heavy Humvees as we have seen and maybe a thousand Rev soldiers left," He announces.

"Oh, and some mechanical dogs. Whatever those are," He adds.

My eyes shoot open. "Those are not fun. Their shells are thick and just like real dogs they're fast with sharp teeth," I inform everyone while shaking my head.

"Wait, are you serious?" Another soldier asks, looking a little surprised.

I raise my eyebrows while giving a sincere nod.

"Bryan, Erin, where do you guys want to be let out?" Blake asks.

"Once you see conflict let us out. Oh, and Bryan, do you have a few magazines for me?" Asks Erin.

"Yeah I've got a few,"

"Well, I will do you one better. I'll swing out a little around the city just to make it a little easier," Officer Blake says.

"Thank you. We appreciate it," I reply.

"No worries,"

About five minutes later we get dropped off in front of a hotel. The street has some cars on it, which is unlike any other part of the area we have seen.

"Thanks again and good luck out there," We watch them leave toward the city.

"What's the plan now?" Erin asks.

"We should see if these cars work," I reply, breaking a window to a red four door car.

She agrees, partially because I am already doing it.

After a few minutes, I successfully hotwire the car. The gas tank is practically empty; it wouldn't be worth our time.

"It's empty," I let the car run the last bit of gas as I get out and slam the door.

"Probably siphoned," says Erin.

"Probably,"

We walk down the street and I try another car. It only has a pinch more gas than the last.

"Yeah, these have been siphoned," I say, disappointed.

We move down the road passing a few more cars figuring they are empty as well.

"This will take us the rest of the day to get there. Even then, we won't have a way to transport that...thing," Erin says.

She is right and I begin thinking that my plan was dumb to begin with. We agree to contact Officer Cortez again and see what kind of assistance we can get.

"Officer Cortez, it's Bryan again. Erin and I are trying to get back to the first camp area, back in the jungle. We need to pick up that strange black stone object we found there," I say hoping he doesn't find it unnecessary

"Okay, it took me a minute to remember what you were talking about, but okay go ahead," Cortez replies.

I guess I need to ask directly for assistance.

"We were also wondering if you could help us get there?" I try not to sound needy,"

"Uh, I don't think we can spare anyone at the moment. I suggest heading to the north side of town. I'm sure there is a vehicle that isn't too beat up," He says

We start jogging, weaving in and out of alleys.

. . .

IT'S about another five miles before we will get there. As we pass various buildings, we notice there are signs of shoot outs. This side of the city must have put up a fight against Rev, or it is the rough side of town.

"Alright, let's take a breather," I stop jogging once we get into an alleyway.

"Yeah," Erin replies, breathing just as heavy as me.

"So, what do you think that thing is?" She asks.

"What thing?" I ask then immediately remember.

"I don't actually have a clue. However, all the evidence from the site says it fell from the sky," I look at her, then right and left, as we cross a street diagonally.

"That's true. Could it be part of a satellite?"

"No, it didn't have any characteristics of an object that was attached to something else," I point out.

"I guess I don't remember much of its details," Erin says.

"Exactly! Because there wasn't much to it. It is black and smooth in shape, comparable to an egg,"

"Oh, and it had a perfectly cut addition sign or a cross on one end," Erin adds.

"Do you remember those weird symbols on it?" I ask looking back at her.

"Yeah, that was the most interesting thing about it,"

THE BOTH OF us don't talk for a few minutes and I just think of the object and what it could be. Of course, the most interesting thing it could be, is some object from aliens. Like myself, I think most people would come to that conclusion on first inspection. However, the most likely answer is, that it belongs to Rev since they are in the business of trying to scare and confuse everyone.

Rev is the most widespread terrorist group the world has ever known. Their influence is also the most widespread. I have to hand it to them, they have done things no one else has done, which is interesting considering they probably don't have the most scientists or engineers of any organization.

WE COME up to a building that has a picture of a bike on it and I begin to get an idea.

"Hey Erin, should we check to see if there are bikes inside there,"

"Sure, but I don't do tandem," She says seriously.

I bust the door down. The door swings all the way open, smacking the wall it's hanging on. The light switch doesn't work but from the window light, I can see a few bikes.

"Hey it's just our luck,"

I pick up a blue and green bike. I test the tires and they still have air in them. Erin grabs a bike, but finds it flat. She tries another and it appears to work.

We take them outside and begin to ride them down the street. Now in pure daylight my bike is obviously old and worn.

"How's your bike?" Erin asks, as each of her pedals squeak when they rotate.

"It's okay. Yours?"

"It's bad," She replies.

I bet we both look ridiculous riding bikes in full combat gear. The bikes aren't even mountain bikes. They're more of a beach cruiser style.

We take the bikes through a few alleys, occasionally having to lift them over trash. Eventually we get to the northside of the city and ditch the bikes just in case they attract Rev soldiers that may be on the outskirts.

We have been trying to listen to the radio about what is happening within the city, but until now the signal has been spotty.

"It sounds like Rev wasn't as strong as they thought," Erin shakes her head.

"They're fools that found enough fools to follow them," She adds.

"How does a crazy organization find or convince enough people to follow them?" I ask, utterly puzzled.

"That's a good question. The answer may be because of the economic crash. Everyone, in some way or another has a group or community they joined to survive. Maybe Rev offered more to the people that would serve them," Erin thinks out loud causing me to wonder if she is right.

After the announcement of asteroids threatening humanity, the economy completely tanked a year later. People joined societies and communities that solely sought the basics of life. Some were lies. Some groups took advantage of people while other groups proved worthy of joining. If Rev had more to offer to families for having the men serve in their military, then maybe that is how they have the numbers.

FINALLY, we are only a few blocks away from a site of used and abused military vehicles.

"Keep your eyes open for stragglers," I pull my weapon up more, prepared for contacts. We check the alleys, looking for any kind of movement. The closer we get to vehicles, we find bodies of both Rev and H.E.R.O soldiers. A vehicle here and there is on fire while some are flipped over or on their side.

"Bryan, are you listening to the radio on station 3?"

"No, why?" I ask.

"Turn to it,"

I quickly turn to station 3 and immediately I am very curious about what is going on.

"No sir, there is no one outside of the chambers," I hear a woman's voice say.

"Don't touch anything. Take a few photos and get out of there. Make sure to lock–" An officer says and then is cut off by the woman soldier.

"No! No! What happened? What did you guys touch? The chambers are preparing to open,"

Voices in the background have the same worrisome tone as the woman.

"Get everyone out, now!" The officer yells.

"Move out! Lock the doors," Exclaims the woman.

Boots of soldiers are heard in the background.

"They're opening!" I hear, accompanied with gunfire.

"Get out now!" The officer orders again.

Then the gunfire stops and the sound of metal doors shutting is heard.

"What is in the chambers?" I turn to Erin. Her face shows nothing but fear and confusion.

"They were talking about...people being inside chambers, asleep. There were six floors each filled with chambers," She says slowly.

"Come on, let's find a vehicle and talk about it on the way," I say, thinking that whatever it is can't be good.

Station 3 is still on in my ear and I hear banging on the metal doors and soldiers yelling.

I find a jeep that is slightly smoking with bullet holes running from the grill to the top of the window.

I try turning it on, but it smokes some more making me unsure if it will last very long.

Then, I notice Erin still moving slowly and not really doing anything.

"Erin!" I yell. She looks at me.

"What are you doing?" I ask, throwing my hands in the air.

"Bryan, they said there were a few chambers empty,"

"We can't do anything about it. We have to go," I try to explain.

"Bryan, those chambers are filled with mutants," She says, stepping towards me with her hand out for exclamation.

I stop and think about what she is saying.

They said there were six floors of chambers. I get the chills and my eyes widen. I swallow hard and begin to look around.

"Erin...we have...have to go," I try to say but my throat has tensed up.

I run to a Humvee, but when I open the door a bloody mess is all over and two soldiers are the owners of the contents. I slam the door and begin looking frantically.

Then I spot it.

A four-wheeler, a tiger I believe, is in an alleyway flipped on its side. I run to it and begin pulling it towards the street.

Erin, now somewhat mentally recovered, helps me pull it out of the alley. I push the start button and it roars beautifully. We jump on and we head off down the street.

Station 3 is now filled with yells and continuous gun shots with occasional groans and strange growls.

"Where is that building?" I ask, yelling over the tiger's engine.

"I have no idea."

We drive a few streets down when Erin taps me on the shoulder and points to a skyscraper. Bodies are falling from broken windows. Then I look a little longer and notice bodies crawling on the side of the building.

"Are there...people climbing the walls?" I turn my head back.

"Yeah!!" she yells back.

I concentrate on my driving, weaving between barricades and burning vehicles. A few minutes go by and then I hear gunshots. I look around, but I can't find where they are coming from.

"Do you hear that?" Erin asks.

I nod my head. "Yeah. Where is it coming from?"

Then just as she begins to deny knowing where it's coming from, she points to a Humvee coming down a perpendicular street. We pass the street but get a glimpse of the Humvee's turret shooting something directly behind it.

"What is it shooting at?!" I ask and nearly hit a barricade.

"I couldn't see!"

Thirty seconds later, we hear more gunshots and another Humvee turns off a street around a corner in front of us. It is then we see what it is running from. A group of strange humans. The mutants, I assume.

The Humvee fires, bursting shots into the group knocking some to the ground. It's obvious that the mutants can't quite keep up, so the Humvee slows down and takes out a couple more before more come out of the alleys causing the vehicle to speed up again.

I turn a corner going further away from the city and pull the throttle back as far as it will go.

My hand is getting tired of cranking back the throttle, so I let up a little and re-adjust. We're far from the center of the city, away from the chaos. I slow down just to talk to Erin.

"Well, that was too close," I say loudly.

"Yeah. That was too many for just the two of us. If we would have been in the mix of it, we definitely would have died,"

I slow down and stop.

"What are you doing?" Erin asks, looking around.

"I have to take a pee. I'll be right back,"

I walk around a building to do my business. Still listening to station 3, I hear the ongoing battle, but I'm pretty sure that the mics I'm listening to are different every few minutes. Occasionally, I will hear groans of a soldier dying or just silence with distant noises.

I walk back and find Erin in the front.

"Are you driving?"

"Yup. Let's go," She replies.

I get on and grab the back of her vest. Erin and I take off again leaving a trail of dust behind us. I start noticing a strange noise coming from the quad, but then it stops. That's weird, I tell myself, but figure it is what it is and if it breaks down, then so be it.

Finally, we reach the west side of town and the base camp. Vehicles and their parts are scattered everywhere. Buildings are crumbled, with much of the debris in the streets. Bodies lie all over the place. Erin maneuvers the quad through the debris, sometimes riding over mounds of concrete or brick. We turn right on a street that leads up to the hill and jungle line where we first came down. We drive slowly, still having to maneuver through the maze of bodies, machinery, and debris.

EVENTUALLY, we get past the bulk of it and begin driving a little faster, only to slow down to check out a mech machine that is lying down, smoking from the back. Bullet dents cover the surface and a few barely break the metal shell. Then I assume a rocket or something hit it from behind, causing it to go down.

. . .

WE REACH the hill and I get off to let Erin ride it up with ease. We take the clearly Humvee driven path back out to the main street. We cruise down the road with the jungle on both sides of us.

"Hey, are we even going to find this place? We have only been there once," Erin turns her head back to me.

"That's a good question. I think it was only a mile out from here,"

I had the image of the location of the fallen black object, but not the actual location on the street where we entered the jungle.

At the mile mark, we begin searching intensely for any sign of something familiar. We go a few minutes longer down the road, but we can't find anything.

"Let's turn around," I say doing a hand signal to reinforce my words, they being hard to hear over the tiger's engine.

Erin makes a U-turn and we head back down the road. We slow down a little bit, going around a corner and it isn't long before I see some ruffled vegetation.

"Maybe right there," I point ten yards ahead.

Erin pulls over and I jump off.

"I'll go check to make sure this is it,"

"Alright, hurry," Erin says.

I jog through the jungle, hoping this is the place. It quickly becomes apparent that trucks have driven here and up rooted shrubs have been placed in the path. I throw the loose plants off to the side to make a neater path for the quad. It only takes a minute or two before I get back to Erin.

"This is it,"

I jump back on and we go into the jungle. Once we get to the campsite, where all the shrubs are laid down, we stop and get off.

"It's over here," I say jogging through some unflatten bushes and trees.

Erin follows behind. As we break through the brush I keep scanning right, left, and down. My mind begins to fear the animals that may be lurking around.

I quickly check to make sure my knife is still in its sheath. It is, so I continue moving with a little more confidence.

We come to the clearing and there it lays.

The black, smooth, egg-like object sits in the exact same spot with dying leaves and branches around it.

"I forgot how bizarre it looks in the midst of a jungle," Erin says.

I kneel down and begin examining the object.

"Be careful," She says

"I don't think it's a bomb. But it does make me nervous not knowing what exactly it is," I agree with her.

"It does look like something Rev would make. However, something about it being so neat and sleek also gives me the vibe that it's not explosive," says Erin.

After a minute of examination, I decide it's okay to move it.

"Let's flip it over and then we'll move it to the quad," I say moving to one side of it and getting my hand underneath it.

I lift it up, exerting all my strength.

"Is it really that heavy?" Erin asks.

"Yeah...it's...that heavy," I reply in between breaths.

"What is that?" Erin points to the underside covered in dirt.

Under the dirt appears an engraving. Erin wipes away the dirt and mud revealing a symbol, the meaning of which is unknown to the both of us.

"Let's just get this thing to the quad. We'll have the lab at H.E.R.O. examine it," I say, tired of trying to figure out everything Rev does.

We each take an end and lift with our legs. "This thing has to be a hundred pounds, at least," Erin says.

Our steps aren't very big but we are pretty quick to get back to the quad. We gently set the black egg on the back of the quad.

"Do you have any rope or straps to hold it down?" I ask.

"Nope. It looks like one of us will have to keep it from falling off,"

It's agreed that I will hold it down first and we'll switch during the drive.

As we drive, it makes me very nervous trying to keep the object from falling off. I tell Erin to drive slowly through the jungle and on any turns while on the road. She does and once on the street, it appears to be okay for the most part.

. . .

THE SUN BEGINS to lower and we drive off after it. Our destination is to return back to the west coast where we were dropped off initially. However, I begin thinking that with Rev being occupied, it's safe to be picked up at the airport in the first city off the bay.

"Grant, can you hear me?" I ask into my mic.

"Bryan, I can barely hear you,"

"We need you to pick us up. And take us back to base,"

"Where are you? Your signal isn't clear," Grant replies.

"About two hours from the west coast. Listen, if you can't that's okay but we need someone to fly us home,"

Then just static and vague sounds of voices come over the signal.

"We have a poor connection to air support," I tell Erin.

"Well, maybe the airport can get a hold of the navy, if they are still off the coast. Let's not worry about it yet. The most important thing is making sure we keep this thing under our watch and get away from the conflict,"

She swerves and I hold the black egg down from rolling off.

"Sorry!" Erin exclaims.

The drive is silent between the two of us for an hour. The jungle gets darker and more mysterious as the sun lowers. Birds fly above the trees chirping and whistling. Clouds from the west begin forming into dark masses.

"You think a storm is coming?" I ask.

"Probably, but I don't think it will hit us,"

We reach a town and only a few people are outside. There is no reason to stop, so we keep going on. Once out of the town we switch roles and Erin holds the black egg. It takes about another hour to get to the city where we experience a fairly busy environment. People are walking everywhere and a few taxis are cruising by.

"Let's get a hold of air support and get out of here," Erin says as she turns to look at the city around us.

The thought that there are no Rev soldiers here seems unrealistic.

16

R ev's Origin

We make sure to take the least busiest streets. Once at the airport and get directed to where military personnel enter with vehicles. It takes ten minutes to figure out that H.E.R.O. air support isn't available and that the airport will get a hold of the navy off the coast for us.

It takes twenty minutes more for a falcon to arrive from the navy ship. Once it comes, we load up the black egg and head out just like that. Besides the fact that we had to show ID, it was pretty easy to get into the airport. They didn't have any planes taking off and I think they didn't have much of a staff, so we weren't interfering with anything.

I sit in the co-pilot seat. "Thanks again for picking us up on such short notice,"

"You must be quite important to be picked up from the navy at a time like this," The pilot says.

"Well, we aren't, but we have an interesting object that needs to be examined,"

"Oh, is that right? Well I can get you to the navy but you need to arrange someone to pick you guys up,"

"Alright, I will get a hold of someone once we land," I say turning to look out the window.

As we lift off I look towards Yaounde to see smoke billowing up into low gray clouds. The disastrous city makes me remember the years that the United States began falling apart. Mostly, high-density cities were subject to burning buildings and people looting stores. I imagine what is going on there in Yaounde, citizens confused as soldiers run around chasing Rev and their mutants. People trying to flee, but being picked off by human altered monsters. I try to change my course of thought. Our soldiers are stopping Rev, their mutants, and saving the citizens. The citizens are being encouraged to remove wristbands and no longer fear Rev.

"Hey Bryan, the egg is beeping in different tones," Erin says, worried.

I unbuckle my seatbelt to go check it out.

"We are about to land, don't stand up," The pilot throws a hand towards me.

I remain in my seat and put my seatbelt back on. A minute later we begin descending. The pilot keeps a conversation going with the control tower.

Once we land, I move to the back of the jet to listen to the beeping noise.

"You hear that?" Erin asks.

"I hear it,"

Faint beeping noises go off in a pattern, almost like an alarm.

"What do you think it is?"

"I don't know. Did you touch it or do something before it went off?" I ask, wondering if she triggered it.

"No," She says putting her hands up. "I didn't touch it,"

As the back door opens we are met with a handful of soldiers with guns ready.

"Alright, you two, out. Put your object here," A soldier says pointing to a cart.

"Wow, we don't think this is dangerous," I try to convince them that they are overreacting.

"Come on. Do as we say, no questions asked," The soldier says. "We have a ride out of here for you two. They will be here in an hour,"

We do as they say and walk where they tell us to walk. The navy has been helpful I guess but not very at ease, with this foreign egg.

As we wait, I try to make small talk with the sailors, but none allow it to get very far.

"So, you guys have been busy, I hear. What have you guys seen lately," I asked.

"Mostly helping remove terrorists by the Meridian Sea," They answer.

"Really? Can you tell me more?"

"No," They kill the conversation.

Finally, our falcon comes and we are escorted to it. The sailors make sure we board it with our mysterious object. As we board the falcon, I notice the pilot looks familiar.

"Grant?" I walk up to him.

"Bryan, I tried getting back to you, but our signal was probably blocked," He says, nodding towards the navy men.

"Well, I'm glad you came. They were acting very strange. I can't stand being here with them. They were treating us like criminals," I say after the door closes.

"How are the others?" Erin asks quickly, coming up from behind us.

"They're okay. I got them back to base and they're in good hands," Grant says convincingly.

"Jace had some internal bleeding I believe, and Jake received some broken ribs," He adds. Grant takes the falcon up and heads west back to the base.

"So, Luke was telling me about the large metal man. He said everyone believed it to be an alien. He said it was dead when they left but they didn't get a chance to find out what it really was. I am really interested in what you guys found out,"

I look at Erin.

"It was a mutant. A man made into a giant," she says firmly.

"I guess it was alien-like to look at, but it was still mostly a man," I add.

"Wow! Really? I have read about the practice of creating mutants, but I thought it would take a lot longer to achieve,"

"Rev has shown us there is a lot of technology they have harnessed," Erin says.

"What they come up with next, no one knows," I say

"From the sounds of it, you're right. Oh, and on a different note, I heard, throughout the U.S., there are mechanical dogs running around. A few people have been attacked for no reason, but these dogs are reportedly keeping people in their homes and preventing people from living life. It's preventing people from going outside to repair their homes or cars or tend fields and livestock," says Grant.

"Really? I haven't heard about that," I say, surprised.

"How many dogs would you estimate?"

"So far we are guessing 2,500 dogs are running around the U.S. On top of that, there was one instance of someone following a dog and saw it go into a shed. When the dog left, only a few minutes later, they saw a man inside the shed," Grant said.

"What does that mean?" Erin asks, confused.

"It means Rev soldiers are also hiding around, running subtle operations," Explains Grant.

.   .   .

THE NEXT FEW HOURS, of flying back to base, we talk about Grant and how he was recruited into the H.E.R.O organization. He explains how he was in the Air Force and he was exceptional at his job. The Air Force told him that they were trying out new aircrafts and invited him to test the falcon line. It wasn't long until he was at the top of his class. It is interesting to hear everyone's story of how they got into the organization. We also talk about the update on the meteorites.

"There isn't much more falling, but who really knows, now that most satellites are down. Communication from observatories out to the public is slow," Grant says.

"What's the destruction on the surface?" Erin asks.

"They have reported massive destruction in Russia. However, everything else has spotty damage," Grant replies.

"Well, now Rev is going about doing more damage," I say.

"My crew and I go up there to destroy the threat but the truth is, we had something growing here on earth all along,"

"Yeah, who would've thought. This plan of Rev's is almost too well planned out. If you think about all the things that had to be put in place for this to happen, it seems improbable," Grant says, shaking his head.

"What do you mean?" Erin asks.

Grant thinks for a moment. "Nine years ago, it was predicted that earth was going to be obliterated, causing the economy to falter. Who invests enough money to help Rev grow their technology? Then two years later the economy is totally tanked and there are still seven years before the earth's end. Rev now is probably stronger than when it started. There has to be more than what meets the eye," He pauses for a second.

"Jake started this organization on the knowledge he had but what if he didn't know everything and there is, a bigger story behind this?"

Then Erin and I look at each other then back at Grant.

"Like what?" I ask.

"I don't know. It just seems like someone had to have enough time to really prepare. Seven, nine, or even ten years seems unrealistic with the technology they have perfected,"

I think about what Grant is saying. He has a point. Rev's story isn't adding up.

"They had to have known like 20 years before everyone else," Grant says.

"Yeah, you might be right," Says Erin.

"The only way to find out, will be to ask the head of Rev," says Grant.

The aircraft, in a woman's voice, indicates that we will be at the base in two minutes.

"Thanks again for picking us up. We were getting worried that we would be intercepted by Rev," I say while making sure my seatbelt is secured.

"Anytime. I will always be on the same radio channel if you need me. You soldiers impress me and deserve the help, especially when all else fails. I could never face combat the way you do,"

GRANT LANDS the falcon on the runway that leads to the inside of the base.

"Here you are, safely home," He says smiling.

"Yeah, give it a few hours and we'll be gone again," says Erin, rolling her eyes.

Erin and I unload the black-egg. Some soldiers wheel over a cart. Metal on metal screeches as we place the heavy object on the cart.

"What is that? One of the soldiers asks.

"We have no idea. Can you show us to the lab?" I ask.

"Yes. Right this way, sir,"

We pass through two metal doors into a hallway. The two soldiers lead us through more doors with various turns throughout until we reach a door guarded by one soldier. The two soldiers with us hand the guard their ID's. The guard runs the IDs through a card reader. A green light appears and the door unlocks. Handing back their IDs, the guard nods and pushes the doors open.

Once inside the soldiers lead us, through another pair of doors and the moment we get in, people swarm us. The officers that I spoke to, the day I accepted to be part of the H.E.R.O. operation, are there watching and giving some orders, behind a plastic sheet. Men and women in contamination suites take the cart. I notice that the room we are in is not a room, but a containment zone. The two officers, Erin and myself are instructed to wait in the room. The door we came through is closed off.

"I feel like this is a bit much," I tell Erin.

"It's a couple hours away from the mundane work," One of the soldiers says to the other. The other nods with a smile.

"Sorry Erin and Bryan but this must not be taken lightly," An officer's voice comes over a speaker hanging from the ceiling. "Just so you know, a few more of these have been found around the world and no one knows what they are. We must take extreme caution until we know what it is and means. Until then sit tight,"

I look at Erin.

"You have to be kidding me," I look back at the officers.

"I...We have been in Africa for the last few days with mutants and a giant...hardly any time to eat or sleep. I want to see my family and I want to eat and sleep," I say sternly, but then I pause for a moment, realizing I am being a little dramatic especially because I signed up for this.

"Sorry...how long do you think this will take," I say calmly.

The officer is staring at me with little care about what I just said.

"It's going to take a few hours,"

I nod and wave my hand then lay down on the ground.

"Officer Dunken, I was hoping you could tell me how Jake, Jace, and Luke are holding up," Erin asks politely.

"They are recovering just fine. We have our best doctors taking care of them,"

"Thank you, Officer,"

Erin sits down next to me and pats me on the back while smiling. I turn my head to face the other direction.

"I don't want to hear it," I say in an exhausted and slightly muffled tone.

· · ·

AFTER A MINUTE or two goes by, the soldiers that led us in, sit down too.

"Hey, so what were you talking about? Did you really see mutants?"

I only raise my head at first to look at them.

"Yeah, we both did," I push myself up to sit.

"What were they like?" The other soldier asks.

"You heard about the "alien" right?" I ask using my fingers as quotations.

"We heard about it," One replies, as the other nods.

"That was no alien but a mutated man. It stood about nine feet tall and had a head quite a bit bigger than mine," I try to use my hands to illustrate.

"Maybe not that much bigger than yours," Erin jokes.

I push her with my elbow.

"Wo! Really? So, it was a giant compared to us. And...did you take him out?" The soldiers ask.

"Yeah, our squad, with the help of some other soldiers, took it down and even with all of us it was a challenge,"

"Our soldiers were taking care of the regular Rev soldiers. It was basically five of us against one giant," Erin clarifies.

Just then three people come in wearing their hazmat suites.

"Everyone, stand up. You two against this wall," One of them says, separating Erin and I from the other soldiers.

"We are going to be taking some tests. Please cooperate or this may take longer than necessary,"

Erin and I follow orders and we go to the other side of the tent.

They take our blood samples and swab various areas, then load up the equipment in a suitcase.

"Thank you," They say as they finish up and leave.

"I never really thought I would be in a containment tent being swabbed to death," Erin says.

"Mutants, giants, and containment tents. Today is your lucky day," I say, as we go to sit down again in the middle of the tent.

"Is that the only mutant you saw or were there others?" One soldier asks.

"There were more," Erin says. "One of our squad members sniped a man that was green and had multiple horns growing on his head. It took more shots than normal but it finally went down," I look at her and she looks back.

"Oh yeah, there was a ton in the city," She says more seriously.

I clench my jaw in anger and grief. I couldn't help those soldiers fighting the mutants, but I was so close to the combat that I feel like I should have tried.

"It sounded like a lot of soldiers were clearing some buildings and ended up scrambling to get out, when hordes of mutants were released from their chambers," Erin continues.

"It wasn't one room either. There were multiple floors that had rooms filled with chambers," I chime in.

"How did you guys get out?" Asks one of them.

Erin looks at me.

"We weren't in the city at the time. We were leaving when we heard the situation over the radio channel," I say.

My thoughts go back to those moments and I wonder if there was anything we could have done. But really, there wasn't. We didn't have the manpower to do what needed to be done.

THE NEXT TWO hours we just sit there waiting to hear back from the lab. I fall asleep for a few minutes only to be woken up from Erin pushing me.

"Hey, are you okay?" She asks.

"Yeah I think so. Why? Are they letting us out?" I look around the tent confused.

"No, not yet. You were jerking and clutching your fists till your knuckles were white," She says, looking concerned.

"Oh, sorry. I...don't even know what I was dreaming about," I look at the other soldiers for a second and they try to pretend they weren't listening.

"Sorry to wake you, I just wanted to make sure you were okay. I didn't know if you were poisoned by that object," She says trying to joke and lighten the situation.

I smile and lay back down. I don't fall asleep, but try to remember what I was dreaming about. It must have been about the last four days of hunting the alien.

I'm lying there staring up at the ceiling now wondering why and how Rev is what it is, when two men with contamination suits and no helmets come into the tent. We all look at them without saying anything.

They stare back.

"You two back to your stations," One of them says pointing to the other soldiers.

"And you two come with us,"

We stand up and follow the men out. They lead us through a lab containing all kinds of vials and machinery pushing fluids through tubs. We then come to a door and they stop.

"Everything you see and hear in here is classified. Nothing that happens behind these doors is permitted to be discussed with anyone else," They tell us.

The door opens from someone inside.

"Come in," An officer behind the door orders.

As we walk in, we see a glass room with robotic arms moving around with precision. In the midst of the arms is the black egg-like object. Erin and I look at each other and then back at the object.

Moving around the glass room we see that there are two incisions on the top of the egg. We stop walking when we reach a control panel surrounded by scientists and officers.

"What is it?" I ask.

A scientist looks back at the officers and with an officer's head nod, the scientist begins to brief us.

"Surface tests show no unordinary germs. We found the material to be similar to titanium yet it's not and proves to withstand corrosion, heat, and other tests titanium would fail," The scientist says, as he uses a joystick and buttons to control a robotic arm.

The arm moves directly above the egg.

"During testing we found two very faint squares on the top of the object. With attempts to push on the squares we found that they were not buttons. We decided to cut into this object. We used 3 blades with only making a quarter inch incision. What we didn't notice at the beginning was that the two squares are made of a slightly weaker metal than the rest of the egg,"

The robotic arm moves down and the hand goes inside the hole which is no bigger than 3 inches in across.

"We found this inside," The scientist makes the arm and hand come out of the egg. It's holding something.

"What is it?" Erin asks.

"A vial. It apparently has the same formula that Rev uses in their machinery, which we also use," He answers with some disappointment.

"So, we think it belongs to Rev?" Erin asks.

"Yes,"

I look at Erin then to the object and back to the scientist.

"Why is it still behind sealed glass walls?" I ask, a little skeptical.

"Once we opened the object we found traces of unknown bacteria that may be dangerous," The scientist says.

"Wait, unknown bacteria?" I say in shock.

"First things first. I found this thing and all evidence says that it fell from the sky. Now you are telling me that it has…"

"Hold on Bryan," An officer says.

Then the scientist puts his hands out as if to say calm down.

"Before you get any wild ideas we believe this singularity is caused by mutations that Rev has experimented with," He says putting the vial back in the egg.

"So, what is the purpose of this thing?" Erin asks.

"We don't know yet, we have only discovered that it is made by Rev and we wanted to let you guys know. They have made extraordinary breakthroughs with metal. If we don't stop their leaders soon, we fear that they will make all kinds of armor and machinery with this metal that cannot be easily penetrated. We would not have the means to over-power them and over time our forces will succumb to their evolutionary ways," The scientist turns to look at the officers behind us.

After a moment of silence, I walk past the scientists toward the glass door leading to the sealed room.

"I want to go in and examine the object," I say with determination.

Some of the officers put on disgruntled faces.

"Who do you think you are? You don't own this place. You're not a scientist, you're a soldier," One of the upset officers says.

"George, that's enough," Says the officer that opened the door for us earlier.

"I don't see why he can't inspect it. In fact, I would like to go in there and look at it as well," The officer looks at the scientist in front of the controls.

"Well, sir we must get you properly dressed to enter the room,"

"Okay, well let's do it and I would appreciate it if you would come in too," He says inviting the scientist.

"Alright, right this way to the suits," He says leading us to some racks filled with contamination suites.

AFTER BEING HELPED with proper suit procedures, we are led through a door into a small room. The door closes behind us and we wait for the green light to open a second door.

Literally, a green light turns on and the scientist, whose name I found out while dressing, is Ben, opens the second door leading us into the glass room. The robotic arms are still hanging in the air. The object looks even more mysterious under the fluorescent lighting.

Using the mic within the suit I begin asking questions.

"Ben, I saw these symbols before. What do they mean?"

"Bryan, I don't know what they mean but we are pretty sure Rev has made a language that only they can communicate through,"

I stop and look at him. I then play it off like I believe him.

"Oh, that would be smart."

However, I don't think the Rev leaders are that smart and especially the soldiers.

I look over the egg and decide that nothing is new to me under this light, so I start with the squares that were cut out. The metal shell has a little more than an inch of metal around the inner structure. I anxiously peer into the egg. In the center, it's hollowed out the size of an NFL football. There lies the vial, attached to a metal tube. Also, inside is a small square bump.

"Hey did you guys see this?" I ask.

I try to remove the object, but my hand can't even reach the bottom.

"What is it?" Ben asks.

"I don't know but I can't get my hand inside to remove it. This hole is too small,"

"Let me see if these arms can remove it," Ben looks in the hole, then goes to a hand and puts a claw on it making it look like it belongs in a box with stuffed animals.

The claw reaches in and opens up its fingers. After a few seconds there's a click. It begins to ascend out the hole but stops when the fingers hit the edges of the hole.

"Just a minor problem," Ben says.

The hand goes back in and drops the object. After a few attempts the object is pulled out. Ben grabs the thin metal square from the claw. The face of it had a strange logo. The logo looks like an odd creature.

"What does that look like to you guys?" The officer asks, squinting his face.

"It doesn't look like anything I know of," Ben says and flips it over.

An engraved arrow points to one side. Ben uses two hands and slides the bottom half off.

"That's a memory card," The officer says. "Let's get it into a secured computer."

People outside of the room begin moving quickly to find one.

I keep searching the insides of the egg to see if there are any more surprises.

I try to make sense of what I'm looking at, but I can't. The sides of the egg are lined with tubes and there are metal boxes with blue glass panels one-eighth inch apart. I step back from the egg and look it over from every angle. Another scientist gets suited up and brings a computer in through the door we came in.

"Here, this is a laptop that doesn't have access to any of our data," He says and hands it to the officer.

The laptop is connected to a T.V. screen for the other officers to see.

"Things just keep getting weirder," The officer says inserting the memory card into the laptop.

The computer screen flickers and a pop-up come's on the screen asking what to do with the memory card. The officer selects "read card". The box is replaced with file folders.

"Captain Verdun, Artillery, Lab Reports..." The officer reads out loud.

"Why are these kinds of files on here?" He clicks on Captain Verdun.

A page comes up with a man in a military suit and a bio next to him. I begin scanning the bio, but Ben begins reading it aloud.

"Captain Verdun is a scientist and engineer...in a time of great turmoil, he was invited to interview for a great opportunity for a company that would allow him to work on his inventions and creations. When he showed up for the interview he was met by someone," The page ends and we change it with a swipe across the screen.

Each of us pull back our heads as we see a photo of Captain Verdun and a creature tall and fit, dressed in an unusual military outfit.

It is an alien. Like you would see in a movie.

Verdun and the alien sit at a table with a T.V screen mounted on a wall. The lighting in the room looks strange. The walls aren't decorated but tattered with areas revealing concrete.

"The two met and learned of each other's ambitions and saw that they could help the other. One wanted to prove to the world they could help humanity through scientific breakthroughs. The other lied and said he was there to help the inhabitants of earth resolve their biggest issue in reaching higher intelligence, unity," Ben reads.

The next page shows pictures of an aircraft taking off and then the earth through a window in the shape of an upside-down trapezoid.

"You are experiencing the plan that Captain Verdun and his new accomplice created. I will refer to the accomplice as Gershon. Gershon informed Verdun of asteroids that were to hit earth in 17 years from then,"

We move to the next page that reveals pictures of Verdun and Gershon walking through a science lab.

Ben reads the next passage. "Gershon showed Verdun advanced science that Verdun was close to discovering. Technology that Gershon had, now Verdun knew and held. The plan was to use this technology to help build up the ability to destroy the asteroids. However, Gershon had more planned than he revealed,"

We scroll down the document.

"Over time Gershon was introduced to Verdun's own associates and more people became aware of the great plan to save earth. During this time Gershon found what he wanted, a person that would betray their own kind for a higher position. His name was Cliff Bronson. Gershon devised a plan to remove those that would get in his way of making the world united. Bronson and others were placed at the head of a new operation to help Gershon bind the human race under his own,"

"What is this?" The officer in the room with me asks. "This is made up to derail us. It is a waste of our time,"

"I don't know if it is true or not but I think it's worth finishing," I say.

The officer looks at me and scuffs.

"Aliens. That's what this has come to? We know that Rev has been trying to use facades to scare those that oppose them. This would just be the icing on the cake, if we believed it," He says, shaking his head.

"Officer Coffman, please let Ben carry on. The rest of us are interested," The other officers on the outside say through the mic.

Ben reads the next page.

"At this time, you must be struggling to destroy the newly called Captain Bronson. This is as planned. Unfortunately, there is little hope of ever gaining back total control. At this time Gershon is making his way to earth and his armies are nothing like humanity has seen. You must wonder who I am to be telling you this,"

We change the page.

"We shall meet soon," Ben reads then tries to scroll more, but that was the last page.

"Let's look at the other files," I say quickly before Officer Coffman blows up again.

"Machinery, Armory, Coordinates of interest..." Ben reads.

"Co-ordinances of interest," I almost yell.

Ben clicks on it.

"Verdun's first visit from Gershon, Operations Building, Armory, Recruitment Center, Food Supply Grounds..."

"Go to the Operations Building," Says Officer Coffman.

Ben does and a map comes up of Northern Arizona.

"Arizona?" Ben says surprised and unsure.

"That's it! We have the coordinates," Officer Coffman says with a wave of his hand.

"Let's get some troops there within 12 hours," He looks to the others outside the room.

They write down the co-ordinances off of the screen. I begin to look over the egg again. I wonder if this really has been sent from extraterrestrials. Nowadays photos and films can make anything look like it's a real thing. What if this is just a hoax to lure us into a trap.

I look outside to Erin, who is staring at me.

"Guys, look at this," Ben says, waving me over.

"There are lab reports of mutants but nothing shows complete success. This says they were done in 2026, which means it has only been recently that they have figured out how to successfully mutate. This report is old," Ben tells us.

"There are factual and fictitious elements here, making their intriguing story difficult to discard," An officer from outside says.

"Go to the machinery folder," Orders Officer Coffman, apparently upset from the other Officer's comment.

The folder reveals structured suits similar to the giant mutant we took down in Africa. Vehicles and the blueprints of a Humvee large and robust fill up a couple pages. Pictures of robotic K-9s of various sizes spread across pages with lines connecting them to captions. On another page, the structure of a jet is laid out.

"I have never seen a Rev jet before," Officer Coffman says.

"Wait a second," Erin says.

We look up and she has grabbed a mic from the control panel.

"This only adds up one way. You guys are finding pretty sensitive information. Some we have seen and confirmed to be true and others we aren't sure. No matter what, this information wouldn't be sent out from Rev. Especially days after they begin taking over the world," She says sternly.

"She has a point," an officer next to her says.

As we discuss what this all means, the laptop shuts down.

"Oh no! We didn't have it fully charged. Guys!" Ben exclaims.

"Let's get a cord on that. In the meantime, we have some other things to take care of," Officer Coffman says.

"Bryan, come with me," He puts his gloved hand on my back as he moves to the door.

"How do we get out of here safely?" He asks, looking at the scientist behind the controls. "You need to exit the doors over there and we'll help you," One of them says, pointing to the back wall.

WE EXIT the room to another that has different compartments within. The process only takes ten minutes before we are back to Erin and the others.

"Alright, everyone in the conference room," An officer orders.

Erin and I let the others go as we hang back.

"This has been quite an interesting day," Erin says.

"Hey, I meant you two as well," The officer says from the doorway everyone walked through.

We quickly follow after him.

THE NEXT TWO minutes are spent walking through a maze of halls and doors to reach the large room filled with computers. On the far end of the room is the glass room where I officially became part of the H.E.R.O initiative. We walk to the fishbowl-like room and everyone finds a seat. We begin discussing what we have just discovered.

"These coordinates could be a trap," One of the officers says.

"They could be," The officer at the head of the table replies.

"So, are we going to just throw our men into an unknown situation?" The first says.

"Don't be ridiculous," A third officer says.

There are five officers and only one seems to be keeping their cool, he sits at the head of the table just staring at his blue glowing glass tablet.

"If we don't find out what is there we will never know if all of the information on that memory card is true or not," The fourth begins getting into it.

"Then let's just send a few soldiers to scout it out for a few days," The first says.

"We can't spare many men from the other zones Rev is present,"

The officers look at each other and then realize their superior isn't in on the conversation.

"Officer Haze, would you like to comment on this discussion?" They ask, staring at him as he continues to use his tablet.

Then he looks up and gently sets his tablet down.

"I will. I know very well of your concerns and we all have questions about whether the character in the photos is an alien or not," He pauses.

As he scans the room, he lingers on Erin and myself.

"Let's be honest. Is it okay if we are honest?" His face gets serious, but not stern.

"The lab reports show living organisms, not known to man, in the object. These lab reports confirm they are not just a mixture of human and animal or anything of that sort. They are not from our planet!"

Everyone stands still. I see the faces of some officers showing skepticism and confusion.

"Officer Haze, with all due respect, I don't think we should be jumping to conclusions, especially as to extraterrestrials," The first says shaking his head.

"The evidence is there. Actually here, in our buildings," Officer Haze says.

A minute goes by with no one saying anything and everyone sits down. I start reading everyone's name badges, figuring I need to address them properly. Haze, Coffman, Velt, Nielson, and Ortega. Collins is the first officer that spoke up. He seems to have a hot head. The rest are just normal people trying to wrap their heads around extraterrestrials.

Officer Haze stands up.

"What is impossible and what is possible? That is a question asked every day. Subconsciously, we ask ourselves this all the time. Anything is possible given that there is enough time. Given that we continually strive for whatever it is we want. Countless space explorations have been sent to find evidence of life. Who is to say, when we may find it," Officer Haze walks over to a large monitor and taps the screen, turning it on. The screen shows the lab room, where the black egg object sits.

"What are the odds that life was always looking for us? Why would that be impossible? We should not be that naive," He looks at everyone in the room..

Officer Coffman raises his hand, head high.

"Permission to speak, sir?"

Officer Haze nods in acceptance.

"It seems to me that we are in a pivotal moment. Our lives may completely be turned inside out. I don't want to be turned inside out, that is uncomfortable," Officer Coffman says, raising his eyebrows. "What I want to say, is that I am very skeptical of this extraterrestrial theory, but that I will follow you to whatever end," He finishes with an appearance that says he is swallowing his pride.

"Thank you, Officer Coffman. I want to assure each of you that this next mission is not a suicide mission and it is not a mission of insanity. This is part of what we do. We help everyone restore order. This is H.E.R.O. 's mission and it applies here too,"

All the officers nod.

Officer Haze taps the navigation buttons on the screen and changes the screen to a picture of a building.

"This is where everything mentioned in that file happened. We know there are more sites Rev operates, but this seems to be the beginning of their existence. We will begin here and find out the truth," He says and activates another screen.

"Flagstaff is cold this time of year. Typically, there is snow at this time, so we need to be aware of any hazards,"

Officer Ortega raises his hand.

"How many men should we send? We don't have very many to spare. That building is huge. They'll probably have a thousand men inside. I think my concern is that we are being spread too thin,"

His voice sounds sincerely concerned.

Officer Haze looks at him and the rest of us then changes the screen.

"This is an overview of my plan I have put together. We have a little over 300 men here in our base. I want to take 50 of them for this mission. The other part of this plan is most important. We will be gearing up four soldiers in our best suits and sending them in with 10 other soldiers. The other 36 soldiers will be outside, securing the perimeter. As needed, we will send in more soldiers into the building. This is, for the sole purpose of finding the truth and understanding Rev's plans. Does anyone have any modifications they would like to suggest?"

We all are silent.

"Great, we will be leaving in 12 hours. Let's find the best 14 foot-soldiers and the best 36 utility soldiers,"

The officers begin writing things down.

"We need 5 personnel that can hack computers, if needed. Let's get two Mechs, four Humvees, and three Tiger quads. We will find the truth!"

The officers get up and start leaving.

Erin and I begin following the other officers when Officer Haze stop's us at the door.

"Bryan, Erin, you two, Luke and Jace are going to need to get down to the armory within the next two hours. Down there they will help suit you up for this mission. We have built extremely resilient armor for the four of you. It will take some time to measure each of you for the armor to fit properly," He says.

"Yes, sir," We say synchronized.

He lets us out of the office with a nod.

Once out of the large computer room and in a hallway, we begin discussing the meeting.

"Officer Haze is pretty convinced that there are extraterrestrials helping Rev," Erin says with shock in her voice.

"Yeah, I understand the evidence he pointed out, but it's hard to grasp," I reply.

I myself am on the fence about what is real or not.

"It could be just another illusion Rev has made to throw us back or worse, throw us into a trap," Erin looks at me as we continue to walk.

"Are we going to the hospital wing?" I ask her as I open a door for her.

"Yeah, we need to see how everyone is doing and tell Jace and Luke about the mission,"

"Right,"

"Well, what do you think these new suits are going to look like? They sound better than these that we have on but these were better than any suit I have worn"

Erin looks at me.

"Maybe it's a placebo effect. Kind of like a kid getting new shoes,"

I just raise my eyebrows a little as I consider the idea.

WE CONTINUE to walk through the halls and go up an elevator until we get to the hospital. A man sitting behind a counter looks up as we push open the double metal doors.

"Hello, can I assist you two?" He asks.

Moans and commotion can be heard down both hallways beyond the counter.

"We are looking for three soldiers that came in about 2 hours ago," Erin says.

"Names will help me find them quicker," He says abruptly.

"We don't have last names but their first names are Jace, Luke and Jake," I say quickly, a little annoyed with the man already.

"Okay..." He says looking at his glass tablet.

"Ah, I see who you must be talking about. Two of them, Jace and Luke, are sharing a recovery room down on the right, in stall eleven,"

"Wait, where is Jake?" Asks Erin.

"Officer Farr is in critical condition. He is not able to take visitors at this time. Also, it sounds like he won't get discharged for a couple days,"

"Thanks," I say and tap Erin's arm telling her to follow me.

We head down the hallway on the right, looking at the stall numbers.

"A couple days?" Erin says.

"He must have gotten hit pretty hard,"

We find stall eleven and push open the sheet. There, the two are next to each other talking as though they're just shooting the breeze.

"Jace, Luke, are you guys okay?" I ask.

"Hey Bryan, Erin. I think we are both doing pretty good," Luke says.

"Yup, they patched us up nicely and gave us some purple junk to numb the pain. It's like morphine but better," Jace says smiling as he sits up a little.

"Great. Do you know what happened to Jake?" Erin asks.

They both look at each other and then at the doorway.

"Well, he was in a lot of pain when we got off the jet. I'm not sure what the cause of it was though," Luke says.

"Where have you two been?" He asks.

We look at each other and without needing to say anything the last few hours flash through my mind.

"We just got out of a meeting and found out the four of us need to be down in the armory getting sized up for new suits. We leave in less than 12 hours for a new mission," Says Erin.

They look at us surprised.

"12 hours?" Jace asks.

"We just got back, completing a huge mission. I almost died. Can't I get at least a day to recover?"

Erin quickly steps forward.

"You know what? Jake is in critical condition and from the sounds of it, he won't be okay for a couple of days! We all almost died, not just you,"

I grab her shoulder.

"Erin,"

She flips around at me.

"It's the drug making them talk like this," I try to calm her down.

With intensity in her face, she walks around me and out of the room.

"Man, what is her deal?" Jace says.

"Listen guys, don't be late for your suit fitting. Within the next hour and half, you two need to be down in the armory. Alright?"

They look at each other.

"Sure," They say, as I walk out of the door.

17

New Skin

I WALK OUT of the hospital wing and find a stairway leading down to the next floor. "What drug do they have those two on?" I ask myself.

"They better be completely recovered by the time we have to go,"

I decide I have some time to take a shower and see my family for a few minutes so I head back to my room.

When I get to the door, I swipe my watch just above the black box next to the door. The light turns green and I gently open the door. I step inside and see my wife sitting on the bed and the kids are playing on the ground. Samantha immediately stands up and puts her hand over her nose and mouth, as though not to shriek. It's then I remember I haven't cleaned up at all. I bet I look terrible.

"I'm okay," I say.

Tate gets up and runs over to me.

"Dad, why are you so dirty?"

I mess up his hair and pick him up.

"It's my job, son. I do what most people don't want to do,"

Samantha comes over to me and I hug her with my free arm.

"You look awful," She says through tears and a hint of a laugh. "I'm glad you're back,"

In my mind I think about how I just got back looking like I was hit by a tornado and I have to go out again in less than 12 hours.

"I'm glad to be back too. Are you guys okay?"

She nods and backs up a little.

"Yes, we are fine,"

I put Tate down and walk over to Caroline, but can tell she is scared of my appearance.

"I should probably shower first,"

I spend a good 10 minutes in the shower. Every time I close my eyes I see a scene from the past few days. People, mutants, machines, explosions and corps. I try to think of other things, like my family and friends, but it hardly helps. I turn off the water and dry off.

As I get changed and ready, Samantha asks me why I don't put on some more comfortable clothes. My heart drops because I have to tell her the unfortunate news. "Well, I have to go out again,"

Her eyes widen and then tears begin to form.

"I have 20 more minutes right now and maybe an hour or two later. I just have to go down to the armory for a little bit," I say trying to make it not seem so bad.

"When are you leaving?"

I look at the watch now on the table.

"About eleven hours from now," She tries to wipe away the tears.

"For how long?" She asks.

"I don't think it will be as long as this last one. Which really, a few days for one mission isn't that bad," I keep trying to spin it to look at the bright side of the situation.

But, we know it's not necessarily about the time spent out there in the field. It's about the activities that go on out there, like the one that made me come home looking like I cheated death.

For the next 20 minutes we spend time with the kids and play a few games with them. I wish I could be more involved with Tate's and Caroline's learning, but my role is different now. Nobody gets to pick what job they get to do, when the safety of their family is on the line.

I say my goodbyes and head out to the armory. As I use my watch to find the room, I notice it is a little slow and not to mention scratched and chipped from this last mission. I should probably request for a new one.

THE ARMORY IS BEHIND two heavy metal doors. Trying to open them, I realize they're locked.

"The armory is for authorized personnel only," An automated voice says.

Seeing there is a black box by the doors, like the one at my own room, I swipe my watch over it. Just when I think it didn't work and I am about to swipe again, the doors click and slowly open, sliding into the walls. This catches me off guard, since I thought they would swing open. On the other side of the door stands a soldier in camouflage attire.

"Welcome, Bryan. We have been expecting you," He says as he shakes my hand firmly.

"Follow me and I will introduce you to the team that has designed your suit. We will have to make modifications depending on what fits you most comfortably,"

He leads me a little way past some isles filled with all sorts of weapons. Metal and wooden crates are stacked three high against the walls. When we get to a new set of doors he opens it with the wave of his watch. The doors are light weight compared to the last, and they swing inward to another room.

Inside are waist high tables with what looks like our suites, lying on top. I see Erin surrounded by a few soldiers, who are putting different pieces of the suit on her.

"I'm sorry, I forgot to introduce myself. My name is Daniel, I will be your assistant for the remainder of the day. This is our new division in armor development. As you know weapons are only getting stronger and current armor can't hold up like they used to," He says as we stop at one of the five tables.

I look down at the pieces of armor on the table. Each is for a different area of the body.

"You see here that the pieces are separate, like most traditional armors. However, you will first put this on, before the rest of the pieces," Daniel points out a rubbery fabric lying underneath the other armor.

"What is this?" I ask.

He begins removing the other pieces.

"This is your skin. It will help keep you from getting too hot or cold, for the most part at least. It will also protect you from shrapnel, better than any other fabric. It is not an armor from most weapons. That is not its purpose,"

For some reason he felt like he needed to emphasize that. I would never in my wildest dreams believe something as thin as half an inch would save me from any firearm round.

"Now you may have noticed some designs on the skin. These are to help keep–"

He grabs one of the many armor pieces from the table.

"--these into place while doing what you do best,"

He places both the skin and armor down on the table and taps his watch a few times.

"Alright, strip down to your underwear and put the skin on. A few more soldiers are coming to help assess how you fit in the suit,"

I do as he says and put my clothes on the table. The skin feels a little strange. The outside is rubbery but the inside is a smooth silky feeling. I also notice that the inside of the skin is designed to expand at my joints yet it doesn't necessarily leave them any more vulnerable than the rest of the suit.

Just as I get the suit over my shoulders, three men and Daniel come pushing a cart filled with tools.

"What's with the tools?" I ask.

"Some of the armor pieces need to be bolted together," Daniel says as he circles me, looking at the skin.

"How does the skin feel?"

I move my arms a little and bend at the knees.

"I'm not going to lie, it feels pretty nice,"

He stands in front of me and pokes my sternum.

"What was that for?" I ask, confused.

He pokes me again two more times. Then I notice faint lights glowing in the skin.

"These are the buttons to activate the features on your suit. It regulates your body's temperature."

He waves over the other soldiers who begin picking up the armor and tools.

They put pieces of armor on me, and asks how it fits and if I can do this or that comfortably. With quite a few bolts and some pieces of armor switched out from time to time, they finish. The total time of figuring out what worked for me and completely bolting the suit together takes 50 minutes. However, honestly, I look like someone you don't want to mess with.

"Wow, that took a while," I say. "But I look pretty intimidating,"

Daniel laughs.

"It won't take as long next time. Let's put on the final piece, your helmet,"

He grabs a helmet from the lower shelf of the table and hands it to me. A full helmet with a large visor in the front and vents just below it. I put it on my head easily.

"Oh, I think it's too big," I say realizing the helmet is shifting around.

"It was designed to be easy to get on and off. Once it's on, you press this button under your left jaw," Daniel says as he presses the button for me.

The helmet begins to get tighter and tighter, then almost too tight and then it loosens a little.

I look around trying to get used to the slightly blue tint of the visor.

"It fits great and it's decently comfortable to wear. I'm just getting used to the blue tint on the visor," I look back at the team that put me together.

One of them reaches forward and pulls a film off of the visor.

"How's that?" they ask.

I laugh.

"Better,"

I see Erin walking around with hers on. Her team of suit builders are examining her motions.

"Do you mind if I take this for a run?" I look at Daniel.

"Go ahead,"

The weight of the suit is heavy, but not as much as you might think for how thick the armor is. I start walking using boots that were also specially made. It feels strange to be almost completely covered by metal, but it doesn't feel uncomfortable. I begin to jog and then I turn around when I get to the end of the room and sprint back to my table. Obviously, my sprint is pretty slow due to the 50 pound suit.

"Wo, take it easy," Daniel says waving his hands.

When I get back to the table I'm a little winded.

"Take it slow before you get too crazy. These suits are meant to give you more time taking out the enemy and allow you to do less running and hiding. Only do a full sprint when necessary, because as you can see it will wipe you out,"

He nods to the three soldiers and they begin using the tools to remove the pieces. Daniel takes the helmet off of me. In a matter of ten minutes the suit is completely removed.

"Now, we want to see you back here in eight hours. Don't be late, there is a little bit of training we will have you and your squad do before you leave,"

"Yes, sir,"

As I leave the armory, I begin feeling extremely fatigued. The day has been long and I have not slept at all. After swinging by the mess hall to grab dinner, I head back to my room. Samantha is waiting for me, so we talk about my day for 10 minutes or so. I apologize and I tell her that I need to sleep. Two minutes after laying down I fall into a deep sleep.

It's eight hours later when I wake up absolutely tired. At first, the slim glass clock on my night stand is blurry but a few blinks and squints I see the time. 4:03 am. I slowly sit up and crack my neck. Then I put my head back down on the pillow wishing I didn't have to move for a few more days.

A minute later, I notice a faint blue light across the side of the night stand. I look to see where its coming from and find my watch had fallen down on the ground between the bed and night stand. I pick it up and turn on the screen, preparing to be blinded by light, but it only glows softly. A message was sent from Erin to the squad.

"Breakfast is at 4:00 am. We need to get suited up at 4:30. 4:45 we will be doing some suit training. At 5:20 we will be going over the mission. 5:45 We leave."

I put the watch down and begin getting out of bed.

"This job sucks," I say quietly.

The watch blinks again.

"Bryan, where are you?" Reads another message from Erin.

I quickly get ready while trying not to wake up my family.

Once ready to leave, I wake Samantha up and tell her that I am leaving.

"Okay. Be safe. I love you," She says and then kisses me.

The kiss reminded me of the better times we have had. I gently pull away.

"I love you," I say and then quietly leave.

I make it to the mess hall by 4:20 and grab some eggs and oatmeal. As I sit down next to my squad, Jace raises his eyebrows.

"We weren't sure if you were going to show up," Jace says before taking his last bite of oatmeal.

Luke elbows him.

"Why are you late Bryan?" Erin asks.

"Sorry, overslept. I didn't see your message before I laid down."

I can tell she doesn't care and is annoyed.

"Alright, well eat as much as you can and then come to the armory."

Erin wipes her face with a napkin as she gets up from the table and leaves.

"Alright, I will be there in a few minutes," I say without sounding phased from her all of a sudden leadership status.

"Who is going to ask Erin who made her..." Jace begins to say, but then is cut off by someone dropping their tray.

"Jace, she's probably just tired like the rest of us and concerned about Jake," Luke says.

I begin eating my oatmeal quickly.

"Is there something going on between them?" Jace asks.

"I don't think so, Jake is married," I say in between swallows.

"Related?" Jace asks.

We both look at Luke.

"I don't know. I think it's best that we just don't get on her bad side," He says.

"Yeah, well she shouldn't be so ridiculous. No one made her in charge of us and she is coming off more as a mom than a soldier," says Jace, lifting his eyebrows again.

He gets up and leaves.

A minute goes by and Luke finishes his apple.

"Is Jace an intense person?" I ask Luke.

"He is. We all can be a little intense from time to time,"

I stop eating and stare at him.

"Well, Jace and Erin can be. I like to think I hold them together. We have only had two other missions together, but I have noticed the way they handle stress. They usually work their issues out civilly," He says and gets up from the table.

I quickly finish my food and leave with Luke.

ONCE LUKE and I get to the armory, we hear some grunts and pounding. Back in the room with tables and suits, we see Erin beating up a dummy. Luke and I get separated to our own tables and the teams begin working on us.

This time around the teams work much quicker and we're done in ten minutes. Once suited up completely, they have me walk around the room to make sure everything is right.

Next, I punch a dummy, first without the helmet and then with it. I notice I am not as fast with the suit, but that I have more power to inflict damage.

After I finish punching the dummy, I take off the helmet and meet up with the rest of my squad now preparing for a foot race.

"You will each start here, run to the end of the room and back," Daniel instructs us.

I line up with them.

"Okay on the count of three. One, two, three," He throws his hand down in front of us and we push off the line.

At first Jace takes the lead and then Erin, but then I catch up. The suits are fairly quiet as the metal armor hardly touches each other.

Luke catches up as we get to the end of the room. The turn-around loses Jace and Luke, while Erin and I transition nicely back to the starting line. However, I start losing energy and Erin does too, but she pulls ahead of me. Then Jace comes up just before I hit the finish line. Luke finishes a second after myself.

"Nice work," Daniel says while appearing entertained.

Each of us are exhausted and trying to catch our breath.

"Shall we take a look at the video?" He says, leading us to a room nearby.

"You all ran very well, however, you should see how you look and the time it took you. I think you'll find it interesting,"

A soldier in a black office chair presses play on the glass table that acts as a keyboard. The monitor above the man begins to play the video of us running. It looked like Luke got a bad push off the line, but then gained speed catching up to us at the wall.

"You see here. You guys aren't running that fast. The suits are obviously holding you back. I wanted to show you this because it's important to know the difference the suit makes when trying to perform typical activities," Daniel points out.

"Great, so we are excellent targets. We're like the heavy kid on the dodgeball court," Jace say's still catching his breath.

"You are partially right, you will be slower and an easier target. However, you won't get out like that unfortunate kid you just described. Your suits are a lot more durable than 95 percent of the suits out there," Daniel replies.

I look at him. "How much fire power can these suits take?"

He gets a little smirk on his face.

"They can take quite a bit. Follow me"

We follow Daniel into a low lit shooting range.

"This is the last thing I will show you and then you will have to go to the meeting,"

He grabs a 50 caliber and bolts it down on the counter. The rest of the lights in the shooting range turn on and reveal two suits.

"Just plug your ears for a moment," Daniel says as he puts on his ear muffs and then turns to aim.

He pulls the trigger and fires approximately 20 rounds into the first suit. Then aims at the second suit and fires another 20 rounds.

The suits are about 40 feet away which is fairly close for a 50 cal. It's a good testing method for the instances where you are being ambushed by vehicles that have 50 cals. He takes us down the range and tells us to inspect the suits. So, we do.

"Man, this one got torn up," Luke says as he inspects the first suit.

"Yeah, I hope these aren't the suits we're wearing," Jace says quickly, turning to look at Daniel.

The first suit has holes all the way through the thin metal plating and the Kevlar that sit behind it.

"Jace, those are the suites that 95 percent of the world has. This is the suit you are wearing," Daniel points to the second suit.

We examine it closely. Although there are superficial holes on the armor it appears that the bullets did not go all the way through.

"Wow, we are close to being invincible," Says Erin.

"Don't believe that for a second," Says Daniel.

"Just be aware you can be riskier than the other soldiers around you. Anywhere else that the armor doesn't cover will be vulnerable to high caliber weapons,"

We leave the shooting range feeling pretty good about our suits.

"Alright let's get to the meeting," Erin says walking past us guys.

We follow her down some halls to a room I haven't been in. As the door opens I hear chattering. However, when we walk in, the noise dies down. Everyone is staring at us.

"Here they are," I hear one officer say.

We are asked to sit in some chairs near the front of the room.

"I guess a lot of people don't wear these suits," Whispers Luke.

Jace holds up five fingers. "We are the five percent,"

A few minutes pass and more soldiers trickle in. None of which have suites like ours. Almost all of them are suited up in armor that we were wearing the last couple days. They were nice and I know that they kept me alive, but I feel a little guilty wearing a suit better than theirs.

Officer Haze walks up to the front and the chatter dies down again. Officer Haze looks up at a monitor and turns it on with a remote. He looks back at us and begins to talk.

"You are all here for a mission that has only been put together within the last eleven hours. Each of you will have an essential task to complete. The main purpose of this mission is to receive more information about Rev's beginnings. We believe there is vital information within this building," He says, while the screen shows a video of the premises of a large concrete structure.

"Only two of our spies have seen the inside of the building and they haven't been able to gather enough information about its true history. This building is located in Flagstaff, Arizona. The temperature is low and snow covers the ground," Officer Haze informs.

He then mentions the vehicles that will be part of the mission.

"All soldiers will be dropped off two miles away from the target location. Once on the ground everyone will make their way to the building from the south and the west. If you are assigned to a vehicle you should stay with it until otherwise directed,"

He changes the image to a blueprint of the building.

"This is a basic blueprint of the building. This is all we have to go off of, and it's not much. Because of this, the soldiers that will be inside, will need to be on their toes at all times and be aware that there could be hallways and rooms that no one knows about. Don't rely solely on the map we sent each of you," Officer Haze pauses for a moment.

"Honestly there could be anything or nothing within the building. Rev has multiple locations where they experiment and build all kinds of things. They could have moved on from this site, but this is where Rev began and we need to know more about it,"

One of the soldiers in the back raises their hand.

"Yes, Moreno,"

"Officer Haze, there are rumors going around about extraterrestrials having been in contact with Rev. Is this mission solely to find out if aliens do exist and if they contacted Rev?"

Whispers begin filling the room. Officer Haze looks around the room as though to spot the person causing the rumor.

"Now it's important to know that some information has been revealed recently that strongly suggests extraterrestrials have been on earth,"

The whispers get louder.

"However, like in Africa, where rumors of an alien being took over an entire city, we have proven otherwise. It was a mutant. A giant man under unique armor, as one would see in a movie," Officer Haze says before being interrupted by the same soldier, Moreno.

"Do you believe in aliens?" Moreno asks.

The room gets quiet.

Officer Haze looks around the room then down at my squad then back up.

"I can't say professionally that aliens are out there. This is not a galactic battle, so don't dream up nightmares. Keep your heads on straight,"

The room gets loud again.

"That is all. Meet up with your commanding officers and head out,"

We stand up and as we do Officer Haze waves us over. We follow him out of the room into an office.

"Alright Squad 7, I need you to listen carefully. You need to find documentation of experiments, weapons, technology, and records of when Rev first began," He says.

"So, are we looking for aliens or not?" Luke asks.

"Well, you four..," He stops as someone knocks on the door.

Officer Haze turns around and opens the door. On the other side is Jake suited up like the four of us.

"Officer Haze, I am not letting my team go in there without myself," Jake says sternly.

"Officer Farr, you were not supposed to be released this early. Don't you think you should take it easy?"

Jake walks past Officer Haze.

"I've healed enough. I need to be here," He says looking at some file on the desk.

"I do ask that you catch me up to speed though,"

So, for the next few minutes Erin and I tell him everything that had happened after he was loaded up on the falcon in Africa.

"So, now evidence stands here in our face, that aliens do exist," Jake says.

"It appears so, but we need to confirm it. The information inside the black egg leads us to believe the truth will be revealed in Rev's building," Says Officer Haze.

"Alright, let's do it," Jake replies.

We all nod to each other and leave.

As we board our falcon, we are handed different weapons than the other soldiers.

"Jace, you will be the berserker with our modified 50 caliber machine gun," One of three soldiers says, standing behind a table next to our falcon.

"Jake, your gun is an improved AK-47. Accuracy is now its strength. Each magazine holds 30 rounds with the tenth from last round being an incinerating round to help you know just how many you have left," Another soldier says.

"Thanks," Jake replies, taking the gun from them.

"Erin, you can't have anything less than the HK-416 with a grenade launcher attachment,"

"You know me well," Erin replies, taking her gun and heading into the Falcon.

"Luke, you also get an AK-47A like Officer Farr. Bryan, you get a HK-416 as well,"

"Thanks," I say taking the weapon.

I know this gun and I would prefer it over anything else right now only because the rest have been modified and I haven't tested them out.

We board the Falcon and wait for our queue to take off.

"You're sure you're good Jake?" I ask, trying to make sure he isn't pushing himself.

"Yeah, I'm fine. I took the ZR3 solution so I don't expect to be sore for very long,"

I assume that is something like the pills he gave me the other day for my sore shoulder.

The two pilots board the Falcon and give us a nod.

"We're taking off in 2 minutes," One of them says as they sit down.

We make sure we are buckled in and ready for takeoff.

"Well, this is it. Our lives have come to debunking Rev is in contact with aliens," Jace says sarcastically.

"What does that make us? Alien hunters? Alien busters? Just call us your crazy uncle," Luke chimes in.

"Yeah, we have to debunk things left and right, but the last mission was pretty alien in its own way. With a giant mutant. Whoever thought that day would come?" Jake says.

"By the way, good work out there. It was hard, and in a way, frightening. I will admit that I thought one of us was going to die," He says sincerely.

"No one is dying on my watch," Jace says.

"Nor on mine," Erin agrees.

Luke and I just nod in acceptance to that standard.

We begin to take off and as we leave the hanger I see it's filled with ready soldiers.

"Do you know the status in Africa?" I ask.

"Jake looks at me and then at the rest of the squad.

"200-300 men died. There were more mutants than we had expected. It's a disaster. I suspect the soldiers who are alive are few and scattered,"

We sit there in silence. I fear that the next thing I say will provoke a depressing topic again. I just think about all the possible obstacles we might face at Rev's base. It almost seems like suicide. I could be mauled by a vicious robotic dog, its metal teeth ripping off my armor as I clamber for my rifle next to me. If this place isn't vacant, how many giants would they have protecting their top-secret information. Do mutants roam the halls? What do the mutants think about? Are they zombie-like or are they able to comprehend things in the same way they did as a pure human?

THE TIME FLIES BY, making the flight seem short. I begin to get anxious.

"Five minutes until landing," Calls out the pilot.

Each of us snap out of our own quiet state.

"Alright, make sure your weapons are ready. There's no turning back when we touch the ground," Jake assures.

"Once we get done with this mission I'm requesting at least two days off" says Jace.

"Good idea Jace. I wish I could, but I'm not allowed," Luke says.

"Why is that?" Asks Jace.

"The world needs me too much," Luke tries to say with a serious voice.

Jake pushes Luke. "Ha, funny,"

Erin shakes her head with a smile.

"Helmets on," Jake orders. We each put on our helmets and look around getting used to the visors.

"Does anyone else have a blue tinted visor?" Jake asks.

"It's a film. You can take it off," Jace replies and then stands up to help Jake.

Just as Jace gets the film off, the pilot announces we're about to land. Jace jumps into his seat and buckles up.

We tip to one side and begin to spiral downward, while quickly reducing speed. The falcon levels out and we hover while descending the last 40 feet to the ground.

"Officer Far, we will be standing by if you need us but make sure it's your last resort," The pilot says.

Jake looks at him and nods. "Understood,"

The door opens and we jump out of the falcon with our weapons in hand. The thick mud ejects out from under our boots as we land on the ground. We trot from underneath the Falcon and into the pine trees 20 yards off. The other soldiers follow us and in minutes there are 25 of us in the trees, waiting for the others with vehicles to come.

AFTER THE LAST Falcon leaves we decide to spread out and make sure the area is safe, even though we are two miles away from the actual building. Rev has no reason why they shouldn't secure their perimeters with extra percussion.

Just as we spread out half a mile in diameter, our remaining soldiers arrive with the vehicles.

"Let's get to the vehicles and get a move on," Jake orders.

I move as quickly as possible to regroup with everyone.

"Bryan, let's go," Jace yells out of the side window of a Humvee.

The door opens and I jump in. However, when I jump in I almost lose my balance and I have to grab Jace to pull myself into the Humvee.

"Woah, don't get handsy now," He says jokingly.

"Sorry, I guess I'm not used to jumping yet. The weight of the new suit makes a big difference," I justify my need to grab him.

I sit down in my seat next to Erin and across from Luke. Jace is sitting across from Erin, but I notice that Jake isn't in the vehicle.

"Where is Jake?" I ask.

The headset inside my helmet transmits it to the others.

"He is in another vehicle," Erin says.

Just as she says that Jake begins to speak.

"Alright soldiers. Everyone can hear me, right?" He asks.

Different responses from a handful of soldiers are heard through the headset. I am guessing he is only talking to the 10 of us that are supposed to go inside the building.

"Good. Let's get these vehicles moving while I give the rundown. We are the ones that will break through the doors of the garage and cause some havoc to any residents of Rev's first home. Once inside, only the five of us in heavy armor, plus the two gunners, will get out and neutralize the garage. Once it's clear, we will signal the rest of you and be on our way,"

"Copy that," says everyone in my vehicle.

"The perimeter will be handled by a few of our Mechs, snipers, and foot soldiers. When there aren't any more Rev soldiers outside, we will have more of our soldiers come in and take point where we have cleared out," He pauses for a moment.

"Any questions?" He asks.

No one asks anything.

"Alright, in a mile we'll have Duncan and Vincent blow up the wall. After that we'll make our way to the garage," Jake finishes.

"You guys ready?" Luke asks.

"I don't think we have a choice, but, yes I am," Replies Erin.

"Readier than you," says Jake.

"I am," I reply.

"Good, because there is no way I'm dragging you guys out of the line of fire while you're wearing that suite," Luke jokes.

We laugh.

"Yeah, because you couldn't if you tried," Jace says.

"Oh, and you think you could?" Erin asks.

Jace doesn't say anything.

"Honestly, I don't think any of us could drag another out alone. These suits are too heavy," says Luke.

He has a point, and for a moment I get a sinking feeling. These suits would become our coffins.

We begin to slow down as we approach a security gate with large metal cylinder barricades sticking up from the ground.

Two soldiers on a four wheeler drive past us. As they get up closer to barricade they stop and hop off their vehicle. In a matter of minutes, they blow down a portion of the wall and we get the signal to drive on. We let the other vehicles go first then follow Jake's Humvee.

Our Humvee teeters back and forth as we drive over the wall's rubble.

"You know these suits are pretty padded for being as heavy duty as they are," I say sitting in my seat.

"They are definitely high-quality suits," Luke agrees.

The driver punches the gas as we hit the pavement again. We each do a little lean towards the back and then we sit up straight again.

I think to myself. "This is it. We are about to fight for our lives again,"

THE ENGINE ROARS as we go up a hill. Then as we roll over the top, we see the building and I spot a few soldiers on the perimeter.

The soldier in the passenger seat comes back and gets in the turret. I unbuckle my seat belt and look out the window trying to see the building better.

I see a large unappealing concrete structure with some medium size windows 15 feet apart from each other on the second level. There aren't many doors on the north and west side of the building.

"Let's do one circle around the building and then hit the garages. It should allow our men to set up the mechs and snipers," Jake commands.

We finally get close enough for Jake's gunner to begin shooting. The bullets rip through the few soldiers standing on the West side of the perimeter. Both Jake's and our Humvee follow the road going to the south side, where we find and pass four large garage doors. Three of the doors are for semis and the other one has a gradual ramp leading up to the garage door. Our gunners fire at a door leading into the building. I'm not sure if they saw the enemy or if they were just intimidating Rev.

As we turn the corner on the East side, a rocket whizzes in front of my Humvee barely missing Jake's. Dirt rains on us and then our driver punches the gas again.

"That was close. Turrets, keep your eyes sharp," Jake yells.

"Hansen, what's our status?" Jake asks.

"We don't see any foot soldiers on the ground, but more and more soldiers are heading to the roof," Hansen replies.

"Alright–" Jake starts to say.

"Wait, something is coming out of the garage," Hansen cuts off Jake.

"Two Humvees just left the garage,"

"Alright, Johnson, turn around and we'll try to flank them," Jake orders the driver of my Humvee.

Our driver immediately flips a U-turn and floors it back around the building. Our gunner is still firing up at the rooftop.

"There are quite a few soldiers up top," He says, sounding worried.

As we come around the corner, we see a Rev Humvee, but it isn't beefed up like the ones in Africa.

"Where are those snipers?" Jake asks.

Once our gunner focuses on the Humvee in front of us, we hear the bullets rain from the building's rooftops. Luke jumps up and grabs our gunman's leg.

"Get down,"

Our driver slams on the brakes and we slide on the snowy muddy terrain.

The soldier crouches as much as possible.

"Our turrets can't handle the soldiers on the roof, while firing at the Humvees. Where are the snipers?" Jake yells again.

"Sir, the position of our snipers can't see all of the men on the roof. I am reorganizing my men now, to give you better coverage, but it's going to be a minute," Hansen replies.

Out of the corner of my eye, I see something move at the base of the building and realize it was a Rev soldier. The Rev Humvee shoots at us as we back up, but it, itself hasn't moved at all. Then, as we are about to back up past the corner, out of the line of fire, I see something come out of the garage.

"They have a mech," I say quickly.

"A mech is coming out of the garage," Hansen says.

A grenade goes off next to our vehicle and then a second. "Get us out of here, we are sitting ducks," Erin yells.

Our driver puts the vehicle in drive and turns around.

"Keep fire on the roof tops," Jace orders.

"Are our mechs ready?" Jake asks.

"We are. We're coming," A soldier replies.

Now that we have retreated back around to the East side of the building, I can see Jake's vehicle, also out of the line of fire from Rev's Humvees. We slow to a roll. Two of our mechs begin opening fire on the side of the building I can't see. Another grenade hits our vehicle.

"Where should I go?" The driver asks.

We look at each other.

"Just keep us out of heavy fire until we figure it out," I reply realizing that none of us really know the best thing to do under these circumstances.

"Hansen, can you get a sniper on the Humvees?" I ask.

"Copy that. We will do our best, but it looks like they are coming for you," He informs us.

Our mechs, still firing at Rev's mech, begin to light up with sparks from the rounds hitting them.

The gunman on our Humvee changes its focus to the enemy's Humvee coming quickly from behind.

"Johnson, give me the wheel. Jace, get him down from the turret," I order and quickly get up.

"What?" Johnson says as he slowly moves to the passenger seat.

I get in the driver seat and give it gas. "Buckle up Johnson,"

One of our mechs is on fire now and it falls on its side onto the ground. I can see now that Rev's mech is larger than ours and able to take more heat. It stands tall on its two metal legs and its pod has no window for viewing out of. It's just a metal shell with large guns on each side of it above the legs. It moves out a little further around the corner and aims both its guns at our last mech. I punch the gas and drive towards the front right side of the enemy mech still focused our mech.

"What are you doing Bryan?" Erin yells.

I just keep driving full speed ahead.

"I'm going to ram that mech's leg. Hold on" I say moments from executing my plan.

But then, the collision happens sooner than anticipated. The second Rev Humvee came around the corner so fast, I couldn't avoid it.

Our Humvee smashes into the back corner of the passenger side of Rev's Humvee. Throwing my course of direction off from hitting the left leg to hitting the right leg of the mech. We slam into the leg with less momentum than originally planned. Then, a loud explosion happens. Metal and fire hit the windshield.

"Bryan, what were you thinking?" Asks Jake.

"We took out the Mech," I reply sheepishly, because I didn't know how it exploded, but tried to take the credit.

"We shot two rockets at it," Jake corrects my story.

A large chunk of burning matter falls on the hood with a loud thud. I reverse, causing the flaming junk to fall off, and drive around the mech. Jake pulls up alongside me, then drives faster ahead of me.

A rocket flies by and hits the ground 30 yards away, as one of Rev's Humvees zooms by. We get a few rounds into the side of our vehicle from their turret.

"Bryan, you could have killed us," Erin says angrily.

"We need to consult together before doing something like that, Bryan," Luke says.

I push their comments out and focus on staying alive.

"Where is that Humvee I hit?" I ask.

"It's on fire. Our guys must have hit it with a rocket," Jace replies.

I try to go faster, but my top speed is 20mph.

"It looks like we are out of the race," says Johnson.

He also appears to be disappointed with my reckless behavior.

"Well, it could be worse," I look around outside to see if it actually could be.

"How's the rooftop above us Hansen?" Erin asks.

"You guys are clear. We just have a few soldiers hiding, but none can get a shot on you. Watch the Humvee coming back around," Hansen replies.

"Woohoo!" Cheering from some different soldiers is heard.

"What was that all about?" Jace asks.

"We just took out the last Humvee," Jake replies.

As we get closer to the garage our Humvee begins to smoke from under the hood.

"Turn off the engine," says Johnson.

"Erin, get to the garage," Orders Jake.

WE JUMP out of the vehicle and make our way to the open garage door. The sound of gunfire lightens up and Jake's Humvee comes around the corner of the building slowing down the closer he gets to the garage.

Jake gets out of the Humvee passenger side and walks around the back of it.

"The five of us are going in first and then we'll be backed up by the other five. Let's move in," He says walking up to us

Together we briskly move up the ramp to the garage.

I hold my weapon steady in front of my face, searching for hostiles possible near the entrance of the garage.

"Erin, come with me to the right. Jace and Bryan stay left. Luke, hang back at the entrance,"

As we get up closer, we can see the garage is filled with vehicles. I approximate the size of the garage is 3,500 square feet in a rectangular shape. In the back of the garage are doors and two set of stairs to more doors.

We enter the garage, when all of a sudden, rounds are fired.

I jump to the ground behind a small concrete barrier.

A man using a Humvee turret, in the midst of the other stationary military grade vehicles, fires shots at Jake and Erin. Jake falls to one knee and then Erin pulls him further out of the garage and out of our view.

"We've got a gunner in a turret 20 yards away," Luke yells.

"I'm okay," Jake says. "This armor is durable,"

"That's a pretty good dent though," says Erin.

"Listen guys, the suits are very durable. We can take some hits and be okay. Spread out and take that gunman down," Jake orders.

I decide that I'll run out first. I nod to Luke and Jace, then run out from behind the barrier to a nearby vehicle. Bullets zip by and cause the vehicle my back is against, to vibrate. Jace stands up and fires a few rounds while I move again, further into the garage.

Again, the gunman sprays his rounds across the garage, trying to suppress Jace and I. For a moment it's quiet, but I can hear a faint voice.

"Is that soldier talking to us?" I ask the others.

"I can't tell what he is doing, but I'm moving up anyway," Jace says.

I stand up and fire as much as I can, before the gunman fires back.

"I'm sending Luke and Erin in behind you two," Informs Jake.

"Copy that," I reply.

As Erin and Luke come in, the gunman fires, but abruptly stops and says something a little louder.

"I think I just heard the soldier say 'hurry'," I let everyone know.

"It sounds like we will have more company in a moment," Jake says. "Take that guy out now,"

"Alright, on the count of three let's let him have it," says Jace.

"One, Two, Three,"

We stand up and fire at the gunman who seems to be overwhelmed, because he crouches while firing erratically. I move more right, deeper into the garage towards the stairs, to get a better shot. Then the man quickly jolts and stops firing and I realize Jace got him from the left side.

It is right then, that I feel a couple rounds on my backside and hear them ricochet.

"Bryan, take cover," Jake yells.

Rounds of gunfire fly above me as my squadron provides cover.

I move forward towards the dead gunman and hide myself behind a tarped object.

"Soldiers are on the stairs!" Jake says.

The soldiers continue to fire at me, so I decide to move further into the garage away from them. My knee armor scraps across the concrete, as I stay low behind various crates and more tarped objects. Less bullets hit objects around me now, so I rise a little above the crates to see what I am working with.

The soldiers are on the stairs, using shields for cover. Their focus is mainly on the others. My angle is good, so I fire up at them, taking out one of them. I duck down as they realize my real position and they fire back. I hear another door open and look over at the opposite side of the garage. On the same wall as the shielded soldier, at the other end, more soldiers push through a door.

"We have more on the other side," I inform the others.

I check my six and make sure I can't be hit from the other soldiers. Rising quickly to one knee, I fire the rest of my magazine, take cover, then reload.

As I try to peek over a crate, bullets hit the crate.

"Keep your head down Bryan!" Jake orders.

No duh, I think to myself. Then I hear a sound I haven't heard in a while. A grenade launcher. A few pops go off and then the boom of each grenade.

"Keep firing. They're retreating!" Erin says.

I peak over the crate again, and see both sets of soldiers slowly moving up the stairs. I fire spurts of rounds before they fully retreat back behind the doors. I get up, still aiming back and forth at the two doors.

"I'll watch the left door," I say moving more to the left.

"I got your back Bryan," Jace says.

"We can thank Johnson and his men for those grenades. That sure made them rethink who they're messing with," says Jake.

"Let's get up to those doors. Bryan, Jace, and three light weights will take the left door while Erin, Luke, myself and two light weights will take the right."

We all agree.

Jace catches up with me.

"Do you want to take point?" He asks.

I nod. "Yeah, I'll take point,"

I hop over a crate and quickly move up against the wall the stairs are connected to. Jace and the other three soldiers move up with me. A moment passes by and I look back at Jake's group.

"You ready?" Asks Jake.

"On your mark," I reply.

"Let's move,"

I climb the stairs trying to be quiet, but they're metal stairs and the weight of my suit makes them creek. I accept the fact that I can't be quiet, and move a little faster. As I get closer to the top, I get a strange feeling that something isn't right. I signal Jace to open the door for me. He quickly gets into position and right before he puts his hand on the handle, the door opens.

The next thing I know, I am falling backwards with a metal jaw clamped to my left forearm.

I land on my back, on the stairs and can hear one of the lightweight soldiers yell, "Stay still,"

Even if I wanted to, I couldn't, because the metal dog whips its head back and forth viciously. I drop my gun and try to push the dog off. Then the soldier closest to me, fires into the dog's metal skull. It only takes a second before the vicious jerks stop. Sparks pop here and there, as the dog becomes motionless.

Mean-while, Jace has been holding the door closed and taking rounds that are being fired through the metal door.

"Help me get these jaws off. They are still clamped down," I say trying to use my right hand to open them.

The soldier that shot the dog, helps me pry the jaws open, using the butt of his gun.

"Bryan, we need to clear this hall!" Jace exclaims.

I look at him and then back to our other group. They seem to be fighting off their own metal dog. I climb back up the stairs.

"Grab my rifle," I say, handing it off.

One of the soldiers gives me a grenade.

"Right, good idea," says Jace.

I nod to him and pull the pin.

He opens the door and I toss it in. Jace closes the door.

Three seconds later the grenade goes off.

I take my rifle from the soldier behind me and get into position. Jace opens the door and light wispy smoke comes out at first. Then bullets zip through the hazy hallway.

"Keep it open," I say, moving in while firing steadily at the soldiers. Some still have shields in hand, but those that don't, I take out quickly.

The hallway is short and the soldiers back up around corners.

"Jace, move ahead," I say realizing I need to reload.

He comes up on my left side and fires at the corner of the walls.

I reload and make sure our men are okay.

"Bryan, let me go ahead and take the left, while you take the right. If I say switch then switch,"

I nod, deciding to let him go with whatever he is thinking. We move into the perpendicular hallway and immediately we get sprayed with gunfire from both directions of the hallway.

We retreat.

I think we both realize our suits are incredibly durable.

Jace steps out into the hallway, and then I do in the opposite direction, and we let rounds reign on Rev. About ten seconds later Jace yells switch left. So, I do. The only soldier left on his side is taking his last breath.

"Grenade!" Yells Jace.

I dive back into the hallway we came out of. As I do, I realize that this suit would probably do just fine, if I was only a few feet away from the explosion. Besides, diving in this suit didn't get me as far as I hoped. There is just too much weight to be agile.

After the grenade blows up, Jace gets right back out there killing the last of them.

"The hallway is clear, check the rooms," He orders us.

We quickly search the few rooms around the larger open office space.

The rooms do look somewhat used, but I am not convinced they are anyone's main offices.

"They're clear," I report back.

"Same here," Jace says from the other end.

"It looks like we have some paperwork in these rooms. You three scan the paper work for important information," I say pointing out the rooms to the three light weights.

I can hear gunshots somewhere else in the building.

"Jake, what is you guys' status?"

"Bryan, we are taking heavy fire. If we keep this up we'll be out of ammo soon enough," Luke says.

"We've got to get over to them," I tell Jace.

"If we catch the soldiers from behind they'll have to surrender," He says confidently.

"You stay here with these three. I'll find a way to get to the others,"

I agree and Jace takes off on a jog that shakes the floor.

I stand between the two rooms where the soldiers are searching for significant documents.

"Anything?" I ask.

"Some information about the inventory," One of them says.

"I've got a document. It has some signatures on it to approve modifications on vehicles," Another soldier says.

"Okay, get what you can. I'll stay on watch,"

A minute, then two, then three, go by and I start to get anxious. I stand in the hallway looking back and forth at the two ends, waiting for some Rev straggler to appear. This place feels very average, just like a normal office. The walls are a tan color and the carpet is a speckled gray.

"That is all the paperwork in here and the computer seems to be connected to a main server that is offline. If we want to search any computers we have to get them online first," One soldier says coming out of the room.

"Huck, I'm going to put this in your backpack," He says, talking to another soldier as he walks into the other room with two more soldiers.

"Alright. We just have one more drawer to look through,"

I stand there for another minute before asking Luke for their status.

"Just finishing off the last few soldiers. We have two that surrendered,"

"We'll meet up with you guys in a minute. We are just gathering up documents," I reply.

"Copy that," says Luke

"That's it. Let's pack this up and move on," Huck says.

"We should find more informative documents in the main offices. These mainly pertain to the warehouse and garage matters," Huck informs me.

"We are going to meet up with the group and go from there," I say.

Huck and the other two soldiers agree and we head off in the direction Jace went.

It takes a few minutes, but we cautiously move through the hallways, until we find Jace and the others. Bodies of Rev soldiers lie all over the hallways.

"Bryan, you guys okay?" Jake asks.

"Yeah we are okay. How did you guys handle that robotic dog?" I ask.

"After it knocked three of us down, which made Luke crush Eric on the stairs, I shot its face off with my AK-47A. It really didn't stand a chance," Jake replies, sarcastically sad for the dog.

"Oh, well, how's Eric?" I ask, looking for him.

"Badly wounded actually. We left him in a vehicle in the garage. We decided he could keep a look out for us until medics get there. They should be there now,"

"Enough chit chat, we've got to get a move on," Erin snaps.

"You're right. It doesn't seem like the documents we want are here. We should continue on," Jake replies.

The nine of us move deeper into the building, checking hallways and rooms for Rev soldiers. Strangely enough, after checking a decent amount of rooms and hallways, we still haven't found another Rev soldier. The hallways have gotten wider and the rooms connected to them are larger.

"Where is everyone?" Luke asks.

"Yeah, this place is starting to feel like a ghost town," says Erin.

"Don't let your guard down. You never really know what Rev is up to," Chimes in Johnson.

"What do you think could be behind this door?" Asks Jake.

He tries to open a set of blue metal doors.

On the door reads. "MR2".

"MR2, what does that stand for?" One light armored soldier asks.

"Missile Room, Muscle Room, Man Room, Rev Robotics…" Another soldier starts randomly spouting off words.

"How about I just crack this keypad?" A third soldier says stepping forward and hooking a handheld device to the keypad on the wall.

"How long will that take, compared to blowing up the door?" Jake asks.

The soldier lightly nods their head once, twice, and on the third time the keypad turns green and the door unlocks.

"Not long," He says.

We get ready and put our guns up while Jake prepares to open the door. Erin takes point, but when the door opens we all pause. The room glows a blue hue from strange tubes. Jake notices our lack of vigor and looks around the door to see why we aren't moving.

"What in the world?" One of the soldiers says.

"Move in and clear the area," Johnson reminds us.

We fall in quickly and check the room for soldiers, or dogs for that matter. The room seems vacant like the last twenty we checked. However, this wasn't insignificant like the others.

The room is two stories tall, and the blue tubes emit light, and are filled with bodies. But not normal bodies. They seem to be growing various things, such as tentacles, horns, bone-like plates. There must be 20 tubes, varying in diameter, in the center of the room. After checking the entire room for soldiers, we find none.

"Johnson, you and your men watch the doors, while we gather data," Jake says.

"What is this place?" Erin asks.

"These are mutants," Jake replies as he looks at a specimen.

A large gray man is hooked up to tubes. On his face grows a thin plate of what seems to be bone, between his eyes. Jake takes out a pouch on his waist, it's a small camera.

"This is important for us to learn about. How long does one of these take to develop? Try and find documents for each of these," He says while taking pictures of the various specimens.

I begin looking around the room for a filing cabinet. Then my eyes pass a shallow hallway, leading to double doors. As I move closer to it, I find cabinet drawers built into the walls before the doors.

"Hey guys, I found something,"

The others come over and we begin pulling folders out.

"Wah bam! These are them," Luke says.

"Yeah there are so many files," Erin says.

"The dates, this one was in a tube for 18 months. They must just rotate specimens every so often," I say, reading a document for a man named Joshua Bateman. He seemed to be fond of reptiles and desired to have scales and possibly..."

"Check out this one. They created a man with bat wings," says Luke, interrupting my reading.

"Great, you found them. Stack up as many as you can and we'll have the others take them outside," Jake says walking over to us.

"Johnson, have your men take these files to the garage and load them up in a vehicle. When you get them loaded up, come back inside and we'll finish the search," Jake orders.

Johnson and his men come over to the filing cabinets and fill a couple small crates with the files.

"Alright, let them do that," Jake says, trying to round us up.

We follow him out of the shallow hallway, back towards the tubes.

"We need to search the opposite side of the building, where the big offices are," He says.

"Wait, do you hear that?" Luke says.

"What is that?" Asks Erin.

"It sounds like a gas leak," I reply.

Then the noise gets louder and louder. All of us are looking around and the other soldiers are too.

"Do you see anything?" Jake asks.

"There, I see them," Johnson replies.

The five of us put our backs together and put our guns up in front of our faces.

"They're jets. Small jets. They are flying around," Luke informs, and I begin to aim higher.

The jets are not much bigger than a hobbyist's model plane, but these are operational.

Everyone confirms that they see them.

"I've never seen a drone like that," Jace says.

The small jets begin to descend.

"Shoot them!" Jake orders.

We fire at them, and bring down three of the eight.

"Ah! Watch out!" Luke exclaims.

The jets peel away back up higher and circle the room.

"What happened?" Erin asks Luke.

"I got hit in the face with something. I think it was a missile,"

We look at him confused.

"Oh yeah, look. You got a crack on your visor," Jace says.

There is also black powder, where the missile hit.

"Well, there are five more. How hard can they be to take them down," says Jake.

The jets fly high in a circle, around the large pipes leading down to the blue tubes.

"We need to get you guys out of here with those documents," Jake says to Johnson.

"Make a wall. And move with them," Jake orders.

We follow his orders. Johnson and the other three soldiers hide behind us as we side step and watch the jets.

Halfway to the door the jets get lower and lower. We pass the middle of the room, in front of the blue glass tubes, holding mutants.

"Missiles!" Exclaims Jace.

We keep moving while we shoot. The missiles hit our metal armor and the last two jets fly off.

"Okay, go, go, go," Jace tells the others.

They run out the door we came in holding the files in crates.

We check our armor for major damage, but the missiles were ineffective.

"Alright let's get out of here," Says Jake, backing up to the door. Just then, the jets come back around to us, chest high. We fire at them, quickly taking them down. However, as they crash and burn at our feet, alarms go off.

"Guys, I think we made a mistake," Luke points to the tubes. Multiple tubes have bullet holes in the glass.

"The fluid is draining," Erin exclaims. "Quickly,"

"Like I said, let's get out of here," Jake turns around and runs through the doorway and we follow behind, closing the door on the way out.

Luke makes sure the door locks before we run down the hall.

"Let's get to the other end of the building. We'll find more information there," Jake orders.

We find stairs and take them to the fourth and top floor. The lights are all off except a few emergency lights. We walk down the hall a little ways and find a large area with desks and computers lined in rows. Along the perimeter are offices and each corner of the large room has more hallways.

"I'll check down here," Jace says point to the right.

"Luke, go with Jace. Erin, come with me. Bryan take that far hallway," Jake says pointing to the hall kitty-corner from us.

I walk with Erin and Jake a little ways to the left, then I break off to the right toward my hall.

We all have our guns up ready for any unexpected soldiers. All the computers are off and the desks are fairly bare. I glance over at Jace and Luke on the other side of the room. I have to say, if I was the enemy I would be terrified of men in our suits.

WHEN I REACH my hallway the day light gently shines through the partially open blinds at the end of the hall. It's just enough to make the situation even more eerie.

I open the only office door in the short hall. A desk, a chair, and an old computer are the only things that sit in the room. There isn't a filing cabinet or a bookshelf or anything else. I look back at the hallway, contemplating if I should try to see what is on the computer. I figure that this is my only room so I can try to find some information on it.

I put my gun on the desk and turn on the computer.

"You guys finding anything?" Asks Jace.

"A few interesting lab reports about mutants. We suspect a few minutes more just in this room will tell us a lot about the process they use," Erin replies.

"Nothing, yet," I reply.

The computer takes a few minutes before I get to the point that it asks for a password. "Come on," I say as I look around the computer for a note or something.

Nothing.

As I get up to leave I decide to look under the keyboard. Nothing.

I look in the drawers of the desk, but find nothing. In desperation I look underneath the desk and wah-la. Taped underneath the top of the desk is a three by five note card with the username and password.

I get in the chair and put in the required information. As the screen loads I get excited and stand up to make sure the hallway is still clear. I can see Luke and Jace on the other side of the room looking through files.

The computer makes a noise, queuing me it's ready. I open up the file folder and find the most recent activity. I have to read it twice to be sure, but a file that reads "New Recruits" was just used yesterday. I double click the spreadsheet file making the program load.

"Does anyone have a flash drive?" I ask.

"You should have a small pouch on your waist that has one," Erin replies. "You should have learned more about your suit before skipping out to take your nap yesterday,"

"Thanks," I reply confused why she is still annoyed with everyone.

I find the flash drive and plug it into the computer. A spreadsheet pops up on the screen with a table full of names, dates, and almost anything you would want to know about a person. I start transferring the file to the flash drive. As it downloads I scroll down and find information that goes back to 2033. I mentally pat myself on the back for finding this information.

Suddenly, I hear a door open. It didn't sound like someone was coming into an office to find files, but more like they were trying to be quiet. I gently grab my gun off the desk and walk to the hall.

Jace and Luke are still in some rooms going through files. I step across the hall and put my back against the wall and move towards the main area, while facing the perimeter of the larger room. I know taking the right would lead me along more offices and to Jake and Erin. To the left, was another shallow hallway that led to a door. I slowly move away from the wall and out of the hall, pointing my gun to the left.

At first, I see nothing, but as my eyes adjust, I notice the door down the hall is partially cracked open. But nobody appears to have come in. I decide to get the file and head back to the others. As I return to the computer the transfer is complete, so I remove the flash drive.

"Everyone, get back to me and Erin right now. I think we are being hunted,"

I walk out of the room and just as I put my gun up to check the left hallway, someone lunges around the corner and grabs my gun, ripping it out of my hands with ease. The gun flies back and hits a pillar. I throw a punch but the person moves out of the way.

I receive a blow to my left ribs, but the suit takes most of it. I swing a second time, and I miss because the person backs up.

Next, they do the unthinkable.

They run up the wall on my right, on all fours and leaps towards me. They are so quick that I hardly move an inch by the time they reach me.

The impact throws me back and I crash into the window. I can hear the others asking if I'm okay, but my mind only focuses on preventing myself from falling four stories to the ground. My head and shoulders are sticking outside and the soldier is pushing me further out. As I bend my legs and use my fingers to grip the wall, I hear gunshots. The pushing stops, but my suit is heavy and I keep sliding.

"Help!" I yell.

My fingers slip past the window seal and my legs are all that keeps me from falling.

"I'm falling out a window. The suit is too heavy for me," I try to be short and concise.

Then terror fills me as I feel someone grab my leg and I try to grip the wall even harder. "Bryan, we've got you," Jace says. Someone's hand grabs mine through the blinds, and I'm pulled up.

My back slides across the window seal and then down against the wall as I fall to the floor. I'm breathing heavy and trying to shake my mind clear.

"You okay?" Luke asks.

"Yeah," I reply.

"Thanks. For a second there I thought I was a goner,"

I look over to the right and see my enemy lying on the ground.

"What the," I say becoming frozen.

"What is that?"

"A mutant, I guess. It has scales and its palms are weird," Jace replies.

I take a closer look at its palm's.

"His hands are like a reptile's feet that can grip things. It climbed on the wall and leaped at me. And that's probably why it had so much power pushing me out the window,"

"I'm glad you're okay, but we have to leave now," I hear Jake say.

Jace and Luke help me up and I can see Jake and Erin standing a little ways off.

"There will be more mutants looking for us. I'll tell Johnson not to come back inside," Jake says.

I grab my gun and we follow Jake back out of the big room, towards the stairs.

"Keep your eyes..." He pauses.

"Sh," He holds his hand up.

A loud bang from a door echo's up the staircase. Then I hear a door smack a wall behind us somewhere across the large room.

"They're surrounding us," Jace says turning around and jogging to the large room.

"Guys, we are surrounded,"

"How many do you see?" Jake says, lightly stepping down the stairs.

"Four, five,"

None of us speak for a moment. Jake, getting to the bottom of the stairs, looks around the corner and then keeps going.

"Let me check the third floor. Luke, see if you can find a ladder to the roof,"

"Six, seven," Jace keeps counting the mutants.

"We have to make a decision. This floor is going to be overwhelmed with mutants before we know it," says Erin.

I look back at Jace and then to the stairs.

"Jake, how does it look?" I ask.

He doesn't reply, but I begin to hear a thud and then another and another, almost in a pattern. However, once I start to feel a vibration at the same time as the thuds I begin to understand.

"There's something big," I inform the others. "Is that what that is?" Erin asks.

Jake re-appears around the corner and gently walks up the stairs.

"You're right. We can't go downstairs. A large mutant is coming up," He tells us.

"What?" Jace says.

"Luke, how's that ladder coming?" Jake asks.

"It's not. I can't find it and I just saw a mutant so I can't go any further unless you're wanting me to engage."

Jake quickly replies. "Don't engage. Come back to the stairs,"

Jake pauses, then calls for back up.

"This is Officer Farr calling for backup. We are pinned on the fourth story of the building. We have mutants crawling all over. We will be in the Northeast corner of the building waiting for a falcon. Our ammo is low, please come as soon as possible," He says.

"Permission to engage?" Jace asks.

"Permission granted," Jake turns around and pops in another magazine.

Luke arrives panting.

"Get ready," Jake says, looking at Luke.

"Bryan, Luke watch the stairs as we move.

Erin, Jace, watch the large room. We'll take out as many as we can before we retreat into a large office I found earlier,"

"We will be there soon," A soldier replies to Jake's message.

"We have company, helicopters are landing on the roof. They aren't ours," Hansen chimes in.

"Hang in there, Squad 7,"

"Great," Jake says, then walks towards the big room and begins to fire.

Jace and Erin also move next to Jake and together they walk towards the east end of the building. Bullets zip by and the sound of breaking cubicles and computer equipment accompanies rapid fire. Luke and I stand in the doorway of the large room and the hall with the stairs leading to the lower floor. We watch the stairs and occasionally a section to our left in the big room.

"Some have guns," Erin yells.

Jace, Jake, and Erin get to the northeast corner of the room and hold their position.

"Watch the right, we have one crawling low!" Jace informs.

Jase's right is mine and Luke's immediate left, and slightly behind. I tell Luke to watch for the crawler, while I check out the hallway. I move out of the doorway and closer to the stairs.

"Bryan!" Luke yells and begins firing.

A gray mutant comes rushing out of a door way across from our post and into the hall. He is suited with a bullet proof vest and appears quite upset.

Before turning my focus towards him I realize three other mutants are reaching the top of the stairs.

I turn and shoot at the gray mutant, because he is closer and approaching rapidly. It throws its arms up to shield its face. I know I'm hitting him but it doesn't seem to do much, until he gets closer, and I see his flesh rip off. The mutant doesn't seem to mind, because it lunges toward me. I quickly move right and use my right elbow to hit his flailing left arm, causing him to land on the ground. Luke shoots the mutant's exposed head causing it to die. I turn to fire at the other three, which are now very close. We mow down another mutant, looking particularly hairy.

It then occurs to me that a large mutant, probably the one causing the thuds and vibrations, has reached the top of the stairs.

Another hairy mutant with large arms and some combat armor, fires a pistol at my head causing a bullet to stick into the top left area of my visor. I feel pieces of the visor hit my face, including my eyelid.

"Let's get in the room," Jake yells.

I make my shots count and shoot through the throat of the mutant. It falls forward on its knees and gasps for air, holding its neck.

Luke takes out the third and we both target the goliath of mutants, as we back up to the large room. Goliath starts to make larger strides towards us. My heart is pounding hard as I contemplate when to stop shooting and sprint away. A few seconds after backing into the big room, the crawling mutant comes around the desks, low to the ground. It skitters around a pillar, but gets pushed out of the way by the over 600 pounds, 7 foot-tall, mutant. We immediately turn around and run down a hall to the door Erin is holding open.

"Come on!" She yells.

A deep abnormal yell fills the entire fourth floor, accompanied by a ground quaking stomp.

We rush in and Erin closes the door, locking the handle. I think to myself how it won't be a challenge at all against goliath.

Jake and Jace place a desk in front of the door and I grab a cabinet.

"Luke," I get his attention to help me.

"This won't hold them for very long," I say as we place the cabinet on top of the desk.

"We need backup now!" Jake orders into his mic.

"Hansen, what's your situation?" He asks.

Boom! The mutants slam against the door. Jace and I lean up against the cabinet to give it more weight.

"There are five helicopters on the roof. Two are ready to take off. We counted 13 Rev soldiers total that made it into the building. Sorry we couldn't eliminate them all," Hansen replies.

"Copy that. What is the status of our Falcon?"

"Not good, I guess they're getting held up by more of Rev's helicopters,"

The large mutant begins pushing the door causing the door's lock to bend. A gap between the door and doorway begins to form. We hear the eerie grunts and sounds from the mutants, as they hungrily break the door.

Jake, Erin, and Luke aim at the door.

"How much ammo do we have?" Jake asks.

It's determined, no more than two magazines each.

"Make your shots count," Says Luke.

A huge push against the door causes Jace and I to slide backward a foot and the door opens wider. Bullets rip through the wall and door as Erin and Luke shoot at the intruding mutants. Jace and I try to push the door back, but it won't budge.

"I think we got a Rev aircraft coming in. We have a red alert from home base. No one is sure what it is but we think Rev is coming in a new aircraft," Hansen says.

Then a grenade flies into the room and bounces off a wall, causing Erin and Luke to take cover. It explodes causing my ears to ring, but I keep pushing against the cabinet.

Jake shoots through the doorway that seems to be getting bigger every minute.

As Luke gets up to resume his position, he catches a grenade and throws it back out. It explodes causing an intermission of major pushing from outside the room.

Jace, Erin and myself push the desk back to close the door. Then a loud explosion breaks the relative silence. Debris and dust fill half the room and then the dust thins out and we hear loud banging and breaking. It appears Rev soldiers have blown a hole in the wall, left of the door. The large mutant is ripping the rest down.

"I'm out of ammo," Erin says after firing her last shots.

"I only have a few rounds," says Luke.

Then the banging and breaking stop and another charge goes off. A second hole is formed and the mutant goes back to work.

"Erin, take my spot," I say.

She does, and Luke replaces Jace. Jake, Jace and I fire through the holes. We hear screams and screeches from the hallway. The mutant does a heavy horizontal punch, breaking the point between the two large holes. The wall now has a longer opening. A soldier fires back at us. He looks more geared up than the ones we fought earlier today. While taking a few of his rounds, we eliminate him.

More and more of the wall is being torn apart as the mutant relentlessly punches and grabs chunks. Blood from the large mutant is all over the edges of the hole. Our rounds seem to hardly phase it.

We shoot through the wall hoping to hit the mutant in a more effective area. Three soldiers run behind goliath and past the hole, out of the hallway.

"That doesn't make sense" I think to myself. "What were they doing,"

At that moment an explosion bigger than before goes off. I jolt back and trip on something, making me fall on my back. The room is now very hazy, but I can see the damage. An eight by ten-foot hole has been created on the right side of the door. I grab my gun and when the soldiers come, I fire like crazy.

"We are going to die," I think over and over. We start receiving more gun fire and I feel it through the soft part of my suit. None of us know what to do, but fire our last shots and pray for backup.

Another explosion happens. However, this time two holes were made at the top two corners of the room of the wall behind us. The holes let a small amount of natural light shine in.

Unsure of what was going on, I keep my eye on the soldiers and fire my last four shots. The hole on the left side of the door is now almost as big as the right side. The sound of a large bullet blasts into various areas of the wall behind us.

Then, as the large mutant shoves his shoulder into the wall and steps into the room, the wall behind us breaks down. Daylight floods the room and the mutant slows down and soldiers stop shooting.

My squad is about to turn around to look for ropes or ladders leading us out of danger, when rounds of fire rain down into the room. The large mutant is pushed back against the desk and wall. Blood splatters all over the room. More mutants try to enter the room but the angel-like gunman stops them short. My squad and I keep our heads down and for good reason, because three pairs of metal boots land right in front of us.

It is right then that we learn the truth. After spending the whole morning fighting and searching for files and for the truth. It decides to show up at literally the last minute.

One tall and fully armored being stands between two slightly hunched creatures. Each blasting down our enemies and taking rounds of gunfire.

"Get up," The tall being says in a unique voice.

"Get in the ship,"

The five of us look at each other. We do as we are told and board the unfamiliar aircraft hovering next to the building.

Only 10 seconds go by before the three life saving soldiers retreat back into their ship with us.

The ship takes off, and the doors close.

Inside the ship, equipment and the control panel look nothing like anything I have seen before. I immediately believe these three beings have all our answers concerning the information on the black egg's memory chip.